Green Light

By
Tom Barber

*****

Green Light
Copyright: Archway Productions
Published: 3rd September 2014

The Sam Archer thriller series
by
Tom Barber

NINE LIVES

26 year old Sam Archer has just been selected to
join a new counter-terrorist squad, the Armed
Response Unit. And they have their first case. A
team of suicide bombers are planning to attack
London on New Year's Eve. The problem?
No one knows where any of them are.

THE GETAWAY

Archer is in New York City for a funeral. After
the service, an old familiar face approaches him
with a proposition. A team of bank robbers are
tearing the city apart, robbing it for millions.
The FBI agent needs Archer to go undercover and
try to stop them.

BLACKOUT

Three men have been killed in the UK and USA
in one morning. The deaths take place thousands
of miles apart, yet are connected by an event
fifteen years ago. Before long, Archer and the
ARU are drawn into the violent fray. And there's
a problem.
One of their own men is on the extermination list.

SILENT NIGHT

A dead body is found in Central Park, a man who
was killed by a deadly virus. Someone out there
has more of the substance and is planning to use

3

it. Archer must find where this virus came from and secure it before any more is released. But he is already too late.

ONE WAY
On his way home, Archer saves a team of US Marshals from a violent ambush in the middle of the Upper West Side. The group are forced to take cover in a tenement block in Harlem. But there are more killers on the way to finish the job. And Archer feels there's something about the group of Marshals that isn't quite right.

RETURN FIRE
Four months after they first encountered one another, Sam Archer and Alice Vargas are both working in the NYPD Counter-Terrorism Bureau and also living together. But a week after Vargas leaves for a trip to Europe, Archer gets a knock on his front door.
Apparently Vargas has completely disappeared. And it appears she's been abducted.

GREEN LIGHT
A nineteen year old woman is gunned down in a Queens car park, the latest victim in a brutal gang turf war that goes back almost a century. Suspended from duty, his badge and gun confiscated, Archer is nevertheless drawn into the fray as he seeks justice for the girl. People are going missing, all over New York. And soon, so does he.

Also:
CONDITION BLACK (A novella)

In the year 2113, a US 101st Airborne soldier wakes up after crash landing on a moon somewhere in space. All but two of his squad are dead. He has no idea where he is, or who shot him down.

But he quickly learns that some nightmares don't stop when you wake up.

To Andy Robinson and Jo French.
For their constant, much-appreciated support
since the first day Archer joined the ARU.

PROLOGUE

The nineteen year old woman was in her apartment when her cell phone started to ring.

Although she'd been expecting the call, the shrill sound still made her jump. Out of communication for the past month, nevertheless she knew that word would have got out about where she'd been. She also knew that certain people would be more than pissed about it. She'd cost them a lot of money.

And with what she was about to do next, she was going to cost them a whole lot more.

Breaking off from her hasty packing, she walked across the room and picked up the phone. She wasn't leaving the city by herself; she had an accomplice, a friend she'd known less than a year but someone who'd done more for her in that short period of time than people she'd known her entire life. That friend had left her just under an hour ago, saying she'd call when she'd packed her own things and was ready to leave. The blonde girl had never been so excited or so nervous at the step they were about to take.

This was finally it.

Glancing at a clock across the room which read *9:45pm*, she pushed the green button then trapped the phone between her ear and shoulder as she walked back over to her bag.

'I'm almost done, babe,' she said. 'Are you ready?'

'Where are you?'

The girl froze, midway through tucking a pair of jeans into her holdall.

The voice on the other end wasn't the one she'd been expecting.

'I said where are you?'

'Uptown,' the young woman lied, stuffing the jeans into the bag then zipping it up. 'I'm getting back to work.'

'Bullshit. I always know when you're lying to me. You're at home, aren't you?'

Pause.

'I'm leaving,' the girl said, dropping to one knee and pushing her arm under the mattress.

'No, you're not.'

'You'd better believe it,' she replied, withdrawing some dollar bills folded in half, which she tucked into her back pocket. 'And you can't stop me. Not anymore.'

She heard a laugh down the end of the phone, which infuriated her.

'Try anything and I'll go straight to the cops,' she threatened angrily, hooking the bag over her shoulder then turning off the light in her bedroom and closing the door behind her. 'I'll tell them everything I know. All the things you're doing here. Everything.'

'Are you threatening me?'

'You bet I am,' the blonde girl replied, moving to the apartment's front door and unlocking it. 'So you can take this as a final goodbye. I'm leaving.'

'No, Leann. You're not.'

ONE

Three hours earlier it had been a normal mid-September evening in New York City. The streets were busy but not unusually so, the temperature pleasantly warm as commuters made their way home after a day's work while others headed into the city, some to start evening shifts, others to hit the town and meet friends.

However, in Brooklyn the usual sounds of the city winding down for the evening were suddenly interrupted.

A black Ford 4x4 with tinted windows slid around a corner, police fender lights flashing and siren wailing, other vehicles pulling over to give it room to pass. The car was heading north-west, being manoeuvred skilfully through the streets, the engine gunning as it propelled the 4x4 forward.

The Ford rounded another corner then headed towards the Atlantic Avenue entrance to the subway station fifty yards ahead, the last stop between Brooklyn and Manhattan. However, traffic was far thicker near the transport hub and the vehicles in front of the police car had no room to pull over; despite its flashing lights and siren the Ford was quickly forced to slow.

Before it had come to a complete stop, the front passenger door flew open and a young blond man in light blue jeans, white t-shirt and a black bulletproof NYPD vest leapt out.

'Go!' 3rd Grade NYPD Detective Sam Archer shouted to the driver.

Slamming the door, he raced through the gaps in the queuing traffic and sprinted off up the street towards the subway. Behind him, the 4x4 pulled a fast U-turn, taking off for the Brooklyn Bridge fifty yards ahead, leaving behind a sea of startled onlookers.

Six feet tall, a hundred and eighty five pounds and fast on his feet, Archer dodged his way past pedestrians, heading straight for the subway. Those who saw him coming did their best to get out of his way, others who were not so alert taken by surprise as he forced his way through.

'Move! Move!'

As he reached the entrance, Archer went for the far right of the stairs, taking them two at a time, the balmy heat of the New York September suddenly intensifying, the air thick with humidity. Cutting his way through the commuters, he vaulted the ticket barrier turnstile, an MTA employee in a glass cabin shouting as she spotted him.

Ignoring her but pausing for a moment to check the directions for a certain train line, Archer took off again towards the Manhattan-bound Q line, twenty yards ahead and down another flight of stairs. As he raced on, he heard the screech of brakes coming from the platform, followed by the sound of doors opening.

The train had already arrived.

Reaching the stairs to the N/Q platform he hurtled down them, willing a late arrival to hold the doors. Passengers who'd just exited the train were flowing up towards him, making his progress even more difficult, forcing him to fight his way through.

He could see the train waiting with its doors open.

Leaping down the last four steps, Archer hurled himself towards the nearest carriage as they started to close, managing to get his hand in the gap. Using all his strength to wrest them back open, he forced his way through and squeezed inside.

Stumbling into the carriage, he quickly regained his balance as the doors clicked shut behind him.

Seconds later the wheels bit down onto the rails and the Q train lurched onwards towards its next stop.

Half a mile above the train, the two detectives Archer had left in the 4x4 were speeding across the Brooklyn Bridge, their flashing blues and siren assisting their progress as they cut and weaved through the Manhattan-bound traffic.

Trains on the New York City subway could reach speeds of 60mph and had the advantage of a clear run to their next destination, something Detective Josh Blake knew he couldn't match as he negotiated his way across the Bridge, drivers ahead unaware of the urgency of the situation as he flashed past them. Sam Archer's NYPD partner, Josh was a thirty one year old black guy built like a bodybuilder or line-backer, his usual calm, relaxed demeanour understandably absent at that particular moment as he gripped the wheel tightly, turning a sliding right and just missing another car.

Beside him sat Detective Alice Vargas, twenty nine years old and half his size, black-haired, brown-eyed, tanned and slender, a beautiful woman with an inner toughness which frequently took people by surprise, many of whom judged her purely on her half-Brazilian, half-American good looks. Having climbed over into the front seat after Archer left, she was holding her cell phone to her ear with her left hand, her right hand gripping hold of the arm support as Josh approached the end of the Bridge.

'Talk to me Vargas!' their team Sergeant, Matt Shepherd, ordered. *'Did you make it to the train?*

'Traffic was too heavy, sir! We left Archer trying to get on board.'

'Did he?'

'I don't know. We haven't heard from him.'

'Where are you?'

'On our way to Canal Street.'

'We're already here but we might not be able to stop that son of a bitch in time. Get to Union Square right now. Back up's already on its way!'

Somewhere below the Bridge, Archer was already making rapid progress through the Q train. The service was moderately full, not overcrowded, twenty or so people sitting or standing inside each carriage. At this hour most people were leaving the city, not entering it, but there were still way too many potential fatalities here on the city-bound service.

As he moved through the train, Archer rapidly scanned each person as he passed, his hand lingering near the Sig Sauer P226 pistol resting in its holster. He couldn't see the suspect or the bag anywhere.

Up ahead, the doors to the carriage suddenly whooshed open and an MTA employee in glasses and a blue uniform appeared and started walking towards him. Moving forward quickly, Archer met him halfway and pulled his badge from his hip.

'I need you to stop the train right now.'

'What? Why?'

'Just do it,' Archer ordered quietly, looking around, aware that they were in earshot of those immediately around them. 'And get everyone towards the rear of the train as quickly as you can.'

As the man pulled his radio, Archer turned to the carriage, showing his badge to everyone inside. The vest strapped across his torso had already attracted the attention of more than a few.

'Ladies and Gentlemen, I'm Detective Sam Archer, NYPD. We have an incident on board; I need you all to start moving towards the rear of the train immediately.'

As people looked at him uncertainly, hearing what he'd said but not immediately reacting, some who were listening to music quickly realised there was something unusual going on and pulled out their headphones.

'Why?' a woman asked.

'As I said, we have an incident. For your own safety, everyone please go, right now!' he ordered, not wanting to waste any more time. *'And tell everyone you pass to do the same.'*

Picking up on his urgency and his tone of command, people started to do as they were told, standing up and moving towards the other end of the train. Beside him, a workman picked up his toolbox as he rose from his seat. Archer grabbed his shoulder.

'Got pliers? Or a knife?'

The man nodded, thankfully not using up valuable time asking questions; he put the box on the bench and opened it up, passing over a small set of pliers. As he took them, Archer glanced at a

green and white plaid shirt hooked across the box
and pointed to it.

'Can I borrow that too?'

The man nodded; taking the garment, Archer
quickly pulled it on and did up the buttons, hiding
his NYPD vest as the workman walked down the
train. Watching him follow the others, Archer
rolled up the sleeves on the shirt then realised the
noise level had changed.

They'd just entered Manhattan.

At Canal Street, Matt Shepherd and the fifth and
final member of his Counter-Terrorism Bureau
investigation team, Lisa Marquez, were rapidly
clearing the platform of passengers who'd just
disembarked from a train on the Uptown-bound Q
platform, working fast with the help of scores of
back-up officers. A thirty two year old Latina 3rd
Grade detective, Marquez was only five foot six
and a hundred and thirty pounds but more than
made up for it with her no-nonsense,
commanding attitude.

'Let's go!' she shouted, herding people out.
'Move it!'

People instinctively responded to her tone,
making their way quickly up the stairs and out
onto the street above. An MTA employee
standing close by listened to a message coming
over his radio then turned and looked over at
Shepherd who was further down the platform,
also directing people out.

'Control say it's not slowing down!' he
shouted. *'It'll be here in under a minute!'*

Swearing, Shepherd turned and ran towards the
front of the train standing in the platform, the

driver peering out of his window anxiously, waiting for instructions.

'Get out of here right now!'

On the approaching train, Archer was starting to sweat. He'd cleared all but one carriage, sending people down towards the rear, but the suspect was nowhere to be seen.

He heard the doors open behind him and the MTA guy reappeared, having successfully shepherded the passengers down to the other end of the train.

'Why are we still going?' Archer asked. 'I said we need to stop!'

'I tried!' the man said. 'I called the driver but he's not responding.'

Archer looked at the man for a moment then turned and stared up towards the front of the train, focusing on the closed door to the driver's cab in the next and last carriage. Pulling his pistol, he approached the connecting link between his carriage and the first. As they thundered through Canal Street, he saw a blur of cops and emergency personnel on the platform, but he barely registered them.

Holding his Sig Sauer double-handed, he entered the front carriage; he had no trouble attracting the attention of the passengers this time.

'Everyone get out,' he said quietly. 'Go down the train as far back as you can go. Don't take anything with you.'

The frightened passengers made no attempt to argue, the drawn weapon having an instant effect as they scrambled past him. A few moments later both he and the MTA employee were alone, the

connecting doors closing behind the last
passenger to leave.

Now just the two of them, Archer checked the
door to the driver's cabin ahead, looking for any
cameras.

'Can he see u-'

Before he could finish asking the question, a
burst of bullet holes suddenly appeared through
the driver's door ahead of them. Archer instantly
threw himself to the floor, dragging the MTA
man down with him, and fired back twice with
his Sig. Keeping down as another burst of gunfire
came from the cab, Archer saw the door swing
open, revealing the driver on the floor with his
hands over his head, the suspect standing beside
him and firing wildly with some kind of compact
sub-machine gun, lighting up the cab.

Firing back and aiming high to try and put the
gunman down but avoid hitting the driver, Archer
scrambled up and pushed the MTA man towards
the carriage behind them.

'Archer!' the MTA man's radio said, bursting
into life. *'Archer, it's Shepherd, can you hear
me?'*

As they moved into the second carriage and the
doors closed behind them, Archer snatched the
receiver just as the suspect let fly with another
barrage of gunfire, smashing the glass out above
their heads.

'Suspect located; he's in the cab!' he shouted
as he pulled the other man down, his voice
fighting to be heard over the wind now howling
through the train. *'But he's got an automatic
weapon; I'm pinned down!'*

'The driver?'

'Still alive!'

16

'Have you found the device?'

'It must be in there with them. I can't get near enough to find out!'

Up on street level, Josh and Vargas screeched to a halt at the top of Union Square on 16th Street, bailing out of their car and moving as fast as they could into the station, the place heaving with evacuating commuters coming the other way. Forcing a path through the crowd, the pair headed for the N/Q Uptown track where they knew the train would be arriving any second.

As they appeared, two cops standing with an MTA employee ran towards them, one of them holding a radio receiver.

'Your guy on the train found the suspect!' one of the cops told them. 'But he can't get near him. The son of a bitch is pinning him down with some kind of machine gun.'

As Josh grabbed the radio, Vargas heard the sound of the train approaching the Q rails below. Knowing they were out of time, she pulled her Sig Sauer and sprinted down the stairs that led to the middle of the platform.

As she reached the last step, the train roared into view and the brakes started to screech, the bomber arriving at his destination. Seeing the suspect in the cabin as the train ploughed along the track towards her, Vargas pushed two remaining members of the public out of the way and fired twice, straight at the driver's windows, the sound of the gunshots and splintering glass lost in the noise of the approaching train.

Holding on as the train ground to a halt, Archer went to fire into the cab again but then realised the sub-machine gunfire had ceased. Peering round his cover, he saw the suspect was slumped on top of the cowering driver on the floor.

Standing up slowly and stalking forward, his sights never leaving the gunman, he saw the man had been shot twice in the head. Seeing the blond man approach, the driver wriggled his way out from under the dead gunman, crawling over shell casings and broken glass.

Reaching the cabin, Archer saw two bullet-holes in the front window, the train only stopping because of the dead man's lever. The front of the Q train had moved through the 14th Street station and was now partially in the tunnel, dark gloom ahead illuminated by the occasional light; but Archer wasn't here to admire the view.

'Where's his bag?' he asked the driver quickly.

'What?'

'He must have had a bag. Where the hell is it?'

As the man stared at him, shocked and confused, Archer turned away to look around the cab. Fifteen feet behind him, the doors to the carriage were forced open, Josh and Vargas climbing inside with their weapons ready to fire and saw their team-mate in the cab.

'Arch!' Josh said urgently.

Archer didn't respond; instead, he dropped down, turned the dead suspect over and pulled open his jacket; frisking him down, he paused, then pushed up a sleeve.

The guy had cylinders of ball bearings taped to his limbs.

'Jesus Christ,' Vargas said quietly, bending down beside Archer.

Working fast, Archer patted down the gunman's torso and frowned. Quickly pushing up the man's shirt, he froze.

'What the-?' he whispered.

The suspect had fresh, angry-looking stitches covering his stomach; the skin was lumpy and inflamed, dried blood visible from the crude needlework.

The explosives were sewn under his skin.

As the detectives stared at the man's torso in disbelief, they saw a flashing green light just under the skin, accompanied by a quiet beeping sound.

And both had just started to quicken.

'Go!' Josh ordered the two MTA men, who not needing to be told twice, turned and stumbled away down the train.

Not wasting a second, Archer rose and pushed open the driver's side door, which swung out into the dark tunnel. Turning back, he grabbed the suspect's arms and pulled him towards the exit, Vargas and Josh picking up the man's legs.

They manoeuvred him awkwardly out of the train, the flashing light on the man's stomach getting faster, the three of them frantically searching for somewhere to dump the body before the explosives detonated. However, there were no obvious access doors, nowhere they could put the body, just dark dirty tunnel stretching onwards uptown.

Holding the dead man's arms, Archer looked around, the speed of the beeping and flashing under the stitches increasing by the second.

'Shit!'

Glancing down, he suddenly spotted a circular manhole cover a few feet in front of him on the lower level of the tracks, camouflaged with dirt and grime from the tunnel.

'There!' he said, Josh and Vargas following where he was looking.

Knowing they only had seconds, they quickly carried the dead terrorist towards the manhole cover; Archer lowered him gently to the ground, grabbed the cover with both hands and heaved it off.

The flashing was now going as fast as a drum roll.

Without ceremony, they stuffed the guy inside the hole, Josh and Vargas holding onto his ankles as they lowered the dead man onto several thick pipes, all three of them praying to God they weren't gas mains. With him safely placed, Josh and Vargas stepped back.

'Let's go!' Vargas said.

Grabbing the lid, Archer quickly lowered it back in place then sprinted back to the train behind the other two, taking care not to step on the tracks.

Pulling themselves up into the cab, they ran through the carriages, trying to put as much distance between themselves and the manhole as they could.

Suddenly there was an enormous muffled explosion, throwing the three detectives to the carriage floor. The whole station seemed to shake, dust and brick falling from the walls, the train rattling like a tin can caught in a tornado. Coughing, Archer looked up through the dust and to his relief, saw the other two moving.

A few seconds later the three of them slowly sat up and turned, looking towards the front of the train which had been annihilated, the wailing fire alarms accompanied by the sound of running water.

'You good?' Josh asked his colleagues over the noise.

Beside him, the other two nodded, Vargas giving a thumb's up. On the far left, Archer exhaled and lay back on the floor in exhausted relief.

'Next time I'm taking the bus,' he said.

TWO

Two and a half hours later, Archer and Josh were standing on the street in Union Square, the entire area illuminated by the flashing lights of emergency services vehicles and the glare of news-camera lights. The place was full of activity, members of the public and MTA employees who'd been directly caught up in the drama being treated for shock and minor injuries by medical teams.

CSU were down in the cavernous station examining the damaged front of the train, the entire place shut down for the time being. The FBI and ATF had shown up too; both agencies were being brought up to date on the situation as news teams both national and international were filming the Square from behind hurriedly-erected barriers, reporters interviewing members of the public trying to get what information they could as they reported back.

Standing beside his detective partner, Archer watched it all unfold; as he stood there he was also very aware that the Square was being doused with a torrent of water, jets spraying up into the air and drenching those in the immediate vicinity. It turned out those pipes Archer, Josh and Vargas had laid the body onto had been water mains supplying much of downtown Manhattan.

He glanced over at the geyser erupting from a storm drain forty or so feet away, aware of several burly maintenance workers looking in his direction; now the situation was safe, word had quickly spread regarding who'd been responsible for the destruction.

22

'Why are they looking at me?' he said to Josh, noting the glares directed at him. 'I wasn't the one with the C4 next to my guts.'

'Word's got round that putting our friend down the manhole was your idea,' Josh said, hiding a smile. 'Apparently Vargas and I were just following your lead.'

Archer raised an eyebrow. 'Oh, it's like that is it?'

'Sorry buddy. You know I've always got your back.' He nodded at the burly, blue-collar group. 'But not with those guys.'

Archer smiled. 'What happened to the driver, by the way?'

'He's OK. Bit shaken up; they took him to hospital. Said the gunman forced him to open up the cab at Atlantic then put a gun to his head.'

'Our boy must have seen me with the Sig on the camera and panicked,' Archer said. 'Guess he didn't want to risk the train being stopped by us before it made it here and he could detonate.'

Before Josh could reply, the two men sensed someone approaching and turned to see Marquez walking towards them, pushing her cell phone back into her pocket.

'Sergeant Hendricks and his team secured the other device,' she said. 'Just. They nailed him at 76th Street, heading for Times Square on the 1.'

'Alive?'

'Dead. He tried to run so Philips blasted him; head shot like Vargas, luckily for them. Same deal, ball bearings strapped to his limbs, explosives and a timer under his skin, loaded to the gills with crystal meth to numb the pain and pump them up. Bomb disposal managed to cut him open and defuse the charge before it blew.'

Archer grimaced. 'How pleasant.'

'What were estimated casualties?' Josh asked.

'Including down here, over a thousand. Times Square was packed.'

'The motive?'

'Same old shit; idiots with a so-called cause. But these bastards were inventive; they knew even if someone found them or put them down, they couldn't get to the explosives and timer. Bomb disposal call it *Franken-bombing*, apparently it's becoming increasingly common.'

As both men absorbed this, Shepherd joined the group, having wrapped up a conversation with two agents from the FBI and ATF.

'Everything OK, sir?' Marquez asked.

He nodded. 'Just about. The Feds are saying we left it late to move in.'

'We only just got this tip-off. Wasn't our choice to cut it so fine.'

Looking at Archer, Shepherd smiled. 'By the way, if you were ever thinking about running for Mayor I'd reconsider it. You're not exactly flavour of the month with the Worker's Union over there.'

He nodded towards the city maintenance guys, who now had the mighty task on their hands of repairing the damage, water continuing to gush up through the ruptured concrete.

'Apparently they only finished work on that pipe last week. They're suggesting sending you down there head-first to plug the hole.'

As the others laughed and Archer started to protest again, the group saw Vargas reappear, stepping out of a portable mobile command truck forty feet away, her pistol absent from her hip. Seeing as she was the one who put down the suspect, she'd been in there for almost an hour giving a statement. She'd had one hell of an evening; not only had she put two rounds in the bomber, but when they'd breached the suspect's apartment in Brooklyn she'd been the one who'd found the schedules of those particular trains with the two stations marked.

She immediately spotted the rest of her team and walked across the Square.

'You good?' Shepherd asked as she joined them.

'All clear. They took my Sig as evidence. I'll get it back next week.'

'They should give you a medal to go with it,' Shepherd replied.

'I'll just take going home for the night.'

'Me too,' he replied, turning to his team. 'I'll head back to the Precinct and start on the reports. Go home and get some rest. You deserve it; good work, guys. I'm proud.'

The group nodded their thanks and Shepherd walked off through the Square, leaving his four detectives alone.

'I need a beer,' Josh said. 'Anyone else?'

'Not for me,' Vargas said. 'I'm spent.'

'Arch?'

'Not tonight, mate.'

'Lisa?'

'Right now I just want to go home and see my kid. Give me a ride?'

Josh nodded, turning to Archer and Vargas. 'See you guys tomorrow. A night to remember, right?'

They both nodded. A beat later he and Marquez headed off through the Square towards one of the two NYPD Fords. Left alone, Archer and Vargas

25

looked at each other, the events of the day starting to hit them both now the adrenaline rush had faded.

'Think I've had enough for one day,' Archer said.

Running her hand through her hair, Vargas nodded. 'That's for sure.'

'Let's get the hell out of here.'

Glancing at the maintenance workers, she managed to raise a smile. 'I'd say that's the second best decision you've made today.'

THREE

Fifteen minutes later, Archer and Vargas crossed the Queensborough Bridge in a black Bureau Ford as the clock on the dash ticked past *9:45pm*, the sun already gone for the day and a thickening veil of darkness drawing across the city.

Archer was behind the wheel, Vargas in the passenger seat beside him with her cell phone in her hands, checking for any messages. Leaving the Bridge and moving into Queens, Archer glanced at her. She still seemed wound up, which was natural, but as she looked at her phone, he saw a tiny shift upwards in her body language and guessed who'd be on her mind; her adopted daughter, Isabel.

'Is she back yet?' he asked.

Vargas smiled. 'She's downstairs with John. He's asking when we'll get home.'

'We got anything in the fridge?'

'Not much. Don't think I could eat anyway.'

'Neither do I but she'll want to. Let's get a pizza or something.'

She nodded and tapped in a reply as Archer took a right turn down 39th Avenue before swinging left into a parking lot, just a handful of cars sitting in the bays with a row of stores fifty feet away. As Vargas sent the message and put her cell away, Archer pulled to a stop in an empty space.

Switching off the engine, he reached for his door handle but then realised Vargas hadn't moved. Turning, he saw she was staring at the dashboard, the momentary lift Isabel had given her already dissipating like mist in the sun.

27

He paused, his hand on the door. 'Everything OK?'

She didn't reply.

Withdrawing his fingers from the handle, he turned to her.

'Hey. Talk to me. What's up?'

'We should have died tonight,' she said after a few moments.

Archer paused for a moment. 'I know.'

'I feel like I end up saying that every couple of months.'

He smiled. 'But you're still alive.'

'It's not me I'm worried about.'

She continued to stare straight ahead, not looking at him.

Archer touched her hand. 'I'm still here. See?'

'Yeah, but only just.'

She exhaled sharply, obviously wound up and stressed; Archer turned all the way in his seat to face her.

'I'm not going anywhere. Shit, Alice, even Wile E Coyote couldn't get me.'

She suddenly smiled. 'He couldn't get anyone, Archer. That was the whole point.'

He grinned back and she laughed briefly, closing her eyes and keeping them shut.

When she opened them again, he could see a slight sheen of tears.

'I'm not going anywhere,' Archer repeated, squeezing her hand. 'I mean it.'

Tears still in her eyes, she glanced at him.

'You promise?'

He smiled. 'I promise. I won't leave you. I'm here for good.'

As he watched her, seeing his words having an effect, she suddenly leaned forward and kissed him, something she never normally did when they were on duty. A few seconds later she withdrew and smiled again, wiping her eyes.

'Come to think of it, Josh was right. We definitely need some booze.'

'I'll get it. My treat.'

Shaking her head, she pushed open her door handle. 'Stay put. This one's on me, Road-Runner.'

With that she stepped out of the car and shut the door, then walked across the car park towards the stores. Watching her go, Archer's own smile lingered for a few moments.

Then it faded as he watched her arrive at a deli and disappear inside.

He and Vargas had been working together since June, Alice brought into the Department from the US Marshals Service. However, they'd met a few weeks prior to that on a warm night in March, a first encounter neither was likely to forget.

Alice and a team of fellow Marshals had been attacked on the upper West Side by a group of armed gunmen. Happening to be passing by, Archer had raced to their aid and ended up taking refuge with the team inside a Harlem apartment block to find the trouble had only just begun, more killers arriving intent on wiping them all out. It had been a nightmarish few hours as they'd fought to survive; considering the odds against them, they should have died, but somehow they'd made it out and that night had forever changed his life.

He'd read a 9/11 anniversary article a few weeks ago focusing on the bonds that developed between survivors from that day, people from vastly different backgrounds brought together by the terrible experiences they'd undergone that no-one else, no matter how sympathetic, could ever truly comprehend. Although under far different circumstances, he felt he had more understanding of that sense of kinship than he did before. Twice in six months he and Vargas had been side by side thinking they were about to die, three times if they included tonight. Surviving those ordeals gave every second they were alive an intensity and clarity that he'd never previously experienced. When he thought back to the past, his life before he'd met her that night in March seemed to have been in sepia tone, like an old Hollywood movie. Her presence had given it colour.

Which earlier tonight had almost cut to black.

Looking up, he watched her leave the deli and step into the pizzeria, a six-pack of beer in a white bag clutched under her arm. Her concerns about his wellbeing weren't unfounded; the Q train wasn't the first time in the last few years that Archer had survived against the odds.

Having come from the Armed Response Unit, one of the two premier counter-terrorist teams in London where he'd experienced some serious heat, Archer had been in New York for fourteen months and the temperature hadn't dropped at all. During that time, he'd been up against everyone from psychotic neo-Nazi terrorists to corrupt cops determined to empty a clip into his skull. Using all his skills, training and every ounce of luck that he appeared to have been blessed with, he'd cheated death more times than he liked to remember.

However, now things had changed. Before, he'd only ever had to worry about himself but now he had Vargas and Isabel to consider, both of whom had their own demons to battle. Isabel had had one hell of a year to say the least and Alice seemed to attract almost as much trouble as he did. With every passing day he felt more attached to the pair and it scared the shit out of him.

I'm not going anywhere, he'd told her. Given the nature of their work, that was a bold statement. Alice was right; it seemed as if every few months they came face to face with death and tonight was a perfect example. Before the call had come in, Archer and the team had been assessing a routine case at the Bureau's HQ, winding down for the day.

An hour later he, Vargas and Josh had almost died.

But how many lives do you have left? a voice whispered at the back of his mind. He'd used up more than his fair share already; as he thought back to all those close-calls, he watched Vargas twenty yards away inside the parlour and felt a jolt in his stomach.

I don't know.

Feeling like some fresh air and doing his best to banish the negative thoughts swirling around his head, he opened his door and stepped out, closing it behind him with a quiet click.

Although there were a number of parked vehicles dotted about, the lot was empty of human activity, a quiet night in Queens. As he stood there, he realised he was still wearing the workman's shirt that he'd borrowed to cover his NYPD vest, the sleeves rolled halfway up his forearms, the fabric still showing the effects of the explosion in the station, dusty and slightly dirty. Patting the chest pocket, he felt the pliers;

he'd have to see if he could track the guy down and return them. *Maybe give the shirt a run through the washing machine first,* he told himself.

He undid the buttons and was about to pull it off but then movement across the car park caught his eye.

He saw a young woman heading quickly towards a car.

She was blonde and very attractive, in her late teens or possibly early twenties, dressed in a plaid shirt and short skirt. She was wearing high-heels that clicked rapidly on the concrete as she hurried towards her vehicle, a beaten-up white Chevy Lumina parked fifteen yards away, sitting on its own in an otherwise empty row.

Archer watched as she nervously checked over her shoulder just before she reached her car then quickly rummaged through her bag, presumably looking for her keys.

There was something about her nervous behaviour that held his attention. He'd always been able to read people well, a skill that had been honed during his time as a cop, and as the woman glanced around her, he recognised the look on her face.

It was fear.

Beyond the woman, Vargas stepped out of the pizza joint, checking her cell with one hand and carrying a box with the six-pack of Budweiser balanced on the top with the other. She walked past the young blonde without even noticing her, engrossed in her phone as the girl found her keys and pulled them out.

'Went for mozzarella and pepperoni,' Vargas said, re-joining Archer by the Ford and putting her phone away. 'No pineapple. God sure as hell didn't invent pizza so we could put fruit on it.'

Archer didn't reply, focused on the young woman, who was now fumbling with the car lock.

'Something wrong?' Vargas asked, turning to see what Archer was looking at.

But before he could reply, it happened.

A black van that had just entered the other side of the car park suddenly roared forward and slammed to a halt beside the blonde woman. As she spun round in shock, dropping the keys, the side door on the van was ripped open, revealing a man in a grey tracksuit and white ice hockey mask holding a grey pistol.

He fired immediately, the muzzle flashing, and the bullet cut straight through her, smashing out the driver's window of the Chevy.

Before the girl even landed on the concrete, Archer's hand was already on the grip of the Sig Sauer P226 on his hip but the gunman had the drop on him and moved fast, swinging the pistol round in Archer's direction and firing twice, a quick double-tap. The two bullets hit him in the chest with the force of what felt like a freight train, winding him and knocking him to the ground.

Six feet from him, Vargas had reacted just as fast but seeing Archer go down caused her to hesitate a split second. She'd already dropped the pizza box and booze and reached instinctively to her hip but there was nothing there except an empty holster. Her weapon was with the Department, left for analysis after the shooting at Union Square.

A second later there was another gunshot and Vargas took the round in the neck, blood spraying

33

into the air, and she hit the concrete hard in a heap.

Lying there on his side, Archer stared at her in horror. He saw his Sig a few feet away but it was out of reach. Fighting to breathe, he looked across the lot and saw the masked man jump quickly out of the van and put two bullets into the blond woman's head, the harsh gunshots booming in the night, someone screaming from somewhere nearby as dogs barked in the distance

Turning, the anonymous gunman then stalked towards Archer and Vargas.

Seeing the man coming, Archer tried to reach for his pistol but the guy made it before he could touch it and kicked the Sig away, the metal gun skidding across the concrete out of reach.

Standing over him, the gunman then aimed his pistol at Archer's head, smoke coming from the barrel and the air stinking of cordite, greasy straggly hair visible either side of the hockey mask.

Waiting for the final shot, staring at the last thing he'd ever see, Archer suddenly saw the brown eyes behind the pistol barrel and hockey mask widen.

'Oh shit,' the guy said, his voice muffled under the mask.

Behind him, the driver of the van leant out and shouted to his partner. *'What are you doing? Kill them!'*

'They're cops!'

'What?'

'They're cops!'

The driver pushed open his door and stepped out, running around the van with the engine still running.

Both Archer's and Vargas' NYPD vests were now clearly visible through the parted fabric of their shirts, as were the badges on thin ball chains around their necks.

'*Shit!*' the driver said, looking down at the pair. '*What the hell do we do?*'

'*Screw it. We kill them.*'

'*Whoa, are you crazy? We'll have the entire NYPD on our asses!*'

'*They've seen us.*'

'*They haven't seen shit!*'

The gunman didn't reply, his gun still aimed at Archer, indecision in his eyes behind the mask as the driver's words had an effect.

Suddenly he turned his head a fraction. The sound of sirens could be heard in the distance, the first responders reacting fast, someone having already called 911 or patrols reacting to the sound of the gunshots.

'*Let's go!*' the driver shouted, running back to the van.

Staying where he was, his pistol still trained on Archer, the gunman hesitated a moment longer, trying to decide what to do as he looked at the downed cops.

Helpless, Archer watched him as he fought for breath, Vargas lying still as she bled out over the concrete a few feet from him.

The approaching sirens in the distance spurred the gunman into a decision.

He swore and ran over to the van, jumping into the back and pulling the sliding door across as the driver floored it, the tyres squealing as the vehicle sped out of the lot and away into the night.

With the van and the two men gone, the car park was suddenly silent, the noise of the receding vehicle fading as the sound of the sirens grew louder.

Still half-winded, Archer hauled himself up and crawled over to Vargas, his forearms imprinted with her blood from the concrete.

She was lying on her back, her head tilted to the right, and was looking up at him. Blood was leaking out in a pool around her, already matting her dark hair, her eyes wide with silent shock and fear as she stared at him.

He clamped his right hand over the wound, holding his left to the side of her head, looking down at her as she bled out.

She tried to say something, her lips moving slowly, but nothing came out, her blood warm against his fingers as it continued to pulse from the wound.

'Hold on, Alice,' he whispered fearfully, looking at her so they were face to face. *'Just hold on.'*

Panic in her eyes, Vargas again tried to say something as she stared up at him.

'I'm not going anywhere,' Archer said, desperately trying to reassure her as her blood ran through his fingers. 'I promise.'

Vargas didn't reply. She couldn't.

And as he stared at her, Archer saw the faintest sheen of tears appear in her eyes again.

FOUR

A month later it was the third week of October. The warmth of the summer was now just a memory, replaced by a chill that seemed to be increasing by the day, the leaves on the trees in the city turning golden, caramel and brown as the city residents began to get ready for the upcoming holiday sequence of Halloween, Thanksgiving and Christmas.

A few blocks from his home on West 78th Street, Josh watched leaves fall from trees across the street and drift down onto the pedestrians below, the branches disturbed by the slight wind. He was sitting inside a coffee shop, a freshly-served cup of Earl Grey tea in front of him. The place was warm and welcoming, smelling of blended coffee and baked goods straight from the oven; as it was mid-afternoon on a Sunday the atmosphere was muted, but under the table Josh's leg was jiggling with suppressed tension as his mind raced, turning over possible scenarios.

Unlike those around him, he wasn't at all relaxed.

He hadn't thought it possible but what had already been a terrible few weeks had, in the last few hours, threatened to take a drastic turn for the worse.

Twenty feet away, the bell rang as the door opened, allowing a sudden rush of cold air into the coffee shop; Josh looked over and saw Marquez walk in, right on schedule. She was dressed in grey jeans, a black and grey polo neck and a black jacket, the pistol and NYPD badge on

37

her hip briefly visible as she closed the door, her dark hair loose around her shoulders.

Spotting her team-mate, she moved forward to join him, taking a seat across the small table and blowing air into her cold hands.

'Any sign of him?' Josh asked, as she sat down.

'Nothing,' she said. 'He wasn't there. You?'

'Not a trace. I checked his apartment, his gym, his local bar, talked to his neighbours. They haven't seen him since yesterday morning.'

Marquez swore. 'So where the hell is he?'

As the pair looked at each other, confused and worried, a waitress approached and Marquez ordered a black coffee, no milk or sugar.

'You think he flew back to England?' she suggested, once the waitress had departed. 'Just forgot to mention it?'

'I thought of that so I called Chalky. He said he and Archer haven't spoken for a couple of weeks. Anyway, Arch's hearing is on Monday. He's not allowed to skip town. He misses that, he knows he could get kicked out of the Department.'

There was a pause. Marquez ran her hand through her hair worriedly, looking out of the window.

'When was the last time you spoke to him?' she asked.

'Day before yesterday.'

'How was he?'

'Pissed off. Really pissed off.' As he spoke, Josh noticed the look on her face. 'What?'

'You think he did something stupid?'

'What do you mean?'

'What happened to Vargas hit him hard. That kind of shit can mess with your head.'

Josh realised what she was thinking. 'Lisa, are you kidding? This is Sam Archer we're talking about. That son of a bitch is harder to put down than anyone I've ever met. No way would he help someone do it.'

'No, no, I don't mean that,' she said hurriedly. 'I mean do you think there's a possibility he went after someone? On his own, without telling us?'

'Why would he? The case is closed.'

'Maybe he found something.'

Before Josh could reply, Marquez' coffee arrived. As the female detective thanked the waitress and picked up the cup, wrapping both hands around it in an attempt to warm her cold fingers, Josh considered the possibility of his detective partner planning to exact his own justice after what had happened in that parking lot four weeks ago.

It wasn't exactly a stretch to see him doing it.

'Let's track back, to the beginning,' Marquez said, cradling her cup. 'See if we can figure out where he could possibly be.'

Josh nodded. 'I'll start. Archer and Vargas are on their way home and stop to pick up a six pack and some pizza. As they're about to leave a van pulls up, someone shoots a girl then takes out Arch and Alice before they could react. Vargas takes one to the neck, Arch two to the chest; the vest saves his life.'

'With the shooting going down in their Precinct's jurisdiction, Homicide from the 114th take charge of the investigation,' Marquez continued. 'But they don't make any progress in almost a month. When we go over there last Saturday to find out what the hell is going on,

39

Archer loses his shit and lays out one of the investigative team.'

She paused.

'A Lieutenant.'

'Archer's suspended on the spot and his badge and gun are confiscated,' Josh continued. 'Four days later, the two leading suspects are found and the case is closed, which was Thursday, seventy two hours ago.'

'And Archer's hearing for assaulting the Lieutenant is tomorrow at 10am,' Marquez finished. 'If he's lucky he'll be demoted. If he's not, which is far more likely, they'll kick him out of the Counter-Terrorism Bureau. That's if he even shows up.'

Josh cursed. 'I don't know much about the guy he punched, but I heard he has a bad reputation.'

Marquez nodded. 'I've got a friend at the 114th; she said if you get on the wrong side of this guy, he's like kryptonite to your career. He's a vindictive bastard and right now, Archer is the number one target in his crosshairs. Lieutenant Royston wants him on a platter with sides.'

There was another pause. Frustrated and worried in equal measure, Josh looked around the coffee shop as Marquez took a sip from her drink.

'How's Isabel?' she asked, keeping the cup close to her lips.

'Confused.'

'What does she know?'

'Nothing. When it all went down, Archer told her Vargas had to go away to see some family. She doesn't understand why Alice hasn't called in a month. Or Arch, now.'

'When was the last time he spoke to her?'

'Three days ago. She keeps asking where he is and why he hasn't called. I'm beginning to run out of excuses.'

Marquez took another mouthful of coffee then reached inside her jacket and pulled out a folded brown envelope, sliding it over to Josh.

'After you called, I stopped by the Bureau. Ethan pulled it for me. It's the 114ths closed case file from the shooting. Check it out.'

Quickly scooping it up, Josh opened the envelope, curious to see first-hand the details of the investigation that they were all so invested in.

The uppermost sheet was a photo of a dead blonde woman slumped on concrete, keys and bag lying beside her, the girl who'd been shot in the parking lot. A small square police mug-shot of her holding a placard was pinned to the top; she was very attractive with a porcelain complexion, arresting green eyes and long blonde hair. She wouldn't have looked out of place on a catwalk or gracing a magazine cover.

'Her name was Leann Casey,' Marquez said, as Josh studied the girl's photo. 'She was a nineteen year old escort.'

'Pretty girl.'

Marquez nodded. 'Expensive too, not street trash. The day that mug-shot was taken, she was arrested in a Vice bust on an Upper West Side hotel. Client unknown due to an injunction, which means he had a profile to protect. But apparently her rate was $5000 a night. She served three months in the women's facility on Rikers Island.'

'A kid like this?' he said. 'She'd be feed in a place like that.'

'She was,' Marquez said, turning the photo over.

41

There were several of the girl's face, this time badly battered and bruised, her lip split, one eye swollen, her beautiful face almost unrecognisable.

'She was lucky to get away with just that,' Marquez added.

Josh stayed silent, looking at the photographs for a moment, then turned the page to her report from the rehabilitation facility.

'She was killed the day she left rehab,' Josh noted, reading the notes.

'Less than two hours after she walked out. She'd admitted herself into Covenant Housing, who supported her through a four week drug rehabilitation program for addiction to pain-killers. The staff there were the last documented people to see her alive, apart from Arch and Alice. And her killers, of course.'

'Homicide talked to the clinic?'

Marquez nodded. 'It was out on Long Island. Near Jones Beach.'

'Was she scared to leave?' Josh asked.

'Quite the opposite,' she said. 'They had nothing but good things to say about her. Said she was upbeat, positive, excited, confident. A different person from the one who'd checked herself in four weeks earlier.'

Flicking back to the first page, Josh glanced at the crime-scene photo of the girl whose life had been so brutally and suddenly extinguished. She'd been shot once in the chest and twice in the head.

Executed.

Turning to the next sheaf of paper, he stared down at a series of photographs clipped to an incident report, these images taken from inside a run-down apartment somewhere, old battered furniture, peeling paint and a litter-strewn floor.

Two Latino men were laid out on that floor, dead from gunshot wounds. They looked to be a similar size and build, both wearing jeans, one with a hooded sweatshirt and the other in a blue Giants football jersey. One had a buzz-cut, the other a longer straggly mop. The guy with all the hair had been shot twice in the chest, the other in the side of the head, a grey silenced pistol lying in his open hand.

Suddenly remembering he was in a public venue, Josh tilted the photo close so no-one around him could see what he was looking at.

'The suspects,' Marquez said. 'Mario Valdez and Hector Carvalho, two low-rate pimps who pushed girls in Spanish Harlem. Both were found dead on Thursday afternoon at Valdez' apartment on 168th and Amsterdam. They matched the descriptions of the car park shooters provided to detectives by several witnesses, including a liquor store clerk and a mechanic who was working across the street when Leann, Arch and Vargas were shot.'

'I thought they were wearing masks?'

'They were but in relation to witness statements, their hair, build and the pistol put them at the scene.'

Josh looked at the photo, focusing on the grey handgun resting in Carvalho's open palm.

'That's a Steyr M9. German weapon.'

'The same gun that killed Leann Casey.'

'They held onto it?'

'Judging by their priors, these two weren't exactly Mensa material. How they died underlined that.'

She tapped the photo.

'Homicide and CSU figured they had a fight, Carvalho lost the plot, shot his buddy then for some reason killed himself.'

Josh frowned. 'Four weeks after they killed Leann and shot Arch and Vargas, they suddenly end up dead with the murder weapon at the scene?'

'And take a look at the suspected motive.'

Josh thumbed through the incident report, quickly finding what Marquez was referring to.

'Eliminating competition,' she said as he read. 'Apparently.'

'But Leann Casey only has a history of working in the Upper West and East Sides,' Josh said. 'And she charged around five grand a night.'

Marquez nodded. 'Completely different patches and a totally different class of girl. Valdez and Carvalho ran street trash for thirty bucks a trick in Spanish Harlem and Leann was anything but. She was in an entirely different league.'

'And even if they were trying to up their game, why kill the golden goose?' Josh said. 'Five thousand a night? She'd be worth a hell of a lot more alive than dead.'

Marquez nodded, but didn't speak, the unanswered questions hanging in the air. Taking a last look at the folder, Josh shut it and placed it on the table in front of him.

'Shit,' he said.

'Exactly.'

'There're more holes in this than a Texas oil field.'

'According to the 114th, it's good enough. They've locked it down and moved on. Ethan said he had to call in a big favour to get this.'

44

'It's obvious that this needs more attention. Something is way off here.'

He paused, thinking.

'Why the hell would they just leave it like this? That's a good team over there.'

'I think the pressure was on from the Department and the city to find who shot Vargas; the press are right into this case too. Homicide was clutching at straws, then suddenly they have a stroke of luck; two suspects dead with the actual murder weapon at the scene. Forget asking questions, the glove fits so it's staying on the hand.'

'Every loose end tied, case closed, everyone happy,' Josh said. 'Not left with an investigation that could drag on for months staining the 114th's reputation.'

Marquez nodded and tapped the file. 'But four weeks after they shoot Leann, Vargas and Archer, this hombre suddenly ups and kills himself after dropping his friend? It doesn't make any goddamn sense.'

Josh sat quietly for a moment, looking at her. 'You reckon Arch is thinking the same way?'

'Count on it,' she replied. 'You and I saw these anomalies in minutes. Imagine what he's had time to dig up with a week's suspension.'

'How could he get the files?'

'Ethan's source at the 114th said someone else asked to see them earlier in the week. My friend told me that apart from a few of his favourites he groomed from the Academy, Royston's hated by most of the guys over there. They reckon he gives them a bad reputation. I think they'd help Arch out if he needed it.'

Josh paused as the thought of Archer reminded him of someone else.

'How's Alice doing?' he asked.

'Still on the private recovery floor. She's improving.'

'Her security?'

'Still in place. Shepherd's insisted on it until she's out even though the case is closed. Two cops outside her door at all times. Archer's been banned from seeing her since his suspension, but hospital staff said he hasn't called either since Friday lunchtime.'

Josh swore. 'That really makes me uneasy. He'd walk barefoot over hot coals to get to her. He'd never just stop checking on her status.'

Marquez looked at him for a moment then focused on her coffee. Across the table Josh stared out of the window, trying to work through this latest information.

It'd been over two days since anyone had seen or heard from his detective partner; Archer seemed to have disappeared right off the face of the earth. Josh imagined him working alone, trying to find out if Valdez and Carvalho really were the killers. Asking questions, digging deeper, possibly finding something or someone Homicide had missed.

And quite possibly getting himself into deep shit, with no-one to watch his back.

Thinking back to his visit to Archer's apartment building thirty minutes ago, he suddenly straightened, realising something.

'What?' Marquez said, noticing the shift in his behaviour.

'His car wasn't outside his place,' Josh replied.

Reaching into his pocket, he pulled out his cell phone and dialled the Bureau.

'I'll get Ethan to run a trace on the plates. If he's parked it somewhere in the city, we can find it.'

Looking at him, her eyes brightening with hope, Marquez drained her coffee. 'Still have the key to his apartment on you?'

His phone to his ear, Josh nodded and tapped his pocket with his other hand.

'Right here. But I already checked it out.'

'Let's go take another look,' Marquez said, sliding off her seat as Josh connected to Ethan. 'I've got a bad feeling about this. Something's really not right.'

As Josh and Marquez left the Upper West Side coffee shop, downtown in Hell's Kitchen an attractive nineteen year old African American girl called Kelly Greer walked quickly into her apartment building, checking nervously behind her before closing the main door.

Turning, she moved up the stairs, her heart thumping as she pulled her cell phone and retried a number.

Once again, it rang out.

Gripping her cell, she tried another number but no-one answered that either. She started to feel sick with fear. That was two more girls not answering their phones.

She paused in the hallway to steady herself, closing her eyes and taking a deep breath. Then moving down the corridor, she unlocked her apartment door and walked quickly inside.

A moment later, a large hand clamped over her mouth. Her scream muffled, she tried to fight back as the door was slammed shut behind her, someone with brutal strength keeping hold of her as she fought and struggled. She realised there was a rag in the hand covering her mouth, some chemical pushed against her nose and lips, the palm of the gloved hand holding it in place.

Unable to breathe, she inhaled involuntarily.

And a second later she passed out.

FIVE

Across the East River in Queens, Josh and Marquez pulled to a halt outside a semi-detached building in Astoria; there was just one apartment per floor, the place Archer shared with Vargas and Isabel located at the top. Josh switched the engine off and the two detectives stepped out of the car, closed their doors and walked over to the building's entrance.

As Marquez glanced around her, noting that Archer's car was definitely missing, Josh withdrew the spare key Archer had given him a while back and opened the front door. They walked inside, made their way up to the 3rd floor and came to a halt outside the apartment.

'He might have come back,' Marquez said, more in hope than expectation.

Glancing at her, Josh knocked and waited for a moment.

There was no response.

A beat later he slid the key in the lock and opened up.

As they walked inside, the pair sensed the apartment was empty; it had that deserted, forlorn feeling homes have when they've been unoccupied for a while. To the right was the sitting area and door to the balcony; straight ahead was the kitchen and to the left were the bedrooms and bathroom. Everything was as it should be, a few personal possessions strewn about but there was no sign of any disturbance, nothing unusual and no obvious clue as to where Archer had gone or where he might be right now.

Turning, Marquez walked down the corridor and towards the main bedroom, easing the door back. The double bed was empty and made, the window half open, making the room feel chilly. Her eyes settled on a bedside table. There was a picture frame sitting there; she stepped forward and picked it up. The photo was of Archer with Vargas and Isabel in a stadium, all three of them smiling at the camera, Vargas wearing a blue Dodgers baseball cap back to front, Isabel standing on a seat beside her, a blue baseball cap on her head matching Alice's with *LA* printed on the front in bold white lettering.

Looking at it, the thin curtains billowing in the wind the only movement in the room, she smiled briefly. It must have been taken at the beginning of this summer.

Then the smile faded.

A lot had happened since then.

Placing the frame back on the table, she glanced around and saw there was nothing here to provide any sort of clue to Archer's whereabouts; she walked over to the window and shut it, then left the room. Heading back down the corridor, she passed another bedroom on her left. Glancing through the open door she could see a pink bedspread, posters on the wall and stuffed animals on a shelf; Isabel's room.

Seeing nothing out of the ordinary, she moved back into the sitting room and glanced around. Everything was in place, nothing disturbed, no clues to suggest where Archer might have gone.

Beyond the kitchen counter in the sitting area, Josh was perched on a chair near the wall, flicking through some papers.

'No case files, no keys, no phone,' he said.

'And no Archer,' Marquez muttered, looking around.

Her fondness for him extended beyond that of a work colleague; she regarded him as one of her closest friends and with that in mind, she was worried. Going dark like this was totally out of character for him. She'd seen first-hand the effect that Vargas' shooting had had on him; despite being suspended, she knew he wouldn't have just let this go. You'd have to kill Archer to get him to quit.

She looked around the empty apartment, that last thought echoing in her mind. She knew Arch; with a closed case that full of questions, he must have found something.

Or something must have found him.

Josh's phone suddenly rang, the sudden noise catching them both by surprise. Pulling out the Samsung quickly, he saw it was the Bureau and put it on speaker.

'Blake.'

'Josh, it's me,' Ethan said. *'I got a hit on Archer's car.'*

Josh and Marquez looked at each other, hope flaring in their eyes. 'Where?'

'It just rolled into the Midtown impound. They picked it up on East 19th. Apparently it's been sitting there collecting tickets for two days.'

As Josh absorbed this information, Marquez remembered something she'd read earlier and pulled out the brown envelope from her jacket pocket. Rapidly rifling through the pages, she found the sheet she was looking for and withdrew it, holding it up so Josh could read it, pointing to an address.

'Any idea why he'd park in the East Village?'
Ethan asked, his voice echoing around the empty apartment.

'East 19th Street,' Josh repeated, looking at where Marquez's forefinger was resting. 'That's where Leann Casey's mother lives.'

Once she enters the sex trade, the average life expectancy for a prostitute in the United States is seven years. AIDS and homicide are the two main reasons for that statistic, but at that moment it was the latter that the terrified young escort called Cece Mills was concerned with.

She was alone in her West Village apartment, her room-mate out of town. With her attention split between gathering her things and watching the front door, she frantically packed her most valuable possessions into an overnight bag, her ears straining for any unusual noises coming from outside the apartment.

At twenty three years old she was already five years into that seven year life-span statistic but she knew if she didn't get the hell out of there right now there was a more than high chance that she wouldn't make it another two.

Almost finished packing, she hurried across the bedroom through the open door and into the kitchen. Ripping open a cupboard, she pulled out a can of tomato soup camouflaged amongst all the others and unscrewed the top. After some advice from one of the other girls a while back, she'd started to store a gradually-increasing wad of money away, an emergency fund. The cash was rolled up tight, six grand in total, her life savings which had taken months to build up, a joke considering she earned $5000 a night for the people who controlled her.

Taking the money, she pulled off the elastic band holding it together then flattened out the half-folded bills and tucked them into her bra. Pulling out a cell phone, she moved back into the bedroom and dialled that friend who'd told her to stow the cash. She had to correct herself halfway through the sequence, misdialling due to her shaking hands, but she finally got it right and pressed *Call.*

'*C'mon; pick up,*' she whispered as she zipped up her bag with one hand.

It continued to ring, no-one answering.

'Pick up!'

'*Hello?*'

'April, it's Cece!' she said hurriedly. 'We're in deep shit, babe.'

'*What's wrong?*'

'Kelly's not answering now,' she said quietly, her voice cracking.

'*Are you serious?*'

She squeezed her eyes shut. 'It's just you and me. We're the only ones left.'

'*Where are you?*'

'At home,' she said, holding the phone against her ear with her shoulder as she picked up her bag, grabbed her keys and moved to the door. 'I'm getting the hell out of here.'

'*Come over to my place right now. We'll get out of the city and figure out what to do.*'

'OK,' she said, opening up. 'I'll be the-'

As she opened the door she was suddenly pushed back into the room by a large figure in a black gas mask and white overalls, his hand around her throat and her scream cut off a second into the sound. As she stumbled back, Cece dropped the phone, the call still connected, and kicked out at her attacker but she was totally outmatched in size and strength. She fought in vain as two other figures similarly dressed moved into the apartment behind the lead figure and closed the door.

As she continued to struggle, the huge figure kept her restrained in an effortless iron grip, then whipped her around, clamping a chemical-soaked rag over her nose and mouth. Using up all her oxygen, her screaming and shouting muffled under the man's glove, Cece was forced to inhale.

Then she passed out.

SIX

Assisted by the relative lack of traffic on the
Sunday city streets, Josh and Marquez made it
down to the East Village in quick time, parking
by the sidewalk outside Karen Casey's apartment
building on East 19th Street. Exiting the car, the
pair quickly moved towards the building's
entrance, Josh running forward and catching the
door as a couple walked out, Marquez following
him inside.

Ten seconds later, they arrived outside 2B. Josh
knocked on the door; there was a delay then the
sound of movement before the door opened a
fraction, catching on the chain.

A middle-aged woman peered through the gap.
They could only see an inch of her but even so
they saw she looked hostile.

'Help you?' she asked.

'Are you Karen Casey?'

'Who's asking?'

'Lisa Marquez and Josh Blake,' Marquez said,
showing her badge. 'We're detectives with the
NYPD.'

A second later the door was slammed in their
faces.

'We need to talk to you, ma'am,' Josh said,
raising his voice so he could be heard. 'Please.'

*'Go away. If this is about Leann, I've said it
all.'*

'This is about one of our detectives,' Marquez
said. 'He's gone missing.'

'So?'

She looked at Josh, trying to find the right
things to say. 'We think he might have come to

55

see you before he disappeared. His car was towed from down the street less than an hour ago. We don't know where he is and we figured you may be able to help.'

There was a long pause, the pair looking at each other. The door remained shut.

Cursing under his breath, Josh shook his head at Marquez and they turned to leave.

'Is that the only reason you're here?' Karen's voice asked.

Marquez looked at Josh. 'No.'

There was the sound of rattling and then the door opened fully this time, to reveal a slim woman somewhere in her forties. She looked tired and worn, dark shadows under her eyes but nevertheless it was easy to see she would once have been very attractive, just like her daughter.

She folded her arms defensively, looking at the two detectives. 'So what's the other reason? Leann?'

'We're from the Counter-Terrorism Bureau. We're taking a look at the case.'

'Jesus Christ, I got a call telling me you found her killers. Why the hell are you still looking at this? And why Counter-Terrorism? You're telling me Leann was mixed up with terrorists?'

'No, of course not,' Marquez said. 'Two of our colleagues were shot that night with Leann. That's why we're involved.'

Karen didn't reply.

'One of them has gone missing and we're trying to find him. His name's Sam Archer.'

'The blond guy?'

'That's him. He came to see you?'

'He did; two days ago. Friday night.'

'What did you talk about?' Josh asked.

56

She took a breath. 'Leann. He told me he was there when she died. All you other people that showed up talked about her like she was an inconvenience, just because of what she did for a living. But he seemed different; more respectful. I liked him.'

'How did he appear? Angry? Upset?'

'More curious than anything. Like you, he said he wanted to make sure they got the right guys but I didn't take that too seriously. I knew they had but his girlfriend got shot and I felt bad for him, so I was happy to talk for a while.'

'How long did you talk for?' Josh asked.

'Twenty minutes or so. Maybe thirty. Then he left.'

'Do you know where he went next?'

'No idea. I stayed up here.'

'His car's been parked on this street for the past two days collecting tickets.'

She shrugged. 'Can't help you, I'm afraid. But you're taking another look at Leann's case?'

'Yes,' Marquez said. 'Just a precaution.'

'Why? Do you have other leads?'

'Just one.'

'Which is?'

'Archer was going around asking the same kind of questions we are. And he hasn't been seen in over two days.'

The comment lingered in the air. Karen nodded.

'Well, I hope you find him,' she said. 'I mean that. He seemed like a nice guy. I liked him. A lot more than I liked the rest of you.'

With that the door was closed in their faces again, leaving Marquez and Josh staring at the wood.

Not far south on the Lower East Side, just twenty four hours after he'd been released from a twenty one day stretch in prison, a thirty two year old pimp called Alex Santiago was lying on the floor of his two-man apartment, his eyes bulging in terror as he watched two figures in white overalls and black gas masks pour a translucent chemical liquid into his bath-tub.

Santiago ran six escorts for his employer, including Kelly Greer and Cece Mills, and had always enjoyed enforcing a certain level of discipline on the girls, ensuring he received the right amount of fear and respect in return. However, right then the tables had been turned; he had a strip of duct tape over his mouth, more wrapped around his ankles, and his wrists were bound behind his back with zip-ties. Gagged and bound, he tried to shout but any noise he made was reduced to a murmur by the duct tape and masked by the sound of splashing as the bath was being drawn.

Sucking air in through his nose, his mouth covered by the tape, his eyes started to water from the acrid chemical smell.

He'd quickly realised the liquid in the tub wasn't water.

Behind Santiago, the front door opened, and a figure in white overalls and a gas mask eased himself back through the door into the apartment, carrying another cylindrical can which he passed to one of the two others filling the bath.

'How we doing?' he asked, his voice sounding disembodied from behind the mask.

'With this, it'll be ready,' one of the others said, a woman judging by her voice, as the third person poured the last canister into the tub.

'Clock's ticking,' he said. *'Both of you, go downtown and get the last girl then bring her back here.'*

He looked over at Santiago.

'I'll get started on this one.'

Nodding, the pair walked out of the apartment, closing the door behind them. Now alone with Santiago, the large figure walked over and stared down at the bound man on the floor, whose eyes widened with terror as they stared back up at him.

'Bath time, Alex,' he said.

Kneeling down, the man settled his heavy weight on Santiago's torso and placed his large hands around the pimp's throat.

Then he started throttling him, Santiago's face turning crimson as he suffocated, the last thing he saw before he died being a gas mask with a pair of dark emotionless eyes looking down at him.

SEVEN

Walking out of Karen Casey's apartment building, Josh and Marquez stopped side by side on the porch step, taking in the scene around them as if it might offer up some clues as to where Archer could have gone.

Vehicles were parked along the street but there were several free spaces available, one of which would have been occupied by Archer's car just several hours ago. Aside from traffic moving along the Avenue, the only movement on the block was the occasional pedestrian and three small girls playing with a skipping rope on the sidewalk opposite.

'Well that was a wasted trip,' Josh said.

'Maybe not,' Marquez said, looking down the street at the intersection, the way they'd come and the route which Archer would probably have taken. She pulled her cell and went to call the Bureau; there were cameras covering each road down there. If Ethan could pick up the car, he might also be able to track Archer after his chat with Karen Casey and figure out where he went next and why he left his car behind.

However, as she brought up Ethan's number she paused, looking over at the group of young girls engrossed in their skipping game across the street. Putting the phone back in her pocket for the moment, she moved down the steps and crossed the road.

'Hi girls; can I talk to you for a second?'

She showed them her badge as she spoke and their game came to an abrupt halt, the three of them looking scared.

'We didn't do anything,' one of the girls said.

Marquez smiled. 'I know. Actually, I need your help on something. It's very important. Do you live here?'

The two holding the rope looked at each other and nodded. 'We do. She lives down the street.'

'OK. Now think hard. Were you here on Friday night?'

Before they could answer, the door to the building behind them opened and a woman walked out, presumably the mother of the two girls.

'Can I help you?' she asked sharply.

Marquez nodded, showing her badge to the woman. 'You live here?'

Seeing the badge the woman softened slightly and nodded, jerking her thumb over her shoulder at the ground floor apartment facing the street. 'In there.'

'Were you around on Friday night?'

'Sure was.'

As Josh joined her, Marquez pointed across the street. 'A colleague of ours was last seen inside that apartment building on Friday evening, around 7:30pm. He's a blond guy, late twenties, good looking. Did you see him?'

'Yeah, I saw him. Hard to miss, right?'

'Did you see him arrive or leave?'

'Leave. I felt pretty bad for him, nice-looking guy like that.'

'What do you mean?' Josh asked.

'I'd just called the kids in and saw two police cars pull up; four cops stepped out. They stood around for a moment, like they were waiting for someone. A minute or so later, your guy walked out.'

'Did they talk?' Josh asked.

'Not exactly. They slammed him against one of the vehicles and put him in handcuffs.'

Marquez turned to look at Josh beside her, her eyes widening as realisation dawned.

'He wasn't too happy about it,' the woman continued. 'They put him inside one of the cars. Then they drove off.'

Three miles south on Delancey Street in the Lower East Side, a beautiful red-headed twenty year old escort called April Evans walked rapidly towards her apartment building, Cece's scream so abruptly cut off fifteen minutes earlier still echoing in her ears. Rounding the corner and moving fast, glancing around to make sure she wasn't being followed, April reached her apartment building with relief.

Letting herself in and closing the door, she took some deep breaths, trying desperately to steady her thoughts and think clearly. Turning to look through the glass, she couldn't see anything unusual, just some passing pedestrians, several cars and a white van parked outside.

She started to climb the stairs, even her slight weight causing the old wood to creak as she made her way up. Arriving on the 3rd floor, she cautiously peered each way down the corridor, making sure it was empty. Satisfied, she walked towards her apartment and reached into her bag for the key, wanting to get inside quickly.

Then she suddenly paused and looked down the empty corridor.

She could have sworn she heard the stairs creak.

She stayed where she was, her key in her hand, listening. The apartment building was quiet. She waited a few moments but still couldn't hear anything.

It must have been her imagination.

But as she was about to insert the key in the lock, she spotted something else.

Resting on the floor by her feet.

The East Village 13th Precinct was on 21st Street, just around the corner from Karen Casey's place, so Josh and Marquez were there in ninety seconds or so. They'd already entered the building and were now confronting the desk sergeant, who although being co-operative was struggling to understand what they were saying.

'Just hold on,' he said. 'Start again. What's wrong?'

'A member of our team was arrested two nights ago by officers from this Precinct. We want him released right now.'

'I just told you I don't work nights. Let me check the system.' Tapping some keys, he clicked into the computer. 'What's his name?'

'Sam Archer. He's a 3rd Grade detective with the Counter-Terrorism Bureau.'

He typed it in, then nodded. 'He was booked in on Friday night. Says he accessed confidential police files whilst on suspension and harassed a family member of the victim. Orders here are to keep him locked up until his suspension hearing at Police Plaza tomorrow morning.'

'We want him released right now.'

'On whose orders; yours? Get out of here.'

'Maybe we should call Lieutenant-General Franklin and tell him what happened?' Josh said.

'That's a bold threat.'

'He likes Archer. A hell of a lot more than he'll like you.'

Looking at them and realising they weren't kidding, the desk Sergeant hesitated then made a decision. He checked the system again.

'As it happens, your man's not here anymore.'

'Was he released?' Marquez asked.

'No. There wasn't enough space here so they shipped him uptown 'til his court date tomorrow. You need to take it up with them.'

'Where uptown?'

The man paused, not quite able to make eye contact with Josh and Marquez.

'Rikers Island.'

Already inside April Evans' apartment, one of the figures in white overalls and a baseball cap stood waiting with a chloroform-soaked rag in his right hand, ready to pull the bitch in the second she stepped through the door.

He'd heard the shitty old wood creaking as someone climbed the stairs and had just received a text telling him the girl was on her way up.

But the door didn't open. Perhaps she'd stopped to talk to a neighbour or something.

The man waited.

A few moments later, getting impatient and not hearing any voices, he eased the door open and looked outside.

The corridor was empty.

Looking to his right he saw his companion suddenly appear from the stairs, having come up from the van.

'Where the hell is she?' he asked.

The other figure stopped.

'I thought you already had her?'

'*You sent him to Rikers?*' Josh said incredulously, leaning over the desk. 'A police detective? Are you kidding me?'

'I didn't, the last shift did. And it says here he's suspended so technically right now he ain't a detective. He's booked in 'til his hearing tomorrow morning.'

He looked at them and shrugged.

'Sorry. Nothing I can do.'

Without wasting another second, the two Counter-Terrorism Bureau detectives turned and ran outside to their car and climbed inside. Slamming his door, Josh fired the engine and took off down the street as Marquez pulled her cell phone to call the prison. Although they now knew where he was, both of them were now infinitely more concerned about Archer's safety than they'd been a minute ago.

He was locked up inside Rikers Island, the city's biggest prison and the second largest in the country.

An unarmed police detective.

Surrounded by the some of the most dangerous criminals in New York State.

Lowering herself down the last rungs of the fire escape ladder, April hung for a moment then dropped onto a large metal garbage receptacle with a *thump*. Sliding off the edge and landing on the ground, she hurried down the small side alley then paused when she reached the end, looking cautiously round the wall.

As she watched, she saw the door to her apartment building on her right suddenly open

65

and two figures in white overalls and Yankee caps hurry out, looking left and right, clearly searching for someone.

She jerked back before they spotted her and thought for a moment, her back to the wall, her heart-pounding.

She stayed where she was for a few more seconds.

Then she turned and ran down the alley in the opposite direction, exiting at the other end and taking off down the street as fast as she could.

EIGHT

Ten miles away, dressed in the orange
Department Of Justice overalls and white shoes
that all inmates were required to wear, Archer
watched as the gate to the busy prison yard
buzzed and then opened in front of him, his heart
thumping and his mouth dry.

'Move, pretty boy,' the guard behind him said,
drawing his baton. 'Rec time.'

With inmates already in the yard turning to
watch and no choice other than to do as he was
told, Archer walked forward and immediately felt
the clock on his life start ticking.

The last four weeks had unfolded like a slow-
moving nightmare but this current predicament
was beyond anything he could have expected, all
triggered by that night in the car park when Leann
Casey, Vargas and he had been shot. Help had
arrived minutes after the shooting and treatment
on Alice had started immediately. Archer had sat
with her in the ambulance and watched as the
medical team fought frantically to save her, her
heart stopping twice on the way to the hospital.
She'd clung to life by a fingernail, Archer not
leaving her side until she was out of immediate
danger, Josh taking care of Isabel.

Once the medics said that she was going to pull
through, followed a short time later by a call from
Shepherd telling Archer he needed him back on
duty at the Bureau, he'd reluctantly left her in the
care of the two guards and the medical team. He,
Shepherd, Josh and Marquez had waited
anxiously for any updates from Homicide,

becoming increasingly frustrated when constantly told the investigation was still in progress.

Last Saturday, eight days ago, their patience had finally run out and they'd headed over to the 114th to try and get some answers. The Precinct boss, Lieutenant Royston, had been both arrogant and uncooperative, in the end ordering them to leave. Shepherd had done his best to reason with the man, but it had been hopeless. He wouldn't listen.

Realising they weren't getting anywhere, they'd headed for the door, but just as Archer had been walking past Royston the Lieutenant had made a derogatory comment about Vargas.

It'd been like holding a flame to a box packed with tinder.

Before he could stop himself Archer laid the son of a bitch out, firing off a vicious right hook that had taken the fat Lieutenant completely unawares, knocking him out cold. Archer had been suspended immediately, his badge and gun confiscated, and was banned from every police Precinct in the city. His hearing was due for tomorrow morning, Monday, but he knew that was just a formality. He was going to be demoted out of Shepherd's team and he knew it. He'd be lucky if they didn't bust him out to some middle of nowhere beat in Staten Island.

But it had also meant that now he had nothing to lose.

Josh had called on Thursday, saying Homicide had finally come through and found the shooters. Finding it all a bit convenient, Archer had broken the rules by contacting a friend at the 114th and persuaded her to pull a copy of the case files for him, the first time he'd seen them since the shooting. After noticing something that didn't ring true, he'd decided to pay Karen Casey a visit late Friday afternoon, thinking she might be able to shed some light on who might have wanted to kill her daughter. She'd been cold, distant and edgy at first, the atmosphere only changing when she accidentally dropped a china cup from a high shelf on the floor, smashing it to pieces. After a pause Archer had bent down and cleaned it up without a word, which seemed to thaw her frostiness towards him.

After that, she'd opened up but hadn't told him anything that wasn't already in the file. Then, just as he was leaving the building he'd found four cops waiting for him on the street, taking him down right outside Karen Casey's apartment building. Royston's handiwork, no doubt; no-one else could have moved in on him that fast.

The son of a bitch must have had me watched, Archer had quickly realised.

He was waiting for any excuse and I gave it to him on a plate.

He'd been cuffed and arrested on harassment charges, which was complete bullshit. He'd been pissed off but not worried, expecting to be taken to the station and released after he made a call to Shepherd and explained what had happened.

However, he hadn't been given that opportunity; he'd spent the rest of Friday and all day Saturday in the Precinct. Then late last night, officers had come to his cell, saying he was being transferred until his hearing on Monday due to overcrowding at the East Village Precinct.

Instead of another police station, they'd brought him here.

The moment Archer realised where he was headed, he'd understood just how badly he'd screwed up and why other detectives had warned him to watch his back after his suspension. As punishment for getting Rach to access the case-file and then speaking to Karen Casey, let alone the humiliation of getting flattened by Archer in front of his subordinates, the fat Lieutenant had pulled some strings and arranged for Archer to be admitted to Rikers for a weekend stay.

And this place wasn't exactly a country retreat.

As the gate locked behind him, Archer continued to walk forward, keeping his shoulders back and staring straight ahead, ignoring some cat-calls and wolf-whistles. From the moment a fresh inmate arrives in any prison, the cycle begins; existing inmates look for ink, ask about background, assess the newcomer physically to judge where he'd fit into the pecking order. Until now, Archer had only ever seen it from the other side.

As he moved forward into the heart of the yard, he realised word hadn't got out yet that he was an NYPD detective. If it had, he'd have known about it already. Putting a cop inside a jail for the weekend was like throwing meat to a pack of starving wolves and Archer had realised last night when he'd been locked in his single-man SHU cell that because he was suspended, Royston could dump him in here with no real consequences. Whether this was teaching him a lesson or exacting the ultimate revenge was irrelevant.

The reality was he was here until tomorrow morning and he knew he'd be lucky to make it that long.

Straight ahead of him were some empty bleachers which he made a bee-line for, avoiding eye contact with anyone and maintaining a totally blank expression despite the adrenaline pumping through his veins. Arriving at the wooden slats, he stepped up and took a seat on the second row, relieved to have his back to the fence and his eyes covering the yard.

It was sunny but chilly, the DOJ overalls providing scant protection against the cold wind and he shivered, goose-bumps appearing on his forearms as he rested them on his knees. The yard in front of him was about the size of half a football field, all concrete with razor wire on the high walls, a basketball court and two free weights sets. The ball game was shirts against skins, the torsos of the men not wearing vests or overalls adorned with scars and tattoos, all thickly muscled and all intimidating.

Taking a quick glance around, Archer was relieved to see most of the activities had resumed but he was aware of several pairs of eyes still fixed on him. He'd already noticed the different races were keeping to themselves, the white boys over on the left with a load of weights, the black guys playing ball, the Latinos using another set of weights on the right. One particularly large and intimidating Mexican guy over there was sitting on a bench staring straight at Archer, so many plates on the barbell racked behind him they were bending the bar.

A guy next to him leaned down and whispered something, the larger man nodding as he studied Archer sitting alone on the bleachers opposite.

Keeping his face blank, Archer felt a jolt of nerves run through him. If one whisper about who

71

he really was spread around this place it would be a feeding frenzy, outnumbered hundreds to one; he'd get torn apart. Luckily he hadn't shaved for a couple of days and his hair was overdue a trip to the barber so he didn't stand out quite as much as he normally would, but time was running out and he knew it.

As he glanced around the prison yard, the sun going down behind him, he pictured Shepherd, Marquez and Josh out there enjoying their weekends with no idea that he was in here.

C'mon, guys, he silently willed, feeling eyes upon him and sensing danger building with every second.

Get me the hell out of here.

'Answer, goddammit!' Marquez shouted, swearing as she waited for her call to Rikers to be answered. She'd been put on hold, the clock ticking as Josh burned it uptown.

'Hello?'

'This is Detective Lisa Marquez, NYPD, acting on Department orders,' she said quickly. 'I need you to pull one of your overnighters right now. I don't know which facility he's in but he's on site.'

'Name?'

'Detective Sam Archer, Counter-Terrorism Bureau.'

As Archer sat on the bleachers, a whistle suddenly echoed around the yard. It immediately ended the activities, the inmates trudging back towards the gate, guards shouting orders as the men formed an orderly line, the ball abandoned on the concrete, slowly rolling to a stop. Archer had only just caught the end of rec time and he smiled; he'd survived.

Staying by the bleachers and ignoring the shouts of several guards for him to move, he waited until most of the other men had gone, joining the back of the line to avoid the possibility of someone getting the drop on him. As he edged slowly forward towards the door, he noticed several of the Latinos looking back at him. He certainly seemed to have caught their attention

'Move it!' a guard ordered, the gates ahead buzzing and the inmates walking slowly into the building. As Archer moved into the prison, looking forward to heading towards the safety of his one-man SHU block cell, the line ahead deviated to the left instead, down another cleanly-scrubbed corridor with grills covering the windows.

As the inmates in front of him walked on, Archer suddenly stopped, one of the guards bringing up the rear bumping into him from behind.

'I thought we were going back to cells.'

'It's 6 o'clock, princess. Shower time.'

'I'm good, but thanks.'

The guard's hand moved to the baton, pulling it out, the metal making a quiet *whish* as it slid out of the leather. 'This isn't a hotel, asshole. And that wasn't a request.'

As he spoke, the man suddenly hit him hard in the gut with the baton, causing Archer to gasp with pain and double over.

'You don't move right now, I'll put you in Gen-Pop after chow and let feeding time commence,' the guard said. 'You've already made some fans.'

Straightening and looking at the man, Archer waited for a moment then walked forward, his heart beginning to thump overtime with adrenaline. In that moment all thoughts of his police team, Isabel and Vargas vanished.

His sole focus was on staying alive for the next ten minutes.

NINE

When in a hostile environment, a human being is hard-wired to seek protection. If the threat is because of the elements, they search for a way to ward off the cold or heat; if the threat is physical, they seek cover or a weapon to fend off an attack.

But as he stripped down outside those prison showers, his heartbeat going like a rock-band's drum solo at the end of a world tour, Archer knew that he'd have none of those things in the block next door. He'd been in extreme levels of danger before; falling out of a plane without a chute, jumping off a twenty two storey balcony onto another, dumping a body sewn up with explosives down a manhole seconds before detonation.

But he was about to be a completely naked, unarmed cop in a room surrounded by some of the toughest, most aggressive criminals in the State, men who didn't need a weapon to kill someone.

He'd never experienced anything like this.

As he peeled off his orange DOJ overalls and white t-shirt underneath, he glanced at the guard who'd hit him and saw the man's eyes flick to the scars on Archer's body, the result of previous altercations. His hand was also resting on the grip of his night-stick, Archer guessed in case he was going to raise any more objections about taking a shower. As he took his time undressing, using every moment to think, he considered telling this guy he was a cop but decided against it, not knowing whether he could be trusted to keep his mouth shut or if he'd even care. His instinct told him he already knew and he didn't give a shit.

Pulling off the remainder of his clothing, Archer stepped out of his white prison-issue boxers and stood for a moment.

Focus, he told himself, adrenaline spiking through his veins and pumping him up.

Breathe.

Watching him, the guard drew his baton again, silently indicating what would happen if Archer didn't move.

Turning, the blond NYPD detective rounded the corner and walked into the shower block.

The place was rectangular, four separate lines of shower heads, eight on each row; it was three quarters full, some men finishing up and moving off, about fifteen or so still in there, inmates from other blocks presumably showering in adjacent areas. Most of them were focusing on what they were doing and didn't pay Archer any attention, low conversations taking place between some of the men whilst others washed in silence.

He saw their bodies were adorned with tattoos, most also criss-crossed with scars; big, threatening men. The older inmates were thinner but like their younger counterparts were covered in ink and scars, with that wizened toughness of men who'd spent their entire lives in and out of jail.

As he walked under a shower head on the far left side, every muscle in his body primed to fight but his face blank, Archer noticed something else.

None of the inmates were showering facing the wall.

Standing under the cascading water and feeling eyes upon him, he took a piece of soap and pretended to start cleaning himself, in reality scanning the room as subtly as he could for anything he could use as a weapon. Choke-holds or joint locks wouldn't work in here. As well as being slippery with soap and water, it took more than several seconds to put someone out and in here, by that point he'd already be dead.

He stood under the jet-stream, never taking his eyes off the stall around him as more inmates finished their showers and walked off.

Water cascading off his head and shoulders, he watched and waited.

Focus.

Breathe.

He noticed a few other inmates glancing over but no-one looked as if they were about to make a move. Archer's guard didn't drop but he realised all his concern might have been for nothing. No-one in here seemed to know who he was.

He started to lather himself up properly, remaining alert, working fast but never taking his eyes off the showers around him.

Then suddenly, he heard a commotion next door, shouting and what sounded like some kind of altercation, the guards turning and running out to handle the situation.

Watching them go, Archer cleaned himself even faster, wanting to get the hell out of here.

But then the room around him went quiet.

At the front gate to the facility, a Counter-Terrorism Bureau Ford was buzzed in and pulled to an abrupt halt in an empty space near the doors. A moment later, a member of the Department stepped out and moved swiftly towards the front entrance, pulling open the front door and walking towards the desk.

'I need to pull someone right now,' the newcomer said, showing his badge. 'You've got a suspended police detective in here and you'd better pray to God he's still in one piece.'

'Wait a minute. You can't just walk in here giving orders.'

'Waste any more time and you'll need a new haircut by the time you wake up,' the detective said. 'Get him out now!'

All conversation in the block stopped. Archer hadn't seen any kind of a signal but it must have been pre-arranged. The inmates showering around him suddenly withdrew like the tide pulling back, turning and leaving the block without so much as a backward glance.

Three remained behind. They were all Latino, big guys, members of the gang who'd been using the weights in the yard. They were all holding a bar of soap.

And they were staring straight at Archer.

Glancing to his right, standing against the wall and out of the direct flow of water, Archer looked for the guards but they were nowhere to be seen, no doubt still handling the situation next door. In front of him he watched as the Mexicans used their large hands to push through the white soap, a shiv becoming visible inside each bar.

Each one was crude but wickedly sharp, soap clinging to the tips and blades.

The men looked at him silently, Archer standing there outnumbered three to one.

The only sound was water splashing onto the tiled floor.

At six foot and a hundred and eighty five pounds Archer was well-built but he knew he wasn't a physical match for these men. He never went looking for trouble, although well able to take care of himself; he was also a man who'd spent the last few years of his life forced to make split-second decisions to kill or be killed. That was the reality of what he did for a living.

And as he stared back at the three gang members intent on ending his life, he knew that if he was going to have any chance of surviving this he would have to match these guys for violence and brutality.

His back against the wall, he focused on the Latino standing in the middle, who appeared to be the ringleader. As Archer watched him, the man glanced towards the fat, tattooed guy on his right.

That was all it took.

The inmate who'd been given the signal suddenly rushed forward and stabbed upward viciously, aiming the shiv for Archer's gut with his considerable strength behind it. Reacting fast, Archer stepped forward before the arm could gain momentum, tucking his stomach back as far as he could and using his left forearm to block the man's arm before it could make contact, the two bones thudding painfully on impact.

The guy was far stronger than Archer but in that enclosed space, technique could even the odds. As he stopped the arm, Archer immediately bent and then twisted the man's elbow around, using him as a human shield from the others, but as he glanced at the other two he knew that wouldn't make any difference.

Pushing the man's arm up hard, the guy yelled and his grip on his weapon loosened. Archer grabbed the shiv from the man's opened palm and thumped it into the guy's shoulder blade just as the other pair rushed him.

As the man shouted in pain, Archer pushed his bulk directly at one of the two men, keeping his grip on the shiv and withdrawing it from the guy's shoulder, blood running down the handle and onto his fist. His attacker collided with one of his friends, both of them losing their balance on the slippery surface.

But the other was moving in fast. He was right handed and swinging his arm in an upward arcing motion, but this time Archer had a weapon too. He desperately tried to block the forearm again but slipped, the man's shiv slicing across his arm. Shouting in anger from the hot pain, Archer buried his own soapy, blood-stained shiv in the guy's chest as hard as he could.

However, the handle was slippery and he lost his grip. As the man dropped his shiv and clutched the weapon buried in his pectoral, Archer grabbed his wet hair and slammed his face into the wall, the man's forehead thumping off as it made contact. The impact cracked part of the old shower wall, small pieces of tile falling to the floor as the guy crumpled and went down.

Shouting with rage, the remaining pair attacked simultaneously, over four hundred pounds of murderous fury bearing down on him. Unarmed, cornered and outnumbered, Archer scooped up a shard of broken tile and rose just as the nearest guy took a swing; he was built like a barn door but not as fast as Archer, who jerked out of the way as the shiv in the man's hand missed his gut by an inch, the blade continuing on its arc. As momentum caught the guy off-balance Archer brought his left hand up and sliced the shard across the man's face, starting at his lower cheek and continuing across his nose and forehead, the porcelain cutting him diagonally lip to brow.

The man screamed, dropping his shiv and clutched his face as blood started to flow into his eyes, blinding him. However, by that point the other inmate had already moved in. Turning to face him, Archer twisted at the last second and felt hot pain across his chest as the shiv sliced him, the guy going for his heart.

Caught in the water pumping from the shower, his attacker lost his grip on the small blade and went to grab Archer but the blond detective was still lathered up with soap and rolled out of the man's grip, hammering an elbow into his face and then pushing him back into the first man he'd stabbed, who'd just got back to his feet.

Panting, soaking wet and with blood leaking down his arm, chest and hand, Archer kept tight hold of the piece of tile and braced himself.

Suddenly a gunshot echoed around the tiled room, deafeningly loud inside the stall, the sounds of the fight attracting the attention from the guards next door. His back against the far wall, Archer straightened and put his hands up as the officers ran inside, their boots splashing on the wet tiles.

Slamming him into the wall and pulling the piece of ceramic from his hand, the two men dragged him out. As they did so, Archer looked back at the aftermath of the fight.

One of the gang members was down with a stab wound to the shoulder, the second had the savage cut across his face and the third had a broken nose and stab wound to his chest. The white-walled block was lined with red which flowed and swirled into the water.

'You're dead, ese!' the third guy screamed as more guards poured into the room, blood flowing from his broken nose and wounded chest. *'You hear me? You're dead!'*

Archer didn't reply as he was hustled around the corner and down the corridor towards the SHU block, naked and soaking wet. His forearm felt as if it could be broken and he was in serious pain from the two cuts to his chest and his arm.

But despite all that, he grinned. The Latino was wrong.

He was still alive.

TEN

Pushed into the single man SHU cell, Archer turned just in time to catch his orange overalls, t-shirt and boxers as they were thrown at him, the door slammed and locked behind him.

Tossing the clothes onto the bed, he ripped the pillowcase off and wiped himself down before pulling on his boxers and slacks, his hair wet and clinging to his head, his body shaking from the cold and plummeting adrenaline. Picking up the pillowcase again, he rubbed it through his hair to dry it off as best he could, then held it to the cut across the left side of his chest.

As it made contact, he cursed under his breath; the shiv had cut about a third of an inch deep, the skin sliced open, blood still running from the wound down his chest. Glancing down, he saw the cut on his arm was bleeding too, the blood dripping to the floor. Now out of danger, the pain from the two injuries suddenly kicked in, in addition to the throbbing ache of his forearm from where he'd blocked that first knife thrust.

He sat down on the bed while he got his breath back. *Jesus Christ, you sure know how to get yourself in deep shit,* he thought, shaking his head. *If it was an art-form, you'd be goddamn Pablo Picasso.*

Then he heard the sound of a key turning in the lock.

Throwing the pillowcase to one side as the door started to open, Archer rose instantly, ready to defend himself in case this was Round 2. However, as the door pulled back he saw two guards standing there, one holding a box containing Archer's actual clothes, the other the man from the shower block.

'Change,' the latter said. 'You've been released. Someone's pulled you.'

'Who?'

'Just get changed,' he ordered, the other guard placing the box down and pushing it towards Archer. 'And don't bleed on my floor.'

The box slid over until it hit Archer's foot; the guards stood there, waiting. Opening the box and quickly pulling his blue jeans, black sweater and shoes back on, Archer replaced them with his overalls then walked over to the men who turned and led him out of the cell. It took some time to get to the exit as they had to negotiate several locked doors and long corridors, but eventually they reached the last door, the three of them waiting for it to be buzzed open.

Walking through that final exit, Archer expected to see Josh, Shepherd or Marquez but was caught completely off-guard when he saw who was standing there waiting for him.

It was Sergeant Jake Hendricks.

*

At six foot two, over two hundred pounds, dark-featured and tough as two dollar steak, Jake Hendricks was the hardest cop Sam Archer had ever met. The man was a walking sledgehammer, his uncompromising approach legendary in the Department. He was also Matt Shepherd's closest friend and ran his own five-person team in the Counter-Terrorism Bureau, the two squads often working side by side. Although Archer knew him relatively well, he wasn't anywhere near the top of the list of people he'd expected to see just then.

He knew Hendricks was intelligent but it was his fearless approach to police work that had built his reputation. There were many stories about him that had done the rounds, some no doubt having grown with the telling, but one Archer knew for a fact to be true was also one of his favourites. A few years back a gang from Cypress Hills had plotted to kill Hendricks after he'd come down on them hard shortly after being transferred there; he'd made their lives a misery and they'd decided it was time for some payback. Two of the gang members had found out where he lived and waited one night to waylay him, but when Hendricks had arrived home things hadn't exactly gone as they'd planned. The incident had taken place a couple of years ago but apparently the two gang members had only recently started eating solid food again. Hendricks wasn't a man to cross and definitely someone you didn't want as an enemy.

Dressed in jeans, a dark sweater, boots and a leather jacket concealing his badge and weapon, Hendricks nodded at Archer as he appeared then turned and led the way out of the building without saying a word. Surprised, Archer followed the dark-haired Sergeant outside and over to a Counter-Terrorism Bureau Ford; Hendricks climbed in behind the wheel as Archer got into the passenger seat beside him. Hendricks fired the engine and they took off out of the compound, being buzzed out through the exit and heading towards the only bridge off the island which led into Queens.

Now he was out of there, Archer finally felt relief wash over him; against all the odds, he'd made it out alive, but only just. As he sat there he started to feel sick and cold, his nervous system exacting payback for the adrenaline spike that had helped save his life in the shower block twenty minutes ago.

Leaning back in the Ford's passenger seat, he felt blood running from the wound under his sweater. Reaching under the garment and the t-shirt underneath, he pressed his hand to his chest and withdrew it. Hendricks glanced over, both men seeing it was red with blood.

'You're hurt?' Hendricks asked.

'I made some friends in there.'

'Is it deep?'

Archer shook his head, remembering how he'd turned at the last second from that final shiv thrust which had saved his life. 'Could have been a lot worse.'

Keeping his left hand on the wheel, Hendricks reached under his seat and tossed Archer a small first-aid kit. 'Fix yourself up. And don't bleed in my car.'

Seems to be a recurring theme tonight, Archer thought as he caught the box. Resting the kit on his lap he opened it up, taking out some antiseptic spray and a pack of wipes. Pulling off his sweater, he shook the canister then pushed it under his t-shirt and sprayed the cut on his chest then the one on his arm, both wounds still bleeding sluggishly. He found some gauze and tape in the box, which he stuck over the cut on his arm, then pulled out a large rectangular bandage and strapped it over the cut on his chest, the whole process taking less than a minute.

His effort at first-aid completed, he closed the box, placed it in the foot-well and sat back in his seat, closing his eyes and taking a long deep breath, his sweater resting on his lap.

'Talk about a weekend to remember,' he said. 'Jesus Christ.'

'How the hell did you end up in there?' Hendricks replied. 'Tell me what happened.'

'I got picked up two nights ago for visiting a victim's mother in the East Village. They held me at the 13th for a day then transferred me up here last night, saying there wasn't enough room at the Precinct or some bullshit like that. I was in my SHU cell all day but got taken out at dusk for rec time and 6pm was showers. Five minutes in the yard and a couple of minutes into the shower was all it took. Three Latinos jumped me.'

'The guards?'

'Pulled next door by something else. I think it was planned. A diversion.'

Hendricks swore quietly as Archer eased his sweater back over his torso, adjusting it awkwardly under his seatbelt, trying not to dislodge his bandages.

'That place can be a real shit-show,' Hendricks said. 'You wouldn't be the first suspended cop to die in there.'

'Thanks for getting me out. How'd you know I was inside?'

'Because I know Lieutenant Royston. He was a sergeant in the same Precinct as me years ago when Shep and I first started out in a squad car. He's always been an asshole.'

As he spoke Hendricks moved off the Bridge into Queens, keeping his eyes on the road.

'Two years before I joined the Department, he was accused of rape but beat the charges on a technicality. When we worked at the same

Precinct he had two complaints of sexual harassment lodged against him but again he got away with it; he's a vicious bully. After I heard you punched him, I knew he'd drop you in more shit the first chance he had. Getting you suspended wouldn't be enough for him.'

'So locking me up in there was the answer?'

'He's done it before. Years back, there was a guy who got aggressive with him. Royston had made advances to his girlfriend at a bar during another guy's retirement bash. The officer was pissed and rightly so, so he called Royston out on it in front of half the Precinct. The next day, the poor bastard was conveniently arrested on some bullshit weapons license charge and locked up in Rikers for the weekend due to *over-crowding*, just like you. However, they didn't put him in the SHU block; he was jammed in General Population.'

'What happened to him?'

'Sure you can figure it out, but let's just say two nights can be one hell of a long time in a place like that. The guy made it the full two days but he was never the same afterwards. Couple of years later he killed himself.'

Archer felt the cuts on his chest and arm burn from the antiseptic. 'All things considered, I got off lightly then.'

'Shep called saying you hadn't been in contact and had dropped off the radar, so I decided to check the prison admission logs during the past forty eight hours and bingo, there you were.'

Archer shook his head. 'That son of a bitch.'

Hendricks paused for a moment, the car continuing on its journey through Queens. 'What did Karen Casey say when you visited? Anything that wasn't in the file?'

Archer looked at him, surprised. Hendricks ran his own team in the Bureau and hadn't been working with Shepherd on the shooting. 'You're familiar with the case, sir?'

Hendricks nodded. 'Shep briefed me. Once he told me what was going on, I asked to see the files.'

'We tried that; Homicide wouldn't co-operate. I had to call in a favour to see them.'

'I've got a couple friends over there.'

Pulling out a brown folder from the well by his seat, he tossed it onto Archer's lap.

'The deceased was Leann Vanessa Casey. Nineteen years old at the time of death, unmarried and no partner, born in Johnstown, Pennsylvania to Karen and Marcus Casey. Was arrested in February on the Upper West Side for nothing since. No idea who she's working for or where she's been except apart from a three-month stint here at Rikers and record of her at Covenant Housing; apparently she was being treated for addiction to pain killers. Did four weeks in rehab out on Long Island and was released four hours before she was shot and killed.'

As Archer scanned the girl's meagre police file again, getting reacquainted with the case, Hendricks pulled up at a red light.

'Maybe she wasn't working for anyone else; just herself,' Archer said, turning the page and looking at the case notes again. 'With the internet, who says a prostitute needs a pimp nowadays?'

'That's very possible.'

Archer turned the page, seeing the girl lying in the car park, her keys and bag beside her and numbered with small tags by CSU.

'The Chevy was hers, all the documents checking out in her name. The bag she was carrying just contained a few spare clothes. Investigative team at the scene found several thousand dollars tucked into her clothing.'

He glanced at Archer.

'Her savings, perhaps.'

Archer nodded, turning the page, and looked at the mug-shots of the two perpetrators.

'The 114th settled on two suspects, pimps from another gang. Both were found dead from gunshot wounds this past Thursday, Carvalho shooting Valdez then wasting himself with the gun that killed Leann Casey. Convenient, right?'

'Exactly,' Archer said quietly.

'Doesn't exactly match up with the behaviour of a man who shot a young woman without hesitation three times and dropped two police detectives,' Hendricks continued. 'But aside from Valdez' girlfriend, no other sets of prints were found at the location and she was doing thirty days for a DUI at the time of death. Homicide asked around but no-one in the building saw anyone in the vicinity of the apartment at the time of the shooting other than the two men. That meant it was case closed, investigation complete. All that was missing was a ribbon on top and a *thank you* card.'

There was a pause.

'So what's your view?' Hendricks finished, looking at Archer.

'The gun was the same that killed Leann Casey. They both had the same build as the two assholes who jumped us. It ticks every box; guys like this have done far dumber things.'

'But?'

Archer pointed at Carvalho's mug-shot, the heavier-set of the two, the man who'd killed Valdez then shot himself. 'The eyes are the giveaway. When I was waiting for him to finish us off, I stared into the killer's eyes. This isn't the same man.'

Hendricks looked at him for a long moment.

'What happened to the van from that night?' he asked.

'Pulled over four hours later in Harlem,' Archer replied. 'Officers arrested the driver, a guy two weeks out of the joint for stealing cars. He had priors, but he wasn't the killer. He had an alibi. He'd been seeing his PO downtown at the time of the shooting.'

'How'd he get the keys?'

'Said he found the van on the corner of 144th and 2nd and they were still in the ignition. He stole it and called a chop shop in Queens who said they'd give him eight hundred bucks for it. He was driving it over there when he was pulled over. The plate had gone out to every cop in the city and a passing squad car tagged it.'

'What about street CCTV? Cameras must have picked up the two suspects leaving the vehicle.'

'Both figures were in dark clothing. They knew what they were doing. A bus stopped off on the near side of the street and obscured the shot for a good thirty seconds. When it pulled away again, both of them were gone.'

'The man who shot you, what was he wearing?'

'Jeans, jacket, hockey mask. Gun was a Steyr.'

'His manner?'

91

'Hard as hell. He took out the girl without any hesitation; it was only when he saw our cop vests that he lost his cool. Even then he was going to kill us but the driver was freaking out and stopped him.'

'You heard them talk?'

Archer nodded.

'Accents?'

'Nothing I picked up on.'

'Anything else you can remember?'

Archer closed his eyes, recalling what he saw. 'That's it.'

Hendricks thought for a moment, the hum of the car's engine filling the silence, the vehicle driving on through the dark web of streets.

'You know my wife was shot once too,' he said. 'Three years ago.'

Archer glanced at him. 'I didn't.'

'After I tuned up a couple of gangbangers who tried to welcome me home one night, three of their boys came to our house a few days later to kill her as revenge. Fortunately they were sloppy and thought she'd be an easy mark. She fired back but took two to the leg; almost died. So I know where your head's at. And you're right; something about this is way, way off.'

Archer nodded then looked around him and frowned, realising they were heading for Brooklyn, not the Bureau or his apartment.

'Where are we going?'

'Somewhere we can get some real information,' Hendricks said. 'Cypress Hills.'

He glanced at Archer as they entered Brooklyn, heading for one of the most dangerous neighbourhoods in the city.

'Let's find out what's really going on here,' he said.

ELEVEN

In the sitting room of Karen Casey's apartment on East 19th Street, Shepherd and a blonde thirty year old social worker named Theresa Palmer waited as the distressed woman recovered from the bout of tears triggered by their arrival several minutes ago.

Marquez had called Shepherd when he was on his way to the Hendricks' for dinner, telling him that she and Josh had found Arch. Apparently he'd been dumped in Rikers having been arrested after visiting Karen Casey, and she and Josh were on their way to pull him out. After a few seconds of stunned silence, having not even realised that Archer was missing, Shepherd had swung his car round and come straight here to speak with Leann's mother, wanting to see if Karen could shed any light on why his detective had been arrested as he left her place and telling Marquez to let him know the moment they got Archer out.

As Shepherd had arrived outside the building another car had pulled up and Theresa Palmer had stepped out, just as surprised to see him as he was her. Palmer was from the Polaris Project, the biggest anti-human trafficking organisation in the United States, and had been brought in by the 114th after it became apparent that Leann Casey had been an escort. Palmer's role required her to counsel the families of those caught up in the sex-trade as well as the victims and Karen Casey had been on her visit list since her daughter had been murdered. Shepherd had been part of the NYPD for sixteen years but apart from his early days in a squad car with Hendricks when they'd arrested a few hookers and pimps, his work since, especially in the Counter-Terrorism Bureau, hadn't involved the sex trade so he was glad she was here, feeling somewhat out of his depth in this unfamiliar territory.

The pair had been let in, walked up together and had now been sitting with the distraught woman for several minutes. Palmer was beside Karen on the couch, a hand resting against her back, murmuring words of comfort. As he waited patiently for Karen's tears to pass, Shepherd glanced at the social worker, even more grateful she was here right now. Green eyed, attractive if in a slightly hard way and with shoulder length blonde hair, Palmer looked just what she was, a competent professional, dressed in a smart, well-tailored grey work suit with a white shirt and black court shoes. He guessed she had to be pretty tough to be involved in this kind of work.

Beside her, Karen would have been a head-turner herself once but Shepherd guessed life hadn't been kind to her. She looked run-down, which wasn't surprising considering her daughter had been murdered a month ago. He could relate to that; he knew how it felt to lose a child. Unlike her daughter, she didn't have a police record for him to check, but the interviewing detectives from Homicide had noted down a few of her details in the file. She'd been born in a small town in Pennsylvania, was unemployed, divorced and the mother of one child, Leann, her ex-husband Marcus proving hard to trace, various Pennsylvania Police Departments still working on finding him to inform him of his daughter's death.

Glancing around, Shepherd guessed she didn't have much money to spare but her place was comfortable enough and well-furnished, if slightly worn and faded, a bit like its owner. As the woman began to compose herself, Shepherd's attention settled on a photo of Leann to his right, the shot taken when she must have been around fifteen or sixteen. Sitting alone in a back-yard, the girl looked slightly strained in the picture although that wasn't surprising considering Homicide's notes recorded that Karen's ex-husband had been an abusive alcoholic. She looked like a nice, sweet young woman, very pretty even then, someone whose life could have been very different under altered circumstances.

Palmer broke the silence, bringing Shepherd's attention back to the two women.

'We're very sorry if our being here upsets you,' she told Karen. 'But believe me, we're both here to help.'

'It just brings everything back,' Karen sniffed. 'I thought you'd found my girl's murderers.'

'We need to make sure,' Shepherd said. 'For your sake, ours and Leann's.'

'That's the second time I've heard that bullshit tonight,' she fired back angrily, frustration getting the better of her. 'Are you saying now those two men may not have killed her? That it was someone else?'

'That's why I'm here.'

Agitated, Karen stubbed out the cigarette she'd lit only a few minutes ago in an ashtray then reached for the pack and pulled another, sparking it then taking a long draw, the embers glowing and crackling as she sucked the nicotine deep into her lungs.

'The file says you're both from Pennsylvania,' Palmer said.

Karen nodded. 'Johnstown.'

'When did you come here?' Shepherd asked.

'End of last year.'

'Why?'

'Leann's father started to knock her around. Piece of shit always drank a lot but then he lost his job and started spending his unemployment on Southern Comfort.'

She took another draw on the cigarette.

'He used to smack me about sometimes, but when he started on Leann I knew we had to get out, so I packed our bags and we left one morning while he was still out cold from the previous night. Haven't seen or heard from him since.'

'So why New York?' Shepherd asked. 'Why not Pittsburgh or Philly? They're closer.'

She motioned to the apartment around them, keeping the cigarette trapped between her fore and middle finger. 'Friend of my mother's had this place and said we could crash here. Her man died a long time ago and she said we could move in with her seeing as we had nowhere else to go; I think she wanted the company. When she died, I found she'd left the place to me. Thank God.'

'Did you know what Leann did for a living?' Palmer suddenly asked.

Karen took another deep drag on the Marlboro, not making eye contact with either of them.

'Life's tough, you know?' she said. 'It was bad in Johnstown but here it was worse. This is an expensive city but at least we had a roof over our heads. And my girl wasn't just some cheap street trash; she had class. She was high-end.'

She closed her eyes.

97

'I got sick and couldn't work. I don't know how she got into it. But she said I didn't need to try and get a job, that she'd take care of it, wanting me to have an easier life. She wouldn't tell me where she got her money but deep down I had a feeling. Then she got busted and I knew for sure; had to watch my little girl do ninety days inside, amongst murderers and gang members. I brought her here so I felt like I was responsible, you know?'

She sniffed again, taking another drag on her cigarette.

'When she got out of the joint in May, she talked about moving on, going to college then get a job. She checked herself into rehab to start the process off. She knew she couldn't do shit if she was addicted.'

She paused, her voice starting to shake.

'She did it too. She beat it. Then she was killed the day she left the facility.'

'When was the last time you spoke to her?' Shepherd asked.

'That day. She called me when she got out of rehab.'

'How long before it happened?'

'A couple hours. She sounded great; upbeat. She said she was leaving town for a while and didn't know when she'd be back but would keep sending me money. I hadn't heard her sound that good in years.'

'Do you know where she was going?'

'No, but then she didn't either. She said she wanted to make a fresh start. Said she'd get a job some place, a proper gig, somewhere where no-one knew her history.'

'Did Leann ever mention a pimp?' Shepherd asked.

'Sometimes. Why?'

'I'd like to talk to him.'

'Too late for that. He's dead. Someone wasted him up in the Bronx a year ago.'

'What about since then?' Shepherd asked, looking at the file. 'Did she have someone new running her?'

'Not that I know of,' she said.

Shepherd looked back up at the woman.

'I lost a child too,' he told her. 'He died last year.'

Suspicious, Karen looked at him. 'How?'

'He was shot. Like Leann.'

'How old was he?'

'Her age. Nineteen.'

'Did you catch who did it?'

'I already knew who he was. And it was an accident; I had to let it go.'

'You forgave him?' she asked.

'Not yet.' He paused. 'But I'm working on it every day.'

He kept looking at her.

'But what happened to Leann wasn't an accident. For her sake, I want to make sure we got the right guys. But I can't do my job if you don't tell me everything you know.'

'I've told you what I know.'

'Who are Carlos and Alex? Her pimps maybe?'

Caught completely off-guard, Karen Casey's eyes widened. 'How the hell do you know that?'

Shepherd gestured at the table between them. Karen's eyes flicked down. There was a paper napkin there with the names scribbled roughly on it in ballpoint pen.

Carlos and *Alex* were at the top.

'Shit, man,' she said, as Shepherd reached forward and picked it up. 'You're good.'

He focused on the names, then glanced back at Karen Casey. 'What happened? Did they threaten you?'

She didn't reply for a long moment, taking a drag instead.

'The night after Leann died, I got a phone call saying that if I told the cops who she worked for, they'd both come here. They knew where I lived.'

Shepherd stayed quiet for a moment; he looked at the napkin.

Carlos.

Alex.

'Did Leann ever tell you their surnames?' he asked.

She shook her head. 'Leann wasn't a big talker.'

Besides the two men's names, Shepherd saw eleven others were scribbled underneath, all female, and he recognised a couple of them immediately.

'These are Leann's associates,' he asked. 'Other girls she worked with. All high-class escorts.'

Karen nodded. 'I figured it wouldn't hurt to warn them. They might be in danger too so I copied down their names off Leann's phone. Felt as if I was doing something useful. Something to help. She'd have wanted that.'

Shepherd glanced at Palmer, who nodded, looking at the list.

'That's the group,' she said. 'I spoke to most of them but they wouldn't tell me anything.'

'They probably got the same phone call I did. Leann going to rehab will have cost Carlos and Alex a ton of money. She was one of their best earners, I think.'

Shepherd looked at the list. 'I'd like to talk to some of these women myself.'

'They might not be easy to find. Once your guy Archer stopped by saying he thought the killers might still be out there, I called around to warn them they might be in danger.'

Looking at the list, Shepherd showed it to Palmer, who reached into her pocket and withdrew her cell.

'I spoke with several of these women fairly recently,' she said. 'They each gave me a contact number.'

'It's worth a shot,' Shepherd said.

Karen shrugged. 'They're scared. Even if they pick up, they might not want to talk to you.'

'We're here to help them,' Shepherd said. 'You can trust us.'

Karen took another drag, seemingly unconvinced, Carlos' and Alex's threat no doubt ringing in her ears. Beside her, Palmer scrolled through her phone then called a number, putting the phone on speaker as Shepherd and Karen sat there in silence.

'Cece Mills,' Palmer said. 'Twenty three years old, from Rochester, NY.'

The call rang through, Cece not answering, the monotonous repetitive rings echoing around the apartment. Glancing at Karen, Palmer selected another number and called it, tapping a name on the list, *Zoe Cross*.

That call rang through too, no-one picking up.

'Looks like you could be right,' Shepherd said to Karen.

She nodded, taking another drag.

'I've got one more number,' Palmer said. 'April Evans.'

While she searched for it, Shepherd flicked through the file of Leann's known associates and pulled out a driving licence photo of a girl who according to the DMV had just turned twenty. She had long thick red hair and green eyes, and like Leann was extremely attractive.

'Cece and Zoe told me April and Leann were good friends,' Palmer said.

Karen nodded. 'They were.'

'I spoke with her a few weeks ago,' Palmer said. 'She didn't tell me anything but she seemed like a nice girl. Smart.'

'Give her a try,' Shepherd said.

Palmer nodded and pushed *Call*, the sound of ringing filled the living space for a third time, echoing around the room.

However, just like Cece and Zoe, after ten rings it went through to answer machine.

April didn't pick up.

TWELVE

In the heart of Brooklyn, Hendricks pulled the black Ford to a halt on a street corner in Cypress Hills, the tinted windows concealing the identity of the occupants. Beside him, Archer looked out at the darkening streets, ignoring the hot pain radiating from the cuts on his chest and arm as his attention shifted to his immediate surroundings.

He'd thought he was clear of danger once he'd been buzzed out of Rikers, but the night was still young and he was Sam Archer. This place was consistently rated the most dangerous neighbourhood in New York; on average, someone was shot every day around here and right then, he couldn't have been more aware of the lack of an NYPD badge and sidearm on his hip.

Various doors were boarded up, walls covered in graffiti and fences topped off with barbed wire, the whole area run-down, quiet and menacing, only a few people in sight. One of them was a solitary African American girl standing on the street, only wearing a pink dress and heels despite the cold.

Studying her for a moment, Archer glanced at Hendricks. She seemed to be attracting the Sergeant's attention too.

'What's the plan?' Archer asked.

'There's a kid down here I use to sweat for information,' Hendricks said, his eyes not leaving the woman. 'I arrested him for assault a few years back and busted him later for running girls. He's two strikes in the hole and knows I'll be there to push a third if he doesn't co-operate.'

He nodded at the girl down the street.

'She's one of his. And if he's here, he'll more than likely be able to tell us who shot Leann, you and Detective Vargas.'

'We're a long way from that part of town. Will he know?'

'He'll know something. Word spreads fast around here; especially if someone shoots a cop.'

Archer nodded as Hendricks put his foot down and moved forward two blocks, pulling to a smooth halt beside the girl.

The sidewalk and road were lit by the occasional street-light but the place was pretty dark, which helped to conceal the rectangular boxes under the fender on the Ford that immediately gave it away as a police car. The black girl on the sidewalk was none the wiser, more interested in the occupants than the vehicle, and right on cue she flicked away a cigarette, stepping forward as Hendricks slid his window down. Despite all her exposed skin, she wasn't shivering; Archer guessed there was a strong chance something out of a bottle or needle was keeping her warm.

'Hey there baby,' she said in a practiced tone to Hendricks, smiling as she reached the car and chewed on some gum seductively. 'Looking for some fun?'

She bent down to emphasise her cleavage, smiling even more broadly as she noticed Archer in the other seat.

'Or is this going to be a party? I charge double rate.'

'We're looking for your boss,' Hendricks said.

'Who?'

'You know who I mean.'

She stopped chewing the gum. Her face hardened, her expression instantly turning hostile.

'Why?'

Reaching to his hip, Hendricks showed her his badge. 'That's why.'

She stepped back warily, realising she'd just been stung. 'Hey man. I didn't do anything.'

'Go get him and I might agree with you.'

As she stood there, looking wary, a young Latino man suddenly materialised from a doorway the other side of the street and headed over towards the car. His baggy jeans were slung low around his backside, a white and green NY Jets jersey over a thick black hooded sweatshirt keeping his body warm and also concealing whatever weapon he most likely had tucked into his belt.

With the sidewalk adding height the guy swaggered over, pushed past the hooker and leaned in close to the window, his right hand lingering near his waistband.

'There a problem?' he said, looking into the car.

The moment he saw Hendricks' face, his eyes widened and his arrogant manner immediately evaporated.

'Oh shit!'

Before the guy could step back Hendricks' arm shot out, grabbed the pimp by his collar, and pulled the man's head into the car as he pushed the button for his window with his other hand. It slid up three quarters of the way, trapping the man's neck; he started struggling, his mask of arrogant hostility replaced by panic as he fought to pull his head free from the window, like a cat who'd got his neck stuck through a hole in a fence. It was useless; he wasn't going anywhere.

'Long time, no see,' Hendricks said, letting go of the pimp's NFL jersey, the window keeping him in place. 'I've missed our little talks.'

The guy didn't respond, too busy fighting to free himself, the window jammed tight under his throat. In the passenger seat, Archer watched impassively, observing Hendricks' well-known style of police work.

'Hand it over,' Hendricks said.

'Hand what over?' the guy gargled.

Hendricks went to tighten the window a hair.

'OK, OK!'

The pimp reached into the back of his waistband and withdrew a pistol. He lifted it carefully, sliding it through the small gap at the top of the window beside his head. Hendricks took it grip first and passed it to Archer, who raised his brows when he saw it. The gun was an Ingram MAC-10, a machine pistol; it was an erratic weapon, one click draining the clip, and was a junk gun, a drug dealer's delight. Archer pulled the top-slide back and removed the magazine on the low-rate weapon, a gleaming copper round slotted on top of thirty one others.

'What do you think?' he said to Hendricks, playing along. 'A year per bullet?'

'Sounds about right,' he replied, turning back to the man in his window. He jerked his head towards the hooker watching from the street. 'I said no more girls. You know what happens now if you get one more charge?'

'I thought you left,' the man managed to get out.

'I decided to stop by and see how you were doing. Now listen to me because I'm not repeating myself. You lie to me or I think you're lying to me, I'll drive back to Queens and we'll book you for carrying a deadly weapon. And you won't be riding in the back. Clear?'

The pimp didn't reply, still struggling to breathe.

Hendricks reached for the keys in the ignition.

'Yeah, yeah, I got it!' the guy rasped.

'Two cops and an escort got shot last month in Queens. You hear about it?

'Yeah man,' the man got out. *'I heard. We all did.'*

'We're looking for the shooter and the driver.'

'I don't know them.'

'Don't lie to me.'

'I swear!'

Hendricks reached forward and started the engine.

'I swear!' the man said.

'What were their names?' Archer asked, leaning across. 'The two guys?'

The pimp didn't reply. Hendricks put the transmission into *Drive*.

'Now might be a good time to talk,' Archer suggested, as Hendricks released the handbrake.

'Goya and Santiago!' he spat out.

'Why'd they kill the girl?' Hendricks asked.

'She was one of their bitches. I heard she was stepping out, leaving the game. They put a green light on her.'

'You're saying her own pimps took her out?' Archer said.

'Yeah!'

107

'Goya and Santiago. Not Valdez and Carvalho?'

'They sound similar?'

As he tried to make sense of this new information, Archer saw they'd attracted the attention of a group of guys standing further down the street. As he watched, a few of them peeled off and started heading towards the police car. Hendricks saw them approaching but didn't seem concerned.

'I find out you're lying to me, I'm coming straight back,' Hendricks said to the man in his window. 'And it'll be your balls in the gap next time.'

'It's the truth, bro, I swear!'

Hendricks looked at the pimp for a moment longer. Then he pressed the window button and the man fell to the sidewalk, coughing.

Turning the wheel, Hendricks put his foot down and pulled a quick U-turn, heading off down the street just as the approaching gang members reached the pimp still lying on the ground.

'So Goya and Santiago were the killers,' Archer said, looking across at Hendricks. 'Not Valdez and Carvalho.'

Hendricks didn't reply and Archer swore, kicking the first aid kit in the foot-well.

'Son of a bitch, I knew it; Homicide got the wrong guys.'

'Leann Casey's own pimps killed her,' Hendricks finished quietly.

*

In the 4th floor apartment on Rivington Street, the three figures in white overalls and black gas masks stood in a line in the bathroom, observing Alex Santiago's body as he lay in his own bathtub. The dead man was fully submerged in hissing clear liquid, the extractor fan helping to clear the eye-watering chemical stink from the air as the concoction in the tub went to work on the corpse.

A few years back, the three killers had chosen pest control as their way of moving around a city easily without the risk of being challenged. People ignored fumigators; it was an unpleasant job but an essential one in the city, which meant no-one wanted to interrupt their work, happy to see the exterminators getting rid of whatever pest was infecting their space. They were anonymous, helped by the masks they wore as part of their assumed role, which were replaced by baseball caps worn low when they weren't on a job or were out on the street.

They'd worked together for a number of years and their routine was so slick and well-practiced they could get on with the task in hand without any communication whatsoever before, during or after. The moment their target opened a door, the leader would shove a pistol in their face. He'd push them back as the second man secured the door, locking it behind them. The third member, the woman, would clear the victim's residence with her pistol, making sure no-one else was there. If they were, they were unlucky.

The target was chloroformed, ensuring no marks were left on their attackers from a blow which could potentially incriminate them. After the targets were restrained with zip-ties, the baths were prepared, the two men bringing up the reinforced pesticide cans from the van outside as the woman kept a pistol on the target or targets just in case they came round.

When the baths were ready, the victims were strangled quickly and quietly.

And once they were dead they were placed in the liquid.

A normal sized bath-tub needed about ten cans to dissolve a corpse and their specific concoction worked fast. In under an hour, all they had to do was turn on the taps and the body was gone, leaving no trace. They always used the victim's own bath to dispose of them when there was one available, which took away the risk of moving the body and potentially providing any evidence for police or forensics. If they had to remove a body, they carried it to their van wrapped in plastic and a box along with their other equipment and disposed of it at a warehouse they used as a base. It was effective as hell.

No-one here knew their names or who they really were.

As the extractor fan whirred and the liquid in the bathtub hissed, the leader of the trio turned and stepped out of the bathroom, glancing to his left to make sure the curtains were drawn, which they were. He then removed his mask to take a deep breath of air and pulled out his cell phone with a gloved hand, checking his messages.

He was pissed off; his two partners had just returned after leaving earlier to secure the last escort, April Evans, but apparently the bitch had slipped through their fingers and got away. Reading a fresh message that had come in ten minutes ago, the large man's eyes narrowed. Deleting the text and pocketing the phone, he turned and looked over at the other two who were standing outside the bathroom, watching him, the hissing from the tub filling the silence.

They'd also pulled off their masks. The figure on the left was a man, about five-ten and lean with a shaved head and a beaked nose. The woman standing next to him was around five foot six, dark-haired with a hard but not unattractive face. She wasn't wearing any make-up and looked pretty ordinary apart from a blackened vein on her neck from a drug overdose a few years ago. He had close ties with both but right now was furious with each of them.

'We good?' she asked.

'No. We're not. Because you two got sloppy, we've got less than five hours to find one woman in the entire goddamned city.'

Neither replied. The larger man looked at them angrily.

'Pack your gear. We need to get moving and find this bitch. She's a risk to this entire operation.'

'What about him?' the slender man asked, jabbing a thumb back into the bathroom behind him.

'Let him soak. We'll come back and flush him away later.'

As the pair pulled their masks back on and moved back into the bathroom to gather the empty cans, the leader also replaced his mask then shifted his thoughts to their last target, April Evans. Despite the fact they'd never met he knew a lot about the woman, where she lived, her patch, her habits, her clients. He knew she'd be scared shitless and low on cash.

He knew she'd be alone and that she'd be making mistakes.

They had five hours to find one woman in New York City.

But considering who they were and the connections they had, that was more than enough time.

THIRTEEN

Driving fast towards the city from Cypress Hills, Hendricks called a Bureau number on the hands-free system as the car carrying him and Archer moved onto the Brooklyn Bridge.

'Sergeant Hendricks?' Ethan's voice responded, slightly tinny over the Ford's intercom.

'Ethan, I need you to run a check for me.'

'What do you need, sir?'

'Priors, charges and addresses on two male suspects' surnames. Goya and Santiago. I don't know their first names but both are involved in the city sex-trade; that should narrow it down.'

'Yes, sir. One moment.'

As he and Hendricks waited for Ethan to come back, Archer watched the Financial District lights rolling into view and saw the newly finished World Trade Center building standing tall and proud, a vibrant blue in the evening sky, a defiant big brother returning after a spell away.

'Sir, Rach told me she just spoke with Sergeant Shepherd; apparently he asked for a check on two names, Carlos and Alex, and she pulled a result. The men you want are Carlos Goya and Alex Santiago.'

'Who are they?' Archer asked.

'Both born in Pittsburgh, early thirties, convictions for some minor infractions. Santiago was just released yesterday after serving twenty one days for a public order offence. According to city files, they share an apartment on the Lower East Side.'

'Got an address?'

113

'Fourth floor walk-up on Rivington Street. Apartment 4E.'

The moment Ethan passed over the specifics, Hendricks ended the call and put his foot down. As they approached the end of the Bridge he glanced across at Archer, that cold ruthless determination he was renowned for on his face.

'These two are the pair who really shot you, Leann Casey and Detective Vargas.'

'So let's go pay them a visit,' Archer replied. 'I've got some catching up to do.'

At Karen Casey's, Shepherd had received the same information from Rach a few moments earlier; after making another brief call, he looked at Palmer and rose from his seat.

'We're on. I've been given the address for Carlos and Alex. It's not too far away.'

Beside them Karen Casey remained on her sofa, looking bewildered, events moving rapidly around her. Eager to get going, the pair nevertheless took a moment, not wanting to abandon the woman too abruptly.

'I'm sorry about Leann,' Palmer said. 'We both are.'

She nodded. 'Appreciated.'

'And we're going to find who really did this,' Shepherd said. 'That's a promise.'

Karen looked up at him but stayed silent; then she nodded slowly, trying to smile. With that, Shepherd turned and walked to the door followed by Palmer who closed it quietly behind them.

Suddenly alone again, Karen stared at the door for a few moments longer then glanced around and saw Leann looking at her from photos around the room. It had been four weeks since her death but only now were the police starting to get their act together and track down who might have really killed her. *We're going to find who really did this,* the Sergeant had promised.

As she sat there motionlessly on the sofa, she couldn't help wondering just how the hell he was going to do that.

Eight miles north at Rikers, Marquez and Josh pushed open an exit to the facility entrance and walked out into the car park, having been told that Hendricks had beaten them to it and left with Archer over half an hour ago. The only access Bridge to the island was from Queens so they'd been forced to loop their way around, using up valuable time.

'Jesus Christ,' Josh said, moving across the tarmac. 'Archer's like the goddamn Sasquatch. Where the hell is he now?'

'And how did Hendricks know he was here?' Marquez asked.

As Josh started to reply Marquez' phone rang, cutting him off. Pulling it out, she saw it was Shepherd.

'Sir, good news,' she said. 'Archer's been released and he's safe. Sergeant Hendricks pulled him half an hour ago.'

As she listened to his response her eyes widened, Josh watching and noticing an immediate shift in her body language. Making eye contact while continuing to listen to Shepherd, she started to move towards their car with more haste, Josh following her lead.

'OK, we're on our way,' she said, ending the call and opening her door.

'What's up?' Josh asked, climbing into the driver's seat beside her

'Karen Casey just coughed up two names, the pimps who ran Leann and her friends,' she told him, pulling on her seatbelt. 'Shepherd thinks they might be the ones who really killed Leann.'

'Addresses?' Josh asked, firing the engine.

'They share a place on the Lower East Side.'

'Just as well the Department's paying for gas,' Josh said, taking off the handbrake, activating the siren and fender lights then flooring it out of the space, heading back into the city as fast as he could.

Not long after, Hendricks and Archer turned onto Rivington Street, pulling up behind an unmarked white van with its rear doors open. A man in white overalls and a baseball cap was finishing stowing some gear in the back; they studied him for a moment, but he didn't match the description of either Goya or Santiago. The guy finished whatever he was doing and shut the rear doors, walking round to the front of the van and climbing inside, disappearing out of sight.

Killing the engine, Hendricks checked the chamber on his pistol then holstered the weapon, Archer very much aware that he was unarmed.

'We wear vests,' Hendricks said, peering up at the apartment building. 'These two won't be happy to see us and we know they've got no problem shooting cops.'

Opening their doors simultaneously, the two men stepped out and headed for the back of the car; Hendricks opened the trunk and passed Archer an NYPD bulletproof vest, taking one himself and strapping it over his sweater. As

116

Archer secured the garment, catching his breath as it pushed against the cut on his chest, Hendricks looked at him for a moment, then reached inside the car and pulled out a black Mossberg pump-action shotgun which he passed to the blond man. Considering he was suspended, that was technically illegal but Archer suddenly felt a hell of a lot more confident with something to protect himself.

'That's for persuasion only,' Hendricks said. 'If shit goes down, you let me handle it and use your hands instead. Don't want you giving Royston any more ammunition.'

Archer shook his head. 'Me neither.'

As Hendricks slammed the trunk lid shut, Archer loaded shells into his shotgun then racked the pump.

'Let's go get reacquainted.'

Two cops just arrived!' the slender man with the shaved head hissed into his cell phone from inside the van, watching through one of the blacked-out windows.

'What? A squad car?'

'Unmarked. I think they're coming up.'

'We're still finishing up. Are they inside yet?'

'They're at the front door,' he replied, seeing the two armed men pause outside the entrance. *'And they're strapped.'*

'With what?'

'One has a shotgun, the other a pistol,' he hissed quietly. *'You've got less than a minute. Get the hell out of there!'*

FOURTEEN

Four floors down, Hendricks pushed a random button on the grid, telling the resident he was UPS delivering a package; a moment later the door was buzzed open. Drawing his pistol he eased his way inside the building, Archer following and shutting the door behind them.

The two men strode over to the stairs, moving rapidly up to the fourth floor, their footfalls light on the stairwell, the building around them quiet save for some music playing from an apartment on the second floor and the muffled sound of a couple arguing on the third.

As they moved onto 4, the two men stalked their way down the corridor towards Goya and Santiago's place, the hallway empty.

Arriving outside the apartment, Hendricks stood with his back against the wall.

He tried the handle silently but the door was locked.

He glanced at Archer, who quickly moved to the other side of the door and buried the stock of the shotgun in his shoulder.

Showtime.

Dipping his shoulder, Hendricks blasted the door open and pulled his pistol back up into the aim a split second later, moving right and followed a step behind by Archer who took the left.

'NYPD!' they both shouted, moving into the apartment.

Looking through their sights, the two men split, seeking to use that initial element of surprise to catch anyone inside off-guard.

The sitting room was empty, the curtains across the room flickering in the slight breeze from an open window. As Hendricks moved right to clear the two bedrooms, Archer moved to the left into the sitting room then stopped and sniffed the air.

There was an unpleasant, acrid chemical smell in the room. He frowned; it was starting to make his eyes water.

What the hell is that?

He saw a closed door to his left. Approaching it cautiously and keeping his Mossberg in the aim, Archer paused for a moment, listening for the sound of any activity, picturing Goya, Santiago or both the other side with a weapon aimed at the wood.

Checking over his shoulder, hearing Hendricks moving about in one of the bedrooms, he stood to one side of the door and reached for the handle with his left hand.

Inside the apartment next door, the female member of the trio had her pistol to the head of the terrified owner as the big guy had his weapon drawn and ready, their black respiratory masks back in place to protect their identities.

The big man was listening intently, the door slightly ajar, but since the noise of the door being breached and the shouts of *police*, there was no sound of movement.

However, Santiago hadn't finished his bath yet.

In Santiago's place, Archer twisted the handle then kicked the door back, snapping his shotgun back into his shoulder as it swung open.

A split second later he saw movement, not in front but behind him, reflected In the bathroom mirror straight ahead.

Two figures, one big, one smaller, in white overalls and black gas masks.

Both were carrying silenced pistols.

And they weren't here to talk.

Spinning round just as Hendricks appeared from the main bedroom, Archer saw the big figure was already lifting his weapon, pointing it straight at him, the smaller figure aiming at Hendricks.

'Get down!' he shouted.

But it was too late. The smaller figure pulled the trigger, firing a quick double-tap, Hendricks taking both rounds in the centre of his chest which knocked him back. Across the room, Archer was already on his way down and aiming his Mossberg but then realised that unless he had a clear shot the powerful shotgun could blast through the wall and potentially kill anyone in the apartment across the hall.

Using every ounce of self-restraint he had, he held off pulling the trigger and scrambled behind a couch as silenced pistol rounds ripped through the fabric, spraying feathers and pieces of wood into the air, the bullets smashing a lamp and a window behind him as he drew the fire of both weapons.

Edging forward, he reached the end of the couch and saw Hendricks lying on the wooden floorboards, shot twice in the chest.

But then the sergeant moved.

Lying on his back, Hendricks suddenly brought up his Smith and Wesson and pulled the trigger, hitting the smaller figure in the arm. The larger figure fired again, hitting Hendricks right at the top of his vest but giving Archer time to aim his shotgun at the smaller figure standing just inside the apartment. He had a shot.

He pulled the trigger. It was a direct hit, straight to the torso, and punched the anonymous figure off their feet, the sudden red on their white overalls demonstrating that unlike Archer and Hendricks, they weren't wearing a vest. The other gunman saw his partner go down and after hesitating for a split-second, abandoned the fight, turned and took off down the corridor.

As Hendricks staggered to his feet, still winded from the gunshots, Archer took the lead, stepping quickly over the dead figure in white to get to the door then snapping out low.

He caught a glimpse of the other shooter reaching the stairs at the end of the hallway before disappearing out of sight.

The Mossberg in his hands, Archer took off after him.

As he raced down the corridor and arrived at the stairs, he suddenly snapped back as a barrage of bullets hit the plaster and wood immediately above his head, the gunman emptying the clip at him from two floors down.

Moments later the fire ceased, replaced by the sound of running footsteps. Descending the stairs two at a time, careful to stay against the wall and out of the line of fire, Archer reached the ground floor, made sure the gunman wasn't waiting for him at the bottom and then sprinted down the lower hallway towards the front door.

He burst out through the door just as the white van parked ahead of the police Ford roared off down the road. He raced after it but the vehicle had a head start and turned the corner, quickly speeding out of sight.

Archer continued to the end of the street, rounding the corner but it was already gone, the faint sound of a speeding engine disappearing into the night.

Mossberg in hand, he stood there for a few moments regaining his breath. Frustrated, he then turned and moved back the way he'd come, pulling his cell to call the Bureau and get them working the plates immediately.

As he drew closer to Santiago's apartment building, he saw two Fords suddenly pulling up behind the one he and Hendricks had arrived in. Shepherd and a blonde woman he vaguely remembered from that day at the 114th stepped out of one, Josh and Marquez getting out of the other, all four looking at him in surprise.

'Too late, guys,' Archer said. 'You missed the show.'

'Story of our goddamn afternoon,' Marquez replied, moving forward with Josh to meet him.

FIFTEEN

Hendricks' unsilenced Smith and Wesson gunshot and Archer's shotgun blast resulted in a flood of 911 calls from both inside the apartment building and from nearby, meaning back-up was already on its way by the time Archer had finished explaining to his colleagues how he'd ended up in Rikers, his confrontation with the gang in the shower block, how he and Hendricks had got the information regarding Goya and Santiago's place ahead of everyone else and the shootout that had just followed.

Officers in squad cars patrolling the area had pulled up outside and were now reassuring frightened residents and concerned onlookers who'd gathered on the street. A Forensics team had also just arrived and were already heading up to the apartment, carrying cases full of their gear.

Walking back upstairs, accompanied by Josh and Marquez, Archer moved down the corridor towards 4E and watched as CSU unpacked their equipment, two investigators taking photographs of the crime-scene, focusing on the dead figure by the doorway while residents down the hall were being ushered away as they stared in shocked fascination at the figure in white sprawled on the floor.

Beside the corpse, Hendricks was talking with CSU's lead investigator, running her through the incident. The three rounds he'd taken to the vest had left holes in the front fabric but they were the only clue he'd been shot. Archer remembered only too well the sensation of being hit in the vest. Hendricks' reputation wasn't undeserved; he was one tough bastard.

Shifting his attention, Archer looked down at the dead figure in white overalls. The gas mask had been removed, revealing a slight, brown-haired woman with several moles visible on the side of her face. Her slack head was lolled to one side, dried blood running from the side of her mouth, her eyes open but the light behind them forever extinguished.

However, even in death there was something about her that was unsettling.

Who the hell are you, he thought, looking into her vacant eyes.

'How many others were with her?' Marquez asked him. 'Just one?'

'Two. The guy I was chasing jumped into the back of a white van. Someone else was driving; the guy we saw when we first pulled up.'

'Where are we at with the plates?' Josh asked.

'Ethan's on it,' Marquez said. 'The local Precinct is sweeping the area searching for the vehicle. We'll find it.'

Archer looked beyond her at the blonde woman who'd shown up with his three team-mates; she was staring down at the body. He remembered seeing her at the 114th eight days ago when he'd laid out Royston and vaguely recalled her name was Palmer, a social worker. Even though they had bigger things to focus on, her presence here bothered him; he'd learned from past experience never to trust someone unless their background checked out.

'Do you know who she is?' Palmer asked quietly to no-one in particular.

'Not yet,' one of the CSU investigators said, bending down beside the body and pushing the woman's fingers onto an electronic pad. 'But I'll send her prints out. She'll have a file somewhere.'

'You can be so sure?' Palmer said.

'You don't do something like that and not have some kind of history,' the guy said, jabbing a thumb towards the apartment's bathroom.

'Something like what?' Josh asked, as beside him Archer suddenly remembered that acrid chemical smell. He hadn't had a chance to take a proper look inside the bathroom before he and Hendricks got jumped.

'Go take a look for yourselves,' the investigator said. 'But be warned; it ain't pretty.' He looked at Palmer. 'Suggest you stay here.'

Archer, Josh and Marquez turned and walked over towards the bathroom. Shepherd was already in there with an investigator; he turned as his three detectives approached and shook his head, a strange look on his face.

Once the trio stepped forward, they could see why.

What remained of what had once been a man was lying in the bath. He was submerged in some sort of chemical cocktail that was eating through his body. It was a horrific sight, made worse by the acrid smell of chemicals hanging in the air, the extractor fan whirring but not man enough for the job.

Staring in horrified silence at the tub, the trio stood beside Shepherd, the only noise in the room the rattling extractor fan.

'Well those are my nightmares sorted for a while,' Marquez muttered.

The investigator in the room rose, looking at the four detectives.

'I present Alex Santiago,' he said. 'Or what's left of him.'

'What the hell is that stuff?' Archer asked, looking at the translucent liquid around the body. 'Acid?'

'It's a lye mixture I've never seen before,' the investigator replied. 'Sodium hydroxide, water and some other chemical that I'd need a lab to identify. Variations of it are called *piranha solution*. I'll leave it to your imagination to figure out why.'

He pointed at the tub with a gloved hand.

'I can tell you already, this particular brew will chew through a two hundred pound body in under an hour. And whoever did this knew exactly what they were doing.'

'How do you mean?' Josh asked.

'Ninety nine per cent of people who try to dispose of a body like this screw up and use acid, which eats through the tub and destroys the pipes. Lye solution doesn't do that and the fumes aren't anywhere near as toxic. Give it sixty minutes and this stuff will eat through anything you put in there. Then you turn on the taps and flush away all the gunk that's left at the bottom. No blood, no trace, no damage to the pipes; nothing. Not even a tooth or bone fragment as forensic evidence.'

He directed his attention to Archer.

'If you'd been thirty minutes later, there wouldn't have been anything left. He'd probably have gone down the drain and you'd never have known he was here.'

There was a pause.

'Have you ever encountered anything like this before?' Shepherd asked.

'Heard about it but never seen it for myself until now. I know Mexican drug cartels have used it to dispose of bodies but that process normally took days, not as fast as this. God only knows what else they've put in it or where they got the recipe from.'

The man indicated to the apartment behind them, at the aftermath of the gunfight, the shot-up furniture and pock-marked walls.

'Did it look like this when you first arrived?'

Archer shook his head. 'No; no damage or sign of a disturbance anywhere. Everything looked normal.'

'If they shot him, hit him over the head or cut his throat, it would have left blood spatter or other evidence for us to work with. That means they restrained and killed him silently, leaving no trace and without anyone else in the building hearing anything. Then they went to work disposing of the body but would have had to fill the tub with liquid they brought with them, from their vehicle. That means they made a number of trips in and out of the building without raising any suspicions.'

'The neighbour thought they were a team of fumigators,' Josh said. 'She saw them when she got back from work earlier and thought they were here for pest control until they knocked on her door and put a gun to her head. White overalls, black boots, gas masks, no other details.'

'So they had this all planned, not only with their disguise but with the lye solution,' the CSU investigator said. 'That requires patience, a cool head, zero conscience and a very strong stomach.'

127

He looked at the foursome.

'Christ, you're dealing with some nasty people here, guys. I've done this job for seven years and encountered some real unpleasant characters. Whoever did this is right up there.'

None of the four detectives replied; a moment later the silence was broken by the sound of Marquez' phone ringing in her pocket. She withdrew it and answered, glad to have a reason to avoid looking at what was left of Santiago in the bath.

'Marquez.'

She listened for a moment, then looked at Shepherd, giving a thumb's up.

'It's Rach. She got the dead woman's prints from CSU and already pulled a result from the NCIC.'

'Who is she?'

'Hold that thought, Rach,' Marquez said, moving back into the apartment and putting the call on loudspeaker, everyone in the room stopping what they were doing to listen. 'You're on speaker.'

'Her full name is Nina Lister. Twenty four years old, born in South-Side Pittsburgh. Five six, a hundred and thirty pounds, former heroin addict. Medical records say she overdosed a few years ago which left a blackened vein on her neck.'

'That's her,' Marquez said, the phone resting in her palm. 'We see the mark.'

'No records of any family. She used to be a prostitute; convicted of first degree manslaughter in San Diego when she was sixteen. Served two years.'

'San Diego?' Shepherd said, frowning. 'The victim?'

128

'A client; turned out he had quite a history.
He'd hand over the money then waste the hookers
in a motel room or wherever afterwards, taking
his cash back. He tried the same with her but she
cut his throat.'

'Since?'

'That's what's strange. That jail time is the last
entry on her record from six years ago and that
was on the other side of the country. No sign of
her since.'

'Associates?'

'Just low-level players in San Diego. As I said,
she was a hooker; most of the crew she ran with
are either dead or in jail.'

'No links with New York?'

'Just Pittsburgh, from what I can see. Parents
aren't on the file, so I'm guessing she was
fostered or orphaned. When they arrested her,
SDPD couldn't find anything more on her
background and she wouldn't tell them anything.'

'Keep looking, Rach,' Shepherd said.

'Will do.'

As the call ended, Marquez slipped the cell
back into her pocket. 'An ex-con street hooker
from Pittsburgh who served time in San Diego.
How the hell did she end up in New York killing
Santiago with this lye shit?'

'And why?' Josh added. 'What's the motive?'

'Before we figure that out, we need to locate
Santiago's partner,' Shepherd said. 'Carlos
Goya.'

'If they whacked Santiago like this, I'd take a
guess they've done the same to his friend,'
Hendricks said. 'We might never find that son of
a bitch. He's probably been flushed down a plug
hole already.'

'Until we have proof of death, we have to assume he's still alive,' Shepherd replied.

'Judging by what's in that bathroom, Lister and her two friends don't leave proof, Shep.'

During the exchange, Archer had gone quiet. As the others continued to debate what to do next, he swung round and walked back towards the bathroom, where the CSU investigator and a colleague had now pulled what was left of Santiago's body out of the tub, dumping him straight into an open black body-bag to take him to the lab.

'Was his phone in his pocket?' Archer asked, covering his mouth from the fumes as he arrived at the doorway, deliberately not looking at what was lying on the plastic.

The investigator nodded, holding up a transparent tagged evidence bag with the remains of a black Nokia inside, the exterior whitened and eaten away. 'It's completely fried.'

'What about the SIM card?'

The man looked at him for a moment; then he opened the bag and took out the mangled cell, turning it over and forcing off the rear case. Unclipping what was left of the battery, he reached inside and withdrew the SIM card, holding it up.

It looked relatively undamaged, like a pearl inside an oyster, protected by the shell, the last thing to dissolve.

'Got a glove?' Archer asked, opening up his own phone as Shepherd, Hendricks, Marquez and Josh stopped talking, his conversation with the CSU investigator catching their attention. The investigator passed him a spare.

Stepping out of the bathroom, Archer snapped it over his hand, took the SIM and slid it into his Nokia, pushing the battery back and turning the phone over.

'C'mon,' he muttered, pressing the power button.

Nothing happened.

Shaking the device, he tried again.

Again, nothing happened.

But then it switched on.

'Son of a bitch,' Josh whispered, watching as the phone took a few seconds to recognise the SIM before syncing with it.

'No PIN or password?' Palmer asked, peering over Marquez' shoulder as she watched.

'These guys use disposables,' Archer said. 'Ninety nine percent of the time, they don't bother with passwords or PIN codes. They use them until they run out of credit then ditch them and buy another.'

Going to the recently made and received calls, Archer saw Santiago had made several to a number yesterday, a three week gap between them and the other most recently-called number seeing as the man had been serving time in prison. Showing the screen to Shepherd, Archer waited as the Sergeant pulled his own cell and called the Bureau, putting it on loudspeaker.

'Ethan, I need you to check a number for me.'

'Go ahead, sir.'

He read it out as the others waited.

'One moment,' he said, the sound of tapping keys coming down the line. *'Searching.'*

Pause.

'Got it. It's from a motel outside Scranton, Pennsylvania.'

131

'Can you connect me to their police department?'

'Yes, sir. Doing it right now.'

As the group waited, Shepherd looked at Hendricks and his team. 'Ten bucks says it's Carlos. He's probably hiding out there, waiting for the heat on him to cool.'

Looking at what was left of Santiago's body as it was zipped up in the black bag, the entire apartment stinking of lye, Archer didn't reply.

If he and the other detectives had located Goya that quickly, no doubt Lister and her two friends could have done the same.

*

'Shit!' the smaller of the two killers shouted as he hit the steering wheel, the van roaring uptown through the dark East side streets. *'They killed her, bro! They killed her!'*

Beside him, his partner didn't reply, finishing tapping a text message into his phone with hands shaking from anger as he gradually steadied his breathing after his escape from the apartment building. What had just happened was not only devastating but also a major problem. Lister had served time in San Diego, which meant her prints were still on file. The cops would know who she was by now, which meant for the first time in years they'd have a sniff of a trail. Once that happened, it was just a matter of time before shit went south, especially on a case involving cop-shooters.

For the first time in a very long time, the extermination team had made a mistake.

Trying to calm down and think clearly, the big guy stayed silent, waiting for a response to his message. Beside him, his partner saw the lights of a cop car reflected off a shop window ahead and swore. Spotting a sign, he suddenly turned a hard left and moved into an underground garage, pulling into an empty space.

Not wasting a second, the pair jumped out, the driver taking some fresh plates and starting to replace the old ones as the big guy opened up the back of their van and pulled out a jet-gun attached to a barrel of water. As his partner changed the plates the larger man turned the tap on the barrel for the jet-gun and then started spraying the outside of the van, the outer white layer peeling off from the force of water and revealing a black coat underneath.

As he worked he fought to stay cool, waiting for the buzz in his pocket indicating a reply to his text. Nina might have been killed but their work tonight was nowhere near finished.

And it meant they were going to need a hell of a lot more lye.

SIXTEEN

Law enforcement arrived at the Pennsylvania motel within eight minutes of Ethan and Shepherd making the call. Scranton PD had their own SWAT team and they descended on the site with military precision, the motel owner already pulled aside and being questioned as the place was surrounded, sharp-shooters covering every exit, the rest of the task force encircling the building.

Around the corner from the forecourt, the SWAT Sergeant was standing with the motel owner beside the police team's truck, an iPad in his hands with Carlos Goya's NYPD mug-shot on the screen.

'This the guy?'

The man nodded. 'That's him. Room 5.'

'How long's he been here?'

'Nine days.'

'Last time you saw him?'

'Yesterday.'

As officers covered the back window in case of an attempted escape, rifle scopes on every exit, one of them came to a halt beside the door, a stream of armed officers behind him poised to enter the room, weapons loaded, body armour and helmets in place.

The point man took the key they'd been given and slid it into the lock.

In one fast movement, he opened the door half a foot and the officer behind him pulled the pin on a stun grenade, tossing it into the room. Pulling the door back, he and the other officers covered up as the flash-bang detonated with a *whump* of light.

A second later the point man smashed the door back and they poured into the room.

'Police!' they shouted, quickly clearing the space, searching for Carlos Goya.

There was no-one in the main room. The trash was full of empty food wrappers, beer cans and take-out containers, the bed sheets were messed up, all a sign that the occupant had been here for a while. The SWAT team ripped open the closet, upturned the bed and pushed back the bathroom door, checking every possible hiding place.

Finishing the sweep, the point man turned to his Sergeant. 'He's not here, sir.'

The SWAT team Sergeant didn't reply. A strong chemical smell was hanging in the air, as if the bathroom had just been cleaned.

Frowning, he sniffed again, the point man doing the same.

'What the hell is that?'

Inside the parking lot in New York, the larger of the two men had just finished taking off the last of the white water-based paint when his phone vibrated in his pocket, indicating a new message. As the other man finished changing the plates, using the set they'd had on the vehicle from their recent trip to Scranton, his partner pulled the cell and read what he'd just been sent.

Find April Evans and do what you have to do. I'm buying you more time.

Whistling to his partner and tossing him the phone so he could read the message, the big guy used the jet gun to sluice away the old white paint on the concrete then quickly stowed the gun and barrel back in the van. Slamming the doors, he jumped into the driver's seat, taking his phone back from his partner as he climbed in beside him.

The larger man fired the engine and releasing the handbrake, headed to the exit with the van now black and with different plates from those it had arrived with minutes earlier. As they pulled back out onto the street and headed north, they passed a cop car to their left parked at a red light, the two officers inside checking out the van as it passed.

However, neither showed any interest in the vehicle and it continued on its way out of the neighbourhood, heading uptown and out of the search area.

At that moment inside a nightclub in South Brooklyn, a black-haired Eastern-European re-read a text message he'd received a minute or so ago, just to make sure he was reading it right. Then he turned, moving quickly through the club towards a booth at the back, past three other members of the organisation and several employees carrying cases of booze to the bars to stock up in preparation for business tonight.

At the back of the club, a thickset black-haired man sitting with a three-quarter full bottle of whiskey in front of him noticed his lieutenant approaching and poured himself another drink. At forty six years old, Vladimir Bashev was a man who'd fought his way up from the bottom. He'd survived because he was intelligent, vicious and brutal; he had no boundaries and no conscience which, coupled with his ambition, had resulted in him achieving his ultimate goal; induction into this prized circle in New York.

The club was in the Little Odessa neighbourhood of Brooklyn, the New York home of this particular Eastern-European Mafia; Bashev was the leader. The network that his crew was part of was far-reaching. The *Prizraki, ghosts* in English, had factions in Moscow, Boston, New York, Pittsburgh and San Diego, and Bashev was the current head of the New York branch, the most respected of them all here in the United States. Although formed eighty or so years ago back home, the gang had first arrived in New York in the 1970s and its members had rapidly built a formidable reputation in the criminal underworld, respected and feared in equal measure. They'd been dubbed *Prizraki* for good reason, operating in an environment of intense secrecy in which membership couldn't be bought but earned.

However, the gang's reputation hadn't protected them from experiencing a shit-storm of a year, Bashev's first and now possibly last in the city. He knew he couldn't survive much longer if this continued. After the events of the past few months, paranoia had settled over the club like smog, flowing over them all as things showed no sign of improving.

The *Prizraki* and Bashev in particular were specialists at making people disappear.

This year, however, the situation had been reversed.

Swallowing a mouthful of whiskey, the strong alcohol slightly easing the foreign anxiety he was feeling, Bashev looked up at his lieutenant as he reached the table. Marat took his silence as an invitation to sit. As he slid into the booth, he pushed his cell phone across the lacquered table towards his boss, the device turned so the screen was facing the larger man.

'Valentin just messaged me,' he said in his native tongue, keeping his voice low. 'Names and addresses. These are the people.'

Bashev paused, his glass halfway to his lips.

Lowering his drink back to the table he looked down, examining the message but not touching the phone.

He studied the list on the screen then glanced up at Marat.

'I thought he was gone. He hasn't been here in over two weeks.'

'Said he's been laying low, trying to find out who's behind all this shit. And he's done it.'

'Who are they?'

'Don't recognise the names. But he said they're behind the disappearances.'

'How'd he get these?'

'I don't know; he didn't say. But at last we have something, boss.'

Bashev scanned the list for a moment longer. Then he made a decision.

'Go with Ilya, Sivic and Nemkov,' he said quietly. 'Call Valentin and tell him to meet up with you. Take whoever you find at these places out to Long Island. When you're on your way, call me and I'll meet you out there. We'll find out if these people are involved soon enough.'

Marat nodded, pocketed his cell and rose, heading for three men by the door. He passed on their orders quickly before they all left the building.

Watching the four men depart, Bashev refilled his glass and swallowed, feeling the alcohol burn his throat and making his temples throb; whiskey always gave him a headache but he hated vodka, something he'd always kept quiet about. Glancing around the club, he looked at the remaining three men who'd stayed with him as security. Three enforcers; all he had left. The humiliation burnt as strong as the alcohol.

Cursing under his breath in his native tongue, Bashev took another mouthful of whiskey and kept his eyes on the door.

SEVENTEEN

At the motel outside Scranton the forecourt had been closed off, the SWAT truck now parked beside two newly-arrived CSI vans, investigators examining the scene.

Inside the room Carlos Goya had been renting, the SWAT Sergeant finished talking with one of the crime scene investigators and then stepped outside. He paused for a moment as he took a deep cleansing breath of air; the room wasn't large and the number of people crowded in there combined with the lingering chemical smell had made it an unpleasant place to be.

Standing by the team's truck thirty feet away, one of his men saw him reappear and approached, a cell phone in his hand.

'Sir, you've got a call,' he said. 'It's a Sergeant in New York. He's the one who contacted the Department about the fugitive.'

Stepping forward, the SWAT team leader took the phone. 'Waters.'

'This is Sergeant Matt Shepherd, NYPD. I'm co-ordinating the search for Carlos Goya. Is he there?'

'Afraid not, but he was definitely staying here,' Waters replied. 'The clerk confirmed it from your man's file photo.'

'How long's he been at the motel?'

'Nine days.'

'No sign of him now?'

'Afraid not, but there's still a bag here. We're thinking he either saw us and split or he's coming back. We're going to pull back and wait in case he does.'

'Is there any kind of chemical smell in the bathroom?'

Waters paused. 'How did you know?'

There was a pause.

'Oh Christ.'

'You know something we don't?'

'Has anyone swabbed the tub?'

'Forensics showed up a few minutes ago. Hold on.'

Walking forward, Waters worked his way back into the motel room, stepping past the teams inside and going towards the bathroom, that acrid smell hanging in the air. An investigator was kneeling by the bath-tub with a testing kit, having just taken a sample. Swilling a small glass vial, he looked at the mixture as it turned pink.

'What is it?' Waters asked, the phone in his hand still connected to Shepherd in New York. 'Bleach?'

The man shook his head, holding up the sample. 'It's mostly sodium hydroxide. Lye.'

'You hear that?' Waters said down the phone.

'I did,' Shepherd said. *'You don't need to pull back and wait, Sergeant.'*

Pause.

'He's not coming back.'

In New York, the blacked-out 4x4 carrying the four Eastern European Mafia enforcers was already on its way through South Brooklyn, heading towards the Bridge into Lower Manhattan. In the front passenger seat, Marat sent Valentin a message ordering him to meet them at their first stop then opened the text with the names and addresses again, burning them into his memory.

141

Thirty two years old, he'd been a mid-level guy until a month back when a sudden lack of personnel meant he'd received a quick promotion to become Bashev's right-hand man. Unlike Vladimir he was New York born and bred, and before his promotion had been carrying out a variety of tasks, including body-guarding, chauffeuring and disposing of people, alive or dead. He had his own methods for the latter but the boss wanted everyone at these residences taken alive tonight so that's what was going to happen.

Marat knew what awaited these people when they got to Long Island. The *Prizraki* were involved in a number of different enterprises; one of them currently being a housing development company used to launder money. Right now they had an extremely wealthy client whose home they were building to his exacting specifications; one of his requirements had been a large swimming pool, which had been dug out but not poured with cement yet. Each person on this list would be tortured for information regarding the whereabouts of the missing men; then their wrists would be broken and they'd be buried alive in a coffin laid in the swimming pool's pit. Cement would be poured over the top, covering the boxes and any trace of the victims. Four inches of concrete and nine feet of chlorinated water was enough to protect from the best sniffer dog on the planet. It was very effective. The method had been used successfully many times before.

Nemkov drove onto the Brooklyn Bridge, the car holding the four mobsters anonymous amongst a stream of others heading in the same direction. Hidden by the blacked-out windows,

Marat pulled out a suppressed HK UMP sub-machine gun from under his seat, slotted a thirty round magazine into the weapon and snapped the working parts forward. Aside from being fitted with a silencer, the gun was fresh out of the box and didn't have so much as a scratch on it, Marat enjoying the distinct and comforting smell of gun oil. Behind him in the back seats, Ilya and Sivic followed his cue and pulled out two other silenced UMPs, the harsh sound of magazines being slotted into weapons and rounds being loaded filling the car.

As well as keeping their police records immaculately clean and their fingerprints rubbed down, the *Prizraki* always cycled their weapons, taking what they wanted from the guns they ran up and down the East Coast. It was expensive but unlike many other gangs in the city, none of them had ever been picked up from old ballistics evidence. To them, it was worth the cost.

No-one spoke, but then again none of them were the chatty type; each was keen to finally be able to administer some retribution. After the events and humiliation of the past few months, it was long overdue. They also knew if they didn't find who was behind these disappearances and stop them, any one of them could be next.

'Where first?' Nemkov asked as they began to approach the end of the Bridge.

'West 78th Street,' Marat replied. 'We take every person at the residence; women, children, whoever. If anyone resists, shoot them in the legs, tape them up and get them in the car.'

'You said the boss wanted them alive,' Ilya said.

'They'll survive long enough.'

EIGHTEEN

Exiting Santiago's and Goya's apartment building on the Lower East Side, Archer walked down the steps to the sidewalk whilst unscrewing the cap on a small bottle of water. The bleeding from the cuts to his chest and arm seemed to have stopped but they were still sore and painful. He popped two painkillers a medic had just given him into his mouth and swallowed them with a gulp of water, feeling the cold liquid hit his empty stomach. He hadn't eaten anything apart from some prison chow given to him at midday in his cell but whatever appetite he might have had had been taken away by the sight of what had been lying in the bath upstairs.

He'd worked on the street for six years and as a counter terrorist cop for over three but he'd never encountered anything as disturbing as the sight of Santiago in that bathroom. It took a special kind of person to work in CSU but even they'd seemed slightly unsettled by what they'd found. There'd been no sign of anything unusual in the apartment when he and Hendricks had first entered, no smashed lamps or overturned furniture to indicate there'd been any sort of struggle, just a dead criminal dissolving in the tub.

Piranha solution, the CSU investigator had called variations of the concoction.

I'll leave it to your imagination to figure out why.

Goya and Santiago were dead, the pair who'd really killed Leann and shot him and Vargas. He should have been elated but he felt almost the opposite; it was a surprising anti-climax.

144

Although they were both gone, their fates didn't change Vargas' current situation or his own prospects, which were looking pretty grim. He also felt slightly cheated; he'd have liked to have had the opportunity to reintroduce himself to the two men, especially after what they'd done to Alice and Leann Casey.

Feeling the bite of the cold wind as it whipped through his hair, he pulled his cell phone and dialled a number saved into the Nokia, lifting it to his ear and looking down the lamp-lit street as it rang. Behind him, Josh walked out of the building, moving down the steps to join his partner.

'St Luke's.'

'It's Detective Archer,' he said.

'Hi Sam. We've been wondering where you were.'

'I was out of Manhattan and didn't have any service. How's she doing?'

'Pretty good; sleeping right now. She should be ready to leave any day.'

'That's great. We found who did it.'

'They've been arrested?'

'Not quite. They're dead.'

Pause.

'That's good news. I mean, that you found them.'

'I'll be in touch. When she wakes up, tell her I called.'

'Will do. Take care.'

He ended the call as Josh joined him on the sidewalk.

'How is she?' he asked.

'Better.' Archer paused. 'Thanks, by the way.'

'For what?'

'For looking for me; the whole time I was in there, I was praying you guys would realise something was wrong.'

'Just sorry it took so long. Neither of us could figure out where the hell you'd gone. Hendricks said you almost didn't make it out?'

Archer nodded. 'Sounds about right.'

'Royston needs to pay for serving you up in there.'

'What can I do? He's a Lieutenant, I'm a detective who punched him out in front of his people. He holds all the cards.'

As Josh looked at him, Archer suddenly grinned.

'It was almost worth it though.'

Josh smiled. 'Try not to mention that in court tomorrow.'

'I'll do my best. Anyway, how'd you find out where I was?'

'Your car was towed from outside Karen Casey's. We went down there and she told us you got picked up.'

'My car got towed?'

Josh nodded. 'Afraid so.'

'Goddammit. There goes another hundred bucks.'

He paused, the two men watching the officers down the street talking with residents of the building who'd been evacuated from the building.

'How's Isabel doing by the way?' he asked Josh.

'She's great; she misses you. She got real worried when you didn't call.'

'She did?'

146

'Of course. She worships you. We've got a moment; why don't you try her now? If she's not asleep, Michelle can pass the phone over.'

Looking at his partner for a moment, Archer lifted his Nokia again as Marquez walked out of the building behind them, moving down the steps to join the two men.

'Ethan's checking Lister's file with SDPD to try and work up some possible associates and potential suspects,' she said. 'Every squad car in Lower and Midtown Manhattan is combing the area for the white van.'

'No sign of it yet?'

'No, but we'll find it.'

She went to continue but noticed Archer was looking at the phone in his hand.

'You good?' she asked him.

Nodding, Archer tilted the phone, showing them both the screen.

Josh Home was flashing there.

'Your wife must be psychic,' he told his detective partner, pushing *Answer* and lifting the phone to his ear.

On West 78th Street, the four *Prizraki* had arrived a few moments earlier at their first stop. The residential street was quiet, which meant they didn't have to concern themselves too much with prying eyes, but they'd concealed their weapons under their leather jackets anyway, their hands tight around the grips, wanting to avoid attracting any unnecessary attention.

Standing on the sidewalk outside their car, Marat looked around the street but couldn't see any sign of Valentin yet. Unwilling to wait and with the other addresses to visit, he turned and looked at the other three men.

'Let's go,' he said quietly in their foreign tongue.

Without another word the four men headed for the front door of *J Blake*'s house, whoever the hell he or she was, pleased to see lights still on. There was someone home.

But although they were alert, none of them noticed they were being watched by a small dark-haired girl two floors up through a small gap in the curtains.

Dressed in her pyjamas and holding the house phone receiver to her ear with both hands.

NINETEEN

In a lot of ways, Isabel Vargas was just like any other nine year old girl. She looked like one, spoke like one and dressed like one. She went to sleepovers and birthday parties; she worked hard at school. She played games, she didn't like boys and she was still scared of the dark.

However, despite all that, she was different from other kids and she knew exactly why. Bad things happened around her. People got hurt and a lot of them died.

It had started in March, in a horrific, violent way. Her entire blood family had been murdered on a Sunday afternoon, gunned down at a villa upstate in East Hampton. She'd been the only survivor and was still dealing with the things she saw that day in her nightmares. However, her ordeal hadn't ended there; a few weeks later she'd been trapped inside a building here in New York, a group of men seemingly intent on hurting her and the people she was with. Assigned to protect her along with three other men, Vargas had defended her as best she could from events in the building that night but she'd still seen more people die, guns fired and explosions, things that a kid her age would never expect to see or experience.

Someone else had protected Isabel in the building that night too. Isabel had got to know Vargas before that eventful day but Archer had appeared out of nowhere, his presence becoming more and more reassuring as events unfolded. After they'd finally made it out and things had settled down, she'd been overjoyed to find out

Vargas was going to look after her; for Isabel, the icing on the cake had been when they'd ended up living with Archer too.

She didn't know why these things happened around her; she guessed it was because of her father. A few months ago, Vargas had explained to her that he'd done some bad things in his life which was why he wasn't alive anymore and that there were more bad men out there too who were his enemies. As a consequence, she'd said that they all had to stay aware in case more of these men tried to come after them. She'd made Isabel memorise her's and Archer's cell numbers, saying if she ever felt in danger she should call one of them instantly.

Both of those things had just happened.

Michelle had told Isabel that she'd only be gone a few minutes while she went to collect her kids from their grandmother's place around the corner and that she was to go to bed. Isabel had brushed her teeth and then walked into the guest bedroom, glancing out of the window as she drew her curtains, having to do them one at a time.

It was then that she'd seen a dark car pull up outside, parking in the spot Michelle had just left.

A group of men had stepped out, looking a lot like the men her real father used to have around him. They were all in jeans and leather jackets. They were all dark-haired and scary, like the gang who'd killed her family.

And they were all carrying guns.

They'd quickly hidden the weapons under their jackets when they got out of the car but not before Isabel had seen them.

However, despite what she'd been told by Vargas, as she watched the men stand there on

150

the street looking around, she'd still wondered whether she should call, for two different reasons. The first was that she hadn't seen Vargas since last month; apparently she'd been sent on a trip somewhere and couldn't be contacted. Isabel had secretly tried to call her anyway but Vargas hadn't answered her cell.

The second reason was different and it was to do with Archer. She hadn't seen or spoken to him in what felt like ages either. Josh had said he was busy with work but she missed him so much and wondered why he'd been so busy he couldn't even call her, just like Vargas. Isabel had never been close to her real father and Archer was the total opposite to him, open and kind, not closed off and angry all the time. However, despite the fact that Archer had always been kind to her, she felt she could never really get close to him. Perhaps he didn't like her, just like her real father. She'd always wanted a dad who actually liked her, something that all her friends seemed to have.

She knew she shouldn't call him except in an emergency. She'd debated what to do, not wanting to get into trouble, but then she heard Vargas' voice in her head.

No matter what, who or when, you let one of us know if you think you're in danger.

So she'd dialled his cell phone number, hoping he wouldn't be mad.

To her joy, he'd been far from angry when he answered.

'What do you see, sweetheart?' Archer asked at that moment, thirty seconds later into their call. *'Tell me in detail.'*

151

'There are four of them,' she said quietly. 'They all have guns.'

'Are they still outside?'

Clutching the phone with both hands she peered cautiously out of the window, then heard two *thumps*, a third followed by the splintering of wood.

'I think they just smashed open the front door.'

'Where are Michelle and the other kids?'

'They're not here,' she said quietly 'Michelle's picking them up from their grandma's but she said she'd only be gone a few minutes.'

She heard the sound of footsteps in the hallway below, boots on wood.

Floorboards creaking.

The four men downstairs, searching the house. Déjà vu.

'I'm scared,' she whispered into the receiver.

On the ground floor, Marat motioned to the other three who immediately separated, looking down the sights of their weapons and searching for the occupants.

Gripping his own MP UMP tight, he walked into the sitting room. He saw from the pictures in the photo frames that Blake and his family were black but living around here ruled out any rival organisation from Brooklyn that he could think of. The *Prizraki* mostly feuded with the Georgians or Ukrainians and that was it; they had no beef with the Italians or Irish who had their own turf in the city, and the Chechens had been gone from the city for years.

But the man who owned this home was African American. Maybe it was personal, or this guy had been hired to carry out hits on the *Priz*. However, although the man in the photos looked to be a big guy he wasn't menacing, quite the opposite in fact, smiling in all the shots, not fitting the persona of a man who'd made eleven *Prizraki* members disappear. When Valentin showed up, Marat wanted to find out how he'd got this information.

As Ilya kicked open the door to the kitchen, sweeping the interior with his silenced sub-machine gun, Marat focused on a certain photo frame in the sitting room and paused. He stepped forward, black boots on the white rug, and peered closer.

It showed the same black guy from all the other photos, this time in police uniform.

Staring at the image for a moment, Marat glanced at Nemkov, who'd joined him and was studying the photo too.

'A cop?' Marat said quietly.

Nemkov didn't reply, looking at the frame then glanced around the room, confused. Beside him, Marat pulled his cell phone and headed for the front door.

He wasn't going to wait for Valentin to show up.

He wanted to speak to him right now.

Cutting across a red light, the police lights on their Ford flashing, Josh roared up 8th Avenue towards his address, Archer beside him and Marquez in the back seat. The Blake's house was the other side of town from the Lower East Side, and although Josh was driving as fast as he could in the heavy traffic, progress was frustratingly slow.

'Hello?' Archer said. 'Isabel? Sweetheart? Hello?'

'What happened?' Josh asked, panicked.

Archer swore. 'It went dead.'

'West 78th!' Marquez said into her cell, on the line with Dispatch. 'Armed men breaching a Counter-Terrorism Bureau detective's home address. Get over there now!'

Ending the call, she pulled her pistol as Josh weaved his way through the traffic and burned it uptown, now just twelve blocks away. The car's hands-free system had synced with his cell phone and he was calling Michelle.

'C'mon, sweetheart, pick up!' Josh said, looking at the display. 'Pick up the phone!'

Easing his way upstairs in the Blake household, Sivic looked down the sights of his UMP. Bashev wanted these people alive but Sivic didn't give a shit; if he found someone here, they'd die. With the list they'd been given, there'd be plenty of other bodies to satisfy the boss later.

Tightening his finger on the trigger of his suppressed UMP, the tall Eastern-European approached the main bedroom first, pushing the door back with the barrel of his sub-machine gun, tracing both sides.

It was empty.

He eased open the closet doors to check there was no-one hiding inside, then went into the bathroom, pulling open the door to the shower cubicle.

There was no-one hiding in there either.

After clearing two other bedrooms and a bathroom, he moved back onto the landing, then entered a third bathroom. He swept aside the shower curtain hanging around the bath but saw there was no-one hiding in the tub. Frustrated, he looked around. It seemed the entire upper floor was clear, but his instincts were telling him otherwise.

Someone was here. He was sure of it.

He stood still, listening.

Then turning, he looked across the landing. The door to the last room to check was slightly ajar. It looked like a guest bedroom, the duvet on the bed disturbed, a toy rabbit lying on a pillow.

A kid.

Smiling, he walked into the bedroom and stood quietly again, listening.

Glancing to his left, he saw the closet door was open. He walked forward and eased the doors back with the barrel of his UMP, but no-one was hiding inside.

His foot creaking on a floorboard as he turned and looked around, Sivic grinned as he realised there was only one other hiding place. Just where a kid would choose.

A moment later he dropped to one knee, aimed his weapon under the bed and opened fire.

On Central Park West, just twenty seconds from home, Michelle had picked up her three kids from her mother's house but wanted to get back quickly and make sure Isabel was safely in bed. Turning onto West 78th, she drove down the street, annoyed to see a black 4x4 had taken her parking space in the few minutes she'd been away.

As she reversed into another space outside her neighbour's house, she saw the display inside the car indicating an incoming call, *Josh* flashing on

155

the screen. Applying the handbrake, Michelle switched off the ignition as the kids undid their seatbelts and piled out, slamming the doors behind them.

She pulled her cell phone from her bag and pressed the green button as she climbed out of the car. Locking the vehicle, she turned towards her house and lifted the phone to her ear.

'Hey baby,' she said. 'Did you find Archer?'

His reply was drowned out by the noise of a police car with a blaring siren as it suddenly screeched around the corner ahead of her off 8th Avenue. The sound caught her and her kids by surprise, all four of them swinging round at the unexpected noise.

Her phone still to her ear, Michelle frowned as she recognised the fast-moving vehicle.

It was a Counter-Terrorism Bureau Ford.

As they rounded the corner on 9th, having boxed Columbus Circle to get here faster, Josh, Archer and Marquez could see Michelle and the three kids on the street outside the house, looking in their direction.

But then to their horror, two large black haired men in dark jackets and jeans suddenly appeared from the Blakes' front door, carrying automatic weapons.

And before Josh could brake or shout a warning, the two men were already lifting the guns, aiming them straight at Michelle and the three kids.

TWENTY

The car was still moving when Archer opened his door, pushing it back with his foot whilst racking a round into the Mossberg. He leapt out and aimed the shotgun at the two gunmen in one fast fluid movement but there was a major problem which stopped him from pulling the trigger.

The two men were standing on the lowest step of the Blake front porch.

But twenty five feet in front of Archer, Josh's two sons were standing directly in his line of fire.

Michelle and the boys had frozen like deer in headlights. The two gunmen had free shots.

Then Archer noticed a large porch-light directly above them.

Lifting his aim, he fired. As the shotgun exploded and kicked back into his shoulder, the lamp took the shell full on, blasting the glass which showered down onto the men. It only distracted them for a few seconds but gave Marquez the opportunity to move away from the car and get a better angle to fire her pistol. However, the two men recovered fast and swept their weapons back up which meant she didn't have any more time. She had to fire right now.

As Josh shouted at his wife to get down, Michelle turned just as Marquez pulled the trigger. The 9mm round missed Josh's wife but hit one of the two gunmen straight in the shoulder, thumping him back as he let off an involuntary volley from the suppressed UMP into the sky, the bullets ripping into a building across the street, peppering the red-stone brickwork.

The other man managed to get a burst off, his muzzle flashing; taking a hit, Michelle spun in a pirouette and fell to the ground. Josh shouted with rage and instinctively unleashed a volley of fire at the gunman with his Sig, walking down on him, forcing the guy to run for cover as the kids crawled towards their injured mother.

Suddenly two more gunmen appeared from the house, immediately opening fire with silenced sub-machine guns. Josh dived for cover behind a parked car as the sudden onslaught forced Marquez and Archer down, the rounds ripping around them, the two men's rate of firepower so far the winner in this exchange. Using that brief advantage the men ran for their vehicle, maintaining their assault but their aim now more erratic.

Archer grabbed that opportunity to look out from around the car he'd ducked behind. He took aim but before he could pull the trigger one of the gunmen unleashed another volley directly at him, forcing him back as the man jumped into the vehicle seconds before it took off, speeding away towards Central Park West.

Rising from between the two cars, Archer aimed his Mossberg and managed to put a shell into one of the tyres, blowing it out. Racking the pump, he went to fire again but the car slid around the corner and was gone, car alarms set off, dogs barking, the sounds of the speeding car fading.

Beside him, Marquez was already running towards Josh, who was kneeling by Michelle. Beside them the three kids were crying and clutching their mother who was on her side holding her arm, her eyes wide with shock. As

Josh started to compress the wound and Marquez pulled her cell to call for an ambulance, Archer raced towards the front door and sprinted up the steps.

The smoking shotgun in his shoulder and gunpowder stinging his eyes, he snapped inside, clearing the lower level. Things had been knocked over, doors kicked in and ornaments smashed.

Seeing there was no-one there, he immediately sprinted up the stairs.

'Isabel!' he called, reaching the 1st floor. *'Isabel!'*

He looked around, praying that she'd hidden just as he'd told her to and he wouldn't see her small body lying on the floor somewhere.

'Isabel!'

He couldn't see her anywhere and there was no response. His heart pounding, he saw a load of shell casings on the floor in the bedroom. Walking forward, he could see the lower portion of the guest bed had been shot to pieces; someone had fired under the bed, aiming at someone hiding underneath.

Kneeling down slowly, he exhaled and looked under the frame.

Just as he bent, the door to the kids' bathroom on the landing opened from behind him. He spun round and saw Isabel appear, dressed in her pyjamas. He just had time to lean the shotgun against the bed before she flung herself into his arms.

Archer ignored the pain from the cut to his chest as relief poured through him, realising she was unhurt.

159

'It's OK, they're gone,' he told her. 'You're safe.'

She didn't reply as he stood up, her arms wrapped around his neck and her legs around his torso, her body trembling. As he held her and rubbed her back comfortingly, Archer looked into the bathroom and saw the lid to the clothes hamper was open.

'That was a good hiding place,' he told her, leaning back and smiling at her

'I've used it before,' she said quietly.

Outside, Marquez ended the call for an ambulance then put her cell back in her pocket and knelt down by Josh's three kids, all of whom were starting to show signs of shock, brass shell casings all over the sidewalk and scattered on the road. Josh was cradling Michelle, talking to her reassuringly and trying to keep her conscious, his hand clamped over the wound as the sound of sirens came closer.

Curtains on windows along the street were flickering, people who'd taken cover from the gunfight risking a look outside to see what had happened now it had gone quiet. The flashing lights on the hastily abandoned Ford were illuminating the dark street with a pulsing red glow. Focusing on Michelle, Marquez pulled off her jacket and laid it over the injured woman.

'An ambulance will be here any minute,' she said. 'You're going to be fine, OK?'

Michelle nodded quickly but didn't reply, her eyes wide and her breathing ragged as the pain and shock kicked in. Doing her best to help Josh and comfort the kids, Marquez suddenly saw Archer appear from the house, Isabel on his hip, dressed in her night clothes and with her head buried in his neck.

She rose and walked quickly up to them, resting her hand on Isabel's back. 'Are you alright, sweetheart?'

Isabel nodded, not letting go of Archer as emergency vehicles started to arrive on the street. Marquez turned and went to follow Archer down the step when her foot kicked against something.

Looking down, she saw a cell phone half concealed in the shadows on the second step. Kneeling, she hitched her sleeve over her hand to protect against smudging any fingerprints and picked it up. Pulling her other sleeve over her left-fore finger, she pressed one of the buttons and clicked into the device.

Just in front of her at the bottom of the steps, Archer watched the arriving squad cars as they ripped round the corner from Central Park West and pulled to a halt on the street, officers climbing out and running towards Josh and Michelle.

'Jesus Christ, where the hell is the ambulance?' he said.

Marquez didn't reply, staring at the phone in her hand. Archer turned to look at her.

'Lisa?'

Suddenly she thrust the cell at Archer, leapt down the step and took off towards their car.

'Warn Shepherd and Hendricks!' she shouted at him, ripping open the driver's door to the Ford.

Archer watched in astonishment as she fired the engine and took off down the street, passing an ambulance coming in the opposite direction as she roared out onto Central Park West and disappeared out of sight.

161

'What's wrong?' Isabel asked, seeing her go.

'I don't know,' Archer said, looking down at the phone Marquez had virtually thrown at him. On the screen was an open text message, a series of names and addresses.

Then he saw why Marquez had bolted. The first address was Josh's.

Then Marquez's.

Then Shepherd's, and Hendricks'.

And finally, his.

It wasn't Lisa's cell.

One of the gunmen who'd just escaped had dropped it.

TWENTY ONE

Like many other cities in the United States, New York was adapting its approach to prostitution. In the past, those who were paid for sex were viewed as criminals but the outlook had changed, those in authority starting to realise the bleak, dangerous lives these people led, most of them with little chance of escape. *Operation Losing Proposition* had been the Department's first major step in trying to strike a balance, seeking to target the johns rather than the girls; arrests had been plentiful, including some of the providers, but it was a step in the right direction.

Another was Covenant Housing, nationwide secure hostel-like shelters where residents could be admitted for a thirty day rehabilitation program with the intention of getting them off the street and into a safer life. Located in Midtown on 42nd Street, the New York branch was one of the main refuges for victims of the sex industry and that Friday night, three of the project's employees were working together at the front desk when the front door opened and a man in jeans, jacket and a sweater wandered in.

The moment he entered the building, all conversation ceased, the three of them recognising the look on the new arrival's face. The vacancy and despair that was so familiar was clearly visible, his face pale, his head buzz-shaved. Women weren't the only sex being trafficked and sold on the street. The man was slightly built, around five ten and a hundred and sixty pounds, someone who without a lot of confidence would be easily controlled.

163

He shuffled towards the front desk, the female shift leader walking forward to meet him. There was a pause.

'I've got nowhere else to go,' he said eventually, staring at the counter.

She nodded, putting her hand on his back reassuringly.

'It's OK,' she told him. 'We have space.'

More than a hundred blocks uptown, the car carrying the four armed *Prizraki* had stopped at their next address, that of *L Marquez* on 120th Street. The journey had been a frustrating ride, hindered by one of their tyres being blown out in the shootout on 76th Street, but they'd still managed to make it up there fast, knowing the cops would be onto them.

Staying where he was inside their car, Marat gritted his teeth and clutched his shoulder, feeling a searing pain coursing through his body, blood staining his hands. The bullet was still in there and grinding against the bone. He swore at his stupidity as he sweated and bled out; not only had he got shot but he'd dropped his cell phone, which meant those cops who'd shown up would have it by now.

He should have tossed it down a storm drain or deleted the message as soon as he'd memorised it; his desire for bloodlust and revenge had made him sloppy and he knew that could cost them dearly. He wasn't planning on telling the other guys or Bashev though; as a newly-promoted right-hand man, it wouldn't exactly build trust and respect and he had no desire to end up in a coffin with his wrists broken for his carelessness.

164

Taking his hand away from the gunshot wound, he swore crudely in his native tongue as he pulled the empty magazine from his UMP and reloaded awkwardly with a spare from his pocket. Loading a round, he looked out of the window and saw the other three guys reappear, moving out of the apartment building, glancing quickly around them as they climbed back into the car, their weapons concealed under their jackets.

'You check it out?' he asked.

Nemkov nodded. 'Looks like a woman and kid live there. The bitch wasn't home. And there's something else.'

'What?'

'Photos in the sitting room of her in NYPD uniform. I think she's a cop too. Or someone who lives there is.'

Marat stared at him for a moment and thought back to the photos of the man inside the house they'd just left. The police had shown up unusually fast.

'Is this a set up?' Sivic asked from the back seat.

Ignoring him, Marat thought back to the addresses he'd memorised; if they were all cops that could be a serious issue. Valentin was a reliable man, so maybe cops had been the ones responsible for their guys disappearing. It wouldn't be the first time.

'We skip #3 and go straight to #4,' he said. 'If a cop lives there too, we head back to the Beach and figure this out.'

'Where the hell is Valentin?'

'Call him and tell him to meet us there.'

'Why can't you?'

'I look like I can use my hands at the moment?' he retorted, clutching the wound to his shoulder with his right and holding his gun in the left.

'You gonna bleed to death?' Nemkov asked.

'No, but you will if you don't start the car.'

A beat later, Nemkov switched on the engine and checked for any movement behind them as he pulled out onto the street.

'Who lives at this next place?' Ilya asked.

Gritting his teeth from the pain and with his anger increasing, Marat forced his mind to focus.

'Some asshole called Hendricks.'

The Midtown Covenant Housing centre had three floors, eight rooms on each. Six of them had bunk beds, the other two rooms were for single occupants, those who for psychological or post-traumatic stress reasons couldn't sleep in a room unless they were alone.

As most of the occupants were women, putting the man in the single room was the only option and fortunately tonight there was one spare. Having signed him in and taken what details they could get out of him, the female employee led him to the room.

'Here we are,' she said, opening up.

The man walked inside slowly, looking around and then turned to face the woman, crossing his arms in a defensive gesture which she was used to. These people had spent their entire lives trying to protect themselves and ward off abuse; you didn't just drop the habit.

'Can I get you anything?' she asked.

The man didn't reply. She smiled.

'I bet you're hungry.'

'I guess.'

'I'll go out and get you some food. What would you like?'

Pause.

'McDonalds would be good.'

'OK. There's one just down the street. You wait here and I'll be right back.'

Smiling at him, she closed the door and headed off down the corridor.

The moment she shut the door, the man's expression changed.

Moving fast, he pulled his cell phone and called his partner, who was on the street in their black van. He answered before the second ring.

'I'm inside,' he told him. 'The one booking me in just left to get me food. Fat bitch, grey hair, grey dress.'

'OK. I'll let you know when she's coming back. Start searching.'

Hanging up, the slight man tucked the phone into his pocket then drew his silenced FN.45 pistol from the back of his belt, loading a round into the chamber. Pulling off his jacket and draping it over his arm to cover the handgun, he moved to the door and eased it open, checking to make sure the woman had left.

She had.

He stalked down the corridor, moving to the first bedroom he came to and pushed it open, his fingers curled around the grip of the pistol hidden under his jacket.

A black girl was in there alone and turned to look as the door was opened. The man glanced at her then after quickly scanning the rest of the room, pulled the door shut behind him before the woman had a chance to speak, moving on to the next.

April Evans was alone, abandoned and scared with very little money and no friends left to call. This was the only major housing centre for prostitutes in Manhattan, the one place they could come to for shelter.

There was more than a high chance that she was in here somewhere.

Inside the Ford speeding uptown from the Upper West Side into Spanish Harlem, the sound of a ringing phone filled the car, Marquez willing Shepherd to answer. Right now his cell was engaged, which she prayed was Archer warning him and getting there ahead of her.

Moments later she tried again and this time she got through.

'Lisa?' Shepherd said, still down on Rivington Street. *'Where the hell did you all go? I need you here.'*

'Sir, you need to get to your house right now!'

'What's going on?'

'There are people targeting us. They shot Josh's wife.'

'What?'

'We made it just in time; looks as if they were intending to kill her and the kids. One of them dropped his cell. All of our addresses were on it!'

Before she'd finished talking, Marquez could already hear the sound of Shepherd calling for Hendricks, followed by the sound of a car door being opened and slammed shut.

'Who the hell are they?' he asked, the engine in the background firing.

'I don't know,' she replied. 'But we were all on that list. You were number 3, then Sergeant Hendricks, then Archer.'

'My family's at Jake's having dinner. Where are you?'

'Pulling up outside my place!' she said, screeching to a halt.

'Marquez, wait for back-up! That's an order!'

Ignoring him and jamming on the handbrake, she pushed open the Ford's door and ran towards the building, opening the entrance and sprinting up the stairs with her pistol drawn. On nights she had to work late like tonight, she called her sister and asked her to look after her daughter until she got home.

She just prayed to God that tonight was one of the nights she'd taken her back to her own place.

TWENTY TWO

The Shepherd and Hendricks families went back a long way. Matt and Jake had ridden a squad car together as rookies when they'd first joined the NYPD and had been the closest of friends ever since, Shepherd's cool and calm manner a perfect foil for Hendricks' more explosive personality, two different approaches to life and police work that complemented each other perfectly.

Their wives were also good friends and that night had just arrived back at the Hendricks' house just across the Hudson River in Hoboken from a school play that both the Hendricks girls had performed in. They were all having dinner together before the Shepherd family headed back to their place twenty minutes away.

In the kitchen, Melissa Hendricks was putting some final preparations to dinner, Beth Shepherd behind her straining some vegetables over the sink as she glanced at the news headlines on the television mounted on the wall beside her, the kids next door watching TV. The two women had been friends for over fifteen years and like their husbands, their temperaments were very different, Beth calm and placid while Melissa was more like a Spartan mother, as strong, determined and resilient as her husband but also as kind as anyone you could ever hope to meet unless you crossed her.

Finishing mixing the sauce, Melissa felt for her cell phone then realised it was next door in the hall, tucked inside her jacket pocket. She wanted to call her husband and see what time he was finishing work, hoping they weren't going to be delayed so he and Matt could eat with their families. Although it was his day off, Jake had headed out earlier saying he wouldn't be long, and she hadn't heard from him since; no doubt he'd been caught up in something yet again. It was a pattern she'd become very familiar with over the years.

Moving the saucepan off the heat then wiping her hands on a towel, she walked through to the hall and picked up the house phone.

Dialling her husband's number, she glanced idly out of the window as she lifted the receiver to her ear, hoping to see him or Matt show up even as she made the call.

On the third floor of the *Covenant Housing* building in Midtown, a red-headed prostitute was sitting on the bed trying to work up the courage to leave the bedroom and go down the corridor to talk to the other residents. She could hear some quiet laughter filtering down the hallway, a sound she hadn't heard in a long time.

It almost made her smile.

She looked down at her hands and saw they were shaking. She'd come here tonight after fleeing her patch; she knew her pimp and his friends would be out there looking for her. If he found her he'd break her arm again; he liked to beat the shit out of the girls in front of the others as a deterrent. She'd seen him half-kill several.

She took a shaky breath, tears brimming in her eyes. The people downstairs had told her she was safe here for at least a month which is when she had to leave. It had taken all her courage to run and now she knew she had to dig even deeper to come up with some sort of plan.

171

Along with the laughter coming from down the corridor, she could hear the sounds of the city through the window, the echoes of horns, the hum of activity that hid so many secrets.

She took another steadying breath, reminding herself of the positives of her current situation.

In here she was safe.

Twenty seven more days that he couldn't get to her.

The house phone to her ear, Melissa sighed. Jake's cell was engaged.

However, a moment later the ring tone of her own cell phone suddenly echoed from her jacket on a hook across the hall. She smiled, knowing it would be him.

Hanging up the main line, she glanced out of the window as she started to walk across the hall.

What she saw caused her to stop dead in her tracks.

On the 3rd and final corridor of the *Covenant Housing*, the man with the silenced pistol had cleared floors 1 and 2, looking into all the bedrooms and scanning the occupants. There was no sign of the missing red-haired bitch, just a load of other whores and some rent-boys, the usual type, down-trodden and desperate.

As he checked another room, the occupants turning to look at him, his cell phone rang. Seeing she wasn't inside, he shut the door and walked on to the next room, taking the call, his face cold and emotionless.

'Yeah?'

'Found her?'

'Not yet.'

'The fat bitch is coming back. Finish up and get out. I'm on 41st.'

Hanging up, he approached the last two rooms, one of which was a communal, the other a single.

As they'd parked on the street outside the Hendricks house, Marat and the other three men had already seen movement inside. Unlike the Blake and Marquez residences, this place wasn't empty and there were no cops around.

They were in business.

Without another word, Ilya, Nemkov and Sivic had stepped out of their vehicle, quickly concealing their reloaded suppressed sub-machine guns under their jackets, leaving Marat alone in the car watching as he continued to try and staunch the bleeding from his shoulder. The three armed men had made their way up to the front of the Hendricks house, hearing noise inside, kids talking and a television.

Now kneeling by the porch, Nemkov turned to the other two men and nodded, all of them withdrawing their UMPs from under their jackets. Silently stepping up to the front door, Nemkov aimed his fully loaded weapon at the lock and half-depressed the trigger.

But then two things happened almost simultaneously. A teenage boy appeared from around the side of the house carrying a sports bag, stopping dead in his tracks the moment he saw the three armed men.

And a split-second later they all heard a familiar sound from the other side of the front door.

The red-headed prostitute inside the Covenant Housing had just risen to go introduce herself to the others when the door to her room was suddenly pushed open, startling her.

A shaved-headed man stood in the doorway and stepped forward, staring directly at her, withdrawing a pistol from under his jacket.

As they made eye contact she took a step back, whimpering in fright.

Right outside the Hendricks' front door, Nemkov froze, having registered the sound that had just come from the other side of the wood.

It was a pump-action shotgun.

And it was being loaded.

TWENTY THREE

A split-second later he was pounded backwards as if he'd been kicked in the chest by a horse, punching him down the steps in a bloody spray, the centre of the wooden door exploding into thousands of splinters and screws as the door and the man both took the shotgun shell.

Before the other two armed men had time to react, Melissa Hendricks racked the pump and fired at the armed figure on the right, through where the front door had been. The edge of the porch took most of the blast, the woodwork exploding as it ate the shell, but the man received the follow-through and was blown off his feet, hit in the chest, another one down.

The shotgun was a CZ USA Model 612 Home Defence weapon, her gun, not her husband's, twelve gauge with six shell capacity and designed to prevent home invasions. She'd seen three armed men get out of a car and approach her house as she'd glanced out of the window. She didn't waste a second wondering who they were or why they were here. No calls to Jake, no dialling for help. It wasn't the first time people had come looking for trouble.

But for these sons of bitches however, it was going to be the last.

As the second man she'd shot fell back to the ground, she crunched another shell into the chamber as the shocked kids huddled down on the floor in the sitting room, Beth scrambling through to them from the kitchen. Stepping forward just as what was left of the door fell off its hinges, Melissa saw the other man throw himself behind the porch and she fired again, just missing him, the wooden post half-obliterated by the shell.

Racking the pump again, she took aim, intending to blast him through the woodwork when he suddenly reappeared, holding his sub-machine gun to her son's head, the boy's eyes wide with fear. He was still dressed in his soccer gear and dropped his bag as the gunman pushed him forward, jamming the suppressor of his sub-machine gun behind Jack's ear.

'Drop the weapon, bitch!' the gunman screamed at her in a strong foreign accent. *'Drop it or I kill your boy!'*

The stock of the shotgun buried in her shoulder, her face expressionless Melissa didn't move, Jack staring at her with wide fearful eyes, the stranger's gun to his head.

'Drop it!' the gunman screamed again.

Suddenly there was the screech of tyres on tarmac from the street behind the man. He instinctively snapped his head towards the noise as a blue and white squad car appeared, lights flashing, closely followed by another, the NYPD arriving at the scene.

Keeping his eyes on his mother, Jack Hendricks suddenly dropped like a stone, right out of the gunman's grip.

Shepherd and Hendricks had just been beaten to it by two NYPD squad cars responding to Marquez' emergency call to Department dispatch. As the Ford carrying Hendricks and Shepherd screeched around the corner, they saw Melissa fire, blasting a man off his feet as he took a shell to the chest,

176

Jack Hendricks hitting the ground just in front of him as the gunman fell.

Before they could slam to a halt, Hendricks pushed open his door and jumped out while the car was still moving, running towards his wife.

Suddenly however, a door to a 4x4 twenty feet away was thrown back and a man holding a silenced sub-machine gun in one hand staggered out, his other hand clutching his right shoulder with blood over his hand and wrist.

'Jake!' Shepherd shouted in warning, reaching for his Sig.

However, before he could fire Melissa swung and blasted the gunman from the front step, knocking him back into the vehicle. As that last shot echoed in the night, two of the officers ran forward and kicked the man's weapon away before flipping him over and handcuffing him as he bled out, still alive but probably not for much longer.

Up ahead, Beth Shepherd peered round the damaged doorframe then ran forward as she saw her husband. Hendricks had just arrived by his wife and taking the shotgun from her hands, held her and Jack.

'You both OK?' he asked them.

They nodded, staring at the dead men littering their front lawn.

'Who the hell are they, Jake?' Melissa asked her husband quietly, trembling from reaction now the situation was over.

Hendricks looked at the three dead gunmen then glanced over at the fourth man who'd been cuffed and was slumped against the 4x4.

'I have no idea.'

On the 1st floor of the Covenant Housing project in Midtown, the female employee from the front desk walked up to the bedroom door and pushed it open, holding the rolled up bag of food she'd just bought from the Times Square McDonalds down the street.

'Here we are-' she started with a smile.

Then she paused.

The room was empty.

Confused, she looked around then down the corridor. The slender frightened man was nowhere to be seen.

'Michael?'

A floor above, his eyes full of frustrated anger, the man stared at the red-headed woman for a long moment then turned and walked off without a word, leaving the bedroom door to swing shut behind him.

Alone again, the girl stepped back then sat down hard on the bed as her legs gave out, shaking with fear from the sudden encounter with the armed stranger.

Once again, she heard laughter echo down the hallway but it didn't have the same effect as before.

Forget introducing herself.

She was staying put.

TWENTY FOUR

Pushing down the bar to the fire exit, the slender man walked out onto 41st Street and headed towards his partner waiting in the van. Crossing the road, he pulled open the door, tossed his jacket into the back of the vehicle, then climbed in and tucked his silenced pistol into his belt.

'She wasn't there,' he said as he closed his door.

'You're sure?'

'Positive. Thought I'd found her in the last room but it wasn't her. Just some other bitch with red hair.'

The bigger man swore as he checked his watch. 'We've got to make the most of this window. The cop heat isn't going to be off us for much longer and we've got a lot of shit left to do.'

As the smaller man stayed quiet, cupping his hands and blowing warm air into them, the big guy thought for a moment. He had an open file in his hand, one of the pile he'd instructed Goya and Santiago to keep on all the girls. It had April Evans' details inside, her vitals, address and clients.

'You think she saw you and Nina at her place earlier?'

'I don't know. Maybe Nina. She was downstairs and watched her enter the building.'

'Well she split so she knows someone's after her. It's cold at night, so she'll be needing to be indoors or she'll freeze her ass off.'

'Subway?'

'Maybe. But which station? We don't exactly have time to check each one.'

179

'She could have gone to the cops.'

'Doubt it. They wouldn't give a shit. And until they find a body, who's going to believe her?'

'What about her clients?' the smaller man asked, looking at the page. 'Did she have regulars?'

'No-one she'd run to or who would listen. Only possible is a judge.' The big guy tapped a man's name with his finger. 'He's been good for almost a hundred k since we started working him I doubt he'd want to help her.'

'Where'd she meet him?'

The larger man nodded. 'Upper East Side. And other clients. In a bar up there, according to this.'

'Which one?'

'West 82nd and Park.'

'Screw it, it's worth a shot,' the smaller man said. 'We got nothing else.'

The big man nodded, starting the engine just as his cell phone buzzed in his pocket from an incoming message.

Standing on Josh's porch on West 78th, Archer watched as the street was closed off and the scene of the shootout investigated by detectives from the local Precinct. The ambulance with Michelle inside had just left, Josh going with her, officers who'd recently arrived cordoning off the street in preparation for a Forensics team who'd be here any minute.

Rather than go to the hospital with their parents, Josh's kids and Isabel had been taken back to the Counter-Terrorism Bureau. Not knowing who these men were and why they were being targeted, Archer wanted to get the youngsters somewhere where their safety was guaranteed.

180

Officers in an NYPD squad car had also been ordered to act as security for Josh and Michelle at the hospital for as long as they were needed. She was going straight into surgery and Josh was understandably focused solely on her, needing someone to watch his back in case this wasn't the last attack on him or his family tonight.

Isabel had been reluctant to leave, not wanting to be parted from Archer, but he'd promised he'd join her soon; because he was suspended, technically he wasn't allowed back into the Bureau but after what had just happened as well as his little sojourn in Rikers, he didn't think that would be an issue. He'd be happy to debate it with anyone who objected.

He watched officers taking statements from frightened neighbours as he thought about what had just happened. When he'd seen the addresses on the phone Marquez had given him, he'd tried to call Shepherd to warn both him and Hendricks but Shepherd's cell had been engaged. When he'd finally got through, it turned out Marquez had beaten him to it, the two sergeants speeding to Hendricks' house where their families were apparently having dinner together.

The cold wind coming from the Hudson River slightly numbed his face and neck as he frowned. The reason for the addresses on the wounded gunman's phone was confusing; gangs and criminals with half a brain avoided targeting police officers. They knew the heat that would provoke, yet the injured man and his colleagues had been deliberately going after the Counter-Terrorism Bureau detectives.

But why?

Were the gunmen involved in Leann Casey's death?

He dismissed that thought almost as soon as it crossed his mind. He'd stake his life on the fact that the men they'd just encountered weren't in any way connected with Goya or Santiago. They just didn't fit together, neither racially nor in terms of how they operated. Archer was familiar with the habits of the higher-level gang activity in the city and knew the one thing organized crime did was keep to themselves, not wanting to attract any police attention; they were pretty intelligent in that regard and had learnt hard lessons from the past.

Whatever the reason, for the moment it didn't matter that they had his address; right now he, Vargas and Isabel were safe where they were. Alice was downtown at a hospital with two cops watching her room, Isabel was with the police and he was standing here on the street.

As he tried to make sense of it, his phone started ringing, the display telling him it was the Bureau.

'Archer,' he said.

'Arch, it's Ethan. I need to talk to you. I tried Shepherd and Hendricks but no one's picking up.'

'There's a situation right now. What's going on?'

'Shepherd told me earlier to ring round all the girls listed as associates on Leann Casey's case file but none of them are answering. I requested some blue and whites check out a couple of the residences, but they said no-one was home.'

'OK.'

'Leann's closest contact in the group seemed to be a woman called April Evans. Apparently she picked Leann up in a taxi from the rehab clinic out on Long Island the day she died. Shepherd just sent me her number from Leann's phone, so I've been trying to trace it and therefore her.'

'Any luck?'

'Afraid not; it's switched off. But using the Bureau's clout I got a warrant with Verizon, who allowed me access to Leann's cell records. She had a voice message on there from April; nothing important, but I took a voice print and ran it over their network, in case she calls someone.'

'And?'

'She just did twenty minutes ago.'

'Who?'

'Karen Casey, Leann's mother. Listen to this.'

'Karen, it's me,' a woman suddenly said, her voice shaky with fear, her accent from somewhere else, not New York. *'I'm so sorry, but I didn't know who else to call. Someone's after me. It started yesterday. A few hours ago they tried to get me at my apartment. All the other girls have disappeared; I don't know what's going on but it's bad. I think someone's running us down one at a time.'*

Standing there on Josh's porch, Archer suddenly forgot all about the activity on the street around him, completely focused on the recorded phone message.

'I'm getting out before they find me,' April's voice continued. *'I'm laying low but I need somewhere to stay tonight. My cell's about to die but I'll call back from a payphone in an hour. Please be there. I really need your help and I didn't know who else to ask.'*

Then the message ended.

'Can you trace it?' Archer asked, running what she'd said through his mind.

'Afraid not,' Ethan replied, his quiet, deep tone an immediate contrast to April's shaky voice. *'But she said all the girls have disappeared, Arch. The other women who worked with Leann Casey.'*

'And none of them can be contacted?'

'Shit, right now we can't even locate any of them. I'll try to isolate the background noises and figure out if there's anything there that could tell us where she is.'

Archer started to reply but then stopped , thinking back to April's call, replaying it in his mind.

'Arch? Still there?'

'Send back-up to the Upper East Side right now!' Archer suddenly said, turning and running into Josh's house.

'What? Where?'

'West 86th Street. I know where she is!'

Ending the call, Archer moved past some detectives and took the stairs two at a time. The Mossberg Hendricks had given him earlier was still leaning against the bed in Isabel's room but he ignored it. Instead, he ran into Josh and Michelle's bedroom and opened up the wardrobe, taking Josh's home defence pistol from its place on the top shelf.

Loading the Beretta, he tucked it into the back of his belt then ran down the stairs and out of the house, heading east.

Ducking under the police tape blocking off the scene of the shootout, he sprinted down the road and when he reached Central Park West he didn't

184

stop, weaving his way between two passing cars and running into the Park.

Ethan didn't need to isolate the background noise; it had caught Archer's attention during the call anyway. There had been a combination of two sounds that he'd heard before on several occasions.

And they meant he knew where April Evans was.

TWENTY FIVE

Inside the bar of the hotel on East 86th Street and Park Avenue, April Evans was sitting facing the entrance, keeping her eyes on the payphone outside and doing her best to stop her hands from shaking. Since her narrow escape at her apartment, she'd meandered her way uptown trying to work out what to do, constantly checking around her, and had ended up here after taking a detour on the subway.

As she sat there, she tried to make sense of what was happening. This had all started the night Leann was killed; Carlos, their pimp, had always had an unpredictable and violent temper but he'd made a big mistake when he shot the two cops as well as Leann. Alex had been the driver that night and not the trigger-man so he'd decided not to leave but lay low in the city instead; however April hadn't seen Carlos now for a while and guessed he'd run. She wasn't too sad about that.

The day after Leann died, Alex had warned the girls that if any of them talked to the cops they'd be next. Shocked and frightened by Leann's sudden, violent death, the eleven remaining women knew it was no empty threat but had hoped that despite their lack of co-operation, the police would figure it out for themselves. Some detectives and a social worker had come round two weeks ago asking questions but they hadn't hung around. April had kept her answers as short as possible, just like the other girls, Santiago's threat ringing in their ears, but had hoped that even without their help the cops would catch a break and find Carlos. Right now she had no idea what was going on with the investigation.

Nervous and worried for each other's safety in case Alex decided they might have talked and carry out his threat, the girls had started to ring round every so often to make sure everyone was OK. Until yesterday, they all were. However, almost thirty six hours ago three of them had stopped answering their phones. When April had gone round to their apartments to check, there'd been no-one home. When that number had increased to five, it became alarming. By the seventh and eighth before midnight she'd been extremely frightened and concerned. She was pretty sure none of the girls would have talked and certainly not eight of them, so what would Alex and Carlos gain by hurting them?

This morning, there'd only been two other women still answering their phones, Kelly and Cece. Any suspicions April may have had that the other girls were hiding out or had left town were dismissed when she'd been on the line with Cece earlier this afternoon.

She'd heard the moment her friend had been attacked, their conversation suddenly interrupted, Cece's scream abruptly cut off and the sounds of muffled activity coming down the phone.

Frozen in horror, April had heard what sounded like the phone being picked up.

She'd kept listening, the sound of breathing coming down the line from the other end.

Then it'd gone dead.

Closing her eyes, April swallowed. Her cell was in her jacket pocket but it was out of battery and she couldn't charge it without going home. Her remaining money was at the apartment too and she didn't have enough cash on her to get out of the city, so her options were slim and right now she didn't trust anyone, including the cops. Her last shot was Karen Casey, who she'd never met but whose number she'd entered into her phone after Leann had died. She was the only person left April could think to call who might be sympathetic and listen.

She had a quick flashback to the two people who'd come running out of her apartment building dressed in white overalls. Maybe it was Alex and Carlos, figuring the girls might have talked or protecting their backs and taking them out just in case. But despite the fact that they'd be cutting off their only source of income, why the white overalls and ball caps? That wasn't their style; they'd just shoot them like they did Leann. It couldn't have been them.

So who the hell were these people? And why were they doing this?

April was getting tired thinking about it, the same thoughts whirling around her head as they'd done ever since she dropped off the fire escape ladder and run for her life those few hours ago. Whatever the reason and whoever these people in the overalls were, April knew one thing for sure.

She was the last girl from the group left.

And they were after her as well.

She glanced at the people sitting either side of her at the bar, all of whom were engaged in conversations. She could feel the occasional gaze settling on her and knew she looked out of place; normally she'd have come here all dressed up just like the women around her, but she was in the clothes she'd run in, an old red dress, leather jacket and black boots.

Despite the fact she stood out, she figured hiding out here was as good a choice as any. She'd been sent to a bar four blocks south of this on several occasions to meet a client but knew Alex and Carlos would surely check there if it was them behind this. Not wanting to take any chances, she'd come here instead, four blocks north. She'd never been in this particular bar before and figured it was a safe place to lay low until she called Karen again to see whether she could stay with her tonight. There were plenty of people here which made her feel more secure; no-one could attack her with so many witnesses around. If Karen didn't pick up, she could stay here till closing and then figure out what to do next.

Taking another sip of water to moisten her dry mouth, she noticed a man on the other side of the bar looking at her. He didn't smile but held eye contact. She immediately glanced away, feeling a sudden chill of fear sweep over her, and drained her glass quickly. However, the amount of water she'd drunk was beginning to have its inevitable effect; she'd been trying to hold off going as it was getting close to the hour when she'd ring Karen back but she couldn't wait any longer.

Sliding off her stool, she turned and walked towards the ladies room quickly, feeling the man at the bar watching her. She didn't look back, readying herself to lock the restroom door behind her the moment she stepped inside.

In a booth fifteen feet away, his overalls left in the van parked down the block, the driver of the black van looked up from his untouched beer and watched the red-headed escort walk towards the restrooms around the corner.

Giving her a few moments to get out of sight, he slid out from his seat and hit *Send* on a text message.

We're on.

On Central Park East, Archer ran out of the exit between West 85th and 86th, the cold air hurting his lungs as he breathed in hard. He stopped for a moment, several pedestrians having to step around him before continuing on their way.

To his left, he saw a grey-haired African American guy in his sixties sitting beside a series of paintings and framed prints of *The New Yorker*, his back to the Park. Every now and then he shouted out an advertisement for his work, accompanied by the sound of a saxophone busker down the street; it was that combination which Archer had heard in the background of April's panicked call to Karen Casey. He'd spent a lot of his spare time around Central Park in the summer with Vargas and had heard the man and the music on many an occasion when he walked past, heading for the subway stops.

Looking around, he saw that the only likely places nearby she could be were two bars, one three blocks to his right and the other a block north.

'*I've got to hit the treadmill more,*' he muttered, sucking in another lungful of air as he made a quick decision and took off across the street.

Inside the ladies restroom, April walked out of a stall and started to wash her hands at the basin, looking at the tired, worried reflection that was staring back at her. If Karen didn't pick up she could stay here until closing, but where would she sleep? The subway? The Park?

And then what? Could she go to the cops? She'd been evasive when they'd questioned her about Leann, which wouldn't exactly help her case. From prior experience, she also knew they weren't hugely interested when dealing with girls like her. She'd tried to get their help a few years back when a friend of hers had disappeared and they'd pretty well laughed in her face, another hooker with a time-wasting story. Unless she had a long history of drug addiction or there were witnesses to an abduction, a prostitute over the age of eighteen was hardly ever declared missing. She knew the reality; they just weren't considered people worth spending time and money trying to find.

Sighing, she dried her hands then moved to the door to get back to her stool at the bar, twisting the handle and pulling the door towards her.

However, the moment she opened it, she took an instinctive step back.

A large man was directly in front of her blocking her way.

Ripping open the front door of one of the two bars, Archer moved inside, rapidly scanning the place to see if he could catch sight of the girl. He'd seen April's picture in the closed case file on Leann Casey's murder and knew she had red hair, sea-green eyes and was twenty years old. She'd stand out.

Looking around, he saw that none of the women here matched her description. Cursing, he turned and headed for the door. Wrong guess.

However, as he reached for the handle he hesitated and glanced to his right.

There was an unoccupied stool at the bar. That wasn't unusual but the cushion on the wood was still partially pushed down from someone sitting there recently and there was an empty glass on the woodwork in front of it which the barman hadn't cleared. No-one had left the place when he ran towards it or in the last few moments.

Looking back at the front door, Archer then noticed something else through the glass panel.

A payphone, ten feet from the front entrance.

TWENTY SIX

Inside the restroom, the big man pushed April back and slammed her into the far wall, ramming his hand around her throat as the door swung shut behind him.

As she clutched at his forearm, desperately trying to loosen his grip, April tried to make a sound in the hope someone in the bar could hear but the man was too strong, his hold on her throat preventing her from making any noise.

Unable to breathe, pushed up so high her feet were almost off the ground, she saw a smaller man duck into the room behind her attacker then turn and lock the restroom door, making sure no-one else came in.

Trapped and helpless, she kicked out with her remaining strength but the large guy didn't even flinch and only tightened his grip, looking at her impassively as he waited for her to lose consciousness.

A beat after he'd seen the empty stool and then the payphone outside, Archer turned to see where the toilets were located, just in time to catch a glimpse of a shaven-headed man disappear into the ladies' restroom. The guy had moved furtively, pushing the door open then closing it behind him quickly; there was definitely something wrong here.

Archer ran forward and tried the handle, but the door was locked. Without hesitation, he dipped his shoulder and rammed into it, smashing the door open.

As it swung back, he saw a second much larger man strangling April Evans against the wall fifteen feet away, a silenced pistol tucked into the back of his jeans. Judging by his build, he had to be Nina Lister's companion from earlier, black-haired, wide-shouldered, his head twisting round as he heard Archer crash into the room.

As Archer reached into the back of his waistband and pulled his Beretta, he was suddenly pistol-whipped hard in the face from his right, stunning him and causing him to lose his grip on the weapon which clattered to the floor. As Archer recovered from the sucker shot, he saw the smaller guy already had his weapon up, aiming it at his head.

Snapping forward and pushing the man's arm to one side, Archer jerked his head back a fraction of an inch before the guy pulled the trigger. That first bullet missed him by a hair's breadth but the man fired repeatedly, the rounds hitting the wall behind him, Archer feeling the hot exhaust from the weapon as he fought to keep the suppressed FN.45 aimed away from his head.

Kicking the guy hard in the groin, Archer hit him with a flash uppercut, popping his head back and stunning him as he fell to the floor. Following up his advantage, Archer stamped on the guy's hand, forcing his grip on the silenced pistol to loosen which the blond detective then kicked into one of the stalls.

Seeing his partner in trouble, the other man released April, who sank to the floor; stepping forward, he swung a meaty right hook which cleaved through the air but Archer saw it coming and ducked under the punch, immediately tackling the guy and driving him back, smashing him hard into a stall. Riding another uppercut that Archer fired off, the larger man connected with a thumping straight left that cut under Archer's eye, causing him to reel back.

Hitting the basins behind him, Archer grabbed hold of one as support, leant back and drove both feet into the guy's chest just as he lunged at him, propelling him back as he ran at him, buying himself a precious few seconds. As his attacker hit the stall then came at him again, Archer let go of the basin and grabbed hold of a hand-dryer on the wall next to him with both hands. In a burst of strength, he ripped the metal box off the wall and smashed it into his attacker's face just as he rushed him.

The man ran straight into the blow, the force of the impact taking him off his feet. As he hit the deck, Archer dropped the box, scooped up his Beretta and turned to April, who was coughing and trying to stand.

Despite the punishment they'd taken, both guys were already moving which meant Archer was left with one choice and it wasn't to hang around.

'Let's go!' he said to April, reaching out and grabbing her hand as the two men lurched to their feet.

Running towards the door, he dragged her out of the restroom back into the bar.

Racing past surprised patrons and bar-staff who'd heard the noise of the fight, Archer and April sprinted for the door, blood running down Archer's cheek from the big guy's punch. However, a concerned bartender had moved round from the bar and was blocking their way.

'What the hell is going on? You can't fight in here!'

195

Before Archer could answer, he heard a shriek from several customers behind him as the restroom door smashed open.

'*Get down!*' he shouted, pushing April and the bartender to the floor a beat before he heard two muffled gunshots, the glass on the front window shattering ahead of them.

As he hit the floor, Archer rolled onto his back, Beretta in hand, and saw the large guy from the bathroom aiming directly at him. However, he got there first and fired twice at his assailant, the guy reacting fast for a big man, ducking back into the restroom as frightened patrons scrambled under tables, the gunshots from Archer's Beretta harsh and loud compared to the muffled shots of the silenced .45 pistols.

With his gunfire keeping the two men back, Archer pulled April to her feet and they ran through the front exit out onto the street. They made it through the door just as the glass behind them was smashed out from more rounds, the bullets burying themselves in a car parked immediately outside the bar, setting off the alarm.

Looking left and right swiftly, Archer couldn't see or hear any cop cars yet; quickly assessing his options, he realised that if they ran either way down the street, they'd be gunned down in an instant.

Without a moment to spare, he grabbed April's hand and took off again, the pair racing across the street, weaving through the traffic and heading straight into Central Park.

TWENTY SEVEN

With a head-start on the two men, Archer and April sprinted into the Park as rain started to fall heavily, the wind picking up, both of which masked the sound of their running footsteps. The path they were on split into two but without slowing, Archer steered them to the left, the route he'd taken on the way here.

Suddenly, pieces of wood and leaves sprayed up beside them, bullets ripping into the trees and pinging off a lamp-post to their right.

'Jesus!' April shouted as Archer pulled her onwards, not allowing her pace to slow.

The path joined a road with cyclists and joggers, apparently undeterred by the rain. The road stretched out straight either way, offering no cover, meaning they'd be target practice for the two gunmen when they caught up with them in a few moments.

Knowing they were out of options and time, Archer dragged April with him to the left, the pair jumping over a metal railing and stumbling down into the undergrowth on the side of the road.

The two men appeared from the path just in time to see the cop and woman disappear. They opened fire again, emptying entire clips, a hail of bullets sending leaves and bark flying into the air as the fleeing pair scrambled out of sight.

Reloading, the large man nodded to his partner, who stepped over the barrier and pushed his way through the thick vegetation, holding his pistol double-handed, his footfalls muffled by the falling rain which pattered off the leaves around

197

him. Staying on the main road and looking down the sights of his own pistol, the big guy waited in case the cop and woman reappeared, the side of his head pounding from where the blond man had hit him with the dryer.

Then he heard two barking gunshots, the cop's unsilenced pistol, and ran forward, jumping over the railing and pushing his way down the small slope.

Behind the protection of a large tree, Archer fired into the earth again so as not to risk hitting any passers-by. Backed up against the trunk, cursing quietly as the increasingly heavy rain continued to fall around them, his mind raced as he desperately tried to come up with a better plan other than firing the Beretta to lure both men towards him and away from April.

He looked to his right, at the steep wet slope. It would take him at least ten seconds to make it up to the railing and path, but he'd have more holes in him than Leann Casey's murder case-file by that point.

That left one other choice.

Stalking in the direction of that gunfire, the two gunmen suddenly saw the cop throw himself down the slope to his left. They fired at him, the large guy scoring a hit but realising he'd only hit the blond man's vest before he slid out of sight. They ran forward and fired again but he'd gone to ground in the thick undergrowth.

'*You get him?*' his partner called.

The big guy ignored him, running forward to check behind the tree. The woman wasn't there.

'Shit! Where's the bitch?'

On road level, having hidden behind another tree as Archer drew their fire, April pulled herself over the railing then put her hands up as uniformed cops ran towards her from the East-side entrance.

'Please help!' she shouted. *'Two men are trying to kill me!'*

As two of the officers moved forward and secured her in handcuffs, there was movement from behind them. Snapping around, the officers raised their weapons as Archer suddenly appeared, his hands in the air as he struggled to breathe, having taken a bullet to the vest.

'Drop the weapon!'

Archer complied, two of the men moving forward.

'Down on your knees!'

'I'm a cop!' Archer gasped, as he dropped down. Reaching him the guy pushed Archer face to the concrete, taking the pistol from the ground and looking at it.

'This isn't Department issue. It's a Beretta.'

'I borrowed it,' Archer coughed. ' I'm with the…Counter-Terrorism Bureau.'

'Where's your badge?'

'I'm susp…ended,' he got out.

'Two guys just tried to kill us!' April said.

As Archer and April were held, two officers appeared from the other side of the railing.

'Anything?' the Sergeant called.

'Nothing,' one of the men said. 'There's no-one down there.'

Frowning as he was dragged to his feet, Archer looked down at the thick vegetation along the side of the road, his hands cuffed behind his back.

All he saw were wet leaves and branches moving in the wind.

The two men were gone.

TWENTY EIGHT

Just over an hour later, a squad car pulled up outside the Counter-Terrorism Bureau, the officer behind the wheel staying where he was as his partner opened up the rear doors to let Archer and April out. Both had just about dried off but the girl in particular was very cold, both from shock and because of her light clothing, her legs bare under her red dress.

They'd been forced to stay at the scene of the shootout in Central Park for a while, Archer explaining what had happened. His claim that he was a suspended NYPD detective had been quickly verified by the Bureau but now he was in even deeper shit for running around while on suspension with a pistol that wasn't his and firing four rounds in a public space. Confiscating Josh's Beretta and bagging it as evidence, the on-site detectives were refusing to let him go but after a very short call from Shepherd, the reluctant cops drove Archer and April to the Counter-Terrorism Bureau without further delay.

After the squad car did a U turn and drove off, Archer walked towards the main entrance, April hurrying beside him. Pulling open the door, he led her inside.

Marquez was waiting for them beyond a security door and she buzzed the pair in, looking at Archer with undisguised relief as he pushed the heavy glass door back.

'You OK?' she asked.

He nodded; she looked at him a moment longer then shifted her attention to April. 'I'm Marquez. Call me Lisa.'

April didn't reply, too busy looking around the interior of the building as the security door shut behind them. The Bureau was a hive of activity 24/7 and pretty overwhelming for someone who'd never been inside before, particularly a woman who in the past had done everything she could to stay out of places like this.

In the meantime, Marquez studied the side of Archer's face and passed him a tissue, filling a cup of water from a cooler to her left. 'Better clean up a bit. Isabel's next door.'

Touching the sore bump from where he'd been pistol-whipped, Archer took the tissue and wiped down his face. A few moments later he looked at Marquez, who grinned.

'Much better. Don't want you frightening small children.'

Tossing the tissue in the trash, Archer and Marquez started walking towards the detective pit, April following.

'How's Michelle?' he asked.

'In surgery. Josh's there with her.'

'Damage?'

'Two rounds clipped her tricep; one was a through and through. She got lucky; if she hadn't spun before he fired, it would have gone right through her chest.'

As they entered the heart of the building, Archer saw the families gathered in the detective pool straight ahead, a pair of officers talking with them and offering them some iced pastries from a box. They all looked shell-shocked after the events of the night but at least in here they knew they were safe.

Observing the group, Archer shook his head.

'What the hell is going on? Why go after them?'

'That's what we're trying to find out,' Marquez replied, motioning upstairs to the Conference Rooms which the detective teams used. 'We're waiting for you; Shepherd sent me down. They're starting in one minute.'

As Marquez spoke, Isabel suddenly appeared from a side room with a female detective and saw Archer. Her face lit up and she immediately ran over, Archer kneeling down as she hugged him, catching his breath as she threw herself against the cut across his chest.

With the girl clinging to him and not letting go any time soon, he looked up at Marquez and April.

'Better make that two.'

*

The mood on the lower level of the Bureau with the family members might have been one of delayed shock, but upstairs in the Conference Room it was tense and focused. After reassuring Isabel and leaving her with Josh's eldest son, Archer walked upstairs and joined the others, immediately registering the change in atmosphere as he entered the room. Hendricks was standing on the right, Shepherd straight ahead, April sitting on the left side of the central table and looking awkward, an NYPD navy-blue jacket draped around her shoulders.

Having been momentarily delayed, Marquez entered the room behind Archer, easing the door

203

shut behind her, the last member to arrive apart from Josh.

'Michelle's in surgery,' she said. 'I also called the other hospital; the gunman's being operated on right now.'

'Has he said anything yet?' Hendricks asked.

'No chance. They had to put him under and get to work immediately. If they didn't, he wasn't gonna survive long enough to answer any questions. The shotgun blast did some major damage; he still might not make it.'

'Looks like we're going to have to figure out who he is and who his friends were ourselves,' Shepherd said. He turned to Ethan. 'Any results yet?'

'Not yet. None of them were carrying ID, so we're working from face and physical stat searches but so far, no matches. None of them have any tattoos or distinguishing marks which I could search in the databases. A few scars, but nothing major.'

'Three of them are dead and one's unconscious,' Hendricks said. 'We can get their prints.'

'CSU tried, but each guy had taken down the end pads on their fingers,' Ethan replied.

'What?' Marquez said.

'They don't have prints; they burned them off with acid. And no records are coming up anywhere. I've tried everything. Shit, they didn't even show up in the DMV.' He shrugged. 'I guess we'll just have to hope the wounded man makes it through surgery and we can get him to talk.'

He tapped some keys and photos of four men appeared on the screen; three were close-up crime scene captures, the dead men lying on the Hendricks' front lawn, and the fourth was the man currently being operated on, someone having taken his mug-shot on the way to the hospital, the white stretcher he was strapped to visible under his head.

All four were dark-haired, hard-faced men with similar facial characteristics implying the same ethnicity, possibly European, but a specific nationality or gang was impossible to identify.

'Anyone recognise them?' Shepherd asked the room.

No-one replied.

'Rubbed down finger prints. No tattoos. Silenced weapons with the serial numbers burnt off. A car with fake plates. These guys aren't amateurs.'

As Shepherd spoke Archer studied the two separate, smaller screens below the large electronic plasma screen. The left screen was dedicated to the investigation into Leann Casey's death. Underneath her mug-shot and several from the scene of the shooting, were DMV photos of two men. Both were brown-skinned and dark-eyed, the one on the left bulky with a fat face, curly unkempt hair and the other leaner with hollow eyes, short hair and a sour expression. *Carlos Goya* and *Alex Santiago* were the names on the licenses. Archer recognised Goya's eyes instantly; he was definitely the guy from the parking lot four weeks ago.

'What happened at the motel in Scranton?' Archer asked. 'We split before they called back.'

'SWAT found an empty room, no Carlos Goya and traces of a lye solution in the tub that was a perfect match for the shit we found Santiago soaking in,' Shepherd said. 'Looks like he went the same way as his friend.'

No-one said anything; it was hardly a moment for celebration. Suddenly the case wasn't as straightforward as just finding Leann's killers. Three new suspects had suddenly appeared on the scene, Goya and Santiago being wasted by three people whose motives were still a mystery, one homicide leading to two more.

And on top of that, a determined attempt had been made to wipe out the families of each detective in the room. Now he'd had time to think, the more Archer thought about how fast those attacks had happened after he killed Lister, the more obvious the reason seemed.

'All this in the same night,' he said. 'We start digging around then stumble on our three friends disposing of Santiago. Lister goes down and then these sudden moves on our families? There's no way that's a coincidence.'

'It could be,' Ethan said. 'Maybe someone else is targeting your team and they just happened to hit on the same night.'

'Then why was Jake's address on the list?' Shepherd replied. 'He runs his own squad. He's only been working with us tonight.'

Ethan fell silent.

Shepherd had a point.

'It's connected,' Marquez said, agreeing with Archer and Shepherd. 'We start asking questions, follow up on some leads, Lister dies and less than thirty minutes later a team of armed gunmen are paying our families a visit? C'mon; I'm all for coincidence, but that's just way too convenient.'

'So whoever these men are, how did they get your details?' Ethan asked. 'That information is restricted. Who the hell gave it to them?'

'Anyone with Department access,' Marquez said. 'It came via cell phone message. The team downstairs tried to trace the origin number but it was from a disposable that's going straight to voicemail. It'll have been ditched by now.'

Looking at her for a moment, Shepherd turned, focusing on the investigation screens.

'We need to rearrange this,' he said. 'Ethan, put our three amateur chemists on the main screen.'

Seconds later Nina Lister's police mug-shot and close-up CCTV pulls of the two men Archer had fought in the bar and Park appeared, the images taken from a street camera covering the Park entrance. It showed each man's face but the shots were grainy and hard to make out, but at least they were a start. One big, one slighter, the big guy well over two hundred pounds, his partner much smaller whose junkyard dog's aggression was clear even from the poor quality shot as he and his companion stalked after Archer and April.

'They showed up to the bar in a black van which CSU is working over,' Ethan said. 'So far they haven't found a single print inside, just a load of empty canisters with traces of the lye solution, a jet gun with a water barrel and spare sets of overalls, gloves, gas masks and magazines for silenced weapons.'

'Tell them to keep combing that thing,' Hendricks said. 'Tear it apart. After what we saw in that bath, we need an ID on these two.'

Shepherd nodded. 'Bring up the four gunmen from the house calls underneath.'

Ethan complied, forming two lines, one under the other; Lister and her two friends, then the four anonymous gunmen.

'Two very separate groups,' Shepherd said. 'But somehow linked.'

He tapped the smaller screen on the right.

'Lastly; victims here.'

Ethan brought up Goya and Santiago's mug-shots then leant back from his computer.

'Wait,' Archer said 'You're missing two.'

'Who?' Hendricks asked.

'Valdez and Carvalho. They were framed, the murder weapon left at the scene, but made to look as if one shot his buddy then killed himself.'

'Yeah, but surely Goya and Santiago must have done that.'

'Valdez and his pal died early this week. Goya's been in Scranton for nine days and Santiago was in jail.'

There was silence as everyone digested that. Realising Archer was right, Ethan hit a few keys and the two men's photos joined Goya and Santiago's.

'But why frame two men to keep the heat off Goya and Santiago then kill them too?' he said.

'To buy Lister and her two friends time to find and get rid of Carlos and Alex before we realised they were involved,' Marquez finished. 'For some reason, they didn't want us talking to them.'

There was a pause as everyone examined the three screens.

'You think they're all part of the same crew then?' Ethan suggested, looking at the two lines of suspects. 'The visits to your homes were attempted payback?'

'Or something to keep us occupied and off their tails,' Archer replied, looking at his watch. 'It's been two hours since Lister was shot, but this is the first chance we've had to sit down and really take a look at this thing. All the home attacks kept us busy and bought the two men extra time.'

'To do what?' Ethan asked.

'Find me,' April said nervously, the first time she'd spoken.

Standing by the screens, Shepherd turned his attention to her.

'Do you recognise her?' he asked, pointing at Lister's photo. 'Or the two men?'

'Never seen them before.'

'Any idea why they'd be so invested in finding you?'

'None.'

'How long have you been hiding?'

'Since this afternoon.'

'Why do you think these men were trying to find you?'

'I don't know.'

'So why'd you run?' Hendricks asked, confused. 'How'd you know?'

She tried to speak but hesitated, looking uncertainly around the room.

'I, um. I…'

She trailed off, clearly overwhelmed.

'Start from the beginning,' Archer said quietly, sitting beside her. 'Tell us what's going on. We're here to help.'

Turning, she looked at him for a long moment. Then she sighed.

'OK.'

TWENTY NINE

'I started doing this three years ago,' she explained. She went to continue but then stopped almost as soon as she'd started, looking at the police detectives surrounding her, clearly unnerved by sitting in a room full of cops. 'I'm not sure if I should be telling you guys this.'

'You won't get into trouble,' Shepherd said. 'You have my word.'

Glancing at Archer for reassurance, he nodded and she continued.

'I'm from Philadelphia. Used to live there with my mother. I started hanging out with the wrong crowd after school, thinking I was cool, all that kind of stupid shit.'

She paused.

'One night at a party, I met some guy in his twenties who I'd never seen before. We hit it off and started seeing each other. He told me he was only around for a few weeks, but that I should ditch school and go back to New York with him. At first I thought he was joking but he kept on. A few days later I had a huge fight with my mother and packed my bags. My boyfriend picked me up and we came here to New York, a week before my seventeenth birthday.'

She picked up her coffee but didn't drink, clutching the mug tightly. Around her, the room was silent.

'He told me he had a big place in Chelsea but when we arrived I saw three other girls lived there as well. I was surprised, but how naïve can you be, right? He told me that I couldn't stay there for free and that I needed to help out with

210

rent and living expenses. *New York's an expensive city,* he said. *It's the way it gets done here.'*

No one else in the room said anything.

They all knew where this was going.

'I was pretty scared but hid it, wanting to be cool. Didn't want the others to laugh at me; stupid naïve kid from Philly, you know? I figured I'd get a job bussing tables or something. But that first night the girls left the apartment and I hung out with my boyfriend and two of his friends. We drank a load of booze.'

She hesitated. Closed her eyes.

'My boyfriend then told me I should screw the two guys. He said he was into it, and he'd like to watch. I said no. He kept asking. I kept saying no.'

'What happened?' Marquez asked quietly.

'His two friends raped me, one after the other. It was the first time I'd ever had sex. Once they left, my boyfriend told me it was my fault. *If you want to stay here, you need to do exactly what I say.* That's what he told me; I can remember it word for word.'

She didn't lift her eyes from the table.

'The next morning he said I was going out to work with the other girls who lived in the apartment. He took the money I'd brought with me. When I realised what he wanted me to do, he said that if I went to the cops his two friends would come back for a second slice. And they wouldn't be so nice next time.'

She hesitated, her voice starting to shake slightly as she fought to get the words out.

'It was like a bad dream, you know? That first day I managed to avoid anyone who approached,

211

gross men who the other girls took. Then my boyfriend appeared and said I had to get into the next car or he'd call his two friends.'

Tears welled in her eyes.

'I made seventy bucks. Lucky me.'

Silence.

'When I got back he beat the shit out of me in front of the other girls. He told me if I ever came back again with so little money he'd kill me. It turned out he was running ten other girls, most of them suckered in like me.'

'What happened to this guy?' Hendricks asked quietly. 'Where is he?'

'He's dead.'

'You're sure?'

'Positive. He got killed in the Bronx at the end of last year just after getting out of prison for assault. But before he went inside, myself, Kelly and Cece were passed over to two of his friends on a loan; some sort of payback for a deal they had going. They were the two guys who'd given me my welcome party my first night.'

She looked up at the victims screen.

'Carlos Goya and Alex Santiago.'

'At first Carlos and Alex ran the same kind of operation but after a few months, it suddenly changed,' she continued. 'They gave us some money and told us to fix ourselves up, then made us start working uptown on the Upper West and East Side where we pulled wealthier clients, going for bigger paydays rather than the street level stuff.'

'How long have you been working for them?' Shepherd asked.

'Since November, last year. Eleven months.'

'When your old pimp died, you couldn't leave?' Marquez asked.

'And do what?' April asked with a short laugh. 'Go where? I've got no qualifications, no friends other than the other girls. I haven't spoken to my mother in three years. She'd hardly want me back now, would she?'

She paused.

'Instead of the corner, we were sent out to meet professional men, you know, like businessmen, guys with money. We were told to keep the curtains open in the hotel rooms they booked for us. Goya and Santiago had it under tight control; we were all convinced they were photographing the clients.'

'Blackmail,' Archer said.

She nodded. 'I know for sure that they worked a couple of guys. One was my client, a judge. We all talked about it, me and the other girls. There were twelve of us, brought in by Goya and Santiago from around the city. That was when I met Leann.'

'You'd never seen her before?' Archer asked.

'No. She was a nice kid; quiet as a mouse, really pretty. God only knows how or why she ended up turning tricks; she wasn't the type. She moved here recently; I used to ask how the hell she got into this shit, but she never said.'

'Leann's file said she was pulling in five grand a night,' Shepherd said.

April nodded. 'At least. We all were. Multiply that by twelve, with us working five or six days a week, and you can figure it out. We were making a killing for those bastards, not to mention the blackmail rackets we figured Goya and Santiago were involved in.'

'Didn't the move uptown mean you were on someone else's turf?' Marquez asked.

'The Upper West and East Side are easy pickings; there are hardly any street-gangs, loads of wealthy guys with secret lives their wives don't know about or pretend not to. Most of the competition is located on Midtown West near tourist-town.'

'You were never busted by cops?' Shepherd asked.

'Leann was, but that was a one-off; Vice were tailing a client of hers for different reasons and she walked right into a sting not meant for her. Did three months and paid a five hundred buck fine. Apart from that incident, we all blended right in. That was part of their business plan and the change I mentioned. Carlos and Alex insisted they didn't want cheap-looking trash on their roster. They told us we'd been chosen because we looked classy and if we wore expensive clothes they could charge a hell of a lot more for us. We were given money to buy nicer stuff; with our hair fixed up, manicures, expensive make-up and all, we looked just the same as every other young woman in that part of town. A lot better, in most cases. '

'So why the hell did Carlos kill Leann last month?' Archer asked. 'From the sounds of it, you and the other girls were giving him and Santiago a great lifestyle.'

April paused. 'The working conditions were better than before but despite that none of us were there because we wanted to be. We were trapped. Our money was tightly controlled, although later on we were allowed to keep slightly more of it in order to maintain our look and live somewhere

214

that wasn't a crack den. Carlos and Alex got some of the sassier girls addicted which gave them even more control. The rest of us were told they'd kill us if we ever tried to escape. We knew that wasn't an empty threat. And what could we do, go to you guys? We'd be laughed out of the Precinct.'

She glanced at the stack of Leann's photos from the case-file, which had been placed to one side on a table, images on paper all that was left of her friend.

'The moment we met, Leann and I hit it off. A lot of girls never attempt to leave, either out of fear or because they get used to the life and enjoy the extra money, but Leann was as desperate as me to get out, maybe even more so. After she did those three months at Rikers, it occupied her every waking thought. So we started making plans.'

'How were you going to do it?' Shepherd asked.

'It was risky but we began keeping back tiny amounts of money so Carlos and Alex wouldn't notice; it took a few months but we built up a reserve. Enough to escape and set up somewhere else.'

She exhaled.

'In August we were ready, financially anyway; we figured if we waited any longer Carlos or Alex might discover what we were planning. But we couldn't leave just then.'

'Why not?' Archer asked.

'Because Leann was addicted to painkillers. She knew she had to get off them before we could go anywhere so she checked herself into rehab where they couldn't get to her. That really pissed them off, especially as she was one of their best earners, but there was nothing they could do. Four weeks later she came out clean.'

She paused.

'I met her at the clinic in a cab and took her home; this was it. No more waiting. We knew we had to leave immediately before Carlos and Alex discovered she was out. We were so excited. The taxi dropped her off at her place then took me back to mine so I could pack. She was going to come pick me up half an hour later in her car. Then we'd be out of here.'

She took a deep breath.

'That was the last time I ever saw her.'

Silence filled the room. Beside her Archer was taken back four weeks, seeing the young blonde walking towards her car, making her escape.

Seeing the fear on her face that split-second before she was shot.

'I don't know how Carlos and Alex found out she was bailing but they did what they threatened to do if one of us tried to leave,' April said.

She paused.

'And now all the other girls have disappeared. Leann wasn't the last to die. She was the first.'

216

THIRTY

'Since Leann was killed, we started calling round to make sure everyone was OK,' April explained. 'Yesterday was my turn and some of them weren't answering their phones. They weren't at home either. I checked. By midday, I couldn't get hold of four of them. By sundown, it was eight.'

She paused.

'This morning, there were just three of us picking up. A few hours ago, one of them, Cece, called me; she was shit-scared and said Kelly had stopped picking up her phone. But while we were talking, she was attacked. I heard her scream.'

She paused.

'After that call cut out, I ran back to my apartment meaning to pack a bag and disappear. But when I got to my door, I saw a paper clip I always push in the gap under the door handle lying on the floor. I saw someone do it in a cop show once; you never know what kind of whack-jobs might find out where you live.'

'Smart,' Shepherd said. 'So that's when you ran.'

She nodded. 'When I saw that paper clip lying there, I kept going down my corridor and went down the fire escape into the alley. I crept back down to the edge of the building and saw two people, dressed in white overalls and ball caps. They ran out of the building and were looking around. I think they were searching for me.'

The moment she mentioned the white overalls, the reasons surrounding the ten women's sudden disappearances suddenly became a lot clearer. Shepherd swore quietly. Hendricks remained

217

silent. Ethan and Marquez glanced at each other but said nothing. April looked down at the table.

Beside her, Archer glanced up at Lister's photo on the big screen, the dead woman holding the placard with her name and ID number on it, the two shots of her two accomplices beside her.

Ten missing women.

Two people, dressed in white overalls and ball caps.

Then he had a quick image in his mind of what they'd found in Santiago's bathtub.

'They killed Cece and Kelly, didn't they?' April said, looking up at the photos. 'Just like they did Alex and Carlos. Just like they tried to do to me in the bar.'

No-one replied, everyone in the room realising that they'd just stumbled upon something far bigger and more complicated than two shot police detectives and a single murdered escort.

'We can send someone round to collect your things,' Shepherd said, breaking the quiet. 'You're safe now.'

'But my friends aren't, are they? Where the hell were you guys four weeks ago?'

'We weren't dealing with the case then. Someone else had it.'

'So it takes ten more of us to die for you to actually do something about it?' she snapped back.

Shepherd didn't reply. She paused and caught her breath, taking a few moments.

'It's not your fault. I'm sorry.'

'So are we,' Marquez said. 'And we only got our hands on this a few hours ago. But we're gonna do everything we can to find who's doing this and why. I promise.'

Across the room Hendricks had remained silent while listening to April; now her account was over he stepped forward, rummaged through the Leann Casey file and withdrew the piece of paper with the known associates on it. Pulling his phone, he dialled a number and stepped out of the room, his voice audible from the walkway as he connected with CSU and requested teams be dispatched to the addresses of the girls to check them out.

'Could they still be alive?' Ethan asked those remaining in the room as they heard Hendricks make his request. 'Just because those two were at your apartment building doesn't mean all the others are dead.'

'I guess we'll find out,' Shepherd said quietly.

At the table beside April, Archer glanced up at the CCTV images of the two suspects who'd lye-bathed Goya, Santiago and possibly ten more women.

'Jesus Christ,' he said quietly. 'We have to find these guys.'

*

Across the city, the two men were patching themselves up at the East-Side warehouse they used as a base to mix the lye solution and store their vehicles, the car they'd jacked to get out of the Upper West Side now abandoned across the hangar.

Both were severely pissed off, not only because April Evans had slipped through their fingers but because street CCTV and cameras from inside the bar would have crystal clear images of them by now. They knew they couldn't wear ball caps inside that upmarket bar without standing out like sore thumbs, but the bar hadn't had cameras at the rear of the building and they'd already located an exit they could use to get April's body out so they hadn't expected it to be a problem.

Once they'd found her, they'd assumed the rest would be easy, but then that cop had turned up.

They'd also realised that with the fight in the bar and the chase that followed, cameras would have captured them without masks or their baseball caps. For the first time since they'd started all this, they'd be identifiable. And as well as their van, the NYPD would probably have their IDs already or would do very soon, which meant that one mistake was threatening to unravel years of meticulous planning. Like roaches when the lights came on they'd scuttled for cover but were now feeling the intense spotlight of attention focusing right on them. Reloading his silenced FN.45 pistol, the bigger man swore, furious. He didn't like to lose; it didn't happen often.

'How the hell did that son of a bitch know she was at that bar?' he said.

'Who gives a shit,' the smaller man replied, pulling away the gauze on his cheek and spitting out blood. 'I'm getting the hell out of here. Forget leaving at midnight; I'm splitting right now.'

'No you're not,' the big guy said. 'We're not done.'

'I don't give a shit. We need to get out while we still can.'

'Have you suddenly forgotten the whole reason we're here? And who you are?'

'You think I could forget that?'

'We don't leave until we close it out. We've waited too long for this. There are still four of them left. Five if you include that son of a bitch who survived the shotgun blast.'

220

'The cops have our faces, on camera,' the smaller man said slowly, raising his voice and emphasising the words. 'It's not going to take them long to find out who we are, if they haven't already. They'll be crawling all over us soon.'

'We'll be careful.'

'These people aren't dumb. They'll track back and make connections.'

'Forget the cops; what about the hooker? You think we can just leave without taking care of her? She knows too much.'

'She doesn't know shit. We're safe enough.'

'She and the bitch who got shot in the car park were friends; they were thick as thieves. Who knows what they talked about? Leann knew a lot. April Evans is dangerous.'

The smaller man paused, trying to stay calm, his body sore from that asshole cop slamming him around the restroom. Inhaling and exhaling slowly, he breathed through the pain, trying to focus and not let it cloud his judgement.

'We can't leave without taking care of the whore,' the big guy repeated, seeing his words were having an effect. 'Not to mention the other *Prizraki*. We're in this together to the end, right?'

The smaller man nodded slowly. 'Shit. You're right.'

'I know. I usually am.'

His partner smiled, calming down. 'So what now? How are we going to get to the bitch?'

'It's being worked on,' the larger man replied, taking his phone out of his pocket and motioning with it. 'But we've got an hour to kill. The last few *Priz* are all holed up in the club and it doesn't open until 10pm.'

221

'So what are we going to do until then? Lay low?'

'Get some revenge on that son of a bitch who killed Nina and did this to us.'

'The pretty boy cop? How?'

The bigger man smiled. 'Think about who got shot in the car park the night all this shit started.'

'The prostitute, the cop-' He paused. 'And his girlfriend. Holy shit.'

His partner nodded.

'Detective Alice Vargas. And she's not behind security at any police station. She's still at St Luke's hospital.'

THIRTY ONE

Once April finished her account, the detective team separated. Asking CSU to call the Conference Room back the moment they had anything from the missing girls' apartments, Hendricks went downstairs to check on his wife, kids and the others involved in the night's events as Marquez called the hospital to get a report on the gunman and speak to Josh to get an update on Michelle's condition.

Upstairs, Shepherd and Ethan were still inside the Conference Room talking with April, Shepherd going over the main points again and making sure he hadn't missed anything that could prove to be useful, as Ethan ran the two suspects' faces through every system at his disposal, searching for IDs.

Standing on the wooden walkway and taking the opportunity of a moment alone, Archer looked back into the Conference Room at the red-headed woman. She was only eight years younger than him but life had dealt them a very different set of cards. No wonder she was scared; if he'd been ten seconds later in getting to the bar or had checked the other place four blocks south first, there would have been a very different outcome.

As he watched her talk with Shepherd and Ethan, his thoughts turned to her friends, the ten missing women, and the three people they were ninety nine percent certain were responsible for their disappearance. Archer had encountered evil on many occasions in his time as a cop, men and women who'd had no value for human life, but dissolving their victims' bodies and then flushing them into the sewers was a new one on him. Totally outmatched, the women wouldn't have stood a chance.

And that really pissed him off. Turning and looking down at the pit below, Archer saw all the investigation team's family members gathered, people who would most probably have died tonight if not for Isabel and Melissa's interventions. Hendricks was down there reassuring them, making sure they were coping in the aftermath of what had happened.

Isabel was with Josh's eldest son, who was listening to Hendricks closely, but she'd spotted Archer and was looking straight up at him, not paying attention to what the Sergeant was saying.

She smiled and gave him a wave, both of which he returned.

As he did so, he felt a pang of guilt. She had no idea that Vargas had been so badly injured. The morning after the shooting, when Vargas's condition was still critical and Archer had literally only just scrubbed her blood off his hands, he'd gone home, picked the girl up from his neighbour and taken her to Josh's. He'd told her that Alice had been forced to go back to LA to visit a sick relative, which was why she'd left in such a hurry.

He'd blundered through the explanation, exhausted and stressed, but Isabel was young enough to have taken it at face value, trusting him implicitly. He still wondered whether that had been fair of him. The only person in the world who arguably cared more about Alice than he did was Isabel; did she deserve to know the truth even though he was just trying to protect her?

Was it his right not to tell her?

With the little girl still looking up at him, Archer heard some movement from the Conference Room and turned as Shepherd approached, having just left Ethan with April. As his Sergeant joined him on the walkway, Archer glanced past Shepherd at April who was looking at him uncertainly. He gave her a quick thumbs up, which seemed to reassure her, but just like Isabel downstairs she kept her gaze on him. Her account had taken a lot of honesty and courage to tell. He liked her for it; she'd not held anything back, even though it can't have been easy telling a roomful of cops what had happened to her.

'Talk about a goddamned Pandora's box,' Shepherd said, standing beside Archer and looking over the railing at the people below. 'We decide to take a look at this case to make sure Homicide nailed the right two guys. Now we find two more victims and possibly another ten.'

'Any word on the surviving gunman?' Archer asked. 'The guy in surgery?'

'Not yet.'

Archer swore. 'They moved on our families within twenty minutes of Lister getting shot. They had those addresses so damn fast and that info is confidential. It had to have come from the Department.'

'But who?' Shepherd said.

'Christ only knows.' Archer glanced at him. 'Where did that social worker show up from?'

'Palmer? She was working with the 114th.' He read Archer's mind. 'Don't worry, I had Ethan run some background checks. She's kosher. Born and raised in Brooklyn, father was a doctor, mother worked in social care, third generation

225

Europeans. She's been working for the Polaris Project for almost two years. She's legit.'

Archer smiled. 'Been screwed over too many times not to be suspicious.'

There was a pause.

'Jake told me what went down in Rikers,' Shepherd said. 'I can't believe Royston put you in there. He's a real piece of work.'

'That's one way of describing him. And now he's got even more to use against me; I fired Josh's weapon inside the bar and the Park.'

'It was self-defence and protecting a witness. I've got your back.'

'That's if I'm still a part of your team by midday tomorrow.'

Shepherd didn't reply. Taking a deep breath, he exhaled slowly and continued to look down into the pit below.

'Isabel still living with Josh?' he asked, looking at the little girl.

Archer nodded, following his gaze.

There was a pause.

'You ever make the same mistakes with your kids that your father did with you?' Archer suddenly asked.

Shepherd thought about it; smiled ruefully and shook his head. 'Some of mine make his pale into insignificance.'

Archer suddenly realised what he'd said. 'Shit, I'm sorry. I didn't mean it like that.'

'I know. It's OK.'

Pause.

'What's worrying you?'

Archer considered the question. 'By the time my dad died, I hadn't seen him in over ten years. He left the UK one night when I was sixteen and

226

never came back. I can forgive but I can't forget it.'

Shepherd glanced at his detective, following his gaze to Isabel. 'You think you might do the same thing? Abandon her?'

'I'd never walk out on her.'

'But?'

'I know how it feels to see someone you care for walk out the door and never come back. And you know what this job's like; life insurance companies aren't exactly fighting each other to sign me up. After everything she's gone through, what happens if she gets attached and something happens to me?'

'What's the alternative; keep her at a distance?'

'Maybe.'

'To that kid, you and Alice are the best parents she's ever gonna have. Better than her original set, that's for damn sure. And she needs you right now; Alice has been gone a month.'

He looked down at Isabel, then to his own son.

'Parenthood isn't about DNA. What matters is how much you'd do for that child. And you showed six months ago in that building how far you'd go for her.'

Archer didn't respond. Shepherd turned to him.

'My advice? Stop keeping yourself distant from her, otherwise one day she'll be the one who leaves. And once that happens, after everything she's been through, she'll never come back.'

Archer didn't reply. A few moments later, the two men became aware of movement down the walkway, the sound of high-heeled shoes clicking on wood; turning, they saw Theresa Palmer walking towards them. The last time Archer had seen her had been at Santiago's apartment, just before he'd received the call from Isabel, but a hell of a lot had happened since then.

'Where've you been, Theresa?' Shepherd asked as she joined them.

'You guys all vanished from Santiago's before I could join you,' she replied. 'I've been talking with my people and trying to get a fix on April Evans. But I just got a call saying you rescued her from an attack?'

Shepherd nodded, indicating towards the Conference Room. 'Arch did. And she's in there.'

'Is she OK?' Palmer asked, stepping forward and looking at the young woman.

'She's fine. Just a little shaken up.'

'I spoke to our office in New Jersey. Apparently Goya and Santiago run a high-class escort service on the Upper West and East Sides. Including Leann, there were twelve women on their payroll last month.'

Shepherd nodded. 'Correct.'

'With Leann and April accounted for, that leaves ten to find. If Nina Lister and her two friends went after April, they might try to do the same to the other girls. We need to focus on them; bring all ten in and get them under protection right now. '

Shepherd glanced at Archer then motioned to the empty Conference Room next door to the one they were using as a base.

'Follow me,' he told her. 'We need to talk. Arch, join us.'

Looking at him curiously, Palmer followed Shepherd into the room.

Taking a last look down at Isabel staring up at him from the detective pool below, Archer gave her another small wave then joined the other two.

228

At the East-side warehouse, the two killers were just finishing packing their back-up van with canisters of their lye solution, the cuts to their faces cleaned and butterfly-stitched.

Loading up the last can, the larger of the two men closed the door and then withdrew his cell, looking at the details he'd just been sent by their inside man. Beside him his partner drew his silenced FN.45 and racked a round, tucking it in the back of his waistband and pulling his jacket down to conceal it.

'Ready?' he asked his partner.

He nodded. 'Let's do it.'

With that, the two men opened their van and jumped inside, slamming the doors and firing the engine. Right then, they might not have been able to get to April Evans or the remaining *Prizraki* hiding out inside their club in Little Odessa.

But they sure as hell could get to Detective Alice Vargas.

THIRTY TWO

It took Shepherd five minutes to explain the situation to Palmer, who was visibly shocked when he told her about the missing girls and even more so when he came to the attempted hits on their families.

'So who the hell were those gunmen?' she asked. 'You think they work with Lister and her two friends?'

'We don't know,' Archer said, standing beside the pair.

Palmer's attention shifted from the suspects to Archer himself, noting the cut under his eye and his mud-spattered jeans. 'By the way, I thought you were suspended.'

'I am. But after everything that's happened today, I think I'm entitled to stick around for a bit.'

She smiled. 'So do I. I think its bullshit what they did to you.'

She offered her hand.

'We were never introduced; I'm Theresa Palmer; I work with the Polaris Project.'

After hesitating for a moment, Archer shook it. 'Sam Archer. What exactly is Polaris?'

'A national organisation which combats human trafficking and slavery; we help victims forced into work or sexual acts against their will. Cases like Leann's often happen in clutches so I requested to be brought to the 114th as an advisor.'

She sighed.

'Judging by what you told me, I failed completely. I was too late. Lister and her crew got to them.'

'Right now nothing is confirmed until we hear from CSU,' Shepherd said.

'That's just a formality though, right? And after what you said April saw at her apartment building? Two figures in white overalls apparently waiting for her?'

Her voice trailed off. Shepherd and Archer didn't reply.

'If you guys had had this case from the get go, these women could still be alive.'

'We pushed for it,' Shepherd said. 'You saw us try. But Homicide wouldn't budge.'

'Yeah, but I can understand that though. If something happened on your turf, would you just pass over the investigation?'

Shepherd paused, then shook his head, conceding her point. 'No. I guess I wouldn't.'

'And they're gonna be pissed when they find out about all this. It took them four weeks to nail the wrong suspects. You guys are on the investigation for a few hours and you find the two real perps in Leann's murder. Then you discover a previously unknown team killed the two of them and now, potentially ten more homicides on top of Goya and Santiago. Which would have been eleven if Archer hadn't made it to April in time.'

'You were working with the team over at the 114th,' Shepherd said. 'You saw the case get closed.'

'I did.'

'Were you satisfied with that? That Valdez and Carvalho did it?'

'It all matched up; they had motive, no alibi and were found with the murder weapon. Homicide said probability was high and Royston ordered them to wrap it up. From what I heard, he'd been getting a lot of calls ordering him to focus on the case because of Detective Vargas getting hurt. There was a lot of attention on that. You can understand why he was happy to have closure.'

'And Leann Casey,' Archer said. 'Alice was shot but Leann was killed.'

'She wasn't exactly the focus, if you catch my drift. That's why I demanded to be involved from the get go, to make sure she got as much attention as Detective Vargas and wasn't side-lined. They didn't want to bring me in at first; we always have to fight to be included to make sure girls like Leann get a fair shake. Otherwise she'd be forgotten.'

'She wouldn't have been,' Shepherd said.

'Be real, Sergeant. That's your compassion speaking, not your common sense. I've done this job for two years; I've worked with different police departments in New York State and all over New Jersey. And the one thing I've learned is that dead girls from the sex trade rank somewhere between overdosed junkies and missing dogs on the police give-a-shit scale.'

'That's not always the case.'

'How many times did April contact the cops before someone helped her?' Palmer asked. 'Shit, did she even bother, knowing what the outcome would be?'

The two men didn't answer.

'Don't get me wrong, I'm not pissed at you, I'm pissed at Royston,' Palmer continued. 'The team at Homicide were too. He settled for something that looked very possible, but instead of making one hundred percent sure he ordered his team to move on. Because of that, ten more girls are most likely dead. And you know the sad part; they'll be forgotten in a matter of days.'

There was a pause. Archer and Shepherd remained silent.

'So what's the next step?' Palmer asked. 'Finding what happened to these women?'

'That's step one,' Shepherd said. 'Step two is we find out who the hell these men were who came after our families.'

'And number three is we track down Lister's two friends,' Archer said. 'And we do it before they give anyone else a bath.'

Like any city hospital, St Luke's in Midtown Manhattan was a busy facility with a constant flow of doctors, nurses, ancillary staff, the sick and the injured through the building. However, the hospital had also seen two new additions of late, a couple of NYPD officers working on rotation stationed outside Detective Vargas' room on the private 14th floor.

The two night-shift guys had taken up their posts at 5pm; they'd been doing the same stint for over a month now and had to admit it was a pretty good gig, ordered to sit outside the room and prevent anyone other than the medical team from entering unless they could prove they were authorised. The two officers were both in their early thirties and had earned their stripes, which was why they'd been assigned what was seen by their colleagues as a cushy role and not given to some rookies out of the Academy.

However, as was natural with any human attention span, the monotony of sitting outside the room hour upon hour had caught up with them and their concentration levels had waned over the weeks. That Sunday night, one was sitting in a chair reading a magazine whilst the other munched on some sunflower seeds, spitting the kernels into a trash can beside him as he leant against the wall. Medical staff and the occasional cleaner moved past the two officers, all of whom had become familiar to the two men over the last four and a half weeks, light-hearted banter often exchanged.

The guy sitting down suddenly chuckled as he leant back in his chair, scanning the advice column of the woman's magazine he'd found abandoned on the seat.

'Ten signs that your man may be cheating,' he read aloud. 'You ready for some of these?'

His partner shook his head, looking down the corridor. 'You know what'll happen if you get caught reading that shit?'

Before the man could respond, they were distracted by the sight of a doctor who suddenly appeared from around the corner. He had a cut across his temple, blood leaking from the wound, and looked flustered.

'You OK, Doc?' the seated officer asked, sitting up straight, the magazine in his hands instantly forgotten.

'Not really. I could use some help.'

'What's wrong?'

'We've got a drunk guy causing trouble downstairs on 13. He just assaulted me and two of my staff. Security's over in the other wing. I'd really appreciate some assistance.'

The two cops glanced at each other.

'He's a big guy and he's out of control,' the doctor added.

'I'll stay,' one cop said, looking at his partner who'd been reading the magazine. 'You got this?'

The other man nodded, rising and putting the gossip mag on the chair, following the doctor who turned and headed back the way he'd come, dabbing at the cut across his eyebrow.

'Thanks, Officer. We'll take the stairs. It's quicker.'

'So what'll happen to April?' Archer asked Palmer, still in the Conference Room. 'She's free now Goya and Santiago are gone.'

'If I don't help her out, she'll be housed for thirty days at Covenant. Then she'll probably be back on the street.'

'Just like that?'

She nodded. 'That's what usually happens; and things are better than they used to be.'

'But that's it?' Archer repeated. 'If your organisation doesn't help, after a month she's tossed back out on the street?'

'That's it.'

'It's bullshit.'

'That's why I'm here. It's what my organisation specialises in; pimps like Goya and Santiago are a dying breed. The Internet's changed the way many of these girls work; it means they don't have pimps controlling them and they decide who they want as customers. They don't share any of the profits with anyone and charge whatever they want.'

'But no-one knows who they're meeting with, or where,' Archer said.

She nodded. 'Not only are they made more vulnerable, they're also prime targets for all the whack-jobs out there. Before, pimps were there to make sure their girls came back in one piece.'

'April said she and Leann were about to get out,' Archer said. 'Start fresh somewhere else.'

'And take a look at what happened. Another prostitute dead. The only reason her death got the attention it did is because two cops got shot at the scene at the same time and don't try to pretend that's not the case. You know I'm right.'

The two men stayed silent. However, in the quiet Marquez suddenly appeared at the doorway.

'Sir?'

Shepherd turned.

'Breakthrough. Ethan just pulled IDs on Lister's two friends.'

Arriving at the stairwell, the doctor pushed down the bar and held the door for the cop.

'Right this way,' he said.

As the cop passed him and started to walk down the stairs, he noticed the door to a large maintenance closet on their right was partially open, something catching his eye.

'Hold up, doc,' he said.

'What's wrong?'

Not replying, the officer pulled his weapon, easing the door back.

On the floor was the body of a man in a shirt and trousers, a doctor he recognised from his weeks at the hospital.

He'd been shot in the head.

Before the cop could reach for his radio, the man in the doctor's coat behind him had already drawn his silenced pistol, putting a bullet through the back of the officer's head, the weapon coughing and blood spattering over the wall beyond the officer as he took the round.

The policeman's body hit the floor; the guy in the doctor's coat then dragged him into the closet, dumping him on top of the body of the man already there.

Tucking the pistol back into the rear of his waistband, the killer closed the door, then turned and walked back up the half-flight of stairs towards 14.

One down; one to go.

The remaining officer had his back to Vargas' door when he saw the doctor reappear, his partner nowhere to be seen.

'What happened, doc?' he asked. 'Where's Cornell?'

'There was a problem,' the doctor replied, walking towards him.

'What is it?'

Stopping, the doctor suddenly grabbed the cop's shoulder, jabbing a silenced weapon into his stomach, pushing it hard into the man's gut.

'Your partner died,' he whispered. 'And don't even think about it.'

The cop's hand paused, an inch from his sidearm. As the officer stared at him, the doctor pushed him back towards the door to the room.

'Open it, Hudson,' he ordered quietly, looking at the policeman's tag on his chest.

With no choice, the cop obeyed, turning as far as the man would allow him and opening the door.

'You pull that trigger, you're finished,' Hudson told him. 'You realise that?'

'It's not me who's finished,' the man in the coat said with a grin, pushing the cop into Detective Vargas' room and aiming the silenced FN.45 at the officer's head.

THIRTY THREE

Re-entering Conference Room 4, Shepherd, Marquez and Archer joined Ethan and April closely followed by Hendricks, Shepherd having whistled at him from the walkway. He shut the door behind him and stood beside Palmer, who was standing just to the right of the door.

'What have we got?' he asked.

As he spoke, a mug-shot appeared on the main screen. Archer immediately recognised the guy as the larger of the two. He had jet black hair, brown eyes and stubble, the photo taken a few years ago when he was younger. He looked sullen and a tough son of a bitch.

'Found them in the California Department of Corrections database,' Ethan said. 'This one is Nicolas Dean Henderson. Twenty six years old, six foot five, two hundred and twenty five pounds. Parents unknown, attended high school in Pittsburgh, was arrested in San Diego for weapons charges. Served a year in Lompoc.'

'From Pittsburgh,' Archer said. 'Like Lister.'

'And arrested in San Diego like her too,' Marquez noted.

'SDPD currently have a warrant out for his arrest for skipping parole,' Ethan continued.

'How old?' Hendricks asked.

'Six years.'

'What about the other guy?' Shepherd asked.

The screen changed to the slighter man, the one who'd almost shot Archer in the head when he broke into the restroom. Physically he was much smaller than Henderson but Archer knew he possessed a wiry strength that made up for his

239

lack of stature. He was all sinew and aggression, the veins on his neck pronounced, his head closely shaved, his eyes angry as he held the placard for the mug-shot.

'Sebastian Tully; twenty four years old. Went to the same high school as Henderson in Pittsburgh, DOB and parents unknown. Five ten, a hundred and sixty five pounds. Got busted with his friend for possession of unlicensed firearms in Cali and did a stretch too.'

'What about since?' Shepherd said.

'Suspect in a homicide but the case is still ongoing. San Diego too.'

'And it's six years old,' Shepherd said, looking at the screen. 'That long?'

Ethan nodded. 'They've been keeping a low profile.'

'Why the hell did they go from Pittsburgh to San Diego?' Palmer asked. 'People like this tend to stay in places they know. And why'd they come back east?'

'Whatever the reason, they must have left a trail,' Marquez said. 'They'd need money and these two don't strike me as the nine to five type. No easy legal way to fund a three thousand mile trip without some kind of illegal activity.'

'Maybe they just got lucky and were never caught,' Archer said.

'Ethan, run a check on the National Crime Info Centre,' Shepherd said, nodding in agreement with his two detectives.

'What for, sir?'

'Traces of lye at national crime-scenes in the last six years. These sons of bitches must have left something in their wake. That body disposal method is so slick I'm thinking they must have had some practice.'

As Ethan set to work, Palmer pulled her cell phone. 'I'll run them through our system too. See if our people in California have anything on these guys.'

As she stepped outside, Hendricks went to follow but then the phone on the desk rang, grabbing everyone's attention.

'Shepherd,' the Sergeant said, answering.

'Sergeant, its Barton with CSU. I've got some bad news I'm afraid.'

'Go on.'

'We've checked out six of those addresses Sergeant Hendricks gave us. We've swabbed the tubs and that lye solution is showing up at each one so far.'

Shepherd stared grimly at the phone as everyone in the room fell silent.

'I spoke to the team down on Rivington who told me what you guys found over there in the bathroom. I know this isn't what you wanted to hear.'

Pause.

'OK. Thanks.'

Ending the call, Shepherd paused for a moment. Then he looked at April.

'I'm sorry.'

She nodded. 'Deep down I already knew, I guess.'

Beside her, Archer swore. 'Why the hell did they kill the women? I can't figure it out. This isn't mindless serial killing. There's a purpose here.'

His face dark, Shepherd looked at him for a moment then turned and studied the faces of the two killers on the screen, the suspects in a list of homicides that seemed to be growing by the hour, up to fourteen by his reckoning; ten women, Valdez, Carvalho, Goya all flushed down a tub and Santiago on the way before they intervened.

'Where the hell are you, you sons of bitches?' he muttered.

Inside her room at St Luke's, Alice Vargas was fast asleep.

She was lying under a sheet in a hospital gown, her head turned to one side, her eyes closed, the room quiet apart from the sound of her heart monitor, which was providing a slow, constant *beep*. Her black hair was a stark contrast to the white gown and sheets, her breathing rhythmic, her face expressionless but peaceful, a small white dressing on the side of her neck.

Wearing their stolen porter's uniform and doctor's coat, Henderson and Tully stood side-by-side next to her bed, staring down at her, Henderson having just come up in the elevator with the gurney after Tully called and told him they were on. Glancing to his left, ignoring the body of the second cop who Tully had just shot, Henderson lifted away the sheet covering the gurney, five of their lye canisters lying on the top.

Walking past the dead cop and easing back the door to the bathroom, Tully checked inside then glanced at his partner and nodded before walking back across the room and letting himself out quietly. He needed to secure the closet with the two dead bodies and make sure there were no other cops lurking before they got to work.

Now alone with the woman, Henderson stared down at her as she slept; he had a flashback to

Nina taking the shotgun blast from this bitch's boyfriend and his anger rose.

Less than an hour from now, there wouldn't be a trace that she'd ever existed.

As he looked down at her, his phone vibrated in his pocket with an incoming message. He pulled the cell out, checking the screen and seeing it was a message from the fourth member of their operation, wanting to know what was happening with the Russians.

He tapped in a reply, the only movement in the room Henderson's fingers as they hit the keys. However, with his head down he didn't notice something.

Vargas' eyes opened.

It took her a few seconds to register the large figure standing there beside her bed, his head down as he concentrated on his screen.

Blinking from the effect of the sleeping pill she'd been given, it took her a few moments to focus. She studied the large man at the end of her bed, seeing a silenced pistol tucked into his belt.

Then the beeping of her heart-rate monitor suddenly increased in speed.

Henderson heard the change and looked up from his phone. Reacting immediately, Vargas' hand lunged for the emergency call button but she wasn't fast enough and Henderson just managed to get there first, blocking her. Vargas tried to roll out of the bed the other side and escape into the adjoining bathroom, but was too weak and fell to the floor as her legs gave out under her, knocking things off the bedside table as she fell, an IV ripped from her hand.

As she hit the floor she saw a cop facing her against the wall; he'd been shot in the head, blood pooling under him. Shocked, Vargas opened her mouth to shout for help but Henderson was already on her and clamped his hand over her mouth, stifling her scream.

Tully suddenly re-entered the room, having heard the crash of the table going over, and drew his pistol. However, as adrenaline pulsed through her for the first time in weeks, Vargas found new strength. She bit down on Henderson's hand as hard as she could, drawing blood, then hammered her elbow back into the side of his jaw, sending him reeling back.

Scrambling forward, she desperately tried to make it to the bathroom but Tully stepped forward and hit her over the head with his handgun, stunning her. As she fought to stay conscious, he quickly overpowered and restrained her by zip-tying her wrists behind her back. After ripping off a strip of duct tape and pulling it over her mouth, Tully started dragging her into the bathroom as Henderson got to his feet.

'*Bitch!*' he hissed, drawing his pistol and moving over to the door, taking a quick look outside in case anyone had heard the noise.

Inside the bathroom, Tully let go of Vargas when he reached the tub, turning the knob to lower the metal plug. Then he picked up one of the canisters, unscrewed the lid and quickly started pouring the lye solution into the bath.

However, as he worked the dead cop's radio suddenly burst into life across the room.

'*Hudson, Cornell, report.*'

Tully immediately paused in what he was doing, looking at Henderson.

'*Hudson, Cornell, report.*'

The two men looked at each for a long moment; then Tully continued to fill the tub, tossing the canister aside when it was empty and opening up another one.

Bound and helpless beside him, Vargas heard the unanswered transmission from Dispatch repeat for a third time as she watched the man in the doctor's coat in confusion, trying to work out what he was doing.

Then her eyes started to water as a strong chemical smell filled the room.

THIRTY FOUR

Two hours behind New York City, the sun was just starting to go down in Colorado, Lieutenant Jack Rosario of the Denver Police Department watching it through the blinds as he sat alone in his office.

Fifty one years old with short grey-hair and a slight paunch that seemed to have appeared out of nowhere in the last couple of years, Rosario was extremely well-liked and respected in the Department, a distinguished career behind him with the finishing-line of retirement now in sight. He'd been a cop for twenty nine years and was in charge of four Homicide squads, was paid a good salary and thoroughly enjoyed his work. However, there was one case that he'd never managed to solve, something which even now several years later still bothered him.

Eight people who'd disappeared without a trace six years ago and who neither Rosario nor the Department had ever been able to locate.

It'd begun with a woman who'd come to the District 2 station where Rosario worked, to report that her boyfriend hadn't come home in five days. Given that he'd been a relatively high-profile pimp based on East Colfax with a bad history and lot of people who would have been only too happy to hear that he was dead, no-one had been particularly surprised or interested.

However, when reports of two more missing men came in within a week, Rosario's Precinct had started to take notice, concerned they had some kind of gang war starting on their patch.

Over the next two weeks, three more were added to the list, all of these people linked, and squad cars had patrolled Colfax, looking for any sign of trouble. But everything had seemed pretty normal. Officers had located two low-level pimps who were associates of the missing men, but they said they didn't know what had happened and didn't seem to care either.

Rosario knew a number of his colleagues had regarded the vanishing of the six gang members as a blessing, feeling their time and resources were better spent assisting law-abiding citizens rather than the scum of the city. However he'd felt differently. To him a missing person was a missing person, no matter who they were; a detective couldn't pick and choose the cases to work. It looked highly likely someone on his turf was taking these people out and that wasn't something he was prepared to tolerate.

So he was the exception in the 2nd District when the six guys had been reported missing. In the weeks and months that followed, the Department had moved on but the family members of those missing sure as hell hadn't. In the early days of the investigation a couple of girlfriends and a mother of two of the missing men had made a habit of coming to the station to ask if there'd been any progress, but there hadn't and they'd been told they'd be contacted if there were any developments. They never received that call.

And just when they thought everything had settled down and whoever was responsible for these disappearances had either left town or settled their score, the last two low-level pimps associated with the missing men also vanished.

The general view in the Department had been that a rival gang had whacked them but Rosario had never bought that. No gang member he'd ever encountered had managed to avoid leaving evidence; murdering someone was a messy business. Guns, blades or bats were usually the weapons of choice, all of which left traces of blood, DNA and often fingerprints, not to mention a body. However, whoever had been responsible for those pimps' disappearances hadn't left so much as a hair fibre. Street cameras had revealed nothing and witnesses were non-existent.

Curious and frustrated in equal measure by the lack of progress, Rosario had pursued the case in his spare time. He'd worked with Forensics, the lab, a criminal psychologist and even tried to get the missing persons shown on *America's Most Wanted* which had nearly cost him his promotion, his Lieutenant at the time livid that Rosario had almost announced to the nation that the Department had eight open case-files from a potential serial killer that they were nowhere near close to solving.

Forget they ever existed, he was ordered.

However, he hadn't. Sitting at his desk, he turned back to his computer and tapped away on the keypad, bringing up the NCIS database and preparing to perform a ritual which he'd done every few days for almost six years.

Crime-scene reports had stated that traces of lye had been detected in the bathtubs of all the victims' residences; apparently lye was quite common when killers try to dispose of bodies, a method drug cartels were known to use. However, that particular concoction had never

248

been seen before. If the bodies had been disposed of in that way, it indicated that the disappearances had been carefully planned and meticulously carried out. These were no random killings.

Since then, Rosario had searched the NCIC every now and then to see if any similar cases had shown up anywhere in the country. If whoever was responsible had done this eight times on his patch, Rosario was sure they'd do it again.

And he'd been correct.

There'd been a spate of similar incidents in Chicago last year a thousand miles east, the top guys of a particular gang disappearing over a period of ten months, three at the same time and two lower-level pimps months later. He'd flown out there on his own dime and time; being a police Lieutenant, albeit from another city, he had some clout and had received access to the missing persons' files. He'd questioned the girls who'd been run by the missing men, but just like back in Denver they hadn't been able to tell him anything.

If Rosario was correct in thinking the same people were responsible, the number of suspected victims was now in double digits. Still no clearer as to motive, he'd been optimistic when he'd picked up that trail last year, but since Chicago it had gone cold. The killer, or killers, had either stopped or moved on, but it wasn't in Rosario's nature to give up.

About to finish for the day, he saw the search taking place on the screen and leaned back in his chair, looking out at the setting sun.

A few moments later, a series of beeps got his attention.

Swinging round, he read the results in front of him and the hairs on the back of his neck stood up.

'Holy shit.'

Crime-scene reports with a lye concoction being found at the scene of a suspected missing person had been filed today, one in Pennsylvania and a spate of them in New York.

All reported within the past hour.

A note on the screen told him the NYPD had requested three files from the San Diego Police Department, one of whom was for a woman who'd been killed on the site of one of the lye discoveries in an East Village apartment in New York. According to the note, she'd been disposing of a body at the scene, working with two other men called Nicolas Henderson and Sebastian Tully, all born in Pittsburgh with previous in California.

San Diego to Denver was a thousand miles, the same as Denver to Chicago. A methodical procession eastwards, where the three of them had been born. He stared at the dead woman's photo, Nina Lister, then searched for Henderson and Tully's files, the system quickly producing results.

He spent a moment examining the faces of the people who could very well have eluded him for over half a decade. Not a gang; a large man, a smaller one and a hundred and thirty pound woman.

Then he snatched up the phone on his desk.

*

Inside the NYPD Conference Room on the other side of the country, Archer, April and Ethan were sitting in silence, looking at the ten new female

250

faces that had joined Santiago, Goya, Valdez and Carvalho on the screen. Only three of the girls had been arrested in the past; the others had had their photos pulled from either the DMV or Covenant Housing records.

As he sat there, Archer suddenly realised he hadn't called St Luke's in a while to check on Alice. Drawing his cell, he scrolled for the number but then Shepherd suddenly reappeared in the doorway, his phone to his ear.

'Can you send them over?' he said, clicking at Ethan to get his attention and pointing at his laptop. As Ethan responded, Shepherd continued to listen to the call. 'I'll keep you posted. Thanks, Jack.'

Ending the call, he pocketed the phone, looking over at Ethan who was opening some files he'd just received.

'Put 'em up,' he said.

Ethan tapped several keys and hit *Enter*. After a second, thirteen new mug-shots appeared on the main screen.

'I just got a call from a detective in Denver who's had an unsolved multiple missing persons file for six years,' he said. 'This is a case-file that's spread across three different states, from Denver, Chicago to here. Henderson, Tully and Lister left a trail.'

'How do we know it's the same crew?' Marquez asked.

'Forensics. The specific lye concoction found at the residence of each missing person was an exact chemical match to the shit we found at Santiago's and what SWAT found in Scranton. And there's another link.'

'Every guy on this board was in some way involved in the sex trade,' Ethan finished, reading the file on his laptop.

'Twenty seven unsolved homicides?' Archer said, looking at the thirteen faces on the screen and the fourteen on the *Victims* board. 'Are you kidding me?'

'Across three cities and three thousand miles,' Shepherd said. 'And this was inner city work too. South-side Chicago, Five Points in Denver, the East Village here in New York. This was done right under the noses of the cities' police forces but they were never caught; the Denver PD Lieutenant said until today he'd never even had a suspect profile.'

'So Henderson, Tully and Lister are serial killers,' Ethan said. 'Randomly targeting people in the sex trade.'

'This isn't random,' Archer said. 'These people were deliberately targeted. There's a purpose here. In ninety nine percent of murder cases in the sex industry, serial killers target the girls, not the pimps controlling them.'

'So?'

'Look at those guys.' He pointed at the thirteen new faces, all hard-faced, tough-looking men. 'They look like the kind of people you'd want to piss off?'

Ethan didn't reply.

'Why mix it up with them if this was just about stacking up bodies or feeding a fetish?' Archer continued. 'Why not just target the girls? They'd be a hell of a lot easier to take out.'

'So they get to New York and start killing the girls too?' Marquez said. 'Why suddenly change their MO? Before, they only killed the male members of the three gangs.'

'Make that four,' Hendricks said as he walked into the room, having been absent for over thirty minutes.

'What are you talking about, Jake?' Shepherd said.

'I went to visit our Russian friend at the hospital,' Hendricks replied. 'And he just started talking.'

THIRTY FIVE

Across the East River at St Luke's, Josh was sitting in the recovery room with Michelle. She was still sedated after the operation to repair the damage to her arm and sleeping peacefully. According to the doctors, all had gone to plan; she'd been clipped by that initial burst but none of the rounds had stayed inside her tricep. She'd been out of the OR for fifteen minutes and he was waiting for her to wake up, wanting to be there when she did. He'd been shot a few months back and knew how much he'd appreciated her support at the time.

Leaning back in his chair, he sighed. It was only 9:35pm but it had been a whirlwind of a day. Towards the end of Michelle's surgery he'd received a call from Marquez telling him his kids were all safe at the Bureau and their address had been the first name on a list that had contained their whole team. She'd also told him about April Evans and their suspicions about the ten missing women; thinking back to how they'd found Alex Santiago, Josh had put two and two together. It wasn't a nice image.

It had been thirty minutes or so since they'd spoken. He was torn between staying beside his wife and wanting to re-join his team immediately to get to work on this case and find out just who'd done this to her. He withdrew his cell to dial Archer and let him know he'd be on his way just as soon just as his wife came to, then suddenly remembered Vargas was also being treated here, up on the 14th floor. No doubt Archer and the others would appreciate an update; now Michelle

254

had been shot, Josh had a much better understanding of how his detective partner had felt.

Squeezing his unconscious wife's hand and only intending to be gone for a few minutes, Josh rose and walked to the door, shutting it behind him quietly. Moving down the corridor, he headed towards the elevators and pushed the button.

It dinged a few moments later and he stepped inside, jabbing *14*.

'The four gunmen who tried to wax our families are Russian Mafia,' Hendricks explained. 'They're part of a crew who operate down in Little Odessa in Brooklyn. The shooter at Mount Sinai claimed that eleven of their guys have gone missing over the past year and this was a revenge attack.'

'Eleven?' Marquez said incredulously. 'And why us? What the hell have we got to do with it?'

Hendricks walked over the desk and picking up the phone, dialled a number.

'I'll let someone else explain,' he said, the receiver to his ear. 'Mark, it's Jake. I'm back; I'm putting you on speaker. You're with the investigation team.'

'OK.'

'This is Mark Massaro. He's a detective at the Organised Crime Control Bureau in Brooklyn. Tell them what you told me, Mark.'

'The four guys who visited your homes belong to a group called the Prizraki*. My team's been working them for months; once Jake told me what happened earlier, I wanted to speak with you*

personally. Hopefully it might help your investigation.'

'What can you tell us, Mark?' Shepherd asked.

'The Prizraki *are one of the most feared of thousands of Russian criminal organisations. These groups used to be outlaws but after the USSR and communism fell in the 90s, more than 6,000 separate Mafia factions emerged and the* Prizraki *was one of them; the literal translation into English is ghosts. We also know for a fact they operated under an old code called Thieves Law.*

'Thieves Law?' Shepherd repeated. 'What the hell's that?'

'It started in the gulags generations ago. Sounds like something out of a Hollywood movie I know, but believe me, it's some brutal shit. It's a load of rules they've been following for hundreds of years. Don't underestimate it.'

'What kind of rules?' Ethan asked.

'A mix; some of them are bizarre. Members of these gangs are never allowed to serve in the military for example. Senior members never pick anything up from the floor.'

'What?' Archer said.

'The leaders regarded the ground as dirty because in those days they lived among animals in the gulags,' Massaro explained. *'Now it's more a sign of hierarchy, enforces position. Another rule is any man being considered to get promoted to the top level, becoming what they call a* vor, *must disown their relatives, because their only family is the group. Many gangs demand their members have their life stories tattooed on their bodies, like business cards.'*

'None of our dead guys had any ink,' Archer said.

'*The* Prizraki *are different; they're called ghosts for a very good reason. Although we think they follow most of the other Thieves rules, only the highest-ranking guys in their organisation are permitted any tattoos, just two stars to signify the guy's a* vor. *They've run the docks on Brighton Beach for decades.*'

'I had some interaction with a group from Little Odessa once when I was at Brooklyn South,' Marquez said. 'They were in a different league to the gangs we normally had to deal with.'

'*They are. And these sons of bitches are as intelligent as they are violent. That's what makes them so dangerous and difficult to deal with.*'

'What's the structure in the crew?' Archer asked.

'*It's not based on personalities, but on networks. The shot-callers are in Moscow, but they have separate factions in scores of major cities, an entire web. They're tough bastards too; other Mafia organisations have been trying to acquire those docks here for years and have never succeeded; most of them stay well clear now. Before the last ten months, we figured the* Prizraki *have only lost one guy in the past two years.*'

'Who?' Archer asked.

'*Their top guy here. Got picked off by a high-powered rifle when he was getting out of a car outside his home in Brooklyn. Shot through the forehead.*'

'You know who killed him? Shepherd asked.

'*Afraid not. Probably a rival, maybe the Georgians or Ukrainians. His replacement took*

257

*over at the end of last year; we think he came
from another faction, like Philly, Boston or
Pittsburgh, but whoever, he'd have been carefully
chosen. That's how they operate. Like I said,
people have been after that piece of Little Odessa
for years. One of my CIs on the street said he
heard there were some Chechens in town
preparing to make a push, but we haven't seen or
heard shit.'*

'Who are they?' Archer asked, 'These
Chechens.'

'Real dark bastards; they call themselves Volki.
*We know next to nothing about them, except our
intel says they're in the city somewhere. But these
attacks on you guys is a mystery. Gangs at this
level will do anything to avoid going against the
police, which is why what they did to you tonight
is so confusing.'*

'No wonder they were pissed,' Archer said.
'They lost eleven guys and wanted to send a
message.'

'The wounded man said they had no idea we
were cops,' Hendricks said. 'I believed him.'

'So why feed you guys to the *Prizraki?*' Ethan
asked. 'Use them to get revenge?'

'Or to give them time to find me,' April
suddenly said quietly.

Everyone glanced at her.

'No disrespect, but that's a hell of a lot of effort
to find just one person,' Ethan said. 'And why
you?'

'I have no idea,' April replied. 'Not to mention
that these sons of bitches killed ten of my friends
and I still don't have a clue why.'

'Do the *Prizraki* run girls, Mark?' Archer
asked.

*'Not on the street, that's for sure. They're
sharks amongst fish; they don't go in for that
small-time shit.'*

'What about high-end stuff?' Archer asked.

*'I don't think so. It would give us something to
put on them. We think they smuggle people in
through the docks and sell them on. That's as far
as their involvement goes.'*

Archer swore. 'That breaks the pattern. If these
disappearances are Henderson, Tully and Lister's
work, which they almost certainly have to be,
these Russians are the first non-street sex-trade
gang they've targeted. Why?'

'And how did Henderson and Tully get those
addresses?' Ethan asked.

*'Christ only knows. These organisations have
people everywhere. I wouldn't be surprised if
they had a hook.'*

Looking at Hendricks as he listened to Massaro,
Shepherd glanced back down at the phone.

'I'll call you back, Mark. Thanks.'

*'OK. Just one request, Sergeant; if you make a
move, you'll let me know? We've been working
this case for a while.'*

'Of course.'

Hanging up, Shepherd shifted his attention to
April. 'Until this is over, you have an armed
detective with you everywhere you go. This thing
stops right now. No-one else is going to die
tonight.'

She nodded; then taking a deep breath, she rose
from the table for the first time in over an hour.

'Excuse me.'

'Where are you going?' Hendricks asked.

'The restroom.' She forced a smile. 'Do I need
security for that?'

259

Hendricks returned the smile and shook his head. 'No, I reckon that's OK.'

She walked to the door, Hendricks stepping to one side so she could pass. Archer rose too and pulled his phone, scrolling for Josh's number, leaving the room to call his partner and get some air, trying to work through how this all tied up. As he left, he looked back at the victims' screen, twenty eight faces, soon to be joined by eleven more.

Three sex-gangs, the top guys and then low-level pimps, killed and flushed away.

Then a Russian Mafia organisation targeted who didn't run escorts and were so tough they'd run the Little Odessa docks for over four decades.

He glanced at Henderson and Tully's mug-shots on the other screen.

Why the hell did you take on the Prizraki*?*

At St Luke's, the elevator opened for the 14th floor and Josh stepped out, walking down the corridor then turning the corner.

The moment he did, he frowned.

There was no sign of the two night shift cops who were normally outside Vargas' door.

Before he could take another step, he heard the bell ding behind him, announcing the arrival of the second elevator. He turned just as two officers appeared in the corridor behind him. Seeing Josh standing there, one of them challenged him.

'Who're you?'

'NYPD,' Josh said, motioning to his badge. *'Counter-Terrorism Bureau.'*

One of the officers stepped forward, checking it. 'What are you doing up here?'

'Came to see my colleague,' he replied, pointing down the corridor. 'You guys shouldn't leave your post.'

'Not us,' the other said. 'That's why we're here. Our two guys aren't responding.'

Josh stared at the man for a moment; then he turned and sprinted down the corridor, closely followed by the two men. Trying the door, Josh found it was locked. Pulling his pistol, he dipped and smashed it open.

The moment they breached the room they saw a cop lying on the floor beside a load of empty grey canisters.

'Oh shit!' one of the men said, immediately calling it in and moving swiftly out of the room to clear the immediate area.

Looking back at the bed and seeing there was no-one there, fear settled over Josh. He was aware of a harsh chemical smell lingering in the air, making his eyes water. Moving forward, stepping over empty cans, he moved into the bathroom and felt his heart skip a beat.

The plug was up and the tub was empty but still wet.

And he could see tiny pieces of white hospital gown stuck around the rim of the bath.

THIRTY SIX

Standing on the walkway inside the Bureau Archer frowned, looking down at his phone. Josh wasn't picking up. He considered trying him again then decided to leave it for the moment. His detective partner's wife had just been in surgery; no wonder he was occupied.

Returning the cell to his pocket, he glanced left and saw April sitting alone in the Conference Room next door, having returned from the ladies' room but taking a moment alone. He guessed she'd wanted some space and knew she didn't feel comfortable surrounded by police detectives; he could understand that. She was still wearing the blue NYPD jacket someone had loaned to her; it was too large but was giving her an extra layer of warmth as well as acting as a literal reminder that the Department was watching her back.

Walking in quietly, he perched on the table beside her; he didn't speak but just stayed there, providing reassurance. All in all, she'd had one hell of a day.

There was a period of silence.

'I can't stop thinking about what happened to them,' April said quietly. 'It's so horrible. I thought Leann getting shot was as bad as it could get.'

She sighed.

'It wouldn't have been quick, would it? To do that to someone would take some time. You said Alex hadn't…finished before you found him. Perhaps they might even have been still alive when they were put in the bath.'

Archer thought back to that bathroom.

'I don't know,' he said eventually.

'They would have known they were about to die. They must have been so scared.'

She looked at him, tears brimming in her eyes.

'Have you ever been in that situation? Thinking you were about to die?'

He smiled. 'Once or twice.'

'But you survived.'

'Somehow.'

'Did you get lucky?'

He nodded. 'And I fought back.'

'What kept you going?'

Archer went to reply but then remembered a Harlem rooftop six months ago when he'd been sure he was finally done for. Vargas had been beside him, Isabel too, the three of them seemingly trapped with no way out.

'Just stubborn, I guess.'

There was a pause. Glancing over, Archer saw April staring at him.

'What?' he asked.

'You're different from the others.'

'It's the accent.'

'No, not just that. You're different. You actually listen to me when I talk to you. I'm not used to that.'

He grinned. 'I grew up with a mother and sister. Had to learn pretty fast.'

She smiled back; there was a pause.

'Do you have any family left?' he asked.

Her smile faded. 'I guess; I don't know. I haven't called them in almost three years.' She paused. 'They have no idea what I do here. I wouldn't know what to say to them.'

'You can change this.'

'No. I can't. I've been trying to leave ever since I got into this shit but someone or something always stops me.'

'Palmer wants to help you.'

'And then what? Be real, Archer. I've got hardly any money; all my friends are dead. I have no qualifications, no real skills. They'll be getting in line to employ me.'

'If you had a choice, what would you do?'

'It's dumb.'

'Tell me,' he said.

She looked at him for a moment, as if daring him to laugh at her.

'I'd like to be a mechanic. I love cars.'

He grinned and shook his head. 'That's not dumb.'

'You think I'd fit into your typical auto-shop?'

'You think I fit in here?'

She looked at him and nodded. 'Yes. I think you do.'

She paused.

'What was your ambition?'

He thought for a moment. 'I'm living it.'

'Was it what you expected?'

He shook his head. 'It hasn't exactly all gone to plan. Right now I'm suspended.'

'For what?'

'I hit someone.'

'So? Who was he?'

'A Lieutenant; he was running the investigation into Leann's death.'

'Did he deserve it?'

'He deserved a hell of a lot more.'

As April went to reply, the pair sensed movement at the door; turning, they both saw

Marquez standing there. She was looking at Archer, a strange look on her face.

'Hey, Marquez.'

She took a breath and tried to speak but nothing came out, tears appearing in her eyes.

Archer immediately pushed himself off the table.

'Lisa?'

*

The news about what had happened at the hospital hit him like a locomotive, leaving him dazed, as if time had suddenly stopped. As Marquez broke it to him April was caught up in the moment too, seeing the devastation it'd caused to these two police detectives who'd been kind to her.

Outside the room, Hendricks watched them from the walkway. He turned to Shepherd, who'd taken the initial call from Josh who was still over at St Luke's with an NYPD team, cordoning off the hospital in the hunt for the two suspects.

'How the hell did they get to her?' Hendricks asked quietly.

'Apparently they killed both cops then put Vargas in the bath,' Shepherd replied, keeping his voice low so Archer couldn't hear him. 'All that was left were a load of empty canisters and pieces of her gown stuck to the top of the tub apparently.'

He took a deep breath.

'Josh said the hospital is on lockdown but the cameras on 14 were busted up; Henderson and Tully will already be gone.'

Hendricks didn't reply as Shepherd walked slowly into the room to join the others, Hendricks following.

Then Shepherd shouted in rage and frustration, kicking one of the chairs, taking it off the ground and thumping it into the wall, making everyone jump.

'Shit!'

A moment later a large overweight man in a suit and with bruising around his eye suddenly appeared in the doorway, looking left and right. The moment he saw Archer, he headed straight for him, Shepherd immediately stepping into his path to block him.

'Son of a bitch!' Royston shouted at Archer, pointing his finger. 'What the hell are you doing here?'

'Not now, sir!' Shepherd said.

'I said what the hell is he doing here?'

'I wanted him here,' Shepherd said.

'I want him out! He's suspended; he shouldn't be on site and you know it, Sergeant.'

'This isn't your case anymore, Lieutenant.'

'You giving me orders?' Royston asked.

He made to step towards Archer again who was standing watching him impassively but someone else stepped forward.

'This isn't your case anymore,' Hendricks repeated quietly.

'Back up, both of you.'

Hendricks didn't move. Neither did Shepherd.

Royston glared at them both, everyone in the room watching the confrontation.

Then after a few seconds Royston dropped his gaze and took a pace backwards, smoothing down his tie and tucking his shirt back into his belt over his gut, his left eye socket yellow and purple from where Archer had punched him a week ago.

266

He stood there for a moment then looked around the room and started clapping sarcastically.

'I just got a call from my Captain telling me the Leann Casey investigation has been blown wide open; apparently my team and I have over a dozen more homicides to solve, and they're still coming thanks to you. Outstanding work, people.'

'Excuse us for doing our job,' Marquez said. 'And are you saying murders don't exist if you close your eyes and stick your fingers in your ears? What are we, ten years old?'

'Watch your mouth, Detective, or I'll suspend you along with this asshole here,' Royston fired back, spitting the words at Marquez but glaring at Archer who was still watching him expressionlessly.

'Forgive me for being blunt but the only reason we uncovered these other murders was because we dug deeper, sir,' Shepherd said, trying to stay cool. 'You got the wrong killers.'

'No, we didn't.'

'Yes, you did. And we did more with this thing in one day than you did in four weeks. If you'd moved faster, these girls would still be alive.'

'Hookers.'

'Human beings.'

'We just lost one of our own too,' Marquez said.

Royston paused. 'Who?'

'Detective Vargas. Not to mention two officers who were guarding her. So are you saying we shouldn't investigate what happened to these women and find out who killed them?'

'A case where all but one victim was a convicted criminal or prostitute? Christ, I thought

267

you Counter Terrorism folks had better things to do with your time. My team will take over and clear up this mess.'

'We should kick this up to the FBI,' Shepherd said. 'This is a nationwide, Federal deal. I've got a detective in Denver and a police department in Scranton wanting regular updates, and I haven't even had a chance to get in touch with Chicago or San Diego's PD yet.'

'No way is this going Federal,' Royston said. 'My team and I will handle it.'

'What, like last time?' Hendricks said. 'And as Marquez said, one of our own just died. That means we have point on this.'

'You arguing with me, Sergeant?'

'You bet your ass I am.' Hendricks replied, jerking his head towards Archer. 'I also know the strings you pulled to get him put in Rikers for the weekend. After what almost happened to him in there, you might want to reconsider your position. Sir.'

'Oh he's in more shit for that. I got a call from the prison telling me what happened in that shower block.'

'Self-defence.'

'Assaulting fellow inmates. He's out of control.'

Hendricks didn't reply, staring at Royston, who managed to hold eye contact this time.

However, he didn't make any further attempt to move towards Archer.

'Fine,' he blustered, looking at the others. 'You're detectives in one of the most important Bureaus in the Department, but go ahead and waste months of your time trying to track down who killed a load of hookers and low-life gang members. You think the world will miss these people?'

'That's hardly the point, is it?' Shepherd said. 'We can't decide whether or not someone's murder is worth investigating depending on what job they do. You get assholes in all walks of life. Sir.'

There was a sudden silence, the comment hanging in the air. Royston chose to ignore it, focusing on Archer instead and jabbing his finger in his direction.

'You can do whatever the hell you like, but two things are going to happen; this investigation stays in the NYPD and I want him out of here. I don't care if this case gets over a hundred bodies deep, he's still suspended. I saw the incident report from the bar earlier tonight too; not only did he fire a weapon in a public space, he also got into that fight in jail. He stabbed two inmates and sliced up a third.'

'They attacked me,' Archer fired back. 'I just gave them something to remember me by.'

'Let's see what the judge says about that,' Royston snapped, shifting his attention to Shepherd. 'He's out of here in the next ten minutes. That's a direct order. You disobey me, I'll write you all up and you'll be on the stand beside him for insubordination. Ten minutes and counting; that's it.'

With that, he stalked out of the room, leaving silence behind him.

Across the city, Tully closed the doors on their van, having just parked up in their East-side warehouse after dealing with Vargas and getting out of the hospital before anyone saw them. He lay the cop's radio carefully on the ground, keeping it switched on so they could keep up with the progress of the manhunt for them.

'I enjoyed that,' he told Henderson over the intermittent chatter, grinning.

'It gets better,' Henderson said, checking his phone. 'I just got a message from our friend who's monitoring the NYPD chatter. The wounded Russian at Mount Sinai died from his wounds.'

Tully grinned again, checking his watch. 'Saves us a job. And the nightclub just opened. Only four of those *Priz* bastards to go.'

Henderson nodded, pulling his pistol and reloading it with a fresh clip. 'No point in any subtlety this time; they know who we are. We can leave some bodies behind.'

'Save one.'

Henderson nodded. 'Save one.' He picked up an empty canister, preparing to fill it with more of their lye. 'We'll kill the last three and take him with us. We'll save him for our friend.'

He smiled.

'After all, they've got some catching up to do.'

At the Bureau, Shepherd had followed Royston down to the detective pit, catching up with him by the coffee machine.

'I really need Archer here, sir.'

'Are you kidding? No way.'

'It was a heat of the moment action. He was wound up. He and Detective Vargas were very close. With the current situation, I really need him right now.'

270

'I don't care if they were joined at the hip. That son of a bitch knocked me out in front of my team. He's going to pay for that.'

'He's a great cop. One of our best.'

'I couldn't give a shit. And he and his girlfriend still managed to get shot in that parking lot, despite both being outside their car and him being armed. Maybe he's not as good as you think.'

Close by, the team's families were watching the exchange, Beth Shepherd looking at her husband with concern as he talked to Royston. She watched as the Lieutenant turned and jabbed his finger in Shepherd's face.

'You know what the problem is, Sergeant? Your detective won't back down. That son of a bitch is too stubborn for his own good.'

'And that's a bad thing?'

'Yes. He needs to learn when he's beaten.'

'Bullshit,' Shepherd replied before he could help himself.

'Excuse me?'

'That's bullshit.'

The exchange had now caught everyone's attention but Shepherd wasn't yet done, his frustration with the fat bullying Lieutenant standing in front of him finally spilling over.

'You know what? I've been staring at the screen up there all night wondering what the point to all our work is,' he said. 'As hard as we try, people like Henderson, Tully, Lister and the Russians are still out there doing shit like this. And even if we put them down, others immediately step up and take their place.'

He gestured to the floor above.

'But I'll never quit trying and neither will my team. And I'd take one Archer, Marquez, Blake, Hendricks or Vargas over a hundred of you.'

Grabbing a pen and paper from a desk beside him, he slammed the items into the surprised Royston's chest.

'And you can write me up on that,' Shepherd finished, turning and striding towards the stairs as everyone watched him go.

THIRTY SEVEN

Inside Conference Room 3, Archer and Marquez were sitting side by side on the table. Hendricks and Ethan had just left, April going with them but looking with concern at Archer as they closed the door behind them.

Still stunned, Archer was staring unseeingly at the wall. After ticking past so slowly during the last four weeks, time now seemed to have stopped altogether. The case, the attacks on the families, rescuing April, all of it seemed so unimportant now.

The day he'd met Vargas had been one of the toughest of his life, and violence and danger seemed to have been stalking them ever since. They'd been kindred spirits, two people who seemed incapable of living quiet lives but in it together, watching each other's backs just as they had that night in the Harlem building.

She'd been defenceless, lying in her hospital bed, everyone assuming she'd be safe with two cops guarding her. Archer pictured Henderson and Tully entering the room; locking the door and staring down at her. Restraining her if she woke up or working quietly if she didn't.

Drawing a bath and dragging her from the bed.

Then pulling her towards the tub.

He swallowed, forcing the images from his mind. 'Shit. I only knew her for six months.'

'But you couldn't have packed more into them,' Marquez replied, beside him. 'You did more in that half year together than most people do in a decade.'

273

Archer didn't reply; he saw Vargas on the Upper West Side, the first time he'd seen her, spinning round as she and her team were ambushed. An hour later, the two of them bloodied and beaten up, alone in a Harlem apartment block and fighting to stay alive.

He saw her lying in the sitting room of their apartment, reading with Isabel asleep beside her, the girl's head resting on her lap.

And three months ago, the look on her face when he'd broken into an office building to save her life after she'd been kidnapped.

There was a pause.

'Juliana wasn't my first child,' Marquez suddenly said quietly. 'I had a boy eleven years ago, just after I became a cop.'

Archer shifted his gaze, looking at her.

'His father ran off not long after I found out I was pregnant. I was alone when I went into labour. There were complications during the birth.'

She looked down.

'Two days after he was born, the doctor told me he wasn't going to make it. I held him for forty five minutes until they turned off his ventilator. That's a TV episode without commercials, or half a soccer match. I was telling him about me, his family, my interests, my life.'

She swallowed.

'When I was done, I realised he'd stopped breathing. While I'd been talking, he'd died.'

Pausing, she took a moment.

'But even though he was only alive for two days, I still have those memories; they're always there for me whenever I want or need them. So do you with Alice; and you have six months of them.'

Archer stared at her, seeing a different side to the normally tough and guarded detective he worked with every day.

For a brief moment, she seemed vulnerable.

A moment later, there was a quiet knock on the door and Shepherd walked into the room, easing the door shut behind him.

'Sorry to interrupt, guys,' he said. 'But Mount Sinai just put the word out. The surviving Russian died.'

Neither Archer or Marquez replied.

'I spoke to Detective Massaro again too. He said the *Prizraki* crew operate from a club on Brighton Beach. We're gonna go down there, round up whoever's left and bring them in for questioning to try to find out what the hell is going on.'

'Wait,' Marquez said. 'Are we going down there to arrest them or save them from Henderson and Tully?'

'A bit of both, I guess.' He sighed and shook his head. 'Arming up to save a group of Russian mobsters. *Normal* and *ordinary* definitely didn't check in for work today.'

Loose ends. They were what separated those who succeeded in any criminal activity from those who were caught. Fingerprints, shell casings, ballistics evidence, witnesses, camera footage, hair fibres, all potentially the difference between getting away with it or getting caught.

If a mistake was made, it had to be fixed; a shell casing had to be retrieved, a bullet pulled from some drywall, an entire crime-scene bleached and wiped down.

Sometimes however, tying off a loose end meant ending someone's life altogether.

The source of Henderson, Tully and Lister's information inside the Department swallowed their nerves while watching Matt Shepherd gather his team. They hadn't picked up on the leak's involvement yet; that they'd been feeding Henderson and Tully information all night. Shepherd was about to lead a group down to Little Odessa where they would be taking the last four surviving Russian mob members into custody.

However, the inside man didn't care about that; those were Henderson and Tully's loose ends.

The leak's concern was focused on just two people. The red-headed hooker and the blond police detective who'd just joined Shepherd and the others on the walkway. News of what had happened to Vargas had already spread; the person currently watching the team didn't know why Henderson and Tully had greased her but fallout from that one action was inevitable.

Archer was still dealing with the shock of what had happened right now but that would switch to focused anger soon enough. With Vargas gone, he'd stop at nothing to find Henderson and Tully and he'd dig deep. He could find everything.

Sliding a hand into a pocket, the inside man withdrew a cell phone and started tapping a quick text message to the Latino gang contact he'd hired, who'd been demanding retribution after what went down in the prison shower block.

Sam Archer was suspended, had been attacked in Rikers, fought off Henderson and Tully, and had just lost his girlfriend.

But his night was about to get a whole lot worse.

Upstairs, Shepherd and Marquez were almost ready to go. Hendricks was gathering his team comprising three men and two women, all hand-picked by Hendricks himself. As Marquez joined the group, Shepherd took Archer to one side, moving a few feet from everyone else on the walkway.

Archer glanced down and saw Royston glaring up at him, standing by the coffee machine a few feet from Palmer who was just tucking her phone away in her bag.

'We're bound,' Shepherd said. 'Your case is still on hold. We can't do anything about that. I have to obey the rules. You've gotta leave.'

'It's OK. I understand.'

'Go home and rest up. When this is over, we'll talk about your situation. I don't give a shit what procedure says; you're not leaving my team.'

Archer smiled. 'Appreciate that.'

Pause.

'So you're going to bring in the last remaining *Prizraki*. What about Henderson and Tully?'

'Massaro and his team are going to bait a trap and wait at the club to see if they show up. With everything that's happened tonight, they'll be desperate to get out of the city. If they're gonna take out the remaining gang members, they'll do it tonight. The news of what happened to Vargas and the two officers at St Luke's has spread fast.

Every cop in the city is looking for them. They'll know they can't hang around.'

April had seen the two men talking and rose, walking out of the Conference Room towards them. Shepherd turned to her.

'We're stepping out for a moment. But you'll be safe here.'

'I thought I heard you telling him to go home?' she asked, looking at Archer.

'That's right. But as I said, you'll be safe here.'

April's eyes immediately widened; she shook her head. 'I want to stay with him.'

'There are over fifty detectives in this building.'

'I don't care.'

'There are people out there hunting you,' Shepherd told her.

'He'll protect me.'

'You know he's suspended.'

'I don't give a shit.'

Shepherd looked at her for a moment; the girl stared straight back.

'OK; if that's what you want,' Shepherd said. 'I guess I can't keep you here against your will. You got a spare change of clothes?'

She shook her head.

'Vargas does,' Archer said quietly.

'OK. Go get cleaned up then go straight to the safe-house. Royston's a piece of work but he's right; you're still technically suspended. Until that gets resolved, you can't remain on site. But stay close to your phone.'

Archer nodded. With that, Shepherd looked over at Hendricks; moments later the eight person team went quickly down the stairs. As they headed for the exit, Archer looked down into the detective pit and saw Palmer talking with some of the family members, Royston ten feet from her and still glaring up at him. The Lieutenant drained his coffee then made a big deal of checking his watch.

Ignoring him, Archer focused on the family group and saw Isabel sitting close to Palmer and Melissa Hendricks, completely unaware that Vargas had died.

Taking a deep breath, he turned to April.

'Just give me a couple of minutes.'

In the tall canyons of the Financial District, Henderson pulled up outside his place in their back-up van, killing the engine and looking over at Tully beside him. The two men had loaded up the rear of the vehicle with the last of their lye solution, ten canisters tightly sealed and stowed beside some barrels of bleach they were going to splash down the interior of the vehicles with, making completely sure every speck of DNA was destroyed.

Shooting his cuff, Henderson checked his watch. The Little Odessa club would already be open and busy, a prime opportunity for them to do what they had to do and then get out before anyone realised what had happened.

'Go sterilise your place,' he told Tully. 'Work fast. Meet me back here as soon as you're done.'

Nodding, the smaller man opened his door and stepped out, slamming it behind him, then jammed his hands into his pockets and headed across the street towards his apartment four blocks away. Henderson also jumped out, locked up then crossed the street and walked towards his apartment building, pushing the door open and keeping his head down to avoid looking into the lens of the security camera that was mounted in the lobby.

After almost a year, the two men and their accomplice were finally leaving this place.

But before they could go, there were just four last Russian *Prizraki* who needed to be dealt with.

THIRTY EIGHT

Sam Archer's mother had died when he was eighteen. Cancer had weakened her body but a blood clot in her lung had been what finally ended her life. She'd been in a hospice in the UK when it had happened and he'd known it was coming, giving him a chance to prepare and say goodbye.

However, he'd only ever lost one mother. Isabel had just lost her second and neither circumstance had been either peaceful or expected; no hospices, no opportunity to say farewell, just bullets and lye, violence and murder, pain and heartbreak.

The day Archer had first met Vargas, she'd almost been killed protecting Isabel. The bond that had developed between the two had been as strong as titanium.

Now, he had to tell her Vargas was gone forever, just like the rest of her blood family.

Taking a deep breath, he eased the door to the room shut and turned to look at Isabel. Dressed in jeans and a white sweater, her dark hair hanging over her shoulders, she was sitting on the edge of the table swinging her legs, a look of childish naivety on her face as she looked at him. Most teenagers and adults could gauge when something was wrong from body language but she was still a bit too young.

For the best-intentioned reasons, he'd lied to her about Vargas' absence for the past four and a half weeks but he couldn't lie to her about this.

Taking a deep breath, he pulled up a chair, sitting in front of her. He felt her eyes scanning his face, beginning to sense something was wrong but not yet sure what it was.

'Did someone hurt you?' she asked, looking at a trickle of blood that had dried by his temple. He reached up and touched it, remembering the pistol-whip sucker shot that had caused it in the Park Avenue hotel bar.

'I walked into something.'

'You're always injuring yourself. You need to be more careful.'

He smiled. 'Yeah, I guess I do.'

The smile quickly faded and he hesitated, trying to find the words, feeling the girl's eyes on him as she waited. The room was silent, Isabel sitting there wondering what was going on but seemingly happy to have Archer all to herself.

'Do you remember those dreams you told me about?' Archer said eventually. 'The ones with your mother?'

She nodded. 'We talk to each other.'

'There's going to be someone else there now too with you both.'

'Who?'

'Alice.'

He paused.

'She had to go away.'

'When is she coming back?'

'She's not, sweetheart. She's in the same place as your mother and the rest of your family.'

Isabel's brown eyes stared at him as she took in what he was saying.

Then they filled with tears as realisation started to dawn, just like Vargas' in the car park after she'd been shot.

'She died?'

Archer swallowed and nodded. 'Yes. She did.'

282

He paused.

'But now she'll be there too when you have your dreams. She'll be with your other mother too; I think they'll already be friends.'

Isabel didn't speak for a moment; then she looked at him again. 'How? They never met.'

'Because they both love you. And that'll bring them together. That never stops, no matter where you are. And that means they'll always be with you, wherever you go. They'll see everything you do, everyone you meet, everything.'

Isabel blinked, releasing the tears from her wide eyes as she realised that Vargas was gone. 'I can't touch her anymore.'

'But she'll never leave you. And you don't need to touch her for that.'

She looked up, her wide brown eyes focusing on him through the tears.

'Are you going to leave me too?'

He shook his head, looking her in the eyes. In that moment, every reservation he'd had about getting close to the child disappeared forever.

'I'm never going anywhere. I promise.'

'Really?'

He nodded, reaching forward and squeezing her hands. Silence fell again as they looked at each other, the little girl sitting on the edge of the table, him on the chair in front of her.

Then Archer leaned forward and Isabel hugged him, her arms around his neck, his own around her small back as she started to cry.

Inside his Wall Street apartment, Henderson was just doing a final wipe-down with bleach, making sure he'd left no trace in case the cops came looking.

He was working methodically but fast; after what he and Tully had done to the cops in the hospital they knew the net would be closing in. Unlike Carlos Goya, who'd been easy enough to track to that Scranton motel, and Santiago, who'd been at his apartment fresh from lock-up when they came knocking, they wouldn't leave a trail for anyone to follow. The NYPD would never see or hear from them again, their job finally done, disappearing like their victims without a trace into thin air.

He looked around the Financial District apartment, his home for the past ten months. The apartment was basic, white walls, plain furniture, black kitchen units. Like the warehouse they used as a base, which was rented under a front company selling pipes, this place was leased for a twenty four month period under a fake name for just over $1.1 million; he still had four months of the lease to go, but Santiago and Goya's killing of the escort four weeks ago had brought that departure forward. It didn't matter; he wasn't exactly strapped for cash.

They'd set out on this path six years ago in San Diego after Lister was released from prison and had been reunited with Henderson and Tully. Each had a different perspective from the same horrific experience, but they'd all agreed on a mutual objective and had set out east.

They'd stopped a thousand miles into their journey in Denver, realising that if they were going to do this they'd need money. It'd been Lister's idea to take over a sex-trade operation; she'd realised how lucrative it could be, making thousands of dollars a day with the right girls and clients. Pimps pushed girls and boys out onto the corner for one thing; money. The higher class the service, the more money flowed in, particularly if you threw blackmail into the mix. Most pimps wouldn't care who they worked for; if they were paid enough, they'd sell their own mother for cash.

So the three of them decided to target one of the more successful operations in the city and take it over.

Lister had assumed they'd just shoot their targets and dump their bodies somewhere but Henderson and Tully had said different. Just before they'd left California, the pair had taken up with a Mesa cartel meth cooker who'd taught them about lye and the best way to dispose of a corpse. Their first target had been a lucrative East Colfax sex gang and when they'd killed the six men who'd headed up the operation, Henderson and Tully had demonstrated to Lister just how well the magic marinade worked. She'd been impressed. No evidence to incriminate them.

When the six men had been disposed of, Henderson, Tully and Lister took over the operation, the middle-men not caring who was running the show as long as they received their cut. However, the money made from the escort service hadn't been enough for them. They were after the big fish and with their blackmail operation soon up and running, a john didn't end up just paying for that one trick.

That year in Denver, the trio had earned just over two million dollars. Changing the operation from high-class hookers into a top-quality escort service, the girls had some pretty important clients captured on camera. Professional athletes, politicians, lawyers; their careers and reputations potentially ruined if their less reputable activities were made public,

Selecting their targets carefully, the money soon started to roll in, tens of thousands each week as they made a fortune from their blackmail racket, their victims having no idea who they were and so unable to exact revenge. A prominent Nuggets player had called their bluff, refusing to pay, and Lister had immediately sold some very interesting photos to the city papers for almost seven figures. His expensive divorce a few weeks later had also been big news.

The girls never met the trio running the show; their pimps did, but they knew better than to talk, taking their extra cash their new bosses were paying them and doing exactly as instructed. They were well aware their previous top guys had disappeared when these three had suddenly turned up and taken over the operation, and none of them wanted the same thing happening to them.

However, things went sour when a prominent politician who had everything to lose hired some people to track down who was behind the extortion racket and take care of the problem. Henderson had killed them both, but hadn't had time to dispose of the bodies, discovering late that night when watching the news that they were ex Denver PD, which meant he'd just opened up a huge can of worms.

Within thirty six hours, the two pimps who'd worked for the three of them were both dead and the trio were out of the State, two million dollars richer and their operation immaculately well honed. They left the hookers; they'd never seen them and therefore couldn't identify them.

A thousand miles later, Chicago was next, and by that point they knew exactly what to do. They picked out a similar South Side operation, taking out the guys at the top and leaving just four lowlifes on the street, the pile of money the group was accruing growing by the day. Most people had secrets; however, for the clients snared in their traps, Henderson or the other two were there with a camera to catch theirs.

They'd stayed in Chicago until the beginning of the year when they'd moved on to their final target, Pittsburgh. However, when they'd arrived they'd discovered things had changed and their ultimate target wasn't in the city anymore. It'd taken time to find out where they'd gone, but they'd finally tracked the leader to New York City. When the trio had arrived in NYC it'd been business as usual, sourcing a successful operation but then there'd been a totally unexpected development. This had worked in their favour, their team gaining a fourth member who'd proved invaluable.

Although the most unexpected and unlikely of unions, the foursome had worked together like clockwork; after all, they were all bound by a mutual hatred of the same group, an enemy that had brought them together.

The Russian *Prizraki* in Little Odessa.

THIRTY NINE

The Little Odessa *Prizraki* were a whole new ballgame; they were vicious, tough and ruthless, other gangs in the city steering well clear of their area by Coney Island. Like Henderson, Tully and Lister, the Russians were also pretty adept at making people disappear so the trio knew going after them was extremely dangerous; if they were caught, they'd pay a very heavy price. However, they'd relished the challenge; this was their ultimate goal and one they'd been planning for years.

Over the last ten months, they'd managed to liquefy eleven Russians, the new member of their team providing invaluable information and helping make the process a whole lot easier. Achieving that number of disappearances without being caught or leaving a trace had been one hell of a feat, but with meticulous planning, inside knowledge and seamless execution they'd pulled it off.

But then the entire operation had been jeopardised by Carlos Goya and Alex Santiago.

Henderson, Tully and Lister had had a rule; never go after cops unless it was absolutely, one hundred per cent necessary. They'd made that mistake in Denver and having only just got away with it, ensured it was the one thing they made crystal clear to the pimps who worked for them. They figured most police departments wouldn't lose too much sleep over some missing gang members but losing one of their own was a different issue entirely.

288

However, that was exactly what Goya and Santiago had done. The escort Leann Casey had checked herself into rehab over the summer, which had pissed them all off; they'd already lost three months of earnings from her this year after she got busted and was sent to Rikers for a ninety day sentence, and with this latest stunt they were going to lose yet more money with her out of the game. However, instead of giving her a beating when they heard she was planning to bail on them, those two brain-dead idiots had decided to kill her. Then, not only had Goya shot her in a public space but he'd also managed to hit two cops in the process. That had been the real icing on the cake.

A team who only operated in the shadows was now the focus of an entire police department.

And they hadn't completed their task yet.

Their normal evac time was thirty six hours; that was long enough to dispose of everyone they'd come into contact with who could identify them, but when the shooting took place there'd still been eleven *Prizraki* left alive and no way were Henderson, Tully, Lister and their new accomplice leaving without taking care of them.

They also had to dispose of Goya and Santiago. However Carlos had gone on the run, laying low somewhere, and Santiago was doing twenty one days upstate for a public order offence, the police with no idea that they had a perpetrator in a police shooting already locked up in a cell.

Steps had been taken by Henderson, Tully and Lister to buy themselves some more time to waste the last few Russians and find the last hooker by setting up the cops and their families. They'd also found two pimps from another neighbourhood and framed them for the Casey shooting using the murder weapon Goya had had with him at the Scranton motel. They'd killed Carlos on Wednesday, framed Valdez and Carvalho on Thursday and had hit Santiago today, twenty four hours after he was released from County.

However, today had to be their last day in the city. Despite their delaying tactics, the police investigation had changed hands and the new team had an impressive track record, not only for getting results but for the speed at which they worked. These cops had proved much harder to deal with and they'd be totally focused now that they'd lost Detective Vargas.

Kneeling by the door, Henderson pushed a rug to one side and used a key to open a safe sunk into the floor. Reaching inside, he withdrew several keyed bricks of hundred dollar bills, each one ten thousand in total, and put them into the pockets of his coat. Relocking the safe and pushing the rug back in place, he rose and took a last look at the apartment, loading his silenced pistol then double-checking he had his knife in his pocket.

Satisfied, he hitched his sleeve and switched off the light, stepped outside and closed the door behind him. Grinning, he pulled his baseball cap down over his forehead and continued down the corridor towards the stairs, thinking of the last four *Prizraki* sons of bitches who were going to die.

He'd been waiting a long time for this.

Once Isabel started hugging Archer she seemed incapable of stopping. He wanted to stay here with her but knew he had to leave; the last thing he needed right now was Royston causing another scene.

Rising, Archer carried her out of the Conference Room, down the walkway and into an empty office. A couch was pushed up against the far wall; walking forward, he laid her down carefully, Isabel finally releasing her hold on him as she lay back. Taking a blanket someone had left at the foot of the couch, he unfolded it and laid it over Isabel, her eyes red-rimmed from crying.

'I have to go out into the city for a bit,' he told her. 'But I'll be back soon.'

'I don't want you to leave.'

'Me neither. But you'll be safe. This is one of the safest places in the city. No-one can get to you here.'

Archer glanced at his watch.

'Anyway, you must be tired,' he said. 'It's way past your bed-time.'

'Am I a curse?' she suddenly asked.

'What?'

'Everyone around me dies,' she said quietly. 'Am I a curse?'

Archer smiled.

'No, sweetheart. You're not a curse. Just the opposite. And whatever happens next, we'll figure it out. OK?'

She nodded. 'OK.'

'And remember; your mother and Vargas will both be looking out for you too. And if you ever have a bad dream, they'll be there to protect you.'

'They don't need to. Someone else already does that.'

'Who?'

'You.'

Caught off guard, Archer smiled. The girl suddenly sat up, hugging him again. Archer held onto her for a moment then settled her back down and rose, leaving her tucked under the blanket in the office.

'I'll be back soon,' he told her. 'I promise.'

She settled back into the couch, staring up at him. 'OK. I'll be waiting.'

Taking a last look at her, Archer turned and walked to the door, twisting the blinds shut so the room was dark.

Then he opened the door and quietly shut it behind him.

FORTY

Inside the rear office of the nightclub in Little Odessa, Vladimir Bashev locked the door then moved over to the wall behind his desk and lifted down a piece of artwork, revealing a safe. Checking a series of CCTV monitors mounted on the wall to his left, his last three men somewhere out there but invisible amongst the mass of revellers, he quickly turned back to the safe and entered the six digit code.

He was getting the hell out of here. As he'd waited to hear from Marat, Valentin and the others that they were on their way to Long Island, one of his men had been checking the news and seen the report of a failed attack at a police sergeant's house in the city, three men shot dead and another critically injured.

Four more losses, half their remaining force put out of the game in less than an hour, but at least on this occasion he knew what had happened to his men. They'd been set up; the tip-off had been phony, and he and his men had been suckered. Going after a member of the NYPD and their family was just about the dumbest move someone in his position could make.

Cursing, he opened the safe, revealing a wad of dollar bills and a handgun. He'd been in the city for less than twelve months, inducted at the end of last year after the previous head had been killed by a sniper. The *Prizraki*'s operation in Pittsburgh had been drying up due to a renewed FBI presence in the city, and Bashev's promotion had signalled the end of that group, the rest of the faction being reassigned elsewhere on the East

Coast, the *ghosts* staying true to their name and avoiding Federal attention.

However, Bashev was the only one who'd become a *vor*, recommended because of the success of his operation in the Steel City; getting his stars was a huge honour, an opportunity many men in the organisation chased their entire lives but never achieved. Working for the New York arm of the *Prizraki* was the ultimate achievement; It was the top faction on the East Coast, outranking Boston, Philadelphia and Bashev's old haunt, Pittsburgh. When he'd been inducted, he'd joined the most feared gang in New York State, whose legacy went back almost eighty years.

But now, from the original seventeen, including himself there were just four of them left.

The first to go down had been three enforcers, all vanishing without a trace in February. The Little Odessa Russians had many rivals, but the leadership at the time figured the Georgians must have been responsible. Four men had been sent to exact retribution. That was how it worked; you get hit, you hit back harder. That was the only way to stay in business.

But then more guys started to disappear. Now, eight months after this shit started, the organisation had been whittled down to virtually nothing. Bashev had never encountered anything like this; he was the one who made people disappear, not the other way around. He also knew that word was out on the street about what was happening and he was becoming a laughing stock; the Mafia leader who kept losing his men. Right now, he was so vulnerable he felt naked; it was just a matter of time before one of two things happened. The shot-callers in Moscow ordered his execution or someone made a move on this portion of Little Odessa and he didn't want to be around when either went down.

Tonight signalled the end. Although Marat and the other men had no traceable ID, soon enough the police would track down where they'd come from. With the threat of other gangs circling, like vultures over a wounded animal, it was time to get the hell out, cut his losses and quit before he was the next one to disappear. He was well aware that running like this would be looked upon as humiliating failure, especially for a man with stars on his shoulders, but Bashev was ready to accept that loss of face if it meant he kept a pulse. He wasn't afraid of anyone on the street, but he was dealing with something out of the ordinary here. He couldn't fight an enemy he couldn't see.

Continuing to push the last of the bills from the safe into his large briefcase, he glanced at the CCTV screens and suddenly stopped what he was doing.

A series of black 4x4s were pulling up outside the front of the club. The doors opened and a group of immediately recognisable figures wearing black Kevlar vests and armed with shotguns stepped out, *NYPD* clearly printed on the front of each vest, the white letters slightly fuzzy on the screen but still unmistakeable.

Lowering the case, he pulled the top-slide on the handgun, loading a round.

Time to go.

Outside the club, Shepherd walked forward, meeting up with Detective Massaro, who had his team in tow. Without pausing, the two men, followed by Hendricks, Marquez and Massaro's squad strode across the street, all carrying loaded Mossberg shotguns.

With what had happened to Vargas on his mind, Shepherd's mood was unusually dark as he approached the front of the club. The combination of the attacks on the families, Royston's treatment of Archer and Alice's death were all roiling around inside him, filling him with an anger that he normally kept well under control. As a leader, losing someone under his command was something he'd experienced once and vowed he'd do his utmost to prevent happening again.

Two bouncers were on the door, large men dressed in black with ear pieces tucked into their right ears, their eyes narrowing as they saw the armed detectives approaching. As one of them called it in, the other stepped forward, his eyes cold.

'You need a warrant, policeman,' he said, blocking Shepherd's path, jabbing a finger in the Sergeant's face to emphasise his point.

Walking into the man's forefinger, which technically counted as assault, Shepherd's arms moved up in a flash, the butt of the Mossberg hitting the side of the bouncer's head with considerable force.

The blow caught him right behind the ear and as big as the man was, his equilibrium went for a wander, his legs turning to cooked spaghetti. As he staggered, two of Hendricks' men quickly stepped forward, restraining and cuffing the guy before he could make any attempt to retaliate.

The other bouncer stepped forward but Marquez racked a round in her shotgun and put the Mossberg's barrel an inch from the man's face. He stopped in his tracks, taken aback by the look on her face; wisely, he stayed put as the remaining three members of Hendricks' team handcuffed him, both bouncers now under control.

Shepherd swept the red rope barrier strung across the entrance out of the way; then he, Hendricks, Massaro and their teams walked into the dark, hot nightclub, Marquez following closely behind, the pounding music and heat hitting the detectives as they entered the room.

Although they were each wearing an earpiece connected to the doormen, Bashev's last three guys hadn't heard the warnings from outside. The music was too loud, the men frowning and pushing a finger into their other ear as they'd tried to hear what was being said.

They were spread out around the club, two downstairs, one upstairs, all three of them tense and on edge. Each was wearing a loose jacket to conceal the sub-machine gun they had on straps hanging from their shoulders.

As they scanned the people in the club, they became aware of a commotion by the entrance, just as some strobes hit.

Illuminated in the flashes, the man positioned upstairs saw armed NYPD detectives suddenly walking into the club, each carrying a shotgun, most of the people on the dance-floor completely unaware of their sudden arrival.

'*Police just arrived, sir,*' one of the men said in Russian over the radio. '*What do we do?*'

Pushing his finger into his ear, the man on the 1st floor waited.

'*Boss?*'

297

There was no response.

Staring down at the two male and one female cops, others moving in behind them, he pulled out his MP5K and hit the cocking handle forward, racking a round.

They didn't look as if they were here to talk.

And neither was he.

The club was full of people, slowing the three detectives' progress as they walked forward and looked for their quarry.

Moving behind Shepherd and Hendricks, Marquez approached the dance-floor, some revellers on the squares seeing her and doing a double-take, the surprised expressions on their faces jumping in the flash of each strobe.

She checked the floor and then lifted her gaze to the floor above.

And saw a man aiming a sub-machine gun directly at her.

From inside his office, Vladimir suddenly heard gunshots followed a few seconds later by screaming, all coming from the other side of the door.

Quickly snapping his case shut, he pulled on his jacket, snatched up his loaded pistol then turned and opened the door to the cellar, a gun in one hand and millions of dollars in the briefcase held firmly in the other.

Sprinting up to the 1st floor, Marquez fought her way through the panicking clubbers towards the man she'd seen aiming the sub-machine gun at her from below. He'd fired but for some reason his aim was off, shooting high as he pulled the trigger, his rounds hitting one of the lights above her head.

When she finally reached him she saw he'd been shot in the throat, clutching the wound with both hands as he suffocated, his eyes as wide as drink coasters as he writhed on the floor, choking on his own blood.

As the man died, she suddenly heard more screams from across the club, more audible now as the music had just cut out.

Turning, she ran to the edge of the balcony and saw Hendricks scanning the crowd as Shepherd knelt by another man. He'd been shot in the head. There hadn't been any sound of gunshots though, only from the guy behind her who'd fired just before he'd been killed.

Looking around, Marquez desperately searched for whoever was responsible.

Then she heard more screams from panicking clubbers directly under her on the ground floor and sprinted for the stairs.

With the noise muffled by the brick, Bashev ran through the dark passageway away from the club, then up another flight of stairs.

Reaching the exit, he put the case down and eased open a metal delivery hatch, glancing around him. He saw people running away from the club at the other end of the street but none of them were paying any attention to this side street, no cops anywhere in sight, no movement other than clouds of steam rising from some construction portholes to his right.

Stepping out and closing the door behind him, he walked rapidly towards his car, pushing the key fob as he approached. Several cars were parked along the street, construction vehicles, an old work truck and a white van.

Opening the vehicle, he threw the case inside, checking around him again before getting ready to climb in behind the wheel.

Suddenly he sensed a whisper of movement behind him and snapped around.

A beat too late.

FORTY ONE

Eight miles north in Queens, Archer was alone in the sitting room of his apartment, April cleaning herself up in the bathroom before they left for the safe-house in Manhattan. He'd just put fresh dressings over the cuts on his arm and chest then changed his clothes, pulling on a fresh pair of jeans and a navy blue sweater after taking off the NYPD vest he'd worn since he and Hendricks had breached Santiago's apartment five hours ago.

With the vest resting on the couch beside him, Archer glanced at the empty space around him, the sound of the shower filling the quiet. Everywhere he looked, he saw different memories of Vargas and they wracked him with the worst guilt he'd ever felt. After all they'd been through, he'd not been there to protect her when she'd needed him most. She'd been vulnerable and alone in that hospital room. She'd survived the gunshot and the trip in the ambulance when her heart had stopped twice, but they'd somehow got to her.

Against his better judgement he'd accepted his orders, stayed away and Alice had died. For a man who spent his life protecting others, he'd failed to save the person closest to him.

Focusing his blank gaze, he glanced at the digital clock on a table to his right. *11:01pm*; eleven hours until his hearing and almost definitely the end of his career in the Counter-Terrorism Bureau. *When it rains, it pours*, so the saying went; right now, it seemed to be a monsoon.

301

To his right, the bathroom door opened and April stepped out, towelling off her hair; she wasn't wearing make-up anymore which made her look younger, just a normal pretty girl. She was wearing the clothes he'd given her, a pair of Vargas' jeans and one of her shirts. The two women were a similar size and the garments were a good fit; Vargas had been wearing that outfit when they'd gone out to Long Island with Isabel six weeks ago.

'Better?' he asked, forcing his mind back to the present, the memories fading and blowing away like the sand from the beach that day.

She nodded. 'Much. So where's this safe-house?'

'Across town at the West Village. You'll be safe there. Those places are off the grid.'

'Will you stay?'

'For as long as I can. Royston won't know I'm there.'

There was a brief silence.

'I'm sorry about your girl,' April said. 'She sounded like a good person.'

She looked down at her new clothes.

'I can give these back when this is over.'

Archer shook his head and forced a smile. 'Keep them. The jeans are a bit tight on me.'

She returned the smile and a silence fell.

Outside the building on 38th Street, a heavy-set gang member called Raul Ortega whistled at one of his guys, indicating for him to go and cut off the back exit.

They'd arrived moments earlier, the order coming from the heads of the gang, the shot-callers in Rikers. The cop had had a green light put on him when he was in the prison, meaning he should never have made it out of there. Everything in the build-up had gone to plan; a guard had been distracted to ensure the guy was alone in the shower block, about the only place in the entire facility where there were no cameras.

But then it'd all gone wrong. Apparently they'd been complacent and underestimated the cop, assuming he'd be easy meat, but he'd managed to put a shiv into two of them and slice up the face of a third. Ortega was pissed; one of them had been a friend of his, who'd now have a scar across his face for the rest of his life. As a consequence, the gang members on the outside had been ordered to blast the cop, sending the message that no-one could mess with them and survive.

Four of them had just arrived, others on their way, all dressed in baggy jeans, hooded sweatshirts and carrying pistols or sub-machine guns, each eager to put this guy down to regain respect. As one of the men went round to the rear of the apartment and another started to climb up to the balcony, Ortega slid a bump key into the lock on the door to the entrance, then tapped it gently with the underside of his machine pistol, jacking it open.

He stepped inside the building, securing the lock to stop it closing. Pulling the cocking handle on his Uzi, he racked a round, thirty two of them in the magazine and one now in the chamber.

Then he started to climb the stairs.

April was in Archer's bedroom, putting her few belongings into a brown Trader Joe's bag. Next door in the kitchen, Archer was tucking some foodstuffs and bottles of water into a holdall, distracted and working on autopilot.

Closing the cupboard, he zipped up the bag and hooked the strap over his shoulder, ready to go. Remembering his bulletproof vest, he headed towards the sitting area where it was resting on the couch; considering how today had been going, it would be foolish not to strap it on again.

But he stopped in his tracks. The apartment was so quiet he heard a sound so faint it was almost imperceptible, one he would have missed if there had been any other noise at all.

Swinging round and forgetting about the vest, he looked for the source and found it.

His eyes focused on the door handle.

It was the sound of a key being slid very slowly into the front lock.

Then there was a *click*.

Hitting the key with the butt of his weapon, Ortega twisted the handle a split-second later and kicked the door back with a *thump*.

Moving inside, he raised his sub-machine gun as he and one of his men who'd followed him up the stairs moved into the apartment, the two men sweeping left and right, their fingers on the triggers.

Behind the kitchen counter, having ducked down a split-second before the door was kicked open, Archer cursed to himself, realising he was unarmed, his Sig confiscated and his home defence gun hidden in the bathroom.

Knowing he only had seconds before whoever it was found him, he edged around the counter that ran between the hallway and kitchen and saw two men reflected in the balcony window, each heavily built and each holding an Uzi.

Shit, shit, shit!

Thinking fast, he silently eased open a drawer next to him, inch by painful inch, praying it wouldn't make any noise and watching the two men's reflections as they separated and started to check the apartment.

He reached in carefully for anything in the drawer he could use as a weapon. He touched the handle of a small, sharp-bladed knife; curling his fingers around it he quietly pulled it out. He hated knives both to use and being used against him, but right now it was either that or a fish slice.

Staying low, he saw the man nearest to him was about to round the corner of the unit he was hiding behind.

He tensed, ready to spring.

But then April opened the bedroom door down the corridor.

Watching their reflections in the window, he saw the two men swing round, aiming their weapons straight at her as she dropped her bag of clothes.

'Hey!' Archer shouted, rearing up.

Taken by surprise, the two men twisted back round just as the Archer leapt over the counter and buried the knife in the chest of the guy closest to him.

As the man shouted in pain and his partner raised his Uzi, Archer shoved the man he'd stabbed into the other guy then dove back behind the counter as the uninjured guy pulled the trigger.

The assault from the weapon was both sudden and extremely violent, wood, plastic and brick ripped to shreds as he fired wildly. However, the guy made the classic mistake with an automatic weapon, draining the clip with just one pull in his desperation to score a hit.

As soon as the deafening fire stopped, Archer ignored the ringing in his ears and grabbed his opportunity, hurdling the counter once again and smashing into the guy just as he reloaded and cocked the gun. Archer caught hold of the man's arms, driving them up but avoiding touching the weapon to save his hands from being burned.

'Pendejo!' the guy snarled, before pulling the trigger again, the rounds hitting the ceiling.

Head-butting him, Archer pushed the gun round while holding the man's finger down on the trigger. The gunman took a burst, dropping as if his strings had been cut, the gun falling from his grasp as he hit the ground and joined his companion, both men dead.

With every sense on high alert, Archer kicked the front door shut, then swiftly bent down and retrieved one of the dead guys' Uzis, the gun powder in the air filling his nostrils and stinging his eyes. Both were brown-skinned men Archer had never seen before, gang members, one with four teardrops tattooed on his face, two under each eye, and the other with inking all over his neck. Not *Prizraki* Russians, and definitely not Henderson or Tully.

The same inking as his attackers in Rikers.

His hearing gradually starting to return after the gunfire, Archer looked down the corridor at April to make sure she was OK.

But she wasn't looking at him.

Alerted by the expression on her face, he spun round to see a Latino guy in jeans and a hoodie on the balcony, raising a shotgun from the other side of the glass and aiming it directly at him.

'Move!' Archer shouted.

As he ducked back into the kitchen and April threw herself into Isabel's bedroom, the shotgun blast annihilated the balcony glass and Archer's bedroom door, the guy racking the pump to load another shell. Leaning around the damaged counter, Archer fired a quick burst back, his aim far better and more controlled than the dead gang-member's; the rounds clipped the gunman in the shoulder and knocked him to the ground, the guy dragging himself out of sight before Archer could fire again.

As Archer went to move forward after him, the front door suddenly slammed back and a heavily-built Latino guy smashed into the apartment. Archer spun and pulled the trigger but the weapon clicked dry; hurling it at the gunman which bought him a precious second, he launched himself forward, knocking the larger man off balance.

The guy fired his handgun, ripping up the wall while trying to turn the gun on Archer, but Archer hit him hard, using all his strength to slam the man's hand into the wall and knock the gun free, sending it skittering across the floor. Terrified, April peered out from Isabel's bedroom and gasped in horror as Archer's attacker retaliated by slamming him into the wall with brutal force. As they smashed into the kitchen, Archer realised he was in trouble. Adrenaline had kicked in, giving his exhausted muscles survival strength, but this guy was far stronger than him and was just as pumped up.

Ducking under an arcing elbow that would have knocked him out, Archer fired a vicious left hook to the man's body, a liver shot. Done right, it completely incapacitates an opponent, causing their body to shut down, rendering them incapable until they could breathe again. However, the guy had spare ammo magazines in his pocket, which not only protected him from the blow but smashed Archer's knuckles as he threw the punch.

As he instinctively recoiled in pain, the man sunk in a crushingly powerful rear choke, tightening the squeeze around Archer's neck. Archer desperately tried to fight his way out of it, clutching at the enormous forearm locked under his chin, fighting to loosen the hold and feeling the squeeze tighten so hard it felt as if his neck was going to break.

Seeing Archer caught in the choke-hold, April darted forward and picked up his attacker's pistol. Straightening, she aimed the weapon at the two men, her hand shaking.

However, she couldn't pull the trigger; Archer was in direct line of fire, the bigger man behind him as he strangled the blond cop.

About to pass out, Archer frantically motioned with his hand to April.

Realising what he wanted she threw the gun towards him, which he caught grip first.

A second later he put the barrel to the gang member's thigh and fired.

A distance shot from a 9mm handgun would produce a severe injury but up close it was catastrophic. The giant screamed like a stuck pig, instantly releasing Archer and falling to the floor, clutching his leg as he started to bleed out, staring in shock at the blood pumping from the wound.

Staggering forward as he sucked in oxygen, Archer stood for a few moments waiting for the room to stop spinning then moved towards April, the sudden quiet filled by the sounds of dogs barking from down the street, the stench of gun-smoke and cordite hanging in the air.

'We have to get the hell out of here!' he said, taking her hand and pulling her towards the front door, blood running down his arm from the re-opened wound.

However, before they could make it something was thrown into the room from the balcony.

It came through the smashed gap where the window used to be and rolled straight towards them.

As April stared in scared puzzlement, Archer's eyes widened.

He immediately dragged her into the bathroom, shoving her into the tub and throwing himself on top of her just as the grenade came to a stop in the hallway.

A beat later the explosion was so loud it seemed to shake the entire world, blowing out every piece of glass in the apartment, setting parts of it on fire.

The wounded gang member moved cautiously through the blown-apart space where the balcony glass used to be, looking down the sights of his weapon and treading carefully through the smoke, looking for his targets and seeing three of his friends down, two dead and the third bleeding out on the kitchen floor.

There was no sign of the cop or the woman.

Rolling out low from behind the bathroom door, still deaf from the blast, Archer shot the guy in the chest with his home defence pistol, hitting him twice and watching as the man dropped to the floor, joining his three friends.

Bleeding, smoke-covered, his clothing partially torn and with his hearing severely affected, Archer staggered to his feet, four bodies laid out in his apartment around him, part of the floor destroyed and sections on fire. Moving forward, he knelt down by the first guy he'd shot and patted him down, pulling out his wallet quickly, wanting to check his ID the moment they got out of here.

Ready to leave, he turned and saw April had staggered out of the bathroom, bleeding from her temple.

'You OK?' he asked her.

She nodded, still half-deaf and only guessing what he'd said, giving him a thumbs up but still badly disorientated. Taking hold of her, Archer half-carried her out of the apartment while keeping his pistol up in front of him as they made their way down the steps.

Their ears ringing, the pair bloodied and covered with dust and smoke, they reached the ground floor and moved to the entrance, the front door ajar. Easing it back an inch, Archer used the fob to unlock the Ford from where he stood, the lights flashing.

He looked down at April.

'Ready?' he asked her quickly.

She nodded.

A moment later he ripped open the door and they began to run.

FORTY TWO

Inside the back office of the club on Brighton Beach, Shepherd was studying CCTV footage from the club's security system. Next door, medical teams had just arrived and checked the three bodies but there was nothing they could do, all three men dead from gunshot wounds, one to the neck and the other two to the head. The shootings had taken place when the NYPD were in the club, yet none of them had heard a thing.

Back-up officers were outside scouring the crowds whilst Shepherd and Hendricks were focused on finding Bashev, who according to the bar-staff had last been seen heading back to his office before the shooting happened. Watching the playback, Shepherd's attention was drawn to sudden movement recorded by the camera covering the back of the club.

As he leaned closer and watched the action unfold, Hendricks and Massaro suddenly reappeared from a door leading from a cellar, accompanied by a male and female member of Hendricks' team.

'I'm guessing he went this way,' he said. 'Son of a bitch. We must have just missed him.'

'But he didn't get far,' Shepherd said, pointing at the monitor he'd been studying and resetting the recording back a few minutes. 'Check it out.'

The five detectives watched, seeing a burly figure carrying a briefcase moving rapidly towards a car, pulling out his keys and unlocking the doors, tossing the case inside.

However, before he had a chance to get into the car, he was suddenly pistol-whipped from behind, two men appearing from out of the frame.

'Son of a bitch,' Massaro muttered.

The group watched in silence as Henderson pinned Bashev to the ground, holding something over his face. Tully ripped open the side of a van and both men dumped the now limp Russian inside. They saw Henderson retrieve the briefcase from the car then a silenced pistol from the sidewalk before pulling off his coat, tossing it into the van and jumping inside, the vehicle taking off a moment later and disappearing out of frame.

'Bet he's wishing he'd stayed around for us right about now,' Hendricks said.

Shepherd nodded, pulling his cell to pass on the plates to Ethan. 'They killed the last of the gang here, right under our goddamn noses. And with Bashev gone, that's every member of his gang wiped out.'

'So what's driving this?' one of Hendricks's team asked, looking at the screen. 'Are Henderson and Tully looking to move in on the turf down here?'

'Just two of them?' Massaro replied. 'They wouldn't last five minutes.'

'Plus they must have known they were on camera when they took Bashev but for some reason they didn't give a shit,' Hendricks said, tapping the screen.

'They know we'll have them from when they went for April and Archer in the bar and Park,' Shepherd said. 'They must be bailing. With three more *Prizraki* dead and taking Bashev with them,

I'm guessing they've done what they wanted to do.'

'But without that escort?' Massaro said. 'After all that effort you told me about to track her down?'

Shepherd looked at the detective. Then, cursing himself at letting her leave the Bureau, he ended his call to Ethan before it could connect and quickly dialled Archer instead.

'No-one else dies tonight,' he said. 'No-one. Not on my watch.'

Eight miles north, Archer was burning his way through to the Queensborough Bridge, the fender lights on the car flashing as he headed for the safe-house. Turning a hard right, April holding onto her seat as the car slid around the corner, he reached into his pocket and pulled out the wallet he'd taken, tossing it to her.

'Who is he?' he asked.

'Raul Ortega,' she said after a moment, reading from his driver's license. 'Born in Juarez, Mexico. Thirty three years old. I don't understand? Did Henderson and Tully hire them to kill you?'

Archer shook his head.

'He had the same gang ink as some of the guys in Rikers. They must have been sent to take me out. Probably as payback.'

As they raced on towards the Bridge, Archer saw queuing traffic up ahead and was forced to slow, checking his rear view mirror for anyone chasing him down. Just then, the intercom inside the car that had synced with Archer's phone started to ring; glancing at the screen, he saw it was Shepherd.

'How the hell did they know where your apartment was?' April asked, looking at him.

Archer glanced at her as he pushed the button to answer Shepherd; she had a point.

But instead of replying, he grabbed the back of her jacket and suddenly pulled her down a second before her window exploded.

Walking out of the nightclub with Hendricks whose team were handling the scene along with CSU, Shepherd looked down at his phone and frowned. Archer wasn't picking up. He glanced at Hendricks beside him but saw his focus was elsewhere, his eyes narrowed.

Following his gaze, Shepherd saw four officers walking towards them, having just climbed out of two squad cars that had pulled up. He also saw they had their holsters unclipped, their right hands lingering near their weapons. Thinking back four weeks, Shepherd recalled seeing the same officers at the 114th; some of Royston's men.

'No need for that,' Hendricks said. 'The action's over.'

'You're right,' one of them said, looking at Shepherd as he spoke. 'It is. For you.'

'Excuse me?'

'You're under arrest.'

'What?' Shepherd said.

'Apparently you assaulted Lieutenant Royston; you're coming with us, sir.'

Shepherd thought back to when he'd slammed the piece of paper and pen into the Lieutenant's chest. He shot a glance at Hendricks, then focused on the men standing in front of him.

'Are you kidding me?'

'No, we're not. You assaulted a superior. We've been ordered to bring you in.'

'He's not going anywhere,' Hendricks said.

'Yes, he is. Right now, he's under arrest.'

The two sergeants and four officers stood facing each other, the body language of Royston's men confident, fed by the knowledge they were acting under the orders of a superior officer. As they faced each other, Hendricks' hand casually slid towards his holster in case they suddenly decided to pull their weapons as extra persuasion.

Stepping forward, the lead officer took out his hand-cuffs. 'Don't make this any harder than it has to be.'

'Try and put those on him and you'll be heading for the ER,' Hendricks replied.

The words were said quietly but with absolute conviction. The officers all hesitated, but only briefly, the fact they were four against two giving them false confidence.

And then they made their move.

Two of them went to grab hold of Shepherd, but seconds later were lying on the ground, one with a busted nose, the other stunned after taking an elbow to the side of the head. The other two went to draw their guns but Hendricks stepped forward and hammered a punch into one man's gut, doubling him over.

The last officer managed to pull his sidearm but Hendricks caught his arm. A split-second later the officer took a straight right to the face and fell back to the concrete, joining his three companions. As they stood over the four men, the fight over almost before it had begun, Shepherd's cell rang and he answered immediately.

315

'Arch?'

'No sir, it's me,' Ethan said. *'But it's to do with Archer. Teams of officers have been dispatched to 38th Street in Astoria. There've been reports of multiple gunshots and an explosion.'*

'What? That's Archer's street.'

'Apparently a police car left the scene shortly after the reports of a disturbance were called in. A blond man driving, accompanied by a woman.'

'But Henderson and Tully were here.'

'There are four dead gang members at Archer's apartment. All Latino's, with gang colours and ink.'

Shepherd swore and ran towards his car.

'It's probably the same crew who tried to drop him in Rikers,' Shepherd said, looking at Hendricks who was keeping pace with him. 'He'll be going for the safe-house. Give me the address, Ethan.'

'It's in the West Village, sir,' Ethan said, handing over the specifics.

Hanging up, Shepherd pulled open his door and jumped behind the wheel.

'We need to get over to the Village. Archer and the girl got jumped by some gang members at his apartment. He's in deep shit.'

'Now there's a surprise,' Hendricks replied, climbing into the passenger seat as Shepherd fired the engine and took off down the street.

On the Queensborough, one of the Latinos who'd been late getting to 38th Street and seen the cop drive off with the woman caught up with Archer's car and fired again, blasting off a wing mirror and shattering the remaining glass. As the guy racked the pump, Archer fired twice over

316

April's back, hitting the driver in the shoulder and knocking him backwards, pulling ahead as his attackers' car started to swerve.

Flooring it, Archer swung the wheel round and headed straight into the oncoming traffic, speeding past the cars that had been stopped by the roadblock. Glancing in the rear-view mirror he saw two cars peeling off and give chase, but focused his attention on the road ahead, dodging the oncoming traffic, car horns blaring as the police car missed them by inches.

'You OK?' he asked April, who'd sat back up in her seat, gripping onto her door for support, wind whipping her hair round her face from her broken window.

'I think so!'

As Archer continued to weave his way through the traffic, he tried to call Shepherd back on the car's system, but it was fried, having been hit by the shotgun blast which had annihilated April's window.

Then his cell started ringing. He went to answer but had to duck as they took more fire from the car behind.

Forgetting the call for the moment, he focused on his driving, fighting to keep ahead of the two cars now right on his tail.

In Little Odessa, Marquez and Massaro walked out of the nightclub just in time to see Shepherd and Hendricks taking off in one of the Bureau's Fords, the 4x4 heading into Brooklyn. They were surprised to see three cops getting to their feet beside their squad cars, all looking the worse for wear, a fourth leaning against the side of the vehicle.

317

'What the hell happened?' she asked the guy leaning against the car as she and Massaro walked over.

Ignoring her, he pressed down a button on his radio receiver.

'This is Spilner. He resisted arrest, sir,' he reported, turning his head to spit blood onto the concrete street. 'Both he and Sergeant Hendricks assaulted us and drove off.'

'Where were they headed?'

'North. We should be able to tag their plates on the CCTV.'

'I know where they'll be going. Follow my instructions and you'll find them. I'm sending back-up; do whatever you have to do to bring them in. Understood?'

'Copy that,' the man said, turning towards the squad car as Marquez and Massaro watched in confusion, the other three clambering to their feet and moving unsteadily towards their vehicles.

'I don't think they're going anywhere in a hurry,' Massaro said.

FORTY THREE

When Bashev came to, the first thing that hit his senses was the sound of running water.

Opening his eyes, blinking to clear his vision, he saw he was lying in the white-walled bathroom of an apartment he didn't recognise. There was a strip of duct tape pulled tight across his mouth. He tried to move his arms, but realised they were bound behind his back, tightly zipped plasti-cuffs digging into his wrists.

Turning his head, he saw two men dressed in white overalls pouring liquid into a bathtub from canisters, a blonde woman sitting on a chair watching them.

The moment he saw her, Bashev blinked again, trying to focus, convinced he was seeing a ghost.

But as his vision cleared and he stared at her in disbelief, his blood turned to ice; he knew now that he was in seriously deep shit.

After a few moments the two men straightened, putting down the canisters they'd just emptied; then the woman spoke.

'You need to get over there right now. They'll arrive any minute.'

'The Mexicans didn't get it done?'

'No. But you will. Do them both. We don't need her.'

As the pair left the room, the Russian *vor* continued to stare at the woman, still unable to believe it was her. Once the other two were gone, she rose and walked forward until she was standing over him.

'Hi honey,' she said. 'Did you miss me?'

With the duct tape over his mouth, Bashev couldn't have replied even if he'd wanted to. Suddenly, everything that had been happening to his men over the past few months made sense.

He stared up at her, his stomach starting to churn with fear as the woman knelt down and looked him directly in the eyes. Then she reached into a pocket and pulled out a butterfly knife. She flicked her wrist, the blade snapping out, and stabbed down hard into his leg. Bashev jerked and screamed in pain, the sound muffled under his gag. As he stared down in horror at the knife jutting from his thigh, the woman twisted the blade slowly, Bashev continuing to scream under his gag as the wound opened.

'It won't close now. I'd say you have about an hour before you die from blood loss. But as much as I'd enjoy watching you die slowly I don't have time to wait, so we'd better speed this up. You're going in that tub alive but I can't have you thrashing around.'

Pulling a silenced pistol, she racked a round and pushed him over onto his side.

'You should have broken my wrists, you son of a bitch,' she told him, aiming the gun at his lower back.

Across the city, Shepherd and Hendricks were just approaching the address of the West Village safe-house, Shepherd's concern for Archer getting them there in almost record time.

Pulling to a halt in the West Village street, the two men stepped out of the car, Shepherd double-checking the address on his cell phone. As Hendricks went to the back of the Ford, opened the trunk and retrieved their shotguns, Shepherd looked around for any sign of Archer. He couldn't see his Ford but then again from the sound of what had happened in Queens, the car may well have taken some gunfire so Archer wouldn't want to draw any unnecessary attention and would probably have parked it in the basement or somewhere else out of sight.

After Hendricks slammed the trunk shut, he tossed Shepherd one of two Mossbergs, and the two men approached the building, Shepherd gaining them access on the key pad by using a six digit code Ethan had texted him earlier. It had no residents at the moment, the conversion of the building from office space to apartments only just having been completed. The NYPD had taken advantage of that, buying one of the apartments as soon as it became available as a secure new safe-house.

Once inside, Shepherd eased the door shut behind him and the two men made their way up the stairs, moving fast, the building eerily quiet. Arriving outside the 4th floor apartment, Shepherd knocked on the door.

'Arch? It's Shepherd and Hendricks.'

Nothing.

'Arch?'

Shepherd looked at Hendricks, who tried the door. It was locked. Stepping back, he smashed it open and the two men entered the apartment.

It was empty.

'Shit; he didn't make it yet,' Shepherd said, pulling his cell. As he went to dial Archer's number, they both heard the sound of vehicles pulling up outside, the quick screech of tyres followed by the noise of car doors opening and closing.

Both men moved quickly to the window, expecting to see the blond detective and the escort getting out of his car.

However, instead they saw a team of officers in protective combat gear and helmets carrying assault rifles stepping out of black 4x4 Escalades, gathering in a group outside the building.

It was ESU, the NYPD's SWAT team.

His phone to his ear, Shepherd glanced at Hendricks. 'Back-up. They got here fast.'

Hendricks didn't reply. Swinging away from the window, he looked around the room then strode quickly towards the NYPD radio found in each safe-house, switched it on and re-tuned the frequency.

'ESU 2 in position.'

'Ethan, it's me,' Shepherd said, turning and starting to head towards the door. 'I need you to trace the GPS on Archer's car for me.'

However, before he could reach the door Hendricks caught him by the arm, stopping him.

'What is it?' Shepherd asked.

'Suspects are armed and extremely dangerous,' a voice over the radio said, replying for Hendricks. *'Use whatever force necessary. Both men have assaulted NYPD officers.'*

Shepherd stared at the radio, frowning. 'What the hell?'

The two men looked at each other.

Then they suddenly realised what was happening.

Outside the building, Sergeant Michael Hicks gave the thumbs up and his team moved forward. Quickly keying in the six digit code, the ten man team flowed inside, heading immediately for the stairs.

Hicks had been an officer in ESU 2 until six months ago when the entire ESU 1 team had been killed in an operation uptown in Harlem that had gone badly wrong; the team had been replaced and Hicks promoted to Sergeant to command it. The promotion had been bittersweet due to the circumstances; as a consequence, those who perpetrated cop-on-cop violence now ranked alongside rapists and child molesters as far as he was concerned, and these bastards had just put down four 114th officers as well as assaulting a lieutenant.

Third in line, Hicks nodded to his point man and they took the stairs, the ten armed men moving quickly and quietly up towards the 4th floor.

'Son of a bitch!' Shepherd said inside 4D, staring at Hendricks incredulously. 'He sent an entire ESU team after us? What bullshit did he tell them?'

'You said Archer's on his way here?'

'If he even makes it. Ethan said he had people after him when he fled Astoria. We have to find him before that gang does. He's protecting the girl with no back-up.'

'You heard the radio. These boys are here to take us in; we'll be taken downtown and held until God knows when.'

Shepherd looked at his colleague and closest friend as they both realised their minimal options.

'That's not going to happen,' Shepherd said quietly.

Hendricks nodded. 'No. It's not.'

The two men continued to look at each other for a moment, both understanding the potential consequences of what they were about to do.

Then they moved.

As Shepherd headed to the door, ending the call to Ethan and holding his Mossberg, Hendricks traced the wall, looking for the fuse box to the apartment. Finding it in a wall cupboard to the left of the entrance, he aimed his shotgun above the box.

He pulled the trigger, the Mossberg booming, the air filled with plaster and pieces of debris as three thick cables were exposed.

Racking the pump he fired again; a moment later the power cut out in the building, shrouding the place in darkness.

FORTY FOUR

On the stairwell between the 2nd and 3rd floors, the ESU 1st team heard the two gunshots a moment before they were suddenly plunged into darkness.

Despite being caught off-guard, they reacted quickly, flicking on the flashlights attached to the end of their assault rifles before continuing to move up the stairs, the light breaking up the gloom, particles of dust visible in their beams. They all shared Hicks' view of people who perpetrated violence on cops and would have no issue putting these two bastards down, badges or not.

Arriving on the fourth floor, Hicks motioned to two of his men to continue to the floors above, to check each one in case the two sergeants had seen them arrive and moved up.

As the two officers continued upwards, the eight remaining members of the ESU team moved down the corridor, four of them continuing past the apartment to cover the stairs at the other end.

Coming to a halt outside the apartment, Hicks took point, seeing the door was slightly ajar.

Raising his foot, he kicked it back hard and snapped his AR-15 up into the aim.

The two members of the team sent upstairs arrived on the 5th floor, following Hicks' orders to carry out a sweep.

Easing their way out of the stairwell, they moved quietly into the long corridor, tracing as they walked, the building quiet.

Then they heard a low whistle immediately behind them.

Both men snapped round, straight into the stocks of two shotguns that smashed into their goggles, rocking their heads back and knocking one of them clean out. As he dropped, stunned, Hendricks ripped the AR15 out of the man's hands, but the officer's finger was already off the trigger. His companion staggered from the blow from Shepherd and managed to regain his balance, but before he had time to react, Shepherd restrained him in a needle and thread choke, quickly rendering the officer unconscious.

Once he was out Shepherd lowered him to the ground carefully. The two sergeants used the downed officers' own zip-tie handcuffs to restrain them then kicked their weapons out of reach, Hendricks taking a couple of stun grenades from the front of one man's uniform.

They suddenly froze as they heard someone coming up the stairwell.

'Shit!' Shepherd whispered, he and Hendricks taking off for the stairwell at the other end of the corridor. Just as they made it to the stairs, a light suddenly appeared from behind them.

'Freeze!' a voice bellowed.

Shepherd and Hendricks dived into the stairwell a split-second before the ESU officers fired, the stitched burst from their weapons missing the pair by a fraction of an inch.

Racing after them, the four men almost fell over their two unconscious colleagues on the floor.

'Suspects sighted!' the lead man radioed to Hicks as he bent to check the two men. 'East stairwell, 5th floor. Siler and Morris are down.'

'*Dead?*' Hicks asked.

'Out cold,' he said, feeling a pulse in both men before rising.

Continuing to the end of the corridor, the four officers snapped out into the stairwell, finding the place shrouded in thick black smoke, pumping out of a smoke grenade somewhere on the floor and filling the stairwell.

'I can't see shit!' the lead officer reported to Hicks.

'Stay there. We're on our way.'

Releasing the pressel on his radio after making the transmission, Hicks led the three remaining ESU officers down the corridor, the men moving quickly towards the stairs, smoke flowing down the stairwell and into the corridor.

As his point man arrived by the stairwell door, Hicks suddenly clicked his fingers, his men snapping back. Bellick had gone quiet.

'Bellick, what's your status?' Hicks spoke quietly into his mic.

No response.

'Bellick?'

Nothing.

Cursing under his breath, he looked up into the mist of the dark stairwell.

Just as he heard the sound of something rolling down the stairs.

Reacting instantly, Hicks ducked back, covering his ears and turning away from the door to the stairwell, but the three men in front of him weren't as fast.

The disorientated officers in the stairwell on the 5th floor had been relatively easy to put down and were now lying zip-tied and unconscious on the landing, the smoke from the grenade still swirling around them. Hendricks and Shepherd waited for the flash-bang to go off and then moved rapidly down the stairwell through the smoke, ready to secure the remaining ESU officers.

Three of them were stunned and disorientated, two on the stairwell floor and the other bent double, leaning against the wall. Hendricks moved forward and quickly cuffed the three guys, then he and Shepherd lifted their Mossbergs and moved forward to find the fourth man.

As soon as both appeared in the corridor, there were two rapid gunshots. Both men shouted in pain as they took a hit, Shepherd knocked back against the wall and cursing as he clutched his arm, Hendricks taking one to the thigh, swearing as he fell to the floor.

'Put your weapons down!' a voice suddenly ordered through the smoke, a beam of light slicing through it. *'Do it or I'll fire again, I swear to God!'*

Holding his arm, Shepherd saw Jake had dropped his shotgun and was on the floor clutching his leg; with no choice, he placed his Mossberg carefully on the floor in front of him.

The last member of the ESU stepped forward and easing round the two injured men, shut the door to the stairwell, stopping the flow of smoke.

Letting go of his wounded arm for a moment to slowly shield his eyes, Shepherd could just make out the stripes on the man's shoulder, meaning this guy was their sergeant.

Peering closer at the man's face as he turned, he recognised him instantly. 'Hicks?'

The ESU Sergeant paused then looked closer at the two men he'd just shot.

'Shep?' Pause. 'What the hell are you two doing here? We had a report a pair of NYPD sergeants had gone rogue. They didn't say it was you.'

'Listen to me,' Shepherd said urgently. 'I didn't assault Lieutenant Royston. He made up some bullshit charge and sent his men to Brighton Beach to bring us both in.'

'Did you put them down?' Hicks asked, keeping his AR-15 up.

'We had to,' Hendricks answered. 'No way were they going to let us go. One of our detectives was killed tonight. Archer's going to join her if we don't get to him right now.'

In the light from the torches on the fallen mens' weapons, Shepherd saw Hick's eyes narrow.

Hicks lowered his gun a fraction. 'Sam Archer? The guy from the Harlem building?'

'That's right. And the detective who died was Alice Vargas. She was in there with him that night.'

'C'mon man, make a decision.' Hendricks said through gritted teeth, holding his thigh. 'We need to move. And I could use a Band-Aid.'

Hicks didn't reply, still keeping his rifle on the pair.

Then he slowly lowered it and the tension immediately eased.

'Where's Archer?' he asked, stepping forward and dropping down to examine the wound on Hendricks' leg.

'He should have been here by now.' Wincing, Shepherd released his arm and pulled his cell. 'I'll have one of our analysts trace his car. No point chasing around the city until we know where he is,'

'Shit, I don't think you guys are going anywhere except the ER,' Hicks said, looking at the wound on Hendricks' thigh.

Hendricks shook his head. 'No way. Help me up.'

Shepherd and Hicks moved either side of him, hoisting him back to his feet; Hendricks gritted his teeth.

'Christ, Hicks,' he grunted. 'You owe us a beer.'

'I only clipped you.'

'Much appreciated.'

Once Shepherd was supporting Hendricks' weight, Hicks pulled a knife and cut the binds on the three unconscious ESU officer's wrists, Shepherd propping Hendricks up as he pulled his phone and called the Bureau.

'Ethan, it's me. Where does Archer's GPS put him?' Shepherd asked, putting his cell on speaker.

'Heading south from Central Park North, sir. I think he's taking her to the safe-house on 66th Street.'

'Has he taken any more fire?'

'There've been no more reports but I don't know.'

Kneeling by his three unconscious men and hearing the transmission, Hicks looked up. 'You'd better get moving and back him up.'

He rose, ready to go upstairs and check on the others.

'If I was you, I wouldn't want to be here when these guys wake up.'

After weaving his way through Manhattan, eventually making it to the west side, Archer had managed to shake his and April's pursuers. He'd just parked in the basement of the building of another Department safe house on 66th Street, a stone's throw from Columbus Circle, somewhere their attackers wouldn't know to find them.

He and April walked quickly across the car park, heading towards the door to the stairs, Archer with his pistol in his hand. Ducking into the stairwell, he checked back quickly to make sure no one had seen them enter, then moved into the stairwell, keeping April right behind him. He needed to get them into the safe-house before anything else happened. The place was equipped with everything he'd need to protect them until back-up arrived.

Arriving on the third floor, he moved down the corridor then drew the keys and unlocked the door, feeling his phone ring in his pocket.

Looking down, he reached into his jeans for it as he opened up.

A moment later, something hit him over the back of the head hard, knocking him to the floor. As April screamed Archer tried to get back to his feet but Tully was on him, clamping a chloroform rag to his mouth with his good hand, burying his knee in his back as Archer resisted.

'No! Get off him!' April shouted, running forward to try and pull Tully away.

However an arm suddenly snaked around her waist and pulled her back, another rag clamped over her mouth by Henderson as he kicked the door shut behind him. Archer was fighting to rise, but this time Tully had the advantage, clamping the chemicals to his nose.

Doing everything he could to fight him off,
Archer involuntarily inhaled.

Then everything went black.

FORTY FIVE

The purring vibration of his cell phone in his pocket roused him from unconsciousness.

Archer opened his eyes and saw he was lying on his side. He could hear liquid being poured into something the other side of the door, a strong chemical smell hitting his nose. He fought the fog in his brain, trying to focus and get his bearings, and then he saw April lying a few feet from him, similarly tied up with a strip of tape across her mouth.

She'd already come round and was staring at him, looking terrified. He fought with the binds on his wrists but they were zipped tight behind him.

The door directly in front of him opened and he found himself looking up at Henderson, his face partially busted up from their fight earlier. The large man stood in the doorway for a moment, hearing the noise of the vibrating phone, then walked over and knelt down beside Archer, pulling the phone out of his pocket and looking at the display. Rising, he dropped the Nokia and stamped on it several times with his boot, breaking it to pieces, some of the flying fragments hitting Archer in the face.

From his horizontal position, he could see into the bathroom across the safe-house. Plastic sheeting was covering the bathroom floor; Tully was carefully pouring something into the bath-tub.

'How long?' Henderson asked his partner.

'Almost done.'

Henderson grinned.

'We're going to cut you up first,' he said, looking down at Archer. 'It's not normally our style but after what you and your friend did to Lister we figured we owe you some extra attention.'

Stepping over Archer, Henderson hauled April out into the main room then propped her up against the wall.

'We'll leave the door open so you can watch. Everything we do to him, we're gonna do twice as bad to you.' He laughed. 'You shouldn't have run from us, bitch. We were always going to get you. You've been a real pain in the ass.'

She sat there staring at him, wide-eyed in terror.

Then Henderson walked back to Archer and dragged him feet-first across the apartment towards the tub.

As he was pulled into the bathroom, the stink of the chemicals got much stronger, making his eyes water. Henderson unceremoniously dropped his legs, the plastic sheeting cold under his back.

'We'll be back in a minute,' Henderson said, laughing again. 'Don't go anywhere.'

Then the two men walked out of the room, leaving him on the floor.

Across the apartment, Archer could see April staring at him in terror as he heard the sounds of drawers being opened in the kitchen next door. As he lay there, he knew two things for certain. Number one was he'd been set up by someone at the Bureau, otherwise Henderson and Tully would never have known about this safe-house or that he and April were coming here. Someone must have traced the GPS on his car. Also, Shepherd and Hendricks should have shown up by now, which meant something had gone wrong.

The Latino gang had known where he lived too, which meant they'd also been fed that information.

Lying there on the cold bathroom floor, the room stinking of chemicals, Archer's eyes narrowed as he realised who it had to be, now understanding why Henderson, Tully and Lister had always been a step ahead of them.

The other certainty was he knew he was about to die.

And there wasn't a thing he could do about it.

Inside his office at the 114th Precinct, Royston stared anxiously at his phone and then the radio. He was waiting to hear from ESU to confirm Shepherd and Hendricks were in custody.

He was also waiting to hear confirmation that Archer and the hooker were dead.

Behind the two gadgets on the computer screen was the NYPD's GPS tracing software, the light pinging on 66th where Archer's car had stopped. It was the only safe-house in that part of town; Royston had guessed that was where he'd be going and had sent Henderson and Tully there ahead of him.

The phone and radio just sat there, almost defiant in their silence. He swallowed, feeling panic building inside him, seeing the intricate web of lies threatening to entrap him despite everything he'd done to avoid exactly that. All this shit had started several months ago but had come to a crisis four weeks back when that whore had been shot in the car park. A hooker getting shot wasn't exactly news in New York, but Royston's phone had rung out of the blue the same night, clear orders issued, the fifty-nine year old Lieutenant being made very aware of the consequences if he didn't obey them to the letter.

Once the shooting of Detective Vargas had come to Royston's attention, her file hadn't been the focus; the man who'd been shot alongside her was. Sam Archer possessed a reputation for being an excellent cop as well as a tenacious son of a bitch and that was a major concern for the people blackmailing Royston. Archer and the rest of Shepherd's team were going to be a big problem and these people needed them as far away from the case as possible.

Stall this or you know what the consequences will be, he'd been told.

With everything they had on him, Royston hadn't had a choice.

The shooting had gone down in his Precinct's jurisdiction which was a bonus, meaning he could call the shots. After delaying the investigation as long as he could, Royston had rolled in to work one day to find Shepherd and his team at the 114th Precinct base on Astoria Boulevard. Panic and a survival instinct had kicked in; he'd confronted the group, reckoning attack was the best option and had deliberately provoked Archer, making some dismissive and derogatory comments about Vargas.

It'd worked. Archer had lost the plot and punched him, giving Royston all the ammo he needed to get Archer suspended and out of the picture.

Or so he'd thought. But true to his reputation Archer hadn't let it go, and despite his suspension, had continued to work the case. Biding his time, Royston had had him watched, waiting for him to overstep the mark. He'd hit the jackpot when Archer visited Karen Casey, giving Royston the perfect opportunity to arrest him.

Using the charges already against him and Archer's impending court-date as leverage, he'd arranged a weekend trip to Rikers for the suspended cop, over-ruling the night desk sergeant from the East Village Precinct who'd been uncomfortable with the Lieutenant's decision.

Staring at his phone, Royston continued to sweat, waiting for it to ring. That son of a bitch should never have made it out of Rikers; Royston had used his knowledge of the city's gang hierarchy and paid good money to some people inside for that to be taken care of. But somehow Archer had survived the attack and then been sprung by Jake Hendricks, going on to blow this case wide open with the rest of the Counter-Terrorism team.

Earlier this evening, just when he'd been expecting to hear that Archer had been wasted in Rikers, the call Royston had taken instead was from Lister ordering him to send the addresses of Josh Blake, Lisa Marquez, Matt Shepherd, Jake Hendricks, and Sam Archer to an unknown number. Well aware of what the consequences would be if he disobeyed, he'd sent them only to find out a short time later that a Russian gang from Brighton Beach had tried to kill everyone at two of those addresses.

When he'd heard what had happened, Royston had a sudden flare of hope that the crew who'd been blackmailing him had been killed, but that hope had quickly died once he received another call ordering him to get over to the Counter-Terrorism Bureau and stall the investigation.

He'd done what he could, and in the process had learned the identities of the people blackmailing him, Nicolas Henderson, Sebastian Tully and Nina Lister, although that didn't mean shit. So what; he knew their names. They still had all those photos and videos of him which would ruin his career, not to mention the graphic threats they'd made to his physical well-being.

Before the hooker in the car park had been shot, he'd had no idea Henderson, Tully and Lister had anything on him. Only when they needed him did he find out exactly what they'd done, threatening to release the photos of him with the young escort to the press if he didn't do exactly as instructed. When the shooting had happened, they'd threatened to expose him if he didn't succeed in stalling the investigation. Things had gone into overdrive tonight, orders flowing in constantly, but he knew he was living on borrowed time and couldn't get away with this much longer.

After Vargas had been killed at St Luke's, he knew it was just a matter of time before Shepherd and his team realised how these people had been getting their information and who was responsible. And whatever happened, Henderson and Tully would always have that dirt on him.

Sitting there in his office, his phone and radio resting on the desk but neither still making a sound, something else suddenly dawned on Royston. The call he'd received earlier ordering him to pass over the cops' addresses had come from a woman. He'd assumed she'd been one of the blackmailers he knew now to be Nina Lister.

But she'd been dead by then.

Quietly pulling his side-arm from his desk drawer, he checked the clip and saw it was fully loaded. Looking up and seeing his people working away at their desks, none of them watching him, he leaned forward, focusing on the GPS tracing software, the circle still pinging on 66th, the safe-house.

Taking his cell phone, he looked at the number that had called him and typed it into the system. It was a disposable, so wasn't registered to a name, but it was still active.

And it gave him a result.

Looking at it, he rose, shut down the computer and moved to his door.

He could access the same software from his car, but he'd need to make a pit-stop at home first.

As Archer lay on the floor of the safe-house bathroom, he felt hazy from the fumes of the special sodium hydroxide concoction in the bathtub beside him.

Images started flashing through his mind. He remembered being in the ARU car park three years ago, a Glock in his hand, facing down a terrorist leader and shooting him in the head just before he cut another man's throat. Standing in a New York airfield, having just avenged his father's death. Saving Chalky and his other team mates on a rainy night last year.

And a few months ago in a tall office building, Chalky saving his.

He saw it all, his friends, his family, all that pain and those moments of triumph, those he'd saved and those he'd lost. He saw Shepherd, Marquez and Josh. Cobb, Chalky, Fox and Porter.

Vargas.

And Isabel.

He pictured her lying on that couch in Shepherd's office, bereft and now totally dependent on him, waiting for him to return.

He pictured her face when she was told he was never coming back.

And he felt anger start to build inside him.

As he lay there tied up on the transparent plastic sheets, the two mass-murderers laughing next door and about to re-join him, Archer felt those tight binds behind his back.

And then he realised Henderson and Tully had made three mistakes.

FORTY SIX

Given their track record of murdering so many people without the police having any idea who they were, it was abundantly clear how clinical Henderson and Tully were in their preparation and execution. They never slipped up; they didn't make errors.

However, unbeknownst to them they'd just made three.

They'd bound Archer's wrists with plastic zip-tie cuffs.

They'd tied them behind his back.

And they'd left him alone.

To most people, zip-tie cuffs seem more secure than duct tape. They're quickly and easily applied, taking just a second to hook and cinch versus binding wrists by wrapping tape around them.

However, zip-ties have a weakness. With a certain technique, they can be broken with surprising ease, something Archer had seen done in London at the ARU two months into his time there, a suspect they'd arrested suddenly breaking out of his cuffs and trying to smash his way out of an interrogation cell. Although he'd seen it, Archer had never had tried the technique himself.

Now seemed as good a time as any.

Rolling silently to his knees, Archer leaned forward and lifted his bound hands as high behind his back as his shoulder joints would allow. He then brought them down hard onto his tailbone, forcing each wrist as far apart as he could manage in order to increase the tension on the cuffs.

But the plastic held.

Archer repeated the manoeuvre but again, it didn't work, the only result of his effort being the ties biting into his wrists, causing them to bleed.

Having selected a large cleaver from the drawer in the kitchen, Tully grinned and turned, heading back towards the bathroom, the handle of the blade gripped in his gloved hand.

Arriving in the doorway, he saw the cop was lying where he and Henderson had left him, his hands behind his back.

'I saw your file, Detective,' Tully said. 'I know all about you. The cop who can't be killed.'

He stepped forward, kneeling down in front of Archer, and looked him in the eyes.

'But you know the one thing that all heroes have in common? No matter how good you are, you all have to die someday.'

The binding on his wrists having finally snapped from the third desperate attempt to break them, Archer curled his fingers around the beaker of lye he'd just scooped carefully from the tub and nodded.

'Yeah,' he replied. 'But not tonight.'

A split-second later he whipped the beaker round.

And rearing backwards, he threw the caustic soda directly into Tully's face.

The moment the liquid hit the man's eyes it started to burn; dropping the cleaver, Tully screamed and clutched his face. Jumping to his feet he staggered blindly around the bathroom, stumbling into now-empty canisters, setting them rolling around the floor.

Hearing the commotion, Henderson raced out of the kitchen into the bathroom only to be hit with a gunshot of a straight right punch that broke his nose and turned his legs into two accordions. In a burst of adrenaline-fuelled anger, Archer dipped down, drove his shoulder through the killer's waist as he picked him up and then slammed him through the door into the space beyond.

Still stunned and taken completely off-guard, Henderson tried to pull his pistol, but Archer grabbed his arm and slammed it onto the ground several times, using his elbow to hit the man in the face. The gun slid out of Henderson's grasp but he managed to get his legs back under him, trying to wrestle Archer back and get on top. However, Archer immediately locked up a front headlock, tying up the man's neck and arm, then rolled to his side, taking Henderson with him in a crushing anaconda choke, with his arms pulled in like a vice around the killer's neck. From what the CSU investigator who found Santiago had said, Henderson liked to strangle his victims before they were given their bath; finally, he was getting a taste of his own medicine.

As Tully continued to scream and thrash around the bathroom, Archer increased the pressure on Henderson, the broken zip ties still around his wrists. The larger man tried to resist but quickly started to fade, blood running into his mouth from his busted nose. The adrenaline-soaked pressure Archer created was savage, thoughts of what this man had done to Vargas flashing through his mind, and he held the lock with total ruthlessness until Henderson suffocated and died.

Still screaming in pain in the bathroom and unable to see, Tully pulled his pistol and started firing wildly in all directions. Two bullets hit the wall above the still-bound and gagged April's head and she tipped over to her side in a panic, another going through the wall where her torso had just been.

Letting go of Henderson, Archer threw himself forward, scooped up the dead man's silenced pistol and shot Tully twice in the chest, the two rounds propelling him back into the tub of lye.

He landed with a splash, liquid spilling out of the bathtub and flowing onto the plastic covering the floor. Then just like that, the room was still, the liquid in the bath sloshing around as Tully's head and torso sank under the surface.

A few moments later, the only sound in the safe-house was a hissing coming from the tub.

Moving into the bathroom and scooping up the cleaver Tully had dropped, Archer re-joined April, pulled off her gag and tilted her forward, sawing through her zip-cuffs. The moment she was free she flung her arms around him, crying and shaking in shock as he tossed the blade to one side.

'You OK?' he asked her.

He felt her nod quickly as she clutched him, so scared and relieved she was still alive that she was unable to speak. Archer held her for a few moments then gently disengaged himself and moved over to Henderson's body. He knelt down and went through the man's pockets, pulling out a phone.

Dialling the Bureau quickly, he waited to be connected to Shepherd, keeping his pistol in his other hand as he stared at the two dead killers,

Henderson in a limp heap and only Tully's legs visible, the rest of the man submerged in the lye-filled tub.

'Hello?'

'Sir, it's Archer,' he said, catching his breath.

'Arch? Are you OK?'

'I'm at the safe-house above Columbus. April's OK. But we were set-up.'

'What do you mean?'

'Henderson and Tully were here waiting for us. They're both dead.'

'What? How the hell did they know you'd be going there?'

'I think its Royston, sir; I reckon he's been working with Henderson, Tully and Lister.

'Are you serious?'

'Think about it. He's been stalling this entire investigation from day one; that's why Homicide weren't making any progress. He was always uncooperative and desperate to keep us away from the case; he still is. You saw him earlier when he barged in; he practically gave himself a hernia trying to take charge of it again. He provoked me into a suspension, he had me put in Rikers and I reckon he paid off the Mexicans to take me out then gave them my home address so they could finish the job. And what police lieutenant would close a case-file with so many questions that still needed answering?'

'But why the hell would he do this?'

'I don't know. But it's him; it has to be.'

'Shit, I think you're right. He sent four men to arrest me at Brighton Beach. An ESU team followed soon after. Jake and I both got wounded.'

'He's on the take, sir. I know it.'

Pause.

'Jesus Christ. I'll put the word out. I hope you're not wrong about this, otherwise we'll both be working at McDonalds by the end of the week.'

'I'm sure.'

Stay right where you are. We're on our way.'

'Got it,' Archer said, ending the call and looking at April, who'd heard everything he'd said.

'The Lieutenant?'

Archer nodded. As April stared at him, Archer realised that Henderson would definitely have been in touch with Royston recently, otherwise they never could have known he and April were on their way here.

He tapped into the phone's *Call History*, and saw a number showing up repeatedly, several calls having been made tonight, the last less than an hour ago.

Selecting it, Archer lifted the phone to his ear. If Royston answered, it was proof Archer was right.

'C'mon, fat boy,' he muttered as the call rang. *'Pick up the phone.'*

Across the city, Marquez was driving through Manhattan, heading after Shepherd and Hendricks and having just picked up Palmer on the way. When the detectives had left the Bureau for Little Odessa, Theresa had gone into the city to pursue a lead, but had called Marquez asking her to pick her up so she could re-join the investigation.

In the quiet of the car, Palmer's phone started to ring. Expecting an update from her people, she answered.

'Hello?'

At the safe-house, standing beside Henderson's body, Archer froze in disbelief.

Sitting beside Marquez, Palmer held the phone to her ear.

Listening.

Thinking.

'OK, got it,' she said, ending the call and pocketing the phone.

'Everything OK?' Marquez asked.

'No.' She looked at the female detective. 'Not at all.'

'What are you talking about?'

'Pull over for a second. We need to talk.'

At the safe-house, Archer still hadn't moved.

Because his call hadn't ended yet.

'Answer me, Dean. Do you have the bitch and Archer?' the female voice repeated. *'I just took care of Bashev. He's gone.'*

Archer didn't make a sound, unable to believe what he was hearing.

Who he was hearing.

'Nicolas?' Karen Casey repeated. *'Are Archer and April dead yet?'*

FORTY SEVEN

Standing in the sitting room of her 19th Street East Village apartment, Karen Casey stopped pacing for a moment, her phone clamped to her ear.

'Nic? Talk to me.'

'He's next door,' Henderson finally replied, his voice sounding slightly strange, almost hoarse. *'He's gone.'*

'The girl?'

'She's still alive.'

'We're running out of time,' she said, looking around her apartment. 'Lye him and bring her with you. We're out of here.'

'OK. Where should we meet?'

'Where do you think?' She frowned. 'You OK? You don't sound right.'

'Throat's a bit sore, that's all. The chemicals.'

'Whatever. Get moving. I'll see you at the docks.'

With that Karen hung up, looking around what had been her home for the past year, her late husband almost finished dissolving in the tub and his blood scrubbed away then bleached off the floor.

Her real name wasn't Karen Casey; it was Sasha Bilic. She'd grown up in Moscow but had paid all the money she could scrape together for a passage to the United States seventeen years ago, seeking a different life. She'd been brought in to the New York docks with a load of other young women, but instead of the bright new future they'd hoped for, they were immediately shunted into the sex trade, no documents, no passports; disappearing without trace.

However, Sasha had known that was what was likely to happen and she'd been prepared. That first night, she'd killed her first client, taking the four hundred dollars she'd found in his wallet and then making her escape. That was how she'd made money her first year; she capitalised on her good looks, pretended to be an escort, lured someone to a motel room and then pulled a weapon, robbing them. What were they going to do, go to the cops and tell them they'd been fleeced by a hooker?

She'd zig-zagged her way to Pittsburgh doing the same kind of shit, searching for an opportunity when suddenly, fate had intervened; she'd held up a client and taken his money, but this time she'd been tracked down. However, the guy who found her wasn't after retribution. Instead, he'd wanted to make use of her. That man had been her client's boss and her late husband, Vladimir Bashev.

And he'd offered her a job.

It turned out Vladimir was a member of the *Prizraki*, an organisation with considerable prestige among the Red Mafia underworld. He'd been sent to Pittsburgh from Baltimore with a handful of men to stake their claim in the city. The FBI had destroyed Mafia presence in Pittsburgh a year or so earlier and the *Prizraki* were ready to fill the gap they'd left.

However, they weren't the only gang making moves. One of the major steel mills was being used as cover for a big trafficking operation by the *Suki*, a rival Russian gang. Bashev had lost two of his best guys to them already, and he knew he had to assert his authority and fast. He was also aware his Pittsburgh operation was being watched by the bosses in Moscow and he needed to impress them. Taking over that lucrative steel mill operation would achieve that.

Female involvement in Russian gangs was almost unheard of, a fact Bashev decided he could make work for him. The *Suki* would never guess that Sasha could be *Prizraki*.

So she'd become a hit-girl for the Russian Mafia.

In the eight years she'd worked for the gang, Sasha had either killed or assisted in the death of twenty three *Suki*; as cover, she adopted the name Karen Casey, using a *Prizraki* contact with Bashev's help to create an entire set of fake documents, including a social security number, DMV profile and birth certificate. Pittsburgh PD had no idea what was taking place right under their noses and the FBI had moved on, considering their work in the city done now they'd eradicated the Mafia presence. Or so they'd thought. The bodies of Sasha's victims were never found, buried deep in unmarked graves, most of them still alive when they were put into the coffins; the *Prizraki* tradition.

Karen's big moment had been when she'd taken out the head of the *Suki*. Her fellow *Prizraki* had realised she was the only one of them who stood any chance of getting close to him and even then it had been a massive challenge with enormous risks. However, she'd shown her commitment to the cause, befriending one of the *Suki* member's girlfriends and slowly infiltrating the gang. She'd gradually built up their trust, becoming a familiar face, her good looks helping her ease her way in.

Then she made the ultimate commitment, getting several *Suki* tattoos, all of which helped admit her into the heart of their club on the South-Side where she was given a job as a waitress. That place was the centre of their operation and finally, after many months, she had access to the old man.

As soon as she killed him and back-up took care of the rest, the *Prizraki* had quickly moved in and seized the steel mill trafficking operation. Although Karen's services were then no longer needed, she'd earned enormous respect by then, her dedication and ruthlessness acknowledged by all the men around her. She was also romantically involved with Bashev by the end of the *Suki* operation, and with his help had turned her attention to the trafficking side of the business; she started cherry-picking the very best of the girls that came in through the mill and put them to work in the city, making a huge amount of money very quickly from her high class escort service. The relationship between Vladimir and Karen had intensified and they were granted permission to get married, only allowed due to Bashev's status in the organisation.

However, Vladimir had baggage, a kid from a previous relationship who he'd neither wanted nor cared about but had been forced to house after her mother had died. Leann was as quiet as a mouse and no trouble, the only reason he still kept her around, but he'd gladly handed over the responsibility of her upbringing to Karen, who'd quickly spotted her potential. She'd forced the little bitch to work in her business as soon as Leann reached her fifteenth birthday. Vladimir hadn't objected but was adamant the cops' attention didn't swing onto him in case she got busted, so Leann Bashev became Leann Cascy.

Life had been very, very good. They lived in a great house, had money rolling in and everything was going well.

Then December last year had rolled around.

It had started like any other. Karen had arrived home, dropped her bag and went to the kitchen to grab a bottle of wine. She'd walked into the sitting room to see her husband standing there looking at her. He hadn't said anything, which she'd thought was odd. Unlike his daughter, Bashev was a talker.

Before she could speak, something had hit her hard over the side of the head, knocking her to the floor. She'd woken up some time later in total darkness, hardly able to move. It smelt stale and dank, and was strangely quiet. As she'd moved her head and opened her eyes, her heart started to pound with fear and confusion as she gradually orientated herself and realised what her husband had done.

He'd buried her alive.

Inside the safe-house, Archer hung up quietly, staring at the phone.

'What's wrong?' April asked.

'It's Karen,' he said quietly. 'It's Karen Casey.'

'What are you talking about?'

'It's Karen Casey. That was her answering the phone. She was asking if you and I were dead yet.'

'Karen? It can't be. She's Leann's mother.'

Putting the phone down, Archer thought for a moment, looking over at Henderson. The dead

352

man was lying on his back but in their fight, his sweater had ridden up.

And Archer could see the edge of a tattoo.

Moving over, he pulled it up, looking at the man's skin. As he looked, he suddenly had a flashback three days earlier to Karen Casey's apartment. When she'd been making some tea for him, she'd reached up to take a cup out of a cupboard and he'd caught a glimpse of a tattoo on her lower back.

Henderson had an identical one on his chest.

Hauling the sweater right up, Archer saw he also had two stars on his shoulders. Taking the man's phone, he snapped a photo of the tattoo then messaged it to Ethan's email at the Bureau, calling him as soon as he'd sent it. While he waited for Ethan to answer, things started to drop into place.

Leann's arrival in the city last year with her mother; members of the Russian gang starting to disappear around the same time. Leann trying to escape from her life of prostitution.

Archer's arrest on Friday, just after he finished talking to Karen.

Henderson and Tully showing up on the Upper East Side bar to get April, minutes after she'd called Karen asking for help.

The Prizraki *have only lost one man in the past few years,* Hendricks had said earlier.

Their top guy.

'Arch?'

'I just sent you a photo,' he said. 'It's of a tattoo on Henderson's chest. I need you to find out what gang it's from.'

'Wait.' Pause. *'I know that already.'*

'How?'

'Massaro sent over a Russian Mafia file earlier for a point of reference. That's a gang tattoo from a crew called the Suki. *It means bitches, literally, in Russian.'*

'That's their gang name?'

'Apparently it was given to them after the Second World War. When the Soviet Union needed more men on the frontline during the war, Stalin offered a pardon for any prisoner who fought. A load stepped up but then Stalin went back on his word once the fighting was over. These guys were thrown back into their cells; the guys who hadn't fought, following the strict Thieves Law of not joining the military, dubbed them bitches, or Suki. *I guess these guys kept the name.'*

'Henderson, Tully and Lister are from Pittsburgh. Is there anything about the *Suki* there?'

'Let me check.'

Pause.

'Yes. The FBI cleared the city of Mafia activity in the 90s. However, a bartender from a South-Side club came forward a few years back and offered up information in exchange for police protection. He said he worked at a Suki *club; they'd been in town for some time, filling the space the Feds had cleared.'*

'Why did he need protection?'

'This goes back a decade. Two days before he turned informant, the Suki *boss was killed in a back room at one of their clubs. The bartender said he only saw one person go back there just before the old guy was killed.'*

'Who?'

354

'A woman; late twenties or thirties, worked as a waitress at the club. Had Suki *ink on her arms and lower back. The guy said the* Suki *had just found the old guy's body when members of a rival gang broke into the place and opened fire. The bartender split through a back door, and went to the cops the next day. Pittsburgh PD moved on the club, but the place was deserted, no bodies, no blood, nothing. The grandchildren of the dead* Suki *boss had also disappeared too, wiping out his blood-line. No-one ever found any trace of them.'*

Archer looked down at Henderson, the tattoos on his torso still visible from his pulled-up sweater. 'How many grandchildren did this man have?'

'Three. Two boys, one girl. Teenagers at the time, apparently. Mikhail, Seva and Ninochka.'

'Michael, Sebastian and Nina,' Archer said. 'Henderson, Tully and Lister.'

'Those surnames must be fake. If it's them, they must be brothers and sister.'

Archer swore quietly. 'Did this informant have any idea who wiped out that *Suki* faction?'

'Yeah. He said only one other gang would have this much of a vendetta against the Suki, *and it went back decades. Pittsburgh PD never found any evidence of them in the city though and haven't since.'*

'Who are they?'

'The Prizraki.'

Trapped in that dark coffin eleven months ago, her oxygen quickly running out, Karen had fought a major panic attack, terror racing through her veins like pure heroin through a junkie's bloodstream.

She'd had no idea how deep she'd been buried but knew there was only one way out and that was up. The soil above her would have been thrown back over the coffin once she'd been laid in place, which meant it was likely loose, not packed hard. She was a slim woman and luckily for her, the wooden box was large, designed for a man, probably another of her husband's victims. Burying people alive was one of his specialities.

After a struggle, and fighting the claustrophobia which was threatening to swamp her, she managed to slowly work her sweater over her head. Panting hard from the effort, she then pulled part of it back down to protect her nose and mouth from being filled with soil in case she ever managed to breach the wooden lid. Drawing her legs up tight, she started to push up as hard as she could with her knees.

The lid felt completely solid, unmoving as she pushed at it, the sheer weight of soil above her holding it down, but she persevered, using all the strength she possessed. Her leg muscles were soon screaming in protest but she didn't stop, knowing it was either get out or suffocate to death.

She lost track of how long she'd been pushing; it was getting unbearably hot and she was fighting for breath, feeling sweat pouring down her skin and claustrophobia about to overwhelm her when suddenly she heard the lid above her creak.

She renewed her efforts, feeling the wood move slightly as it started to give way, all the weight of the soil waiting to pour down over her.

Then it had shifted.

She'd carried on pushing, forcing the lid up slightly.

Karen had lifted her hands over her sweater to protect her nose and mouth, but the soil had poured down in a relentless stream over her body and legs, trapping her and packing her in tight. Unable to move her legs and only just able to breathe in the tiny pocket of air her hands and the sweater provided, she forced an arm upwards, working it through the loose dirt, feeling the suffocating weight above her as it pushed against her stomach, her air almost gone. She managed to start shoving some of the soil into the lower portion of the coffin with her right foot, giving her some wriggle room.

Her body covered with earth, Karen spent what seemed like an eternity working her fingers through the cold earth, using all of her strength to push her arm upwards and every ounce of will she possessed to avoid hyper-ventilating from fear. Knowing she was close to suffocation, she suddenly felt all the resistance against her fingers disappear, replaced by glorious space and cold air. They hadn't buried her too deep.

Her hand had breached the surface.

With renewed hope, she quickly started to scoop handfuls of earth to one side. Pushing up with her legs, stamping down on the earth and using it to lever herself up, she'd finally been able to force her way out of the coffin, finally erupting through the earth and sucking in oxygen like a drunk with his first drink in years, lying in a field in the middle of nowhere. For a few minutes she just lay where she was, unmoving, just getting her breath back and sucking the cold air deep into her lungs.

She was still alive.

'When was the last time the *Suki* were here in New York?

'Not for a while. They were run out of town. Same as in Philadelphia, Boston-'

'And Pittsburgh,' Archer finished.

'That's right.'

'What happened at the club in Brighton Beach? Did they apprehend the men down there?'

'They didn't get there in time. Three got shot; we think it was Henderson and Tully. We've got them on camera abducting the last guy; the bartenders are saying he's the leader.'

'Do you have a photo of this man?'

'Hold on. I'm sending it now. It came from Massaro.'

'OK,' Archer said, ending the call. Opening the picture, he looked at the image of the man, immediately seeing the likeness.

He turned the phone so April could see the image.

After a moment or two she looked up at him, shock on her face.

It was unmistakeable.

Finally seeing how it all fit together, he thought back to the conversation he'd just had with Karen. She'd said *meet me at the docks,* thinking she was talking to Henderson.

But which docks, West or East?

Redialling Ethan, Archer started speaking the moment he answered. 'I need you to trace the GPS on Karen Casey's cell.'

'What's her number?'

Archer did a quick check on the cell then passed over the nine digits.

'Which way is she going, Ethan?'

'She's heading east on East 19th.'

Ending the call, Archer rose and reloaded the pistol he'd taken from Henderson.

'What are we doing?' April asked.

'Karen's going to the East Side Docks. I need to get over there and stop her right now.'

'That might not be so easy,' April said, standing by the window. 'Look.'

Moving alongside her, Archer looked down at the street.

'Oh shit,' he whispered.

The two cars carrying the Latino gang members hunting him down had just screeched to a halt outside the building, blocking off their exit.

FORTY EIGHT

Once she'd made it out of the coffin, it had taken Karen all night to get back to the centre of Pittsburgh. As soon as she'd figured out where she was, she'd collect-called Leann, instructing her to come get her. The girl had been stunned when she'd seen her step-mother covered in soil, scratched and bloodied, her hair wild and her face filthy.

Using the cash Leann had on her, Karen had checked into a motel, cleaned herself up, then picked up a pistol from a safety deposit box she kept in the city and went home to kill that son of a bitch. However, he was gone, along with everything of value in the house. Taking her gun, she'd gone to Bashev's lieutenant's home and confronted the man, who'd been minutes away from leaving himself, his entire house stripped bare.

With the gun in his face he'd told her everything. Karen had already known the Feds were back in Pittsburgh on the hunt to crush any Mafia presence, which meant the *Prizraki* either had to keep an extremely low profile or get the hell out of there. Apparently the leadership had been watching Vladimir for a while, the success of their operation at the steel mill and the vast sums of money it was bringing in attracting their attention.

When the leader of the New York faction had been killed the week before, Vladimir had been offered the position.

For every *Prizraki* member, induction into the Little Odessa organisation was highly coveted;

the chance to actually lead it was an unrivalled honour and responsibility. Prospective inductees were carefully observed for some time before any offer was made. If an inductee was later judged to be inferior, it wasn't unusual for them to be killed along with the member who'd recommended them. It ensured only the most ruthless and successful survived.

Bashev's lieutenant then told Karen the reason why Vladimir had disposed of her as he had. She knew of course that in the Russian Mafia a prospect was required to shed blood to signify his allegiance, but the New York *Prizraki* were particularly brutal, demanding an extra level of proof of Bashev's dedication. The Thieves Law they still adhered to stated that no true *vor v zakone* could have a family of his own, thus ensuring total loyalty, no distractions or providing an enemy with a potential means of blackmail.

As a consequence, the *Prizraki* leadership had put a green light on Karen.

If Vladimir wanted to join them, he'd have to get rid of her.

Evidently this hadn't posed a problem for her late husband. That ultimate betrayal after so many years of marriage and working together, coupled with the experience of being buried alive completely unhinged her, the professional killer who'd lain dormant for so many years, back with a vengeance. She'd dedicated years building up their operation with her husband and she'd been repaid by being buried alive, the only mercy he'd shown was not breaking her wrists, Vladimir not wanting to torture her but dispose of her. A cold, calculated business decision.

In turn, she made one of her own. Her husband was going to die, but only after each and every member of his new team. She'd inflict the ultimate humiliation on him as leader of the uppermost *Prizraki* faction, knowing that by removing his crew, Bashev would appear completely inept to both the leadership and also all the men around him. Then and only then would Karen take her revenge on him, if the bosses didn't kill him first.

She'd started her campaign immediately, knowing she couldn't leave Bashev's lieutenant alive, so she'd shot him and taking Leann with her, headed for New York. As soon as they'd arrived, Karen rented an East Village apartment then called up two of her old pimps from Pittsburgh who she'd set up in Manhattan, Carlos Goya and Alex Santiago. They'd been forced to leave the Steel City due to police attention and owed her big time; they also had no idea what had happened to her and were extremely fearful of her powerful connections, no idea that they'd been severed. When she told them she was taking over their operation, they didn't argue. It wouldn't have been wise.

The two men ran eleven women, twelve after Karen forced Leann to join the roster, the girl not a problem now Karen had gotten her addicted to painkillers and kicked her out of the house to find her own place. However, even though money started to roll in, Karen had stayed in her East Village apartment in order to maintain her cover, spending every waking minute meticulously planning her revenge.

Her first task was to learn everything she could about the Little Odessa *Prizraki*, the structure, where Bashev and the other men lived and operated and how many of them there were. It was a challenge and she was well aware of how dangerous it was; the men were notoriously hard to get information on and she knew if they got wind of Karen's presence in the city, or even the fact there was someone asking questions, the consequences would be fatal. They wouldn't make any mistakes the second time.

She'd been patiently gathering information for five weeks until something totally unexpected had happened. She'd arrived home one afternoon to find three people in white overalls waiting for her.

Gas masks over their faces and silenced pistols in their hands.

Outside the Columbus Circle building, four Latino enforcers were sitting in a car, all of them pissed off and confused about what had gone down tonight.

Four of their guys had been killed in Queens and two more had been hit on the Queensborough. They'd lost the cop car as it left the Bridge but they'd been sent the address of the safe-house where the cop was heading. The passenger in the front seat looked up at the building, hearing sirens in the distance.

'Shit,' the guy behind the wheel said. 'We're running out of time. Do we check it out?'

As he spoke a black 4x4 suddenly screeched out of the underground parking lot immediately ahead of them, smashing through the barrier and swinging right.

Two of its windows were already smashed out, the vehicle riddled with bullet-holes. It was their target.

'Go!' the guy in the passenger seat shouted, loading his gun.

Arriving at the East Side docks, Karen pulled in through the front gate. The place was huge and as she drove in she saw Henderson and Tully's spare van forty feet to her left the giant piping warehouse they used as a base another fifty feet beyond it.

She couldn't remember exactly what had happened after she'd been confronted at her place in the East Village, but she realised later she been chloroformed and had woken up to find herself restrained with zip-ties, a strip of duct-tape over her mouth, the three figures pouring a chemical liquid into a tub which she'd quickly realised was meant for her.

As she'd lain there terrified, desperately trying to figure a way out of this, she'd noticed the smaller of the three had been staring at her. After a few moments the figure had turned to speak to the other two who stopped what they were doing. The ensuing argument getting heated, the figure had removed the mask, revealing an attractive woman with a blackened vein down the side of her neck.

Searching back through her memory, Karen had suddenly recognised her, and then by association, the two men although they'd both changed dramatically since she'd last seen them.

When she'd killed the head of the *Suki* just over ten years ago, his two sons had also been wasted by the *Prizraki* that same night but his grandchildren had been spared, not out of compassion but because they could be sold. Good money had been offered in California for the teenage captives, Mikhail, Seva and Ninochka, the grandchildren of a *Suki* boss. Vladimir had concluded the deal and been preparing to ship them west to San Diego.

Karen had arrived just as the three kids were being moved; fortunately for her now, the three of them had been blindfolded and hadn't seen Karen. They had no idea who she was.

The woman was looking at her *Suki* tattoos instead.

She'd pulled up Karen's shirt, seeing the rest of the inking on her back. A rapid conversation had followed, the strip of tape across Karen's mouth removed, aware that if she said the wrong thing now then this would all be over and she'd be going into the tub.

Lying through her teeth, Karen said that her husband had been killed by the Pittsburgh *Prizraki* and that she was here to exact revenge on the crew who were responsible in Little Odessa. To her relief, the trio had fallen for it, starting to ask her questions, wanting details.

After a tense few moments the girl with the pronounced vein, Ninochka, had removed Karen's binds. Once again, she'd somehow managed to escape what had seemed to be certain death.

And the enemy of her enemy had just become her friend.

FORTY NINE

Driving fast up 8th Avenue, Shepherd only had
one hand on the steering wheel, the other resting
on his lap; the injury to his arm was painful but
he and Hendricks had patched themselves up as
best they could. Right now they couldn't afford
the time to go the hospital so both were running
on painkillers and adrenaline. Beside him,
Hendricks was wrapping a bandage round his leg,
swearing each time Shepherd took a corner.

A squad car suddenly screeched into view from
their right, speeding alongside them and just
missing a white van coming the other way.
Frowning, Shepherd glanced at the car then
looked left to see what they were chasing and saw
a Counter-Terrorism Bureau Ford burning down
9th.

'That's Archer!' Hendricks said.

Shepherd wrenched the wheel over, causing
Hendricks to let fly with another stream of
expletives as they raced towards 9th Avenue after
Archer.

Henderson, Tully and Lister may have untied
Karen but she wasn't out of danger yet; they
tested her, wanting to hear a lot more about her
time in Pittsburgh. Fortunately for her, Karen had
a good memory as well as a silver tongue and it
didn't take long before she'd loosened them up
enough to discover why they'd been intending to
kill her. It wasn't because of what she and
Vladimir had done to them; she was very lucky
they had no idea she'd been involved in that.

The *Suki* brothers and sister been shipped to San Diego for a total of thirty five grand; then they'd been split up and sent to three different clients. However, a problem for pimps when hustling boys was puberty. Nic had been a scrawny and lanky teenager but two years into his captivity he'd filled out rapidly, growing to over six feet, his weight soon reaching over two hundred pounds.

His pimp was five eight and maybe a buck sixty by comparison.

Twenty four months after his abduction, Henderson had killed the man, making his escape. He'd managed to track Tully down, helped him escape too and the pair began to look for Lister. It turned out that she'd killed a john and was doing a two year sentence for manslaughter.

Waiting for her to get out, the two young men had needed cash and had ended up working for a Mesa drug cartel involved in a bloody war with another organisation from Culiacan. Used as enforcers, the pair had worked with the cartel's muscle charged with fighting off the Mexicans and was where they'd learnt the lye recipe to dispose of bodies. The other men had figured they were just Russian thugs, no idea they were actually *Suki* Mafia royalty.

There were two reasons for that. The first was their names; knowing they were vulnerable as children and wanting to protect them from rival gangs, the three kids had always been called by their Western first names, each given a different legalised surname too to add another layer of protection.

The second reason was they'd been too young when they'd been abducted to have *Suki* tattoos.

However, having reached manhood Henderson and Tully changed that, getting their stars as well as other ink they'd earned after serving a joint sentence at Lompoc for weapons charges, one month after Henderson's twenty first birthday. Lister had still been in jail at that point and had never had any ink-work done.

Once she'd been released, her two brothers had ditched the cartel work and the brothers and sister had focused on one thing.

Finding the men responsible for both destroying the Pittsburgh *Suki* and for trafficking them out to the West Coast.

They'd left San Diego and started working their way across the country, heading for Pittsburgh. Realising they were going to need significant funds if they were going to succeed, they quickly identified a lucrative way of making money; sourcing a high-level escort service in a city, removing whoever controlled it then taking over the operation. Consequently, when their pursuit of the people who'd trafficked them out to California brought them to New York, they'd looked around for a high-end service they could acquire.

Karen Casey's lucrative operation had caught their eye.

Once they found out they had the same goal, they quickly realised they could increase their chances of getting to Bashev and the rest of the *Prizraki* if they worked together. Soon establishing a working relationship, they focused all their energies on achieving the outcome they all wanted, the destruction of the New York *Prizraki*. Karen had discovered how scarily efficient the trio were in disposing of their victims and the fate she'd narrowly escaped.

However, because of all the hard work and planning involved in killing her husband's new team and disrupting his operation, Karen had been distracted and it'd cost her. She'd taken her eye off her step-daughter, who'd been arrested in February on a police bust and served three months inside. She'd only been out for eight weeks or so when she suddenly checked herself into rehab in August without any warning.

Karen had been furious. The day Leann had been released, Karen went to the facility to pick her up, making sure she got her straight back to work, but found the girl had already left. She'd called her immediately and it was then Leann had told her she was leaving and threatened to expose Karen and the real reason she was here in the city if she didn't let her go without a fuss.

The moment she made that threat, she'd signed her own death warrant.

When Leann had hung up on her, Karen had still been on her way back from the rehab clinic in Long Island and so couldn't deal with the issue herself. With Henderson, Tully and Lister fully occupied in Little Odessa, she'd contacted Goya and Santiago, telling them to handle the problem. However, the imbeciles had managed to shoot two cops when they killed Leann, both of whom worked for one of the most powerful divisions in the city. That stupidity had suddenly brought a very unwelcome spotlight of attention onto Goya and Santiago, their girls and potentially, Karen and Henderson, Tully and Lister.

The problem was, at that point they'd still had seven *Prizraki* left to take care of, including her husband, and there was absolutely no way Karen was leaving until he'd paid the ultimate price for what he'd done to her. She'd looked at their escort service client base and the men they had footage of, trying to find anything or anyone she could use to help rescue this situation long enough to finish off the *Prizraki*.

Then, like manna from heaven, she'd found the tape of an NYPD lieutenant with one of the girls, Kelly Greer.

Across town, the Counter-Terrorism Ford roared down 9th Avenue, shooting red lights, swerving past traffic with just inches to spare.

However, it suddenly took a burst from a sub-machine gun from the car behind which blew out a rear tyre. The Ford slammed into a lamp-post, knocking the post back slightly on its heavy base; the front fender of the vehicle crumpled and smoking, the horn blaring and the glass in the windshield and doors shattered.

Pulling to a halt behind it, the four Latinos were already out of their vehicles, loading their weapons as they approached the crashed car, the sound of police sirens getting closer.

Stalking forward, the lead passenger focused on the driver's side, his Ingram Mac-10 held sideways and in the aim.

Arriving by the door, he looked through the blown out driver's window and paused, holding his weapon up with the sights on the driver's head.

'Son of a bitch!'

Now just over four weeks after Leann's death and Lieutenant Royston's reluctant but valuable assistance, the New York *Prizraki* had all been disposed of.

Sam Archer was a done deal too. Like the Russians' moves on the detective team's homes, Vargas' death had successfully distracted her boyfriend and kept him off their backs for a while, but Karen had known that wouldn't be enough and that he needed to die. She'd previously ordered Royston to pull the files on the Counter Terrorism team and had seen Archer's exemplary record. She'd instantly realised he'd be a major threat, but not anymore, finally. Henderson and Tully had seen to that.

Apart from her involvement as Leann's supposed mother, she'd managed to keep attention off herself, despite the visits from the police detectives. Before any of them had come knocking she'd found several framed photos amongst Leann's things she'd brought from Pittsburgh and put them in the sitting area, giving the impression of a happy mother-daughter relationship. Playing each encounter with the police moment by moment, she was either hostile or turned on the tears, and it had worked like a charm. With Goya and Santiago gone, no-one could ever have guessed that she'd been the person who ordered Leann's death.

She already had a new identity for herself and she'd handle Henderson and Tully later, wasting them on the road once they were out of the State. The cops knew their names which meant she had to get rid of them; they'd served their purpose and were now a liability. If she let them live, at some point they could figure out she was actually former *Prizraki,* heavily involved in the deaths of their father and grandfather and she couldn't allow that to happen.

Tossing the empty container of bleach to one side, Karen slammed the door and checked her watch.

It was time.

On 9th Avenue, the Latino gang member lowered his weapon and stared in confusion at the driver of the crashed Ford.

Rather than the blond NYPD detective he was expecting to see, instead there was a red-haired woman sitting behind the wheel, leaning back in the seat and away from the airbag, blood trickling down her face from a cut to the side of her head.

'Wrong guess, asshole,' she said, smiling faintly.

Enraged, the gang member raised his gun again, aiming it at her head.

'Drop the weapon!' a voice suddenly bellowed from behind him.

The man whirled around, his weapon still up, giving Shepherd no choice but to fire.

The gunman took two rounds to the chest, knocking him back against the vehicle before he fell to the ground. As two other officers quickly detained the other gunmen, Shepherd and Hendricks moved forward quickly, seeing April inside the shot-up car. Shepherd opened the door, catching her as she toppled out sideways. Grunting with pain from his wounded arm as he lowered her to the ground, he looked up at Hendricks, who was peering inside the car.

'Anything?'

Hendricks shook his head, staring at the empty seats, no sign of Archer.

'Where the hell is he?'

FIFTY

At the East-side docks, Karen was impatiently checking her watch when Henderson's and Tully's back-up van finally pulled into the yard. Swinging right, it drew to a halt directly in front of her with the lights on full beam. Shielding her eyes with her forearm, Karen caught a brief glimpse of the driver, who was wearing a black Yankees cap with the peak pulled down and thick green coat; Henderson.

She walked over to the newly-arrived vehicle and pulled open the sliding door, lifting out a large container of bleach and unscrewing the cap. As she started to splash the contents inside the van, she heard the driver's door close on the other side, followed by footsteps as he walked round the front of the vehicle.

However, with the stink of bleach filling the air, Karen suddenly froze, the container still in her hand.

She turned slowly.

Wearing Henderson's coat, the baseball cap tossed to the ground, Archer was standing there, his pistol aimed at her head.

'Your two boys aren't gonna make it,' he said. 'Henderson's taking a nap and Tully's having a bath.'

She didn't waste time with a reply, her face expressionless as she stared at the cop, her brain racing as she computed this completely unexpected development.

Looking through his sights, Archer stared back, seeing a very different woman from the one he'd left behind in her apartment two days ago. Gone was the cowed and grieving mother.

This woman looked to be exactly what she was, a hard-faced killer.

'Turn around,' Archer said.

Karen didn't move; he cocked the hammer.

'Last chance.'

Moving slowly, she turned around until she had her back to him.

'Lift up the back of your shirt.'

She did, revealing an elaborate white rose pattern just above her waistband.

'That's a *Suki* tattoo,' he said.

She turned back around. 'Very good.'

'Henderson had an identical one. So did Tully, on his chest. I checked. Just in time.'

'You got me.'

'But you're not *Suki*. You're *Prizraki.* That tattoo is bullshit.'

Her eyes narrowed.

'OCCB told us the New York *Prizraki* had only lost one major figure in the past two years; their head of trafficking. Two months after he's replaced, Brooklyn South picked up some unusual activity; apparently members of the gang had started to disappear. I'm guessing Henderson, Tully and Lister's handiwork. Those tattoos confirmed they're members of the rival gang; *Suki.*'

'Why the hell would they take on the *Prizraki*?'

'Payback. We were told the Pittsburgh *Suki* were wiped off the map ten years ago. According to a bartender who turned informant, their leader was killed by a woman in a South-Side nightclub; she was blonde, late twenties or early thirties,

375

worked as a waitress and had *Suki* tattoos. I think that woman was you.'

Karen stayed silent.

'According to this bartender, the *Suki* leader's sons were killed that night but his grandchildren all disappeared; Mikhail, Seva and Ninochka. Michael, Seb and Nina.'

He fixed her gaze.

'Henderson, Tully and Lister.'

Karen snorted. 'They have different surnames.'

'Which they probably adopted to avoid being identified for who they really were. The *Suki* have been persecuted for decades. But that's why the three grandchildren suddenly appeared in San Diego after being born and raised in Pittsburgh. That's why they're here now.'

'So how do you get to them apparently killing men in New York?'

'Because the man who was responsible for what happened to them is right here. He ran the show in Pittsburgh; he was the guy brought in to take over the *Prizraki* operation here when the original boss was killed.'

Karen didn't reply for a moment. 'So where do I fit in to all this?'

'You ran April and Leann's escort service. Goya and Santiago worked for you. They were probably running it but April told us the whole operation suddenly changed at the beginning of this year, the exact same time that you moved here with Leann. But you didn't come here to escape an abusive husband, did you? Instead, you came here to find and kill him.'

'There's no proof of that.'

'OCCB sent us a picture of the *Prizraki* boss in Little Odessa; Bashev. He and Leann had

376

identical eyes; it was obvious. They had to be related, which meant she was probably his kid. And your husband. But I'm guessing you're not her mother.'

She stayed silent.

'Anyway, we found Henderson, Tully and Lister had a history of targeting successful prostitution rings and taking them over, killing the people who'd originally run them. Goya and Santiago worked for you, which made you the head and therefore a target. I can guess the only reason they spared you was because they saw your tattoos. They couldn't kill a fellow *Suki*; they had no idea you're actually *Prizraki*, the woman who killed their grandfather. If they had, you wouldn't have lasted five minutes. You both had a common enemy, so you struck up an alliance; you bullshitted them, claiming you were on their side, and used them against your old crew.'

'Why would I want to put moves against my own crew, dumbass?'

'The Thieves Law, that's why. I heard about it, a code of honour that Russian Mafia live by. A detective from Brooklyn South gave us a few examples and one stuck in my head. A true *vor* can't have a family, isn't that right?'

Karen stayed silent.'

'So if Bashev was inducted, he'd have to get rid of his family. We haven't found any evidence that Bashev showed any interest in Leann; if she worked as an escort, he probably didn't give a shit about her. She didn't need to die. However, you were his wife so you did. Despite the fact that you killed the head of the Pittsburgh *Suki*, the *Prizraki* betrayed you in the end.'

377

'You still haven't told me why you think I'm one of them. This is all guesswork.'

'When I came to see you, you dropped that cup on the floor, remember? But you made no attempt to pick it up. You didn't even react when you dropped it. Because the code you live by as *Prizraki* forbids you picking anything up from the floor, doesn't it? Seems crazy to me but Detective Massaro says you guys live and die by that stuff. But apparently *Sukis* don't live by the same rules, being outcasts and all. Am I getting close? I think so.'

Her lips thinned but she didn't reply.

'Your husband's not a drunk, and he's not back in Pennsylvania. He's here in New York. You're here for the same reason as Henderson, Tully and Lister; revenge.'

'He buried me alive in a coffin. I'm supposed to let that pass?'

'What about the men who disappeared? All these *Prizraki*?'

'To humiliate him first and scare the shit out of that son of a bitch, to have him watch his entire faction disappear around him before he joined them, last of all. I wanted him to suffer.'

'What about the escorts? And Vargas? Did they deserve to die too?'

'I had my reasons. And your girlfriend was just a bonus.'

'You had something on Royston too, didn't you?' Archer continued, refusing to be goaded. 'You needed more time to finish off the *Prizraki* and told him to delay the investigation. That's why he ran interference from day one. That's why our homes received a visit tonight.'

'Real shame you're never getting your girl back,' Karen replied quietly, staring him in the eyes. 'What was her name; Alice?'

Archer didn't take his eyes off her. 'It wasn't a coincidence I got arrested when I came to see you either. You must have messaged Royston and told him I was there. You told him to get me into Rikers and make sure I didn't leave.'

'Yet you survived,' Karen said. 'You're just like me, Detective. We're both survivors. So put that gun down and let's talk about it.'

'You're done.'

She smiled. 'You have no idea how many times people have tried to kill me. But I'm still here. Just like you.'

'I'm nothing like you.'

The moment he finished speaking there was a racking sound a foot from his head, a shotgun being pumped.

He froze, then quickly glanced to his right. Royston.

Looking back at Karen, Archer saw her smile.

'Well now look at this,' Karen said, Archer's advantage of a few seconds ago gone. 'I was wrong, Detective. You and I aren't alike after all.'

'You stupid bitch,' Royston said, not taking his shotgun off Archer as he addressed Karen. 'I'm not here just for him. I'm here for both of you.'

He'd barely finished speaking when Karen suddenly moved, throwing the container of bleach towards Royston and taking him by surprise. Pulling his aim off Archer, the lieutenant swung the Mossberg and fired but Karen had already darted behind the van as the shell destroyed a trash can just beyond where she'd been standing.

Archer immediately snapped his elbow back into Royston's face as the Lieutenant racked the pump. With a silenced pistol she pulled from her jacket, Karen fired, aiming at Archer, her biggest threat, but he was already moving and she missed, hitting Royston in the leg instead. Shouting in pain, the Lieutenant fell back but before Archer could grab the shotgun from him, Royston turned it on him.

Exposed, Archer threw himself behind a concrete bollard in the middle of the yard, the only cover available, but the shot never came.

Snapping out, Archer went to fire but hesitated when he saw Royston had ducked for cover behind another bollard.

Just as a grenade rolled to a stop fifteen feet from Archer.

It exploded a second later, blowing Archer off his feet and back onto the concrete, leaving him lying in a limp heap.

Seeing the blond detective go down, Royston rose from his cover and racked the pump to finish him off but then heard the screech of tyres behind him, a fast-moving car pulling into the yard. Turning, he fired, blowing out a front tyre on the Bureau Ford. As the car skewed to a halt, Royston fired again at the front windshield then racked the pump; ignoring Archer, who he could see was either dead or unconscious, he turned and looked for his tormentor, Karen Casey. Realising there was only one place she could be, he limped forward into the warehouse.

The shotgun was one he'd lifted a while ago from the Precinct's lock-up, as well as the grenade, after the blackmail had started; already trying to track down who was working him at that point, he wanted weapons that could never be traced back to him in case he struck gold and could put moves on his blackmailers.

Retrieving them from his home and arming up, he'd parked outside the docks and stolen in through the gate. He'd heard Archer and Karen's entire conversation and now understood what was going on. Apparently Henderson and Tully were dead, he could finish off Archer shortly, which left Karen Casey and the cops who'd just arrived.

After months of misery, he was finally going to finish this.

Inside the Ford, Marquez and Palmer had caught sight of the explosion, watching Archer go down, and could now see him lying unmoving on the concrete. Marquez had also seen Royston limping into a warehouse to her right after being shot in the leg by Karen Casey.

That call Palmer received had been from Polaris telling her that two girls in Pittsburgh had been arrested for prostitution last night, working a street-corner. Their English had been poor, but they'd understood the threat of deportation, and with an interpreter brought in, one of them had opened up. Apparently they were both from Moscow and had been trafficked through the South Side docks, then forced to work in the city as high-end prostitutes for a blonde woman called Karen, who'd suddenly disappeared without warning at the end of last year. The cops had put a search out for the name and contacted Polaris to check their records; one of Palmer's colleagues in Pittsburgh who'd already checked out Leann Casey's history at Theresa's request took the call, saw the timings and worked on a hunch. He sent over Karen Casey's DMV photo, asking the police to run it past the two women. Apparently they'd both immediately identified her as the woman who'd run the escort ring they'd been forced to join.

Marquez had called the Bureau to pass on in the information, when Ethan told her Archer was following Karen Casey to the docks.

Ripping open her door, she started to run towards Archer then realised Palmer was following her.

'Get back inside!' she ordered, pointing towards the car. *'And stay down!'*

Reluctantly Palmer turned back, but not before glancing worriedly at Archer lying unmoving on the ground.

'Is he alright?' she called.

Not bothering to answer, Marquez arrived by her team-mate and saw he wasn't moving, blood running down his neck.

'Arch,' she said, kneeling down and checking for a pulse. 'Arch?'

He didn't respond.

Pushing him over gently, she saw he was out cold; she felt for a pulse again and was relieved to feel it under her fingers, constant and strong.

Looking down at her colleague for a moment, unwilling to leave him lying there, Marquez suddenly heard a gunshot from inside the warehouse.

She had to make a choice.

Looking down at Archer again and knowing he'd make the same decision, she turned him onto his side then rose and made her way quickly towards the warehouse, the lapping of the East River waves filling the silence behind her.

FIFTY ONE

Inside the warehouse, Karen darted behind a
container, just avoiding a second shotgun blast
from Royston. As the sound reverberated around
the hangar, she ran down the aisle, ducking
around the corner then listened, training her
weapon on the gap as she waited for Royston to
appear

She'd seen Archer go down, but she'd also seen
the Ford arrive and knew more police officers
would be here any minute. Weighing up her
options, she quickly checked her surroundings. A
large truck was parked across the warehouse, a
beer company logo painted on the side, the
vehicle she, Henderson and Tully were going to
use to get out of the city. It was too slow though,
weighed down with cargo.

The warehouse seemed to be a holding area for
metal pipes, stacks of them piled neatly around
her, several on a metal forklift waiting to be
moved outside and onto waiting ships.

Looking at the aisles, she saw the pipes were
held in place by plastic binding straps, several for
each stack.

And beside her, the forklift still had the keys in
the ignition.

Stalking between the tall corridors created by the
stacked pipes, Marquez was moving silently,
holding her pistol double-handed. The noise of
the city was muted in here, the only sound a quiet
whisper of wind through the large space.

From what Ethan had hurriedly told her, she
now knew that Karen and Royston had fed

384

information to the Russians, helping them put moves on the families of Shepherd's team, resulting in Michelle getting shot. Apparently, having failed to get Archer killed in prison, they'd arranged to finish the job at his apartment. And these two had been responsible for Vargas being lye-bathed. That made this more than personal.

Pausing, she stopped and listened, the place silent.

Suddenly she heard the sound of an engine bursting into life.

Spinning round, trying to locate it, she heard something smash into the other side of the aisle on her right. Looking up, she saw the entire column above her start to rock.

Then there was a *ping* of metal on metal as the furthermost wrap holding a stack of pipes on the rack above her suddenly gave way.

Now free from one side, the pipes started to tilt, their weight causing the other straps to snap one after the other. Turning and running as fast as she could, Marquez sprinted for the end of the corridor and threw herself out of the aisle just as scores of pipes clattered to the ground behind her.

The sound ringing in her ears and echoing around the warehouse, Marquez went to rise.

But then found herself looking at a pair of feet.

Looking up, she saw Royston standing over her, his shotgun aimed straight at her head. She froze as she stared down the barrel and he racked the pump, a shell jumping out of the Mossberg.

'You should have stayed out of this, bitch,' he told her, his finger tightening on the trigger.

'So should've you,' a voice suddenly said from behind him.

As Royston swung round, Josh fired twice, putting two bullets in his chest, the Lieutenant dead before he hit the ground. The gunshots from the Sig echoed around the warehouse then faded away. Staring at Josh in surprise and relief, Marquez took his hand as he helped her back up.

'You OK?' he asked.

She nodded quickly. 'How did you know?'

'Arch called and told me on his way over. I just got here. Where is he?'

Before Marquez could reply, the pair heard a noise near the door and turned, snapping up their weapons.

Royston was down but Karen was still out there somewhere.

Back on the concrete dock-front, Archer opened his eyes.

His neck was wet; reaching up to touch it, he saw blood on his fingers. He vaguely remembered the grenade exploding and guessed something must have sliced him open. His clothing was hot from the blast, smoke on his face, blood on his hands and wrists from the broken zip-ties, the cuts on his chest and arm from the prison shower fight opened up once again.

The concrete was cold and unforgiving under him. He tried to sit up but his body wouldn't obey, his vision blurry.

Glancing to his left, he saw his gun, resting on the concrete.

Get up, Archer.

Gritting his teeth, he managed to push himself up into a seated position, the waves hitting the dock-front wall behind him.

He shook his head, trying to rid himself of the nausea and dizziness washing over him, focusing on the pistol lying there by his hand.

He reached forward, curling his hands around the grip.

Get up.

Moving through the warehouse with Marquez, Josh couldn't see any sign of Karen.

But then ahead of them through the door they both caught a glimpse of movement outside, Karen heading for the police Ford Marquez had arrived in. Pistol in hand, she was moving fast straight towards Palmer, who hadn't seen her. Theresa was on the phone and had her back to Karen, facing away from her as she spoke.

'Oh shit!' he hissed.

Stalking towards the unsuspecting social worker, Karen lifted her pistol as she drew nearer. With cops on her tail, she'd need a hostage.

'Theresa!' Josh suddenly warned from the warehouse doorway.

Karen spun round, firing at the two cops with her silenced pistol, the pair ducking back behind the cover of the hangar. Swinging back towards the police Ford, she suddenly froze in disbelief.

The blonde social worker was now facing her.

And she was holding a pistol aimed directly at Karen's head.

FIFTY TWO

As Josh and Marquez snapped out from behind the warehouse door, ready to drop Karen Casey and protect the social worker, they saw Palmer shoot Karen between the eyes. Thirty yards away, they froze in stunned disbelief at what they'd just witnessed as Karen's body hit the ground.

Without hesitation Palmer switched her aim and fired twice more, dropping them both, hitting Josh in the chest and Marquez in the leg. As the sound of the shots faded she walked slowly towards the two detectives, her pistol trained on them as she loosened the buttons on her jacket with her other hand.

She kicked their guns away then stood over the pair, watching as Josh tried to breathe and Marquez clutched the wound to her thigh.

'Theresa?' Josh grunted.

'She was the last one,' Palmer said, jerking her head back in Karen's direction.

'What the hell are you talking about?' Josh managed to get out.

Palmer smiled. 'You know what the prison guards back in Russia did in the 1940s when the gangs fought each other?'

She paused for a moment, looking down at the two detectives who were staring at her blankly.

'Nothing. They let them kill each other and stepped in when there were only a few left standing.'

Behind her was a flash of headlights at the gate as another van entered the yard, pulling to a halt twenty feet away. Four men stepped out, two of them starting to walk towards the group.

Watching them approach, Marquez stared in confusion.

They were the doormen from the Little Odessa nightclub.

Looking at the other two she recognised the third man as an officer who'd arrived as back-up after they'd found Santiago's body. And the fourth was a CSU photographer who'd been present at Nina Lister's crime-scene all those hours ago.

All of them looked very different now, dressed in dark clothing, automatic weapons in their hands. She switched her gaze back to the social worker, trying to breathe through the pain from her gunshot wound.

'Our organisation has wanted that piece of Little Odessa for years,' Palmer explained, smiling down at the two injured police detectives. 'It's prime real estate for those of us involved in the trafficking trade, but the *Prizraki* were always too powerful. However, our bosses decided to make a push at the end of last year; I capped off their top guy, put a bullet between his eyes with a rifle after he was driven home one night. They replaced him of course, as we expected, but it shook them up. Then just as we were planning our next move Henderson, Tully and Lister suddenly appeared. They might have been *Suki*, but they did a great job; saved us a world of work.'

'You're *Volki*,' Marquez coughed. 'Chechen Mafia.'

She nodded. 'We've been watching you all night, trying to keep you focused on the missing women and give our *Suki* friends time to finish off the *Prizraki*. Which they did admirably.'

389

She glanced over her shoulder and nodded at the two men by the van. One of them dragged open the sliding door, revealing metal barrels stacked inside. *Ether* was printed on the chemical stamp, along with a flame warning due to the highly-flammable contents. The pair each took out a single barrel and walked towards Palmer, Josh, Marquez and the other two *Volki* members.

'The Russians have had that piece of the Beach for decades,' Palmer explained. 'You can't just walk in and take it over. We've been watching and waiting for an opportunity for almost eight years; we got jobs under fake identities, we became pillars of the community. All funded by our people back home.'

She smiled.

'Now at last, it's there for us to take.'

The two men placed the barrels down beside the two injured NYPD detectives, then backed away.

'If you want to dispose of a body successfully, you have to think of the elements,' Palmer said, 'We *Volki* prefer fire. So much neater than waiting for a body to dissolve or burying people alive. Our people have already started to move in on Little Odessa. We'll stay in our roles; me working for Polaris. Such a help being on the inside.'

With the barrels sitting on the concrete directly beside him, Josh looked at Marquez. She was clutching her leg but looking at Palmer. They watched the five Chechen mobsters, four male and one female, move back out of the blast radius.

They came to a stop thirty yards away.

'I'm sorry it had to end this way for you two,' Palmer called out, as the group raised their guns. 'Sooner or later, we all run into someone stronger, tougher or smarter than us.'

She shrugged.

'It's nothing personal.'

'It is for me,' a voice suddenly said, forty feet to Palmer's right.

Snapping her head round, she saw a blond-haired figure standing in the loading bay, holding a pistol double-handed.

But he wasn't aiming it at her or any of the four men beside her.

Focusing on the ether cans stacked in the van immediately behind the group of Chechen Mafia, Archer aimed his sights on the central barrel.

'You've been green lit, bitch,' he said.

Before the four men and Palmer could react, he pulled the trigger.

A split-second later the entire van exploded, knocking him back off his feet once again as the vehicle went up in a huge fireball, the heat intense. The van hit the ground with a crash, a flaming mass of metal.

Pushing himself back to his feet, Archer looked at the wreckage and the billowing flames.

Palmer and the four men were gone.

Then he looked at Marquez and Josh. Having been far enough away not to be seriously affected by the blast, Josh hauled himself to his feet and moved over to Marquez who was lying on the ground, blood pooling out from the gunshot wound to her leg. Running over, Archer and his partner did what they could to staunch the flow, sirens in the distance confirming that back-up would be with them very shortly.

'I never trusted that bitch,' Archer said, compressing the wound.

'You're hurt...too,' Marquez said, looking at Archer, Josh glancing over and seeing blood running down his partner's neck.

'It's just a scratch.'

'Liar,' she whispered, screwing up her face in pain as Archer applied pressure to the gunshot wound. *'Maybe it's about time...we found another career.'*

'And give all this up?' Archer said, smiling at her. 'No way.'

Pause. The sounds of sirens in the distance could be heard clearly now over the waves and crackling flames from the burning van. It was strangely peaceful. As emergency vehicles pulled into the dockyard, Josh rose and ran towards them, attracting their attention.

Staying with Marquez, Archer suddenly realised he was still wearing Henderson's coat, which was keeping him warm but was also bulky. There was something in each pocket.

'Remember what I told you?' Marquez said quietly, catching his attention. *'About my son?'*

'Of course,' Archer said, seeing the paramedics climb out of their vehicle.

'I never told anyone...else in the Department...that.'

He smiled. 'I won't say anything.'

'You'd better not. Or I'll...kick your ass.'

Laughing but keeping the compression on her leg, Archer watched as paramedics ran over towards them, the operation finally over, the

burning van crackling and casting their
silhouettes out across the dockyard behind them.

After the fight in the Rikers shower, the
shootouts at Santiago's and Josh's homes, saving
April at Park Avenue, the attack at his apartment,
Henderson and Tully's ambush at the safe-house,
Royston's grenade and the explosion which killed
Palmer and the other Chechen Mafia, he figured
he could use another bandage or two himself.

FIFTY THREE

After ensuring April was safely under police protection and the surviving Latino gang who'd attacked Archer were in custody, Hendricks and Shepherd made it to the docks twenty minutes or so after the paramedics, fire service and other officers from the NYPD. They found a burning van, a dead police Lieutenant and a dead Karen Casey.

By the time the two sergeants arrived, Archer and Marquez had been taken by ambulance to the nearest hospital, Josh left to fill them in on the showdowns with Royston, Karen Casey and Theresa Palmer. They were stunned to hear of Palmer's involvement and of what had happened to her and her companions thanks to Archer. Almost by way of poetic justice, their bodies were nowhere to be found and never would be.

As Josh explained, the full scale and depth of the evening's events started to become clear to the two men. Karen Casey had been the wife of a Russian mobster, Leann Casey's father, a man called Vladimir Bashev; he'd been ordered to kill Karen, all part of this Thieves Law Detective Massaro had told them about, to prove his total loyalty. He'd failed, and Karen had survived.

The consequences had been far-reaching; the end of the New York *Prizraki* faction Bashev had been inducted to lead. It turned out that not only had Karen intended to destroy the faction, but Henderson, Tully and Lister had also targeted the gang for totally different reasons. Grandchildren of the leader of the Pittsburgh *Suki*, the *Prizraki*'s hated rival, they'd been sold by the *Prizraki* in

394

Pittsburgh to people in San Diego when they were teenagers, finally tracking the man responsible to New York City, Vladimir Bashev. Responsible for twenty seven homicides across three different states, Henderson and Tully's bodies had been found at the NYPD safe-house, Henderson's in much better condition than his brother's by the time officers arrived at the scene.

Inside the warehouse, the NYPD found equipment for making the lye solution, empty canisters and a van containing a significant number of files. It soon became clear the trio had carried out their blackmail business in two other cities while always managing to remain anonymous. The van had contained meticulous records and boxes of explicit photos and DVDs they'd used to blackmail the men caught in their carefully prepared operation. Royston had been one of them and he'd ended up paying the heaviest of prices for his corruption.

Theresa Palmer and the men who'd been with her had operated completely under the radar. Detective Massaro had been right in that the *Volki* had arrived in the city some time ago, but the level and extent of their influence and power had been completely underestimated. Palmer's phone which she'd left in the car and her partial explanation had given him plenty to work with and he and his team were setting up operations at the Beach, waiting for the unsuspecting Chechens to turn up. They also now had a wealth of valuable information on the *Prizraki* organisation, which still had ties in other cities across the country; the FBI had already been in touch.

Josh left to go to the hospital to see how his wife, Marquez and Archer were doing and the two sergeants were finally being seen to by medical personnel, Shepherd on the phone as they worked on him, wanting to find out what Marquez and Archer's statuses were.

'You need to get to a hospital,' one of the medics told Hendricks.

'I'm fine.'

'You got shot, Sergeant. You need to get checked out.'

'I tell you how to do your job?'

Beside him, Shepherd ended the call and thanked the medic treating him.

'How are they doing?' Hendricks asked.

Before Shepherd could reply, his attention was caught by a commotion taking place across the warehouse, right by Henderson and Tully's truck. Standing up, he made his way over, the other officers making way for him.

As soon as he saw what they were all looking at, he stared in amazement.

'Oh my God.'

He swung back to Hendricks.

'Jake! You need to come take a look at this!'

*

At Grand Central Station the next morning, dressed in a new pair of jeans, top and jacket, April stood beside Josh on the platform. For the first time in a very long time, she was feeling upbeat and with very good reason; she was getting out. She'd only suffered mild whiplash in the crash last night but fortunately nothing more serious. She'd experienced far worse at the hands of the pimps who used to control her.

And now she was free.

'Archer was sorry he couldn't make it,' Josh said. 'He had a court date.'

'They're still going through with that?'

Josh smiled. 'I reckon he's got a good chance of beating the charges now.'

He looked at her.

'You know you don't have to leave so fast.'

'I don't want to stick around. I've really had enough of this place.'

He smiled. 'I can understand that.'

'I'm nervous,' she said.

He smiled. 'That's a good thing.'

He passed over a jacket.

'Archer told me to give this to you. He said you might get cold on the train.'

Frowning, she held it up. 'It looks big.'

'Trust me; just take it.'

'Tell him thanks.'

'I will.'

The last call for the train echoed around the station.

'I'd better go,' she said.

They shook hands, then April turned and headed down the platform. However, after a few steps, she turned and looked back.

'You think I deserve a second chance?'

He smiled. 'I think you deserve a hell of a lot more than that.'

She grinned; then moving through the crowds, she showed the conductor her ticket and stepped onto the train, walking down the aisle and taking a seat.

Settling back, her neck aching slightly from the crash last night, she thought back to the moment when she'd roared out of the parking lot. Taking the car had been her idea and she'd had a hell of a job persuading Archer it was a good one; she was well aware he'd only given in because he needed to get after Karen Casey.

She looked down at the jacket he'd asked Josh to give to her and was confused; it was definitely a man's, too large for her slim frame, and she was puzzled why he'd insisted she take it.

As it rested on her lap, she felt something in the pocket under her right hand. Reaching inside, she took hold of something and pulled it out.

It was a banded brick of hundred dollar bills.

Caught completely off guard, she snapped her hand back inside the pocket, checking around to make sure no-one had seen. Satisfied the other passengers' attention was elsewhere, she stared down at the jacket. She tentatively felt in the other pocket and found another large brick of notes. Then the same in the inside pocket, what had to be thousands and thousands of dollars in total.

Feeling something else pinned to the inside lining, she saw it was a note.

Figured all this belonged to you anyway. Take care of yourself.

Ax

P.s: Next time you're in town I could use a good set of eyes looking over my car.

Covering her mouth in shock, she closed her eyes as tears started to roll down her cheeks; suddenly, she wasn't penniless anymore. Archer must have found the jacket inside the van when he'd raced to the docks, along with the money she and the other girls had been made to work so hard for.

Outside there was a whistle and the train lurched forward as the wheels engaged.

A few moments later it slowly pulled away from the platform and began to gather speed, taking April Evans towards a brighter future, far away from New York City.

Outside the courthouse on Pearl Street near One Police Plaza, Josh pulled up in a replacement Bureau Ford to find Shepherd and Hendricks standing in the Square, both men looking upbeat despite their injuries.

'What happened?' he asked.

'The case was thrown out. After it was reported what Royston did, no way was Archer going to be punished. The judge commended his actions instead.'

'Did you speak to him?'

'Not yet.'

Josh grinned. 'So where the hell is he? We need to talk.'

'We don't know. We've been waiting here for him for twenty minutes. He's disappeared.'

'Again? Where the hell is he this time?'

On the Upper West Side, people walking down Central Park West glanced at the good-looking blond man sitting alone on the bench in the black suit, looking slightly incongruous with the bandage on his neck and the marks on his face. He should have worn his NYPD uniform for his hearing, but much of his apartment had been trashed in the shootout with the Latino gang and he'd bought the suit in a hurry on the way to the court-house.

Archer was looking across the street at a building as people flowed past either side, the branches on the trees beside him waving in the gentle breeze, leaves falling to the ground around him. He'd been cleared of all charges, but he couldn't remember much about it, the hearing passing by in a blur; he'd left the moment it'd ended, wanting to come up here and be alone.

Sitting on the bench, he remembered the moment he saw a team of Marshals exit that building across the street, a child with them, a group of four gunmen stepping out of a car intending to mow them down.

He remembered rising to intervene, the following events changing his life.

He remembered the first time he'd seen her.

Marquez was right; he still had those memories. No-one could ever take them from him. And he'd have to make some new ones, Isabel counting on him to do just that. The look on the girl's face when he'd come back from the docks this morning had been one he'd never forget, the same as April's when he'd cut her hands free after he'd taken out Henderson and Tully. Sheer relief. That was why he did what he did. For every bad guy, there were a thousand good ones out there. There was a point to all this.

And he was still here. He'd dust himself off and do it all again. He'd never quit until his last breath. He'd never stop fighting.

And he'd never forget the time he'd spent with Alice.

Glancing at his watch, he rose and started walking downtown towards the train.

And found Vargas standing ten feet away, looking straight at him.

She'd come up the path without him noticing. Dressed in jeans and a black sweater, the white bandage around her neck gone, she looked at him for a moment then smiled.

'No one knew where you'd gone; I figured you might be up here.'

Completely speechless and rooted to the spot, Archer just stared at her.

There was a silence, filled by the noise of the neighbourhood and the wind in the trees beside them.

'They were going to put me in that chemical shit but they ran out of time,' Vargas explained. 'They decided to take me as insurance in case they were stopped and were going to kill me when they were out of the city. They were keeping all the other girls for their next stop; they wanted you guys to not look for them and believe all ten women were dead. Shepherd said it worked.'

Unable to speak, Archer's brain was still trying to comprehend that it was Alice, alive, standing in front of him and wasn't really registering what she was saying.

Then as he stood there staring at her and she smiled at him again, the final pieces fell into place. Karen's greed; the high value of that particular group of escorts. Running out of time to fill the bath and soak Vargas at the hospital.

'Are they OK?' he asked quietly. 'The women?'

'They're all fine. And Polaris is going to make sure it stays that way. They're off the street, for good.'

Pause.

'Does Isabel know?' Archer said.

'She knows. They all do. You're the last one.'

She smiled, then stepped to one side, giving him room to pass.

'Were you going somewhere?' she asked.

He shook his head, still unable to believe she was real.

'Not right now.'

They looked at each other for a few more moments.

Then stepping forward, Vargas threw her arms around his neck. Archer pulled her close, ignoring the pain as her body pressed against his. However, she heard him catch his breath; pulling back, she opened his jacket and saw the bandage through his white-shirt, then noticed the other on the side of his neck.

'Jesus, Archer,' she said. 'What the hell happened?'

'I got hurt.'

'No shit. How?'

'I took a shower.'

'Are you serious? Only you could manage to injure yourself while washing.' She continued to examine the shirt. 'Let's get you home and cleaned up.'

Archer suddenly thought back last night to the gunfight and grenade explosion at their apartment, both of which had destroyed most of their home. He then realised Vargas would have no idea about everything that had happened to him since she'd been shot; his suspension, getting locked up in Rikers and all that had happened yesterday.

As Vargas watched him, he motioned to the bench beside them.

'You'd better sit down for this.'

THE END

About the author:

Born in Sydney, Australia and raised in England and Brunei, Tom Barber has always had a passion for writing and story-telling. It took him to Nottingham University, England, where he graduated in 2009 with a 2:1 BA Hons in English Studies. Post-graduation, Tom followed this by moving to New York City and completing the 2 Year Meisner Acting training programme at The William Esper Studio, furthering his love of acting and screen-writing.

Upon his return to the UK in late 2011, Tom set to work on his debut novel, *Nine Lives*, which has since become a five-star rated Amazon UK Kindle hit. The following books in the series, *The Getaway, Blackout, Silent Night, One Way, Return Fire* and *Green Light* have been equally successful, garnering five-star reviews in the US and the UK, France, Australia and Canada.

Green Light is the seventh novel in the Sam Archer series.

Follow @TomBarberBooks.

Made in the USA
Middletown, DE
18 November 2020

24418962R00241